ADEPT

ADEPT

BOOK ONE OF
THE ESSENCE GATE WAR

Michael J. Arnquist

This is a work of fiction. Names, characters, places and incidents are either products of the author's imagination or are used fictitiously. Any resemblance to actual events, locales or persons, living or dead, is entirely coincidental.

For my family, with eternal gratitude for
your love and steadfast support.

ACKNOWLEDGMENTS

Many thanks to my test readers for your enthusiasm and for braving the hazards of a first draft as it was in progress. Knowing your eager, grasping hands awaited each new chapter kept me pushing forward.

I would also like to thank CreateSpace and Amazon, and the other independent publishing platforms as well, for providing new authors the means to reach new readers.

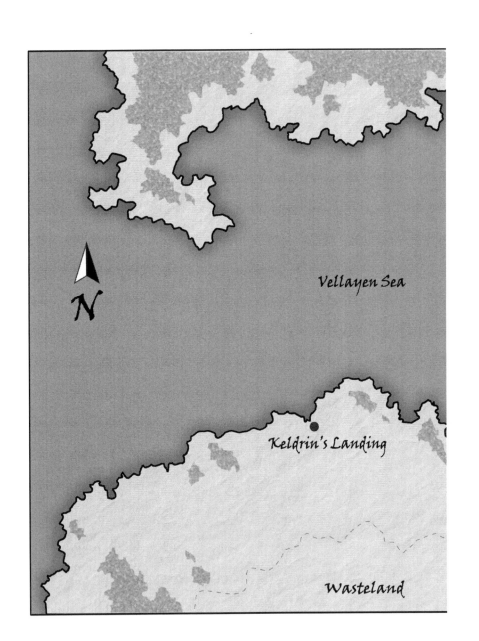

N

Vellayen Sea

Keldrin's Landing

Wasteland

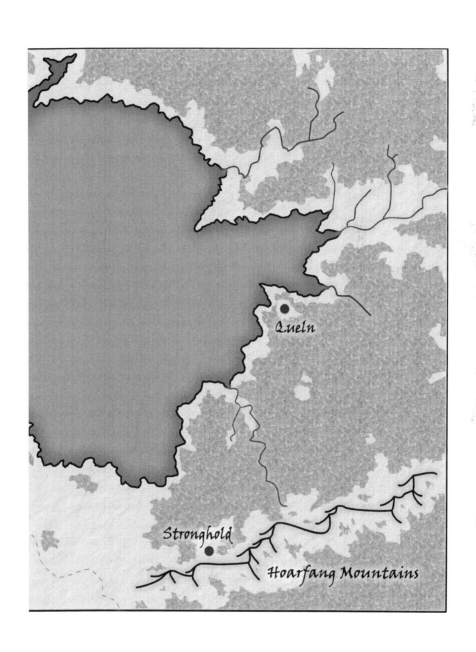

Queln

Stronghold

Hoarfang Mountains

CHAPTER 1

Halthak watched the sword arc through the night air toward him. He resolved once more to deny his assailants the satisfaction of seeing him struggle further, and braced himself to accept the strike. At the last moment, however, his survival instincts betrayed his will, and his arms rose of their own volition to cross over his head in feeble defense. The blade bit into his flesh, a kiss of fire the length of his forearm, laying it open. Halthak bit back a cry and fell to his side in the dirt, curling around the injured limb.

His attacker rocked back on his heels, roaring with laughter. Several of the other men brayed their own amusement from their positions around the camp. The wildest part of Halthak roared to the surface, gibbering in animal fury for the blood of his assailant, but he quelled his savage lineage with a control born of a lifetime of practice.

Drawing a shuddering breath through clenched teeth, he examined his arm. The bleeding was profuse, but the blade had not quite reached the bone. For a moment he considered not repairing it, considered allowing this wound and the ones that would follow to weaken and kill him. It would put an end to their entertainment, and the thought brought him a grim sense of satisfaction.

Again a spark of defiance within him flared against giving in so easily. He blew out a shaky sigh. In any event, the pain from the gash was severe, and he need not endure such discomfort while he waited for a clean killing blow.

He concentrated for a moment and felt the familiar suffusion of warmth spread through his injured flesh. The wound sealed up before his eyes, his pebbled grey skin pulling closed and becoming whole again. Even the faint white scar would be gone within a few days, he knew, under other circumstances. Halthak pushed to his knees once more, drew the perspiration from his heavy brow with a sleeve, and raised his eyes to his assailant.

Mercenaries, bandits—whatever they might call themselves, they were human predators, drawn to the region by the promise of reward from a wealthy port city in need. Unfortunately, Keldrin's Landing was very remote, being at the farthest edge of explored territory, and travelers on the way were vulnerable to more than just the strange creatures rumored to besiege the area. Especially lone travelers who were far too trusting by nature, Halthak thought bitterly. Being a half-breed, visibly only half human and an outcast of two societies, did nothing to help matters.

Not all of the bandits took delight in his torture. He saw a few, in fact, shift and exchange uneasy glances. Even if they were uncomfortable with the proceedings, however, they still stood back and allowed it through their inaction. Any distinction between these men and their leader, he decided, was too fine to matter much at the moment.

Vorenius, the bandit leader, dropped to one knee before him, still chuckling. He propped an elbow on his forward knee and leaned in close. A confident leer twisted his coarse features, but Halthak noted the way his trailing hand tightened on the hilt of his sword. This close, Halthak could smell the liquor that hung on his breath and soaked his unkempt beard, but he knew better than to blame its influence for the man's actions. The mercenary had intended this betrayal from the outset, he was convinced of that much now.

"Proving your bravery by straying within reach of your unarmed captive, Vorenius?" The words were out before his sense of self-preservation could strangle them, but the sarcasm he intended sounded more like pity even to his own ears.

Vorenius's grin vanished, and he scanned his men for reaction before returning to Halthak, eyes narrowed. "You are in no position to mock me, you filthy—"

"I am in position to do little else," Halthak interrupted, keeping his voice level.

"I can rid the region of one hideous menace, right here and now," the bandit snarled, "and without any need of payment."

Halthak shook his head, casting his gaze about the camp at the rest of the bandits. "Do what you will out here, away from all authority, Vorenius. But do not insult us all by pretending there is anything courageous or noble about your actions."

The bandit's jaw clenched and he stood, drawing himself to his full height. He raised his sword, murderous intent writ large upon his features. Halthak met his gaze, ready to let the sword land without deflection and end this charade. Just as the man's arm tensed to descend, however, a startled oath from one of the other bandits spun Vorenius around. From his position on the ground, Halthak had to peer around the bandit leader to get a look at the source of the disturbance.

A stranger appeared out of the night, seeming to coalesce from the very shadows as he strode forward into the campfire light. Clad in dark leather and an oiled black mail shirt, he moved with the leonine grace of a swordsman. All nine of Vorenius's men drew their blades and oriented on the newcomer, but the latter made no move to draw his own swords, the hilts of which jutted from his back over each of his armored shoulders. He padded to a halt within a few feet of Vorenius, hooked his thumbs over his belt and stood at apparent ease. Without seeming to notice the bandit leader's sword leveled at his chest, he addressed everyone.

"Good evening. My name is Amric, and I am traveling to Keldrin's Landing."

Vorenius's sword point never wavered, but his gaze slid from the newcomer to search the darkness beyond the fire's reach. Halthak realized he must be wondering how Amric had entered the camp without raising a cry from his sentries, and if he was truly alone.

"What do you want here, stranger?" Vorenius asked.

"A few moments of warmth from your fire," Amric replied, seeming to notice him for the first time. "And I would pay well for a hot meal, if you have anything to spare for a fellow traveler."

"Take a slice from the spit and be on your way," Vorenius said. "We are in the midst of something here."

Amric glanced at Halthak. "So I see."

"Do not think to intrude, stranger," the bandit leader growled. "This is a matter between us and this creature."

"It is doubtless none of my affair," Amric said, but he did not move, and instead continued to study Halthak.

"Bloody right it's none of your affair," Vorenius said. "Now be on your way, before you join our troublesome friend here."

"Troublesome? Is this creature dangerous, then?"

"Are you blind, or merely a fool? This is an Ork, a savage and mindless beast!"

"Half-Ork," Halthak corrected, from the ground. *And not half the beast that you are, Vorenius,* he thought.

The bandit leader swung half toward him with a hiss as if reading his thoughts, and then snapped back around to Amric. He shifted his grip on the sword and made a curt gesture back toward the forest darkness beyond the campfire light. "I say again, stranger," he grated, "be on your way."

Halthak grimaced, an icy twist returning to his gut. A brief respite, then, but not salvation.

Amric met the bandit's eyes for a long moment and then returned his gaze to Halthak. "May I speak with it?" he asked.

An irrational hope flared within Halthak, but he walled it away. This stranger had no reason to intervene on the behalf of one such as him.

Vorenius's tongue slid across his lips. His eyes darted about, once again taking in each of his men around the camp and scanning for additional intruders. He seemed perplexed as to when he had lost control of the situation. His men murmured and glanced at each other, as uncertain as their leader what to make of the stranger. After a moment's consideration, Vorenius jerked a shrug and slid back a pace.

Halthak tensed as the stranger stepped forward and sank to his haunches before him, resting lightly on the balls of his booted feet. Grey eyes locked onto his own and pinned him in place. This close, he knew how different he looked from human: the coarse grey flesh, the gnarled hands ending in tapered nails, the close-set eyes beneath a too-heavy brow, the jutting lower jaw encasing the protruding nubs of his tusks. All of these features and more betrayed him for the half-breed monster he was. Had he been a full-blooded Ork, he would have been broader and heavier of build, but as it was he would never be mistaken for human.

Halthak tried to read Amric's expression, looking for any trace of revulsion, or hatred, or even pity. He found nothing of the sort. Even the stranger's piercing eyes betrayed no hint of the thoughts behind them.

Amric stared at him, motionless and silent, long enough for the bandit leader to shift in impatience where he stood. Finally he asked, in a low, soft tone, "Why do you not fight back?"

Halthak's mouth dropped open, and then he snapped it shut. He was not certain what conversation he had expected, but it was not this. The warrior's voice was gentle, almost friendly. Recovering from his surprise, he said, "I will not give them the satisfaction. The more I struggle, the more it fuels their sport."

"You look healthy and able," Amric said. "Your limbs are strong, perhaps stronger than a human's. Your claws and teeth appear formidable, though you strive to conceal them." Halthak winced as the swordsman continued. "And yet your captors bear no injuries. Did you not struggle when they took you?"

"What bloody purpose—" Vorenius protested, taking half a step forward, but he drew up short as Amric raised a hand for silence. The swordsman's gaze never left Halthak's face, and he appeared unconcerned about the weapons arrayed around the camp against him.

"I am a healer," Halthak said, lifting his chin. "I heal injuries, I do not cause them. No matter what manner of monster you may see before you, I have dedicated my life to healing. I will not take the life of another."

"Even to save your own?" Amric asked.

"Even then."

Amric tilted his head to one side, but his expression still betrayed nothing of his thoughts.

"I met Vorenius and his men on the road to the port city this morning," Halthak continued, the words now tumbling out in a rush. "Some of them were injured, and I offered them my services in exchange for protection on the journey, since we shared a common destination. They— "

His words slurred, and he ground to a halt in frustration. His mouth was poorly formed for the more delicate human language, and finer pronunciation suffered when he grew agitated. He drew a steadying breath and continued. "They were friendly enough at first. But as night fell and they confirmed I traveled alone, it became evident that I was, to them, just another monster to be slain. Or perhaps just a vulnerable traveler, foolish enough to believe our arrangement would be honored. My healing abilities, rather than earning their gratitude, became additional spice for their entertainment."

Even as he spoke, he was uncertain if he was stalling for time, merely wishing to delay the inevitable, or if he wanted this stranger—someone, anyone—to understand at least this much of him before his death. A fearful part of him recognized that he had involved the man too deeply in his plight already, and that his selfishness might cause the death of another here at the last, but it was too late and so he surged ahead. His eyes raked the circle of men around the campfire and he stabbed a clawed finger at one of the bandits.

"*That* one would have lost his arm to infection at the very least, had it not been for my efforts. And he repays my kindness by cheering my torture and death." The target of his attention started and involuntarily flexed his now healthy hand, glancing about at his comrades. The men began to mutter amongst themselves, their growing discomfort plain, their blades wavering.

Vorenius snarled an oath, seeming to realize that the situation would soon be beyond repair. He lunged forward at the crouching stranger, sword flashing down. Amric spun to his feet and drew one of the swords from his back in a blur of motion. There was a flicker of steel and Vorenius cried out in pain, his own blade tumbling from his hand. Staggering back, he clutched his arm to his torso as a spreading sheet of blood soaked the front of his tunic. Halthak noted with a start that the cut to Vorenius's arm was nearly identical in placement and severity to the one the bandit leader had inflicted on Halthak mere minutes before. He returned his stare to the newcomer.

Amric stood motionless, sword held down and away, and he met the gaze of each of the stunned bandits in turn. When none of them advanced, he gave a sharp flick to the side to clear the blood from his blade, and sheathed it over his shoulder in a practiced motion. He hooked his thumbs over his belt once more, and his voice rang with command as he addressed them all over Vorenius's agonized groans.

"I have seen and heard enough," he said. "You have the opportunity now to make amends for a poor decision, and to let the healer leave this camp with me, without any further harm."

The men exchanged glances. Vorenius cast about, eyes wild, and saw no one leaping to his defense. Lurching away toward the darkness, he screamed, "Sentries, to me! Strike this man down!"

Amric chuckled. "Sentries might be a generous description, given the job they were doing. Your crossbowmen are not coming."

Vorenius spun back, gaping, to face Amric. "You killed them?"

"They were not slain, but disabled. And not by me."

"Who, then?"

Amric smiled and raised one hand high in a beckoning motion directed beyond the campfire light. All eyes turned in that direction as a second figure detached itself from the night and stepped forward.

"Sil'ath!" one of the men exclaimed.

Halthak heard a collective gasp from around the camp, and realized he was part of that chorus. The figure that entered the camp was reptilian, tall and powerfully built, but it walked upright like a man. A wedge-shaped head topped its thick neck, and a sinuous tail lashed behind muscular legs that were jointed differently than a man's and ended in broad, splayed toes. It wore two curved swords crossed on its back, as Amric did. With hardened leather pauldrons and a broad baldric over its chest, it bore less armor overall, but Halthak eyed its scaly green hide and decided that it appeared no less protected.

The Sil'ath stopped just at the edge of the light, inclined a solemn nod to Amric, and then ran its glittering black eyes over the bandits.

"You travel with one of the Sil'ath?" Vorenius said at last, his tone incredulous.

Amric nodded. "This is Valkarr, my sword-brother."

Sword-brother? The term meant nothing to Halthak, but several of the bandits muttered further exclamations of surprise. The Sil'ath were a reclusive race, said to be without fear, mercy or peer in battle. Halthak, like most, had never seen one of the lizardmen before, but there was no refuting the evidence before him.

"You have a decision before you, friends," Amric said, as the murmurs died down. "Choose now how your night will end." Both of the newcomers appeared relaxed, almost unconcerned, but Halthak could not shake the perception of lethal readiness lurking just beneath a calm surface. He noted as well that Amric and Valkarr were spread far apart in the camp, dividing the bandits and leaving themselves plenty of room to operate.

Speechless for once, Vorenius looked repeatedly from Amric to Valkarr and back to his own men. Blood continued to seep through his fingers where he pressed his injured arm to his torso. For their part, his men swallowed hard and held quivering weapons before them in postures that now looked more defensive than otherwise.

The moment stretched out, the only sounds the crackling of the fire and the steady hum of insects in the surrounding night. Finally, one of the bandits—the man that Halthak had singled out earlier as a recipient of his healing—sheathed his weapon with deliberate care, raised his hands before him and took a step backward. The man beside him did the same, and in short order the rest followed suit. Vorenius made no move to stop them, his face drawn in pain but otherwise carefully impassive.

Amric nodded and turned toward Halthak, extending a hand. Staring about in wonder, Halthak accepted it and allowed the swordsman to pull him to his feet. Moving past the men, he gathered his pack and staff from the ground before returning to stand next to the warrior. Shouldering his pack, he considered Vorenius. The bandit leader met his gaze with some hesitation, and the healer could see the malice in him, still present but buried deeply under a sense of defeat.

Halthak approached him, and reached one clawed hand out to the injured arm. Vorenius flinched away from his touch, but Halthak ignored this, and gently but firmly drew the arm away from the man's torso and turned it over to examine the cut. After a moment, he met the bandit leader's eyes once more, reading the mix of surprise and hopefulness there. They both knew he could heal it, that it would be the work of mere moments to draw the injury onto himself and repair it as rapidly as he had done before.

"You should cleanse that wound before you bandage it," he said finally. "And have a poultice applied when you get to town, to stave off later infection." Vorenius's features contorted with rage for an instant before reverting to an expressionless mask. Halthak released the arm and turned away, returning to Amric's side.

A smile played across the swordsman's features. "There may be hope for you yet, healer."

The Sil'ath warrior Valkarr turned as if to depart, and then paused. He swung back and stalked through the camp with purpose, startling the bandits into falling back another step. Rather than attacking, however, he reached down with one clawed hand and wrenched the spit from its cooling stand, complete with the generous portion of roasted boar haunch that remained on it. He bit into it with savage abandon, tearing loose a large mouthful, the muscles around his powerful jaws and neck bunching as he chewed noisily. He seemed to have forgotten the men in the camp, and no one moved to stop him. Finally he uttered a satisfied hiss and took another prodigious bite as he walked out of the camp with his prize and disappeared into the darkness.

Amric turned with a chuckle and strode from the camp without a backward glance, and Halthak followed close on his heels. The healer's last glimpse of the camp showed the men all turning to face Vorenius. From their stances and the wide-eyed look on Vorenius's face, he surmised that the balance of power within the band of mercenaries would be the subject of intense discussion that night.

As he tracked the pale glints of moonlight on the sword pommels over Amric's shoulders, Halthak was forced to consider his own immediate future. He was following two strange and fearsome warriors into the unknown, one of them of a race renowned for its ferocity, love of battle, and intolerance of others. By all rights he should have been terrified, but instead he felt strangely at ease. The Sil'ath was in the company of a human who called him a brother of some sort, and in any event, Halthak knew from his own experience that assumptions based on race were not always accurate. He admitted to himself that he might simply be leaping at any change in his situation, but there was something in the swordsman's unexpected treatment of him that instilled a newfound confidence. Whether or not that confidence was warranted remained to be seen. Regardless, his die was cast, and he was not exactly spoiled for options at the moment.

Halthak focused on his footing and keeping Amric in sight before him. They moved on and were swallowed by the night.

Halthak lay on his bedroll, staring up at the star-speckled sky. The campfire had died down to embers, but the sliver of moon gave enough light by which to see, once one's eyes were adjusted. Several yards away, Amric sat cross-legged on the ground, cleaning with meticulous care the sword he had used in the mercenary camp. He faced outward into the night and lifted his gaze often from his task to scan the darkness. Valkarr was stretched out on the opposite side of the fire pit from the healer, his even breathing almost a purr as he slept.

The two warriors had made camp in the lee of a rock outcropping, with no wasted motion and nary a word spoken, while Halthak stood aside and felt useless. The three shared the roasted boar haunch from the bandits' camp, and then with no apparent communication between them, Amric stood the first watch while Valkarr dropped to the ground without ceremony and fell asleep. Halthak took to his own bedroll, but his mind continued to race over the events of the night, and sleep eluded him. His fingers drummed, feather light, on the haft of his gnarled ironwood staff as he contemplated breaking the silence.

In the end, Amric beat him to it.

"Speak your mind, healer," he said, his tone wry.

Halthak jumped, shifting his gaze to the warrior. He cleared his throat, and began in a low tone, "I want to thank you for saving me from those men earlier. Not many would have intervened on behalf of a stranger, especially one with my appearance, and outnumbered as you were."

"Think no more on it," Amric said, waving a dismissive hand. "It was not a scene we could pass without becoming involved. And appearance is like so much clothing; it can accentuate or conceal the truth beneath it, but is not itself the truth."

Halthak noted the plural 'we', and wondered at the Sil'ath warrior's involvement in the decision. "Nonetheless, it was a courageous deed," he insisted. "I owe you my thanks, and my life."

Amric paused in cleaning the sword and looked over his shoulder. "You owe me nothing, friend. It was your words as much as our blades that made those men reconsider their actions, in the end. They knew the wrong of their deeds. But I accept your gratitude, as offered." Turning back, he resumed running a cloth the length of his blade.

Halthak turned his gaze back to the night sky. Try as he might, he could not puzzle the man out. His actions and speech were unlike any soldier he had met. Bolstering his courage, he cast a furtive glance toward the sleeping Sil'ath and spoke again, more softly.

"Is it true, what they say about the Sil'ath?" he asked.

"No," Amric replied at once, without turning his head.

"How can you know which part I mean?"

"I don't need to. I have lived among the Sil'ath for many years, and I have also traveled broadly enough to know that whenever 'they' talk about the Sil'ath, they invariably get it wrong."

"You live—have lived among them?" Halthak blurted, rising to prop himself on one elbow.

Amric snorted. "What tales have you heard, healer? That they eat their own offspring? That they attack other races without provocation? That they are incapable of reason or honor?"

Halthak reddened, hoping his discomfort was not visible in the poor light. Amric's derisive comments did indeed align with some of what he had heard, and he was beginning to worry that his curiosity and ignorance might have angered his savior. From the dismissive tone of Amric's next statements, however, he had little cause for concern.

"Nothing more than hot air that could just as easily have emanated from either end of the speaker, for all the wisdom it contained." The warrior held up his sword to sight down its edge, looking for nicks. Satisfied, he sheathed the blade and set the crossed scabbards aside but within easy reach. They sat in silence for several moments, and Halthak thought the conversation was at an end until Amric finally spoke again.

"There are no doubt elements of truth in what you have heard of the Sil'ath, healer. They are indeed fearless and implacable in battle, and their warriors are trained from birth with any weapon they can lift. Contrary to the tales, however, they are not motivated to conquer or pillage, and they are never unnecessarily cruel. Any such behavioral flaws are dealt with swiftly in Sil'ath society. They are a pragmatic people in all things, and so when they are provoked to conflict they aim to put a decisive end to it. They bend the knee to no one."

"That does not sound very pragmatic. What if they face an over-whelming force?"

Amric chuckled. "That depends on your point of view. When I call them pragmatic, I do not mean to say they will take the easiest path. Far from it. They are uncompromising in their principles, and every last one of their warriors is worth several of their enemy on the field of battle. Make no mistake, each will fight until he can no longer draw breath. As a result, no one enters lightly into conflict with the Sil'ath. Think of it as promoting peace by advertising the high cost of the alternative. In the end, all they want is to live and raise their own without interference or encroachment from other races, which they find generally baffling and unpredictable by comparison."

Halthak considered his words for several moments. "And despite their dislike of other races, they accepted your presence among them?"

"To be fair, they gave me a home among them when I was quite young, so I had few behaviors to unlearn as they raised me."

Amric glanced over his shoulder at Halthak when he heard no reply, and laughed.

"Close your mouth, healer, it is not so terrible a fate. The Sil'ath raise their own with the principles of honor, integrity, capability and dedication. Not just the words, but ingrained in their core. They treat each other with the deepest affection and loyalty. No, I have spent time among humans as well, later in life, and I am fortunate for the upbringing I had."

Halthak started to object, and then paused. He considered his own past treatment at the hands of both men and Orks, and his arguments faded before him like so much smoke. Who was he to defend the merits of being with one's own kind, when he himself had never found such acceptance? He stole another look at the sleeping Valkarr, and then turned back to Amric.

"How did you come to dwell among them?" he asked.

But Amric shook his head. "This is a barter system, my friend, and it is time to balance the scales."

Halthak swallowed his disappointment. "Very well, what would you know of me?"

"Your healing, is it magic?"

"I am no expert on magic, but I believe so, as I have never seen anyone else with the same ability."

"How did you acquire it?"

"I've had it as long as I can remember, so I expect I was born this way."

Amric glanced back at him again, and Halthak was taken aback by the man's sudden hard expression. "Do you have any other magical abilities? Or any magic artifacts in your possession?"

"None," Halthak replied softly. "But if I had anything of worth, I would offer it to you in exchange for saving my life earlier tonight."

"You misunderstand," Amric said. "The Sil'ath have a deep distrust of all thing tainted by magic, and I suppose I have inherited much of that aversion. Among humans, I have seen magic lead to little other than corruption and lust for more power. I think it cannot be safely controlled by the likes of mortal men, and I want as little dealing with such dark and unpredictable forces as possible."

Halthak was silent a moment, staring at the swordsman's back. "You think of my ability as a disease, a taint on my soul? Well, it's no worse than I have thought myself, many times. While I made no dark pact to gain this ability, it has still been more a curse to me than a gift. As long as I must live with it, however, I will at least put it to good use by helping others in need."

"And if your ministrations are in fact spreading this taint to your patients?"

Halthak was again taken aback. "I–I had never considered it. I draw the injuries into myself and heal them there, but there is much I do not know about...." He trailed off, and then spoke again with resolve. "But it is a part of me, and I have to believe my intent counts for something."

Amric sighed, and the tension eased from his posture. "Please forgive me, healer, for I meant no insult. You are a kind soul, and I agree with you that intent should matter. Regardless, you deserve finer treatment from the likes of me. I will see you safely to the city, and I will not again let my prejudice get the better of my manners."

"Think no more on it," Halthak said, echoing back Amric's own words. "Keldrin's Landing is said to have drawn all manner of experts and artisans to itself in its hour of need. No doubt scholars of magic will be among them. Perhaps I can learn more of my ability there."

"Such knowledge could be useful indeed," Amric agreed, "if you can trust its source. Be wary not to fall under the sway of a scholar with his own motives."

"What do you mean?"

"Magic, wealth and martial might are forms of power, and they have all been congregating at Keldrin's Landing. The city's cry for help has likely drawn as many jackals as defenders. The greatest threat may still be from the surrounding lands, but the dangers within the city walls are no less real. Be guarded in lending your trust to anyone there."

"You talk as if you've been there," Halthak said.

"No, but like any soldier who hopes to live long enough to see his own hair become grey one day, I have gathered information as to the terrain ahead. Word has spread far from the ailing city, as you are no doubt aware, and its afflictions follow the tales. Its plight is expanding quickly to the rest of the land."

"It sounds as if my safest course would be to remain in your company, for a time," Halthak ventured.

Amric gave him a sharp look. "That is not our agreement, healer. I will see you to the city, and then we part company."

Halthak looked away. He had expected no different, but still he was stung by the abrupt rebuke. The swordsman stood, stretched his arms over his head, walked a few paces back and forth, and then resumed his seated position.

"I do not know your purpose in Keldrin's Landing," Amric said in a more gentle tone, and he held up one hand to forestall Halthak's response, "and I do not want to know. Valkarr and I have our own purpose there, and I cannot say where the trail will lead, but we will need to move quickly and it will be hazardous. You do not want to accompany us."

"If your path will be as hazardous as you say, you may be injured—"

Amric shook his head. "Enough, healer. Some secrets must remain between us yet. Now get some rest. If we break camp early on the morrow, I believe we can reach Keldrin's Landing by midday. In any event, we have made too much noise already and there are things out there that will take an interest in us if we continue to beg their attention."

Halthak felt a chill at Amric's words, and he rolled to his side to put his back to the rock outcropping while his gaze raked the surrounding darkness. He had heard many tales of the horrors assailing the lands surrounding Keldrin's Landing. Those tales were scarcely credible, but even if they had grown in the retelling, they were likely based on some small kernel of truth. And any basis in fact to what Halthak had heard was sobering indeed. He wondered, not for the first time, at his own judgment in coming here. He was certain sleep would not come, certain he would lie awake all night waiting for some grinning nightmare to claw its way out of the night and come for him. In the darkest hours of the new morning, however, exhaustion worked at his conviction with its measured touch and proved him wrong.

CHAPTER 2

Amric swirled the tankard of ale in a slow circle, staring into the dark liquid ripples. Two days in this blasted city chasing every stray rumor, and a galling lack of progress to show for it. He felt a twinge of regret for turning Halthak away when they arrived in Keldrin's Landing. For all the healer's naiveté, he had seemed far more comfortable within the confines of the city walls than Amric felt. The warrior had to admit that despite the information he had gathered in advance, despite his efforts to prepare, the sheer magnitude of everything here was overwhelming.

He knew the city's origins decades ago as a military camp established by the dauntless explorer, Keldrin. It was the barest toe hold on the coast of a wild and ancient land dominated by primordial forests. One could still see those martial origins in the grid-like layout of the oldest sections: the docks, the military quarter and the trade district, in particular. From there, with the discovery of the abundance of mineral riches in the region, the growth of Keldrin's Landing had been far too rapid to maintain its orderly structure. The trade district had spilled over its containment, flowing into new thoroughfares. The huge estates of the wealthiest merchants squatted on a long bluff overlooking the city center, each one an opulent walled fortress in its own right. The residential district encircled the others in a great arc, and the outer wall surrounding everything had been collapsed and rebuilt at various times to accommodate the city's expanding girth. These days, refugees were arriving from the countryside by the hour, further swelling the city past capacity.

No, Amric had expected the city to have grown from its modest origins, but not this much. Faced with this unexpected sea of humanity, his plan—to enter the city and ask around until he located the specific information and individuals he sought—had produced nothing so far, and the approach now struck him as far too ingenuous to be effective. Valkarr was still wandering the city, hoping to discern a comment or other reaction to his presence that indicated some knowledge of the Sil'ath that had passed this way. His efforts might pay dividends, but suffered from the same problem; it was like attempting to track a particular fish through a vast ocean. The invading sense of futility set Amric's teeth on edge.

He realized he was swirling the tankard in curt, rapid motions, and its contents threatened to slosh over the lip. He leaned back with a sigh, setting the vessel on the oaken table before him. The din of the Sleeping Boar's grand common room pressed in about him once more. He pushed a hand through his close-cropped hair and took a steadying breath.

He needed a new plan.

He scanned the crowded room, searching again for new inspiration. Like the rest of the city's occupants, the patrons of the Sleeping Boar Inn hailed from many races and regions. While the majority of them were human like him, Amric observed a short bird-like creature at the great stone hearth, three furry broad-shouldered figures exchanging whispers at a table near the bar, and a cloaked figure at a corner table whose snout protruded from its deep cowl. Amric frowned at the number of individuals he observed in ornate robes. He assumed them to be magickers of some sort, and wondered how many more were not so clearly marked. There were, of course, no Sil'ath to be seen.

The owner of the inn, a stout Duergar named Olekk, was polishing the bar with devoted ferocity. He paused, his swarthy face flushed with effort, and squinted down its length. Straightening, he threw the cloth over one broad shoulder, and expanded his possessive scan to include the rest of the room. Finally, with a satisfied nod, he swung away and passed through the doorway into the kitchen. As he went, he exchanged a slight nod with the hulking figure standing at the back wall, a Traug—a truly massive specimen of its kind—that he employed to remove troublemakers from the premises. It was a job the Traug did with dispassionate efficiency, as Amric could attest after two days of hunting rumors among the inn's itinerant patrons.

Amric's roving gaze caught on a grey-haired man seated alone in the shadows of a corner table. The fellow wore a sardonic smile, and as he locked eyes with Amric, he inclined his head in a slight nod toward him. The swordsman had passed through this common room countless times in the past two days, and did not recall ever seeing the man, let alone conversing with him enough to reach familiarity. He shrugged to himself. Perhaps the man had overheard him seeking information, and felt he had some to share or sell. Regardless, given the lack of competing leads, Amric could not afford to let any potential opportunity go unexplored.

As he gathered himself to stand, he noticed two tall, slender figures wending their way toward him between the tables of the common room. Clad in dark leather, they moved with graceful purpose, balanced and alert, remaining precisely arm's length apart at all times. Practiced predators accustomed to hunting together, Amric noted. He settled back into his chair, donning a neutral expression above the table while beneath it he palmed a throwing knife from its concealed sheath behind his belt. The stranger in the corner would have to wait.

They drew to a halt as they reached him, fanned out on the opposite side of the table. Their arms hung relaxed at their sides, their postures confident, almost insolent. They gazed down at Amric with matching smiles but did not speak, and Amric took the opportunity to study them in this close proximity.

They had fine builds and finer features. Their eyes were larger than a human's, liquid glimmers beneath long, delicate brows. That they had Elvaren blood was evident at once, but they were at the same time unlike any of that lineage he had seen before. They had striking white shocks of hair, and their pale skin held a dusky tinge, like layers of translucence over something darker. From features to dress to mannerism, they appeared identical in every detail.

They waited, their manners mocking and expectant, and Amric somehow felt that to speak first was to cede some obscure advantage in this encounter. He passed an unhurried stare from one to another and waited as well. He realized that the room had become hushed as the duo's odd behavior had drawn attention. Or, Amric reflected, they were known well enough to the inn's patrons to warrant the reaction; all the more reason to exercise caution. He felt a sudden nagging itch at his perceptions, and on impulse he flicked a glance toward the old stranger in the corner. The man had withdrawn even further into the dimness there, arms folded across his chest, his enigmatic smile a mere suggestion in the shadows. He appeared to be regarding Amric still across the room, and some trick of the light gave his eyes a lambent glow.

Yes, Amric mused, he would definitely need to understand this man's interest in him soon. He returned his attention to the pair before him.

It seemed that taking his attention from them, even momentarily, had accomplished what exchanging stares did not. Amric read irritation plain upon their features at being ignored so, and the one to his right finally spoke.

"It is churlish for not offering us to join its table," he said.

"Indeed so, brother," replied the other. "And here it sits, compounding its stunning lack of manners with every breath." They cocked their heads to the side in unison, studying him as if he were some loathsome insect.

Amric raised an eyebrow. "I do not believe we have met—" he began.

"The umbrage of our employer is, certainly, less of a mystery now," one continued, as if he had not spoken.

"Agreed," the other intoned, the solemnity of his delivery belied by the cruel twist of his smile.

Try as he might, Amric could not make sense of their statements. It? Employer? He decided to venture another entry into the conversation. "Do you bring information for a price? If you know the whereabouts of those I seek—"

"Still it prattles on," one exclaimed in mock surprise. "So oblivious to the gravity of its situation, is it then?"

"I fear so, brother. Be it our duty to educate it?"

"Ah, you raise an interesting question, and I stand here shamed that we did not think to clarify this point with our employer."

"And I as well. But he is a busy and important man, and cannot be troubled to clarify every little obstacle we might encounter as his agents in this matter. Perhaps we can infer his wishes?"

"An excellent line of reasoning, brother. Let us extend that line further, then. Think you he would wish it to expire in ignorance as to its affronts, or to pass into that dark with eyes opened?"

The other put a long, slender finger to his chin in thought. "Given the strength of his feelings on the subject, I surmise that he would wish it to know, to realize the fullness of the sentence that has been passed over it, and to agonize in vain over the fate its companions will share."

Amric sat forward. "Companions? Do you mean the Sil'ath party I seek, that came this way—"

Again he was ignored, as the sibling gave an earnest nod. "I must concur. He impressed us as a man of highly cultured tastes, inclined to savor this familial indulgence."

"Then we are decided, we must converse with it first."

The pair returned their attention to Amric, the infuriating smiles spreading across their features once more. Amric, for his part, met their stares as his mind raced to assemble the fragments of their strange conversation. He assumed himself to be the *it* featured in their dialogue, though the choice of pronoun was still a mystery. They were in the employ of some as yet unnamed individual who bore him a grudge, for unspecified reason, and that enmity extended to Amric's companions. The plural of that latter designation was intriguing; his only current companion was Valkarr, but if they knew or assumed his connection with the Sil'ath party he was tracking, they would be the first he had encountered in Keldrin's Landing with any such knowledge. As his first and only lead, he was compelled to pursue it, despite the fact that these two clearly considered themselves tasked with exacting vengeance on behalf of his unknown adversary.

With his free hand, he gestured at the chairs before them, on the opposite side of the table from him. His other hand remained below the table, the throwing knife held ready. The table was too heavy to kick up into them without proper leverage, so he would need another distraction to increase the odds of his throw finding a mark that would disable or kill. Their lithe, certain movements hinted at great speed, and he would need precious time to stand and draw his swords as well as room to wield them. He had no allies here, and in fact being involved in an altercation inside the Sleeping Boar would elicit for him the same unwelcome attention his opponents would face from the inn's enforcer. With his peripheral vision, Amric verified that the mountainous figure of the Traug was still by the bar, gimlet eyes focused upon the confrontation.

The pair slid into the chairs with identical movements.

Amric decided to vacate the role of the flushed quarry. If he was to be off-balance, he could at least return the favor. "Keep your hands in sight!" he commanded, raising his voice sharply to draw attention.

They exchanged an amused glance. "And if we do not?" the one on the left purred.

Amric brought his throwing knife into view and brandished it before them, high enough to be visible to all. With a rumbling growl that shook nearby tables, the Traug moved forward in a surge. The room went silent. The heads of the Elvaren whipped around, and they took in the advancing giant.

"He is much faster than his size would indicate," Amric observed. "And that hide is nearly impervious to blades. But I would wager you already know that."

Their heads swiveled back to him. Amric wore a wolfish smile now.

"Yesterday I saw him throw someone about your size out those front doors, and the fellow didn't touch down until he struck the building across the way. To be fair, I cannot say which of his broken bones resulted from the landing and which were from the initial grapple. I am certain I heard snapping sounds when those huge hands wrapped around the poor sot."

Their smirks had vanished, replaced by icy glares. Their hands flashed to the table's surface. "It has made its point. It will put away its blade now, so that we may converse with it."

"Yes," Amric said. "Let us not involve the whole place in our conversation." He lowered the knife, slipped it back into the concealed sheath behind his belt, and then raised both hands in a slow wave to the Traug. The latter halted, studying the table for a long, mute moment, and then made a ponderous turn back to the bar. A subdued murmur seeped into the silence of the room and built from there, and more than a few patrons cast inquisitive looks in their direction.

Amric lowered his hands to the table, and met the seething gazes of the Elvaren.

"I will be direct," he said. "I have no quarrel with you. I do not even know you. I am newly arrived to this city, and to my knowledge I have offended no one, unless by asking after the whereabouts of missing friends. Whom do you represent?"

"His identity is his alone to share, should he choose to do so," one snarled. "But it is incorrect, for it has indeed offended, and our esteemed employer must preserve family honor by defending the wronged."

The familial reference again, another puzzle. So he had made an enemy of someone with a powerful relative? "You mentioned my companions sharing my fate," he continued. "Do you know the whereabouts of the five Sil'ath I seek?"

"It attempts a ploy!" came the accusing reply. "We are neither fooled nor intimidated. Its *one* Sil'ath companion will be no easy mark, but it wanders the city unaware even now."

Amric frowned. "But you mentioned more than one companion."

The Elvaren shrugged. "The Half-Ork is no warrior and of little consequence, but it shared in the offense and therefore will share in the penance."

Amric's thoughts spun in a new direction. They meant Halthak! He and Valkarr had parted ways with the healer immediately upon entering Keldrin's Landing, and they had not seen him since. The only acquaintances they shared were the guards at the city gates and the mercenaries in the camp the night they had met. Amric followed the line of reasoning to its most probable conclusion. *Vorenius.* The fool had known where they were headed from their own comments; he must have enlisted local resources and set out to avenge his wounded ego. Amric considered for a moment whether he should have taken the man's head back at the bandit camp. No, he decided, it had not been warranted at the time. But now the man seemed determined to raise the stakes.

"So there is a price on all three of our heads now?" Amric asked.

"It wastes breath on questions that have already been answered," one of the Elvaren chided, "when there are far more pertinent ones to be asked." Their eyes glittered with malice.

His stomach plummeted. Knowing the answer, he said anyway, through clenched teeth, "Enlighten me."

The Elvar on the right licked his lips in an exaggerated motion, as if savoring an exquisite flavor. "It must now wonder, how many more such as we are stalking it and its companions? When will the strikes come? Are they taking place at this very instant, as it sits here trading words with us?"

Amric cursed to himself. They were right, of course. They might even be here for the sole purpose of detaining him, while other agents of Vorenius and his benefactor made attempts on the lives of Valkarr and Halthak. Isolate and destroy; an effective strategy when hunting dangerous prey.

In a blur of motion, he kicked his chair back and bolted to his feet, both swords seeming to appear in his hands. Eyes wide, the pair slithered from their chairs, backing several rapid paces from the table. Their hands hovered at their sides, but they drew no weapons.

"You came here for my life," Amric said. "So come and take it."

So sudden was the act that the Traug's startled response came a long moment later. From the other side of the room came a sound between a choking gasp and a roar, and then the huge creature was striding forward, brushing aside a heavy table that fell with a crash. The Duergar owner, Olekk, emerged from the back room, his bristling beard whipping about as he sought the source of the commotion.

The Elvaren were smiling once more. "It has succeeded admirably in convincing us how unsuitable is the current setting for our task. We will relish it looking always over its shoulder, until one time soon it looks an instant too late."

With mocking salutes, they turned and glided out the front doors of the inn. Calming his breathing, Amric resisted the urge to pursue them. An unnecessary conflict here in the open would only serve to involve the city watch, and he could ill afford any such delay if he was to warn Valkarr and Halthak of the danger to them, in particular if more hired blades waited out there in the shadows.

The thunderous approach across the common room reminded him of the risk he had accepted in forcing the hand of the Elvaren. He sheathed his swords and raised his empty hands in apology. The Traug slowed and his rumbling growl subsided in volume, but still he approached, his great thick hands flexing open and shut. Amric looked past him to find Olekk at the bar. He met the Duergar's suspicious glare as he produced three heavy coins from his money pouch, and then laid them with exaggerated care upon the table. He then raised his open hands and took a step back.

Olekk glanced down to the coins, and then back at Amric. After momentary consideration, he barked an order and jerked his bearded chin back toward the bar. The Traug ground to a halt and fixed Amric with a scowl that spoke volumes about an exhausted supply of free warnings, and then lumbered back to his favored corner of the room. On his way, he righted the table he had overturned, and the care he exhibited in handling it showed he considered the stout oaken furniture as fragile as finest porcelain in his grasp.

Amric started to leave, but paused for a glance back at where the elderly stranger had been sitting. That corner table was empty. Odd, he thought. All the exits from the common room were well visible from Amric's position, and he had not seen the man pass through any of them. Amric shook his head; the man was a riddle for another day. He strode through the doors and into the afternoon swelter.

Halthak worked his way through the thick of the trade district. A shop owner pressed in at his side, pacing him for a few steps as he hawked his wares with a broad, ingratiating smile. Halthak continued on, shaking his head in what he hoped was a courteous manner as he passed. He knew better than to smile back; baring a mouthful of sharp teeth inevitably caused others to read unintended aggression in his features. He inhaled the rich, heady aromas of spices and cooking food, and his eyes drank in the colors and activity around him. Although his errand in the trade district had been unsuccessful, he had lingered for hours afterward and found a growing affection for the place. Here in Keldrin's Landing, with its diverse collection of different races and cultures, he was just another in the crowd, no more or less unusual than the next traveler.

He saw several full-blooded Orks standing in a cluster apart from the other races. They were thicker of limb and deeper of chest than he, and they bristled with crude weapons and studded armor. They turned scowls upon him, but did not follow up with the prejudice he could expect in a different setting. He kept a wary eye on them until he was well past, and as a result he did not see the elderly man in his path until he slammed into him.

The air whooshed from Halthak's lungs and he staggered back, doubling over. Leaning upon his staff to catch his breath and his balance, he looked up to see a slender old man in grey robes. The fellow's silvery hair was slicked back along his skull, and despite his evident age, his pale, smiling face radiated an intense vitality. The man appeared unaffected by the collision, and Halthak peered past him in disbelief. It felt like he had run headlong into a boulder; surely he had contacted something more solid than this kindly old fellow! The man stooped forward and helped him upright with a grip like cold iron.

"I—I am—" Halthak managed to gasp, still struggling for breath.

"Please accept my humblest apologies, young sir," the man said, his voice low and yet somehow cutting through the din of the crowd. "The years have made me clumsy indeed."

The old man released Halthak's arm and gave a gentle pat to his shoulder as he moved past, disappearing into the crowd. The healer stared after him for a moment until his breath came unhindered again, and then he resumed walking.

It was but moments later that he heard an angry shout followed by a commotion behind him, and he turned to look. The crowd parted to give him a clear view of the scene several shops back. He saw the same old man with whom he had collided reaching down to help an irate individual up from the ground as two other men looked on in surprise. The old fellow's familiar words carried across the distance as if Halthak stood beside him.

"Please accept my humblest apologies, young sir! The years have made me clumsy indeed."

The man on the ground surged to his feet, spitting oaths and swatting aside the proffered hand. He faced the silver-haired fellow, leaning forward with fists clenched, and his two friends moved to join him. Halthak noted their cruel demeanor and their unkempt appearance, and he knew them in an instant for common cutthroats. He felt an immediate fear for the old man's safety, and he took a step in that direction. Even as he did, however, the three brutes faltered and fell back a pace. The old man's posture was mild, but the men cowered back from something in his expression. They made a wide circle around him, glancing at one another, and then all three of them looked in Halthak's direction. No, not in his direction, he realized; they were looking directly *at* him. Seeing him looking back at them, their expressions hardened and they averted their gazes, feigning sudden interest in the nearest shop.

Despite the oppressive heat of the early evening, Halthak felt a chill run down his spine.

The old man turned to look back at him and held his gaze with unnerving intensity. His smile was gone, and he gave a slow nod to Halthak before turning and melting into the crowd.

Halthak studied the cutthroats once more. They cast furtive glances at him, growing restless under his scrutiny. He searched for a familiar face, perhaps from the bandit camp, but did not recognize any of them. He could not fathom their interest in him, but he had a growing certainty as to its nature. They would not need to skulk about if they meant him well, and robbery was unlikely, given his poor attire and obvious lack of coin. No, they intended harm or capture, and he had no desire to ascertain which. Regardless, he doubted he would have spotted them without the commotion, so he was indebted to the strange old fellow for the warning that might have saved his life.

Though he was only saved, he reminded himself, if he managed to evade them.

He debated his course. He could remain in public here, staying close to highly visible store fronts. This might prevent capture, but the ebb and flow of the populace here might leave him vulnerable to a stealthy blade in the press of the crowd. He could go to the city watch, but they were nowhere to be seen at the moment and would require more to act on than his suspicions and some hard looks cast in his direction. He wanted to flee the trade district, as its welcoming atmosphere had palled of a sudden, but he was unsure how to prevent them from following, or even where he could go to be safe. He had almost exhausted the last of his meager funds, and the stable he had been sneaking into each night to sleep seemed quite exposed, all of a sudden.

He found himself wishing again that he had been able to stay longer with the warriors Amric and Valkarr, as he had little doubt they could handle these cutthroats as easily as they had managed the bandit camp. His every interest in their mission here had been rebuffed, however, and they had insisted on parting company with him once he was safe inside the city walls. They had seemed so determined, so purposeful.

He had no such solid plan of his own; he had traveled to this remote, dangerous place in the hopes that his healing talent could be of us in the conflict here. It seemed foolish to him now. Of what use was he? He could not even get here safely on his own. He had hoped to find his purpose, and yet he was just as adrift here as anywhere else, it seemed. And so he had bid the warriors farewell, removing at least one unnecessary burden from their path.

Halthak shook himself. Standing there dumbstruck was doing him no good. He set off at a quick pace, staying close to the stores. If he could put enough distance between himself and his pursuers, he could duck down a side alley and lose them. If he chanced upon a city watch patrol before then, he could shadow the watch until another opportunity arose to escape.

He peered down the alleys between shops as he passed. They were narrow and deep in shadow already, and would only get less inviting as the sun continued to set, but they were his best chance of disappearing. One yawned ahead, a dark portal just past a busy food market. He veered toward it. At the corner, he craned his neck for a look back and felt another chill. The men were shoving their way through the crowd and closing the distance with alarming speed, their gazes fixed upon him. They were far too close, almost at his heels, and entering the alley would be sheer folly now; no one would witness the attack there, and his assailants could flee its aftermath in relative safety.

Halthak turned away from the mouth of the alley, but a figure loomed at out of the shadows. With a startled cry he swung his staff in an overhand chop at the figure's head, but his opponent batted it aside. A powerful arm shot out and seized his robes, yanking him forward into the shadows and sending him staggering down the alley. Halthak threw a hand against the wall to keep from falling, and spun to put his back to it, raising his staff before him. He cursed his own stupidity. Of course they had more than the trio he had seen in the open, encircling him to ensure he could not escape so easily. His fists tightened on the burled ironwood staff. It was a stout weapon, but he was no fighter. He had no illusions about the odds of him fending off one skilled attacker, let alone four or more.

The three thugs entered the alley at a run, becoming black silhouettes like the figure before him against the still bright sun of the main street. They skidded to a halt as they entered the shadows, daggers held low and ready, and for a moment all was still. Halthak had just inhaled to shout for help when the scene exploded. He heard startled oaths as the cutthroats lunged forward at the figure who had hauled him into the alley, and there followed a flurry of activity too fast for him to follow in the poor light. There was a loud grunt and one shape went down heavily. The mysterious figure cut between the other two, and another shape was propelled across the alley to slam into the wall, where it crumpled. The figure spun around the last of the thugs and then approached Halthak at an unhurried pace. Behind him, the final thug pitched face-first to the ground. The entire fight had taken only a few seconds.

Halthak realized that his hands were shaking, and his cry for help had died in his throat. As his eyes adjusted to the gloom and the figure drew near, recognition dawned.

"Valkarr!" he exclaimed.

The Sil'ath halted before him. In a thick, guttural voice the lizardman said, "Come, we must join Amric."

Halthak swallowed and nodded. Striving to emulate Valkarr's casual demeanor, he followed the warrior out of the alley. As he passed, he noted the cutthroats lying in spreading pools of blood, their own daggers jutting from their still forms. He shuddered. Valkarr bore not a scratch, not a stray drop of blood; he had not even drawn his own weapons in the brief scuffle.

Back on the main street of the trade district, Valkarr received a few curious looks, but no one appeared alarmed. Like Halthak, the cutthroats had not even managed to raise a cry before the action was over. Amric emerged from the crowd and flashed Halthak a grin.

"I am relieved you are still well, healer. It seems you will be safer in our company for a time after all, as there is a price on all our heads." He held up a hand as Halthak's mouth dropped open. "Save your questions for now. We must leave the streets immediately. I sent the watch patrol to the docks with a false report of a disturbance there, so that we could operate without interference here, but they will be returning soon with a host of uncomfortable questions. And those buffoons in the alley were merely the most impatient and least skilled of those who will be after us."

Halthak shot a panicked glance to either side. "Where can we go to be safe?" he stammered.

"Safe? Nowhere in this city, I'm afraid," Amric replied. Then a boyish grin spread across his features. "But until we have a better plan, I know where we can go that will make most attackers think twice."

Amric pushed the food around on his plate, lost in thought. Across the table, Valkarr was wolfing down his meal with typical abandon, and Halthak showed almost as much enthusiasm for his own. Amric hid a smile as he pretended not to notice the abashed glances the healer shot in his direction. It was evident that the healer did not frequently enjoy a full belly, and hunger had overwhelmed his manners on a meal he accepted with outward reluctance and inward relief. The warrior found it hard to fault him, as the Sleeping Boar served excellent food indeed.

The Duergar Olekk emerged from the kitchens and cast a baleful eye in their direction, but made no more strenuous objection to their presence. Amric had paid their stay for the week in advance, though it had taken much of his remaining coin, and in so doing had bought a measure of the Duergar's good will by way of providing insurance against their continued good behavior. He had gone so far as to promise Olekk that they would initiate no trouble on the premises, and if the Duergar noted the careful wording, he let it pass.

The Traug hunched against the far wall like some massive boulder, impassive as ever, but Amric noted with some amusement that the creature's gaze lingered most often in their direction. In return, Amric exercised the warrior's reflex by scanning the bark-like hide for vulnerable points. He had no quarrel with him or his employer; they were merely protecting their business against an often unruly crowd. All the same, there might come a day when he had to face that mountain of muscle and be unable to talk his way out of it. No, it would grieve him to slay the Traug, but neither could he allow those huge mitts to clasp him and reshape his spine.

Amric turned his attention back to the matter at hand. The price on their heads was a complication he did not need. They could ignore it and be harried every step of the way, or seek out their faceless adversary and become more deeply embroiled in whatever pointless local conflict was behind it. Either way, it served only to delay them from their true objective, that of finding their missing compatriots.

He was certain of one thing, at least: they could not remain here, as the trail was only growing colder.

Movement caught at the corner of his eye. The tall, iron-bound front doors stood open and, along with all the windows, pulled a cooling breeze through the Sleeping Boar and drew away the hanging heat of the day. A sliver of night detached itself from the darkness outside and passed through the doorway. Amric's fork stopped on his plate; Valkarr's did not, though he tilted his wedge-shaped head to take in the new arrival. It was the old man in grey robes from earlier, and he favored them with a broad smile as he walked through the common room and claimed a secluded corner table.

Halthak noticed the sudden stillness of the two warriors, and followed Amric's stare to the silver-haired gentleman trading words with the serving girl. The old fellow followed her with his eyes as she went to the kitchens with a pretty flush and a flustered smile, and then he settled back into the shadows to boldly return the swordsman's gaze. As before, his eyes caught the light in a strange way, casting it back at the observer like tiny pinpoints of flame.

"That's him!" Halthak exclaimed in a whisper. "That's the old man I ran into in the trade district, the one who identified the cutthroats following me!"

As he said this, the grey man touched two fingers to his forehead in a salute. Amric frowned. The timing made it appear he had somehow heard Halthak's hushed words across the clamor of the busy room, but that had to be coincidence. In any event, the man had made his interest in them evident enough, and Amric's own curiosity was certainly piqued. Amric exchanged a look with Valkarr, then stood and left his companions at their table. A low growl from the Traug trembled the floorboards beneath the swordsman's feet. Gimlet eyes set deep under a heavy brow ridge tracked his every step across the room, but the creature took no other action.

The old man waited with that expectant smile. Amric stopped before his table, and asked, "Sir, may I join you?"

"I would be most disappointed if you did not," the other replied. "Please, take a seat."

Amric did so, leaning forward to rest his forearms on the table as he studied the fellow. This close, he appeared less aged, possessed of an uncommon vitality that was almost palpable. Eyes so pale they were almost white regarded him with a piercing intellect that gave no ground to the advance of the years. His expression was warm but controlled, somehow authentic and calculating in equal parts, and Amric decided at once that the man's outward demeanor was a tool he employed with scalpel efficiency.

"My name is Amric."

"And I am Bellimar," the man returned. The name tugged at Amric's memory, but he could not place the reference. Bellimar studied his expression, waiting. The serving girl came to their table, setting a large tankard of ale before them both.

"Thank you, my dear," Bellimar murmured in velvet tones, eliciting another pink blush. His eyes tracked the girl for a moment as she hastened away. Amric's scalp prickled; had he imagined a faint thrum of power there in the man's voice? And it did not escape his notice that the fellow had placed an order for two drinks before Amric even stood to approach.

"Are you a sorcerer, Bellimar?" Amric demanded.

Bellimar cocked his head to the side, but his smile did not falter. If anything, it broadened instead. "A curious opening to our conversation, friend Amric."

The swordsman took a deep breath. "I apologize for my poor manners, but I have little trust for things magical, and you have that air about you. My friends and I owe you a debt of gratitude for your intervention in the trade district. You seem to have taken an interest in us, and I would like to understand why."

Bellimar shook his head. "I took no offense. It is fair to say that magic was a field of study for many years for me, but I do not tamper with such forces any longer."

"And your interest in us?"

"How could I not be interested in you, Amric? You are a fascinating riddle."

Amric folded his arms across his chest. "That is not an answer."

"True enough," Bellimar said. "Allow me to elaborate, then."

He put forth one pale, slender hand and began to punctuate each point with a finger tap on the surface of the table. "You travel with a Sil'ath warrior who calls you sword-brother. Most Sil'ath can barely tolerate humans, finding them unpredictable and soft, and this one names you with a term of highest respect and affection. Moreover, he defers to you without reservation as he would his tribal warmaster, and you are an outsider of unique stature if you occupy such a position among the Sil'ath. Quite unheard of, in my recollection."

Bellimar paused to chuckle. "Do not look so surprised, Amric. Knowledge of the internal workings of Sil'ath society is rare, and my learning on the subject is meager since I have not lived among them as you have, but I was an avid student of history and this world's various cultures long before you were born. And I am not finished."

He continued to tick off points, each a staccato click of one of his nails on the table. "You bear a price on your head and the enduring ire of a powerful nobleman for having rescued a penniless half-breed from a band of brigands. You did not take the life of that worthless bag of gas Vorenius in the bargain, showing remarkable restraint, if not sound judgment. You faced down two notorious assassins in this very room without apparent fear, and have now taken the Half-Ork under your protection, despite his obvious inherent ability and your personal aversion to all things magical. You show uncommon tact and wit for a simple swordsman, and you gather enigmas as you go."

Amric raised an eyebrow. "So you would have me believe that I am irresistible to a scholar such as yourself because I use words on occasion before swinging my blade, or because I keep company that would be unusual in any other city? I have seen races in Keldrin's Landing that I cannot even identify. The diversity gathered here and the tales I hear of nameless things outside these city walls make one wandering swordsman seem mundane in the extreme."

Bellimar laughed and gave the table a resounding slap. "By the gods, but I like you, swordsman!" He made a sweeping gesture, as if brushing aside all his previous points. "You are correct. Everything I have just listed has only deepened my initial interest, which is owed to something else entirely."

"And that is?"

Bellimar leaned back and regarded him over steepled fingers. "You have no aura."

Amric blinked, and waited for elaboration.

Bellimar studied him for a long moment before nodding. "I wondered if you knew, if it was somehow done intentionally, but I believe you. Every living creature has an aura, varying greatly in magnitude depending on many factors. It is the breath of primal essence intrinsic to the individual, marking one's life force and affinity to magical forces. Call it the spark of life, if you will."

"Then there is no great mystery," Amric said. "I do not have, and do not wish for, any aptitude for magic."

"Your dislike for magic has little relevance as to its affinity for you, swordsman," Bellimar said, leaning forward again. "But there is more to it than that. As I said, *every* living creature has an aura. It can be faint or potent, but it is always present. For that matter, every unliving creature will have an aura as well, though it would be imbued or converted rather than inborn."

"Unliving? You mean the animated dead, ghosts and wights and the like?"

"And the like," Bellimar agreed. "Do you think me a foolish old man, telling fireside tales when I speak of such creatures? Or that they haunt only the dusty crypts of ancient kings, as heroic fables would have us believe?"

Amric shook his head, expression grim. "I might have disregarded your words mere months ago, and been skeptical of the tales of the things lurking in the forests here, but I can testify that the same taint has begun to spread much further south as well. No, I do not doubt that Keldrin's Landing makes its plea for help in earnest."

"Good. I find it tiresome penetrating that kind of ignorance. And many of the ranks of Unlife are drawn irresistibly to strong auras as a source of sustenance, so they are relevant to our topic in more ways than one."

"We have wandered from that topic, Bellimar. You were telling of your interest in me?"

"So I was," Bellimar said. "As I was saying, every living creature has an aura, and its character, intensity and magnitude define that creature. Or from another perspective, that creature's defining attributes are reflected in its aura. Whichever stance you take, there is a strong and undeniable connection. Beyond even affinity for magical energies, many attributes are reflected in one's aura, such as charisma, magnetism, leadership, drive and empathy; other creatures respond to these attributes and to that intrinsic energy out of reflex."

"And you can see these auras around creatures?" Amric asked.

"Yes, I can. Of the many fields of research my long years have afforded me, you could say that the study of auras is my greatest enduring passion. It requires concentration and training to see them, akin to engaging another sense, a separate kind of sight, if you will. But this is not a unique skill, as countless practitioners of the arts can do the same."

Amric's jaw tightened. "I thought you had nothing to do with magic any longer."

"You may as well resolve to abstain from gravity, swordsman!" Bellimar said with a laugh. "Magic is inherent in this world, and surrounds us at all times. No, you misheard me; I do not *manipulate* such forces any longer, but I retain my learned skills to observe them. Is that more clear?"

The warrior relaxed somewhat and gave a curt nod. Bellimar leaned forward further yet, his expression intent. Seeming to operate of their own accord, his long fingers began tracing idle patterns on the table between them.

"Which brings us back to you, my friend. Judging from your interactions with others, your ability to draw others to you, the uncommon skill you must have to reach your rank with the Sil'ath, and what I suspect is a very colorful personal history, I would wager you to have a potent aura indeed. And yet I see none at all when I bring up my Sight. You emanate as much visible life energy as the chair you are sitting upon."

"So I am dead, then?" Amric meant the query in jest, but he fidgeted despite himself. He could not decide which topic he found more disquieting, the thought of pervasive magic surrounding him at all times or the revelation that he had no discernible life force. Anger followed on the heels of discomfort. Why should it bother him, the absence of something of which he had not known until moments ago? He had eschewed interaction with sorcerous forces his entire life, and he should feel relief that he had none inside him.

"No, clearly not," Bellimar replied with no trace of mirth. "You are a man of uncommon vitality, and so you represent an enigma that I must unravel. Amric, you must let me accompany you for a time, to study this phenomenon. I have knowledge and skills that will prove invaluable to you. I know, for example, that you are seeking a party of Sil'ath that came through Keldrin's Landing two months ago, and that you have had little luck in determining their whereabouts or their fate. I can help with this. I know this city well, and I know how information flows here. I can gather in hours what would take you weeks to obtain. I know the identity of Vorenius's benefactor, the man behind the price on your heads, and I might be able to call in favors to ease that vendetta. Even if you leave the city, I am a hardy traveler and will be no burden to you, and I will be a great asset inside or outside the city. What say you?"

The man had a feral, unwavering intensity to his gaze. Amric glanced down to where Bellimar's fingers moved faster and faster in their patterns on the table. In the old man's rising fervor, his nails had somehow scored the hard oak and raised long, thin curls of wood behind them. Following Amric's eyes, Bellimar took in the marred surface of the table, and the hand retreated to his lap. He cleared his throat, and it seemed an effort to pull his equanimity back about himself. When he spoke, however, his eyes still gleamed.

"What say you, swordsman?"

CHAPTER 3

Amric stood before iron gates twice his height and thirty feet in width, painted black and framed by the massive reddish stone wall surrounding the sprawling estate. Huge black lions, regal and forbidding and finely wrought of iron as well, glowered down from the outer bars of the gate. Light rippled across them from the torches set to either side, giving them the illusion of life, of hot breath and fluid muscle. From what Amric had heard, the man inside was as menacing as these, his chosen totems, but he shared none of their nobility of spirit. Halthak stood at his side, both hands curled tight around his knotted staff.

"This is folly," said Halthak. "We are sheep, come to twist the whiskers of the lion in his own den."

Amric chuckled. "I am no sheep."

He looked askance at the healer. In his distress, the Half-Ork's face was so pinched that he looked like a toothless old crone, and his outthrust lower lip seemed in the midst of swallowing the upper half of his own head. Amric considered jesting about it to lighten his mood, but dismissed the thought. Halthak's hold on courage was, at the moment, too tenuous for levity.

"You need not be here, healer. It would be safer for you to remain at the inn."

Halthak snorted. "You tried already to dissuade me. I am going with you. You will need an extra pair of eyes watching your back in there."

Amric nodded and clapped him on the shoulder. He left unsaid what they both knew anyway: the inn offered scant enough protection from a stealthy blade without Amric and Valkarr present, and the healer had few options to escape the city alone if this all went poorly. His best odds of survival remained with the warriors, even in this venture. Halthak cleared his throat and changed the subject, his voice low as he glanced about him to ensure the street was empty save for them.

"I do not trust this Bellimar fellow," he said.

"Nor do I," Amric replied.

"This meeting he arranged could be a ruse, and he a more devious form of assassin meaning to collect the price on our heads."

"The thought had occurred to me as well."

Halthak turned toward him. "Then why do we trust him to lead us under the dominion of the man who set that price?"

"There is more to Bellimar than we have yet seen, and I am convinced that he has not been fully forthcoming as to his motives, but I do not believe he is deceiving us in this. He has been as good as his word thus far, and his contacts indicate that the trail of our Sil'ath friends leads here, to this merchant, Morland."

"And is it coincidence," Halthak said, "that the trail of your missing party ends at the door of the same wealthy merchant who then put a bounty on our heads?"

Amric adjusted the leather bracer on his forearm, his gaze never wavering from the gates before him. "One of many questions I intend to ask Morland. We have little choice, healer. This is our only lead, and even if it proves false, it might at least bring the merchant within reach to end this vendetta threat at its source."

Halthak paled and fell silent.

"It may not come to that, healer," Amric said. "Morland has guaranteed our safety for the duration of this meeting. Is that not true, Bellimar?"

"Quite true," the old man's voice came from behind them, and Halthak jumped.

Bellimar drew up beside them, a merry twinkle in his eye as he grinned at Halthak. He took in the iron gates and the black lions, and muttered, "Gaudy. We get a glimpse of the man's titanic ego."

"Any further word, Bellimar?" Amric asked.

Bellimar stepped forward and turned to face them. "Even piecing it together from multiple sources, there are gaps in the story. The Sil'ath warriors you seek were in the city only briefly, and during that time they met with Morland. The merchant is evidently a distant relative of Vorenius and has put a price on your heads at his behest. After their meeting, the Sil'ath were known to have departed the city through the eastern gate, according to sources that make it their business to monitor such things. From there, the trail grows uncertain. Their destination was unknown to any of my contacts, as the Sil'ath spoke to no one else after Morland, and they have not returned. They left weeks ago, by all accounts, but there is disagreement upon the exact day of departure."

Halthak frowned. "So they left here alive, at least, and Morland is not to blame for their disappearance."

"Let us not rush to conclusions," Bellimar warned. "Morland is a serpent, and may still have sent them to their deaths. Word is that they were in Morland's employ when they left."

Amric shook his head. "They did not come here to sell their blades to the highest bidder, or to run errands for the wealthy."

"Do not be so quick to dismiss the thought," Bellimar said. "The rich grow increasingly frantic for their safety, between the spreading darkness outside the city walls and their rivals gathering personal armies within. Sil'ath reputation at arms being what it is, your friends could amass a fortune here. As could you and Valkarr."

"That was not their purpose," Amric insisted.

"How can you be so certain?"

"Because the Sil'ath care little for such things, and I share that sentiment. And I know their purpose because I sent them here, to Keldrin's Landing. No, they would not abandon their task. If their goals coincided with Morland's, a common purpose or at least mutual benefit was responsible. As I have mentioned, the Sil'ath are pragmatic; if they struck an accord with the likes of this Morland, he represented the best path they could find toward completing their task."

"And that task was…?" Bellimar prodded.

"For now, suffice it to say they were to gather information to aid our people, information we believe is only available here. More detail will have to await our leisure, but it seems their search led them to the east."

"Perhaps," Bellimar said, tilting his head in thought. "But your thinking might be too linear on this, swordsman. If Morland had information they required but he refused to disclose, would your friends have bartered their effort in exchange?"

"Aye, that is possible," Amric admitted.

"Then they may still have departed on a task not directly related to their goal, effectively in the employ of the merchant."

"I cannot argue the logic," Amric said with a sigh. "Tell me of Morland."

"From all I hear," Bellimar said, "he finds the truth very malleable. Be aware that he is avaricious and calculating to the core, and if he is putting aside his public need for vengeance—even for a time—it is because he is after a greater prize. When I discovered he was behind the bounty, I made conciliatory advances through third parties to see how he would respond, and to my surprise found them well received. This public show followed by quick agreement suggests to me that we might have been steered to him."

"Or it is a trap," Halthak put in.

"It could be a trap," Bellimar agreed. "Though if it is, I do not know why he should bother to open his doors to us. Why not just let the bounty do its work?"

Amric gave a slow nod. "Let us discover what he wanted of my men, and what he wants now of us."

Bellimar inclined his head, then moved to the gates and reached for the bronze bell affixed to them, but it proved unnecessary. Two pairs of burly guards in studded leather armor stepped in from their posts on either side, long spears in their fists.

"Your master is expecting us," Bellimar said, exuding a haughty air of impatience.

"Names?" came the gruff query. Bellimar supplied all three.

"There were to be four," the same guard responded, peering past them. "Where is the other?"

Amric smiled without warmth. "Regrettably, he is otherwise occupied, and could not accept the invitation. It will be the three of us."

The guard gave him a long look, and finally grunted. "Wait here." He moved to the side of the gate, took a torch from the wall, and waved it high over his head several times before returning it to its sconce. It was long minutes later that a carriage rumbled up the estate drive and into the ring of torchlight, drawn by large draft horses and surrounded by ten mounted soldiers. The gates swung inward with a heavy groan, and the door to the carriage opened. Amric exchanged an amused look with Bellimar, and gave Halthak a squeeze on the shoulder. Even in the poor light, he could see the Half-Ork had gone almost white, but he was at Amric's heels as the swordsman strode forward and climbed into the carriage. Bellimar followed, and the carriage was moving before the door had shut behind him.

Amric scanned the darkness through the open windows, but could see little of the estate grounds. Members of their escort carried torches ahead of and behind the coach, but they penetrated the darkness only enough to reveal a broad tree-lined lane carved deep with wagon wheel ruts. Amric felt a touch of awe steal over him. Judging by the carriage's rate of travel and the length of time it took to cross the estate grounds, he had seen many towns of not inconsequential size that could be contained entirely within the walls of this place.

"Because he can," Bellimar said from the velvet seat across from him.

Amric swiveled his head to look at him. "What?"

"In answer to the question you were just musing over, why would any man claim so much for himself, more than he could use in a thousand lifetimes? Because he can."

Amric laughed. "Was it so obvious? Or do you read minds, old man?"

Bellimar smiled and shook his head. "No, but it is a rational reaction to this much excess. More importantly, I want you to understand something of this man before you meet him. He has long since shed any need for rationality; he does not question whether he has enough or whether an agreement is equitable. For him, there is only the next conquest. If he can take something, or profit from it, or if he can eliminate an obstacle with no more than acceptable risk to himself, he will do it simply because he can."

"Is Morland the wealthiest and most powerful in the city?" Halthak asked.

"I am not certain. He is climbing the ladder, if not yet at its top rung. From our vantage as the mice in the fable, however, all the elephants are interchangeable." Bellimar's features creased in a wicked smile before he continued. "Of one thing I have no doubt: Morland's plans extend beyond this city. For all its recent growth, it is still a weed at the remote edge of civilization when compared to the great cities of the east like Tar Mora and Hyaxus. There is wealth to be gained here, but wealth alone will not be enough for Morland forever. I suspect he plans to buy his way into nobility and rule."

Amric returned to contemplating the darkness outside the carriage. He had spent most of his life beneath the open sky, or in forests or on battlefields; Sil'ath tribes built modest structures, and tended toward nomadic behavior. He had spent time in human cities, certainly, to learn of his own kind and to supplement his education in ways the Sil'ath could not. He had thought himself prepared for a city larger than he had yet seen, but the immensity of Keldrin's Landing had been bewildering. To discover there were still larger cities dwarfing Keldrin's Landing was sobering indeed.

"Ah," said Bellimar, interrupting his reverie. "We approach the manor at last."

Amric craned his neck forward and beheld a veritable fortress looming ahead. Tiny flames bobbed along the high battlements and peeked through the crenellations atop the towers, marking the patrols. Torches set in sconces at ground level cast a lurid amber glow and sent long black shadows crawling up the walls, giving the appearance of a great bonfire of stone set stark against the night.

The carriage and its escort clattered across a bridge and under the raised portcullis, into a well-lit courtyard. They drew to a halt, and the carriage door was opened. Amric stepped out, followed by his companions. The carriage trundled away, and the ten soldiers formed around them and ushered them into the manor proper. They passed through stout outer doors and into a large marble antechamber where the elaborate engravings almost fully concealed the archer slits in the walls, and on again into a more opulent grand entry. Broad marble stairways and ornate balustrades curved up and away on either hand, but they were marched straight through to another set of brass-bound double doors.

The guard in the lead signaled for a halt and gave a respectful rap to the door with one studded fist. A moment's pause, and then the doors were opened from within to reveal a new set of guards in finer garb than their current escort. Crisp and professional, the interior guards motioned them inward and shut the doors, leaving their erstwhile attendants outside the room.

They were at one end of a majestic hall with furnishings as lavish as the other rooms they had passed through. As with the preceding rooms, Amric paid little attention to the décor, though his roving gaze lingered on the towering tapestries that brushed the floor, and he speculated at what they might conceal. An enormous table of dark wood stretched into the room; Amric did not bother to count the high-backed chairs, but he estimated that a full company of soldiers could eat at the table without fear of bumping elbows. A lone figure was seated at the far end of the table, an ornate goblet in one hand as he studied an array of papers spread before him. The guards, ten strong as the last group had been, encircled them.

"Weapons," said one, in a tone that retained a measure of courtesy without offering the illusion of choice.

Amric glanced back at his companions, and found them watching him intently. The corner of his mouth quirked upward in a smile. He unbuckled the baldric that held the two swords across his back and placed it on the end of the table. He drew the knife from behind his belt and laid it beside the swords. After a moment's hesitation, Halthak stepped forward and relinquished his gnarled staff as well. The guards eyed Bellimar, who spread empty palms and smiled, the peculiar intensity of his stare seeming to invite a challenge. The lead guard met that stare for a long moment, perhaps searching for deception, and then he suddenly leaned away from Bellimar and fell back half a step. Shaken, he cast about to his men as if to gauge their reactions, or to reassure himself of their presence. Then he recovered and made a curt gesture. The guards formed around them, and they moved as a group in formation through the room.

As they approached, Morland pushed the papers from him and raised the goblet to his lips, studying them with dark, dispassionate eyes over its jeweled rim. Amric was seated in the chair nearest Morland but still well out of arm's reach, Halthak to his immediate left, and Bellimar next. The guards took stolid stances behind their chairs, hands resting on the pommels of their swords.

Amric took a moment to study the merchant. He was a tall man, lean and hard like a twisted piece of iron swathed in silks. His dusky complexion, aquiline features and sunken cheeks gave him a cadaverous appearance, and his dead eyes seemed to be weighing whether to eat his prey and be done with it or try to wring some utility from it first. Amric felt an immediate and abiding dislike for the man.

The silence hung taut in the air as they regarded each other. Finally Morland spoke in a voice like dry leaves. "Do you know why I am here, swordsman?" he rasped.

"It is your house," Amric replied.

Morland's eyes tightened at the corners. "Here, in Keldrin's Landing?"

"For the scenery?" Amric hazarded. He heard Bellimar stir in his seat, but he did not glance aside.

"You are baiting me, here, at the center of my power?" Morland demanded.

"My apologies," Amric said. "It seems I left my manners in an alley, skewered on the point of an assassin's dagger. Forgive me for saying it, but you and Vorenius look nothing alike."

"Ah yes," Morland said. "Now is as good a time as any to put that distasteful matter behind us. The boy is an utter fool. I can scarcely believe we share a bloodline, however distant it might be. The only use I can find for him is gathering hired swords to me, and even that is largely just to keep him out from under foot."

"If he is so onerous to you," Bellimar said, "why retaliate on his behalf, when he was prevented from committing a heinous act, and still allowed his life in the end?"

Morland waved a dismissive hand. "Vorenius's actions out in the wilds are his own affair, provided he does not invoke my name. Had you slain him, swordsman, I would have been well rid of him and the matter would be closed. As it is, you spared his life, and he returned to Keldrin's Landing squawking of the assault to all who would listen. To my eternal chagrin, his relation to me is somewhat well known here, and thus propriety had to be observed."

"Then it was a matter of etiquette?" Amric asked, bristling.

"I am pleased you understand. More importantly, I have devised a means by which we can clear the debt between us."

"I owe you no debt," Amric growled.

"Sadly," said the merchant, "that is not, strictly speaking, the case. You have caused me a loss of face, however indirect, and I cannot be seen to brook such defiance. It would erode my business dealings."

"What do you propose?" Bellimar interjected before Amric could retort.

"I understand you seek the Sil'ath warriors who came to me weeks ago," Morland stated, then paused. "Speaking of which, where is your other Sil'ath companion?"

"Oh, he is about somewhere," Amric said. "He sends his regrets that he will not be meeting you face to face this evening."

The implication was not lost on Morland, who gave a tight-lipped smile. "How unfortunate. May he come to no harm in his wanderings tonight. As I was saying, you seek the Sil'ath warriors who came to me weeks ago. As circumstance would have it, they undertook a task for me but have not returned. You can absolve your debt to me, and theirs as well, by completing this task. This will be of mutual benefit to us both, since you must realize your best chance to locate them will be to follow in their steps."

Amric bit back another angry response contesting the debt. He needed to glean as much as he could from this man, so instead he asked, "What is this task?"

"I am coming to that, swordsman. First I must return to my initial question: Do you know why I am here? No? It is not, as you put it, for the scenery." Morland's lip curled in disdain. "Geographically, this city is an inconsequential little dung heap. It is making me rich, I must admit, but I will celebrate the day I leave this place behind. Being here in Keldrin's Landing is like living in a demon's armpit. Strategically, however, this city enjoys a number of unique properties that warrant close consideration. Very close consideration indeed."

He trailed off, one finger caressing the base of the goblet. After a moment, Bellimar cleared his throat. Morland's brow creased in irritation and he turned to the old man as if noticing him for the first time.

"Your name is Bellimar, yes? How did you come by it? Surely no parent would bestow it, given its history."

Bellimar's smile was fixed upon his face, and he did not return the sudden looks from his companions. "You were extolling the strategic properties of this city, Morland?"

"So I was," Morland murmured. "Of this region, more accurately. This wart of a city just happens to be the nearest speck of civilization to the phenomenon. Are you aware that the greatest scholars among the nations are observing a marked drop in the world's magical energies, of late?"

Amric and Halthak exchanged a blank look. Only Bellimar seemed unsurprised at the turn of the conversation.

"It is true," Morland said. "It was gradual at first, a year or more ago, but in recent months it has accelerated. The most powerful sorcerers in all the lands are expressing concern as they can no longer draw on the same reservoirs of power they have in the past."

"I fail to see the problem," Amric said in a dry tone.

"Do not be a fool, boy," the merchant snapped. "Magic is power, and our civilizations are in no small way built on that power. If this trend continues at its current rate, we face chaos and upheaval on a heretofore unseen scale."

"There are many who theorize," Bellimar said, his voice soft, "that magic is so intrinsic to life that, were that energy to ebb too low, our world would become a barren husk, devoid of life. Remember our discussion of auras, swordsman. Magic resonates with other magic, humming together like harmonic vibration, and we exist in accord with the energy that permeates our world. Not only will the fantastic creatures suffer from its loss. None of us would survive."

Amric said nothing, unconvinced. A world with less magic, or no magic at all, sounded very much like an improvement to him. Morland, however, was nodding grudging approval.

"An educated man," he said. "Furthermore, are you aware that this region is seeing an even more marked *increase* in magical energies, as they decline everywhere else? So much so that sorcerous endeavors in this area have become hazardous due to their unpredictability, their sheer instability. Imagine, if you will, lighting a candle only to have it blaze up and fill the room with flame. It is as if all the magical energies in the civilized lands are being drawn to this region."

"Perhaps even," Bellimar said, "all the magic in the world."

Amric shifted, uncomfortable at the thought. "Why is this occurring?"

"No one knows," Morland said, with another appraising look at Bellimar. "But it is also behind the swell of wealth here, in Keldrin's Landing. The area was discovered to be rich in natural resources quickly enough after Keldrin first landed here. Now, however, the gems and minerals here are imbued with essence energies at a much higher rate than anywhere and anytime in recorded history. The nations have boundless appetites for such baubles: focus jewels to enhance rituals, magic alloys that never dull or cannot be pierced, and countless more. Those with mining rights, such as myself, were until recently making money as quickly as we could pull it from the ground."

"Why no longer?" Amric asked.

"Our crews have fled their work sites, and many have departed the region entirely on the first ship that would have them. Chance or not—and I tend to think not—the meteoric rise in magic has coincided with a spreading contagion of dark creatures. We lost many workers, vanished or found torn limb from limb, and now no amount of promised wages is sufficient to coax them into performing their duties."

Morland shook his head and sighed, and Amric ground his teeth. The merchant cared nothing for the loss of life, only his own profits.

"And thus," said Bellimar, his tone wry, "the wealthy elite of Keldrin's Landing found themselves at the golden spigot, now clogged, and put out a plea for assistance to the lands. Ample reward offered to any blades that would travel here and pit themselves against these creatures. Payment terms in arrears, naturally?"

"Spare me your moral arrogance, Bellimar," the merchant sneered. "If you share anything with your namesake, you are on shifting sand of your own."

Bellimar pressed on, his grin broad and predatory. "But times of strife call out to avarice, and one's rivals can be so wonderfully vulnerable when all attention is facing outward. So the wealthy must fortify against each other, and continually more so as the armament continues; for every coin spent on the public defense, two go to outfit the estate. Stop me when you wish to resume the narrative yourself, Morland."

"How does all this relate to my Sil'ath warriors?" Amric interrupted. "They would not have been diverted to serve as hired swords so that you could return to exploiting laborers."

"You are correct, swordsman. Irksome, but correct. Your friends refused any offer of employ, but we found a common goal nonetheless."

Amric snorted. "I doubt that."

"Immaterial, as it is still true," Morland remarked. "You see, your reptilian friends were seeking the source of the disruption in this region, for reasons they refused to divulge. I too have been seeking its source, investing considerable resources into research on that very subject. I offered to put your friends on the right path, provided they returned to me with any information they discovered regarding the fate of a business associate of mine who has been closely studying the phenomenon. The mineral wealth in this region has become secondary to a deeper game now."

Amric's jaw tightened. "Controlling the flow of magic."

Morland gave an approving nod. "Very good. Your brains are not all in your sword arm, then. As magic grows scarce elsewhere and bountiful here, there may be opportunity to control the flow, the supply, the very future of magic on this world. Unfortunately, your friends failed to fulfill their end of the bargain by perishing somewhere out there, and still I lack the information I require."

Amric felt the rage that had been simmering inside him swell against his restraint, cause a spider web of cracks, and burst through like a searing geyser. His vision swam before him, and he darted a look at his companions. He thought his expression under strict control, but they read his intent nevertheless; Bellimar's eyes narrowed an almost imperceptible amount, and Halthak swallowed hard.

Morland was saying, "Now, we could transfer that accord to you, as would be only—"

Amric twisted in his seat and struck the guard behind him in the throat with rigid fingers in a hard upward motion that catapulted the man backward. In a flash, the swordsman was out of his chair and across the table. Morland had a split second in which to gape in shock before Amric hammered into him, overturning the merchant's chair and landing astride him with hands locked about his throat as they slid to a halt on the marble floor. The jeweled goblet hit the floor with a wet clang and skittered away. Amric witnessed a fleeting gamut of emotions flicker through Morland's bulging eyes: terror, pain, fury, appraisal, scheming. Then they were hooded once more. The man must have ice in his veins, a detached part of Amric marveled, to retain his sneer in the face of his own demise. The explosion of movement occurred with such blinding speed that the remaining guards were rooted in astonishment for a long moment before putting hands to sword hilts and charging forward.

"Come no closer!" Amric commanded, his grip tightening on the merchant's throat. "I can snap his neck before you take another step."

The guards stumbled to a halt, uncertain, and then fell back as the merchant gave a surreptitious signal with one pinned hand. Morland's neck was very near its breaking point, and yet he managed a glare through the agonized wince.

"You," he said, his breath wheezing through his constricted windpipe, "are a very fast man."

"And your indifference to the fate of my friends offends me," Amric said. He leaned his face closer to the merchant's, until the tips of their noses almost touched. "All this wealth, all this power, and I can end it right here in an instant. I wonder, does Vorenius stand to inherit it all?"

"Now you are being purposely cruel, swordsman. You have my attention, but you still need something from me. How shall we proceed?"

"Remove the price from our heads, and give us the sum of all information you supplied my friends, so that we may follow their trail. If they live, we will find them, and they will deliver the information they owe you, as per whatever agreement they struck with you."

"I will suspend the price on your heads," Morland countered in a rattling gasp, "and remove it once the information is delivered to me by your friends or by you. It will be reinstated if you return empty-handed."

They remained frozen for interminable seconds, Amric glowering down at the merchant while the latter scowled back in defiance. The guard that Amric struck in the throat thrashed onto his side on the floor, drew one short, whistling breath, and vomited with conviction.

"Agreed," the swordsman said finally. "But before I release you, bear in mind that my Sil'ath friend Valkarr is inside your manor at this very moment, having infiltrated unseen earlier this evening, and he is faster than I am. He will depart your estate grounds after we have done so, safely."

Morland's black eyes glittered. "Understood."

Amric released him and sprang to his feet. The merchant sat up with a grimace and put ginger hands to his throat, drawing deep, ragged breaths.

His angry gaze raked over his guardsmen waiting with their fists curled tight around their sword hilts, then to the weapons piled at the far end of the table, then to Bellimar and Halthak standing before their chairs, and at last back to Amric, poised on the balls of his feet.

Finally he spoke in a rasp, "Get them the maps, and get them out of my sight."

The interior of the carriage was primarily silent on the ride back to the estate perimeter, as the three companions each sat lost in their own thoughts. Amric held tight to the leather satchel containing the merchant's maps and papers, his mind already racing ahead over the necessary preparations for the coming journey.

There was but one interlude of conversation.

"Amric?" Halthak whispered.

"Yes?"

"Was it true, what you said about Valkarr?"

"No, I am slightly faster."

"I meant about him being in the manor house, ready to act."

"Ah, yes, that part was true."

Morland sat in the high-backed chair, tapping the heavy ring on his finger against the base of his goblet. Each tap was accompanied by an audible clink that echoed through the great hall. He did not move otherwise, but his gaze sifted through the corner shadows as he waited. Remembering Amric's words, he quelled a spark of unease that the warrior's Sil'ath friend might have stayed behind after all, might have evaded all the searching patrols and come here for him. He had sent all his guards from the room, as his next guests were peculiar, and the common soldiers found them unnerving. They always made his flesh crawl, despite their devotion to him, but now he felt too vulnerable alone and just found himself hoping they would arrive before some faceless intruder found him instead.

When they appeared, it was from the opposite direction he was facing. It always was, he thought, irritated; but then, that's what made them so good at what they did. He spun around at the low sound of their laughter. Twin shocks of white hair above pale, mocking faces seemed to hang disembodied in the air, and then dark leather-clad forms formed beneath them. Nyar and Nylien, the twin Elvaren assassins, stepped from the shadows.

"I do not like to be kept waiting," Morland snapped.

The Elvaren said nothing, and Morland felt a chill. He relied on their speech patterns to know when their ever volatile natures were turning against a target, and he did not want to inadvertently become one. He tried a different tact.

"You heard everything, I trust?" he said.

"We did, lord," one replied. Nyar or Nylien, he could never tell them apart. "You were very tolerant of its boorish behavior."

"Then you heard our arrangement as well. They are to complete a task for me, and then they will be yours once more. They must live for now."

"We understand, lord." There was a petulant quality to his voice.

"You need not worry, my boys," Morland soothed. "I will find targets for you until they return."

"As you command, lord," one of the Elvaren said, mollified. They turned, faded back into the shadows and were gone.

Morland began to sift through the papers on the table, paused at a thought, and spoke into the air. "The guard who was struck down tonight and failed me, I have no further use for his service."

The reply was a whisper, directionless. "Thank you, lord."

Morland sipped from the goblet and resumed reading.

CHAPTER 4

Gormin wiped the sweat from his brow, surveying his crops in the failing light. He was down to just two of his largest fields, all he could manage alone, but they were thriving and he felt a fierce exultation. He had finished harvesting the oats today, and could start on the barley with the morrow. It would take several days by himself, but then he could load his wagon and commence bringing loads to the city, and both vindication and profit would be his. Then his gaze slid over his other fields, all lying fallow, and his mood soured.

He beat the day's dust from his wide-brimmed hat and cast a look back at the barn he had just finished locking up for the night. It was difficult to recognize as a barn any longer, with all the fortifications he had added: boarded windows, reinforced doors, buttressed walls and a ring of outward facing stakes. His early years in the Marovian infantry had served him well, though he had never expected his experience defending military camps and forts to be used later on his own farm.

From inside the barn came a coughing grunt and the protesting creak of wood. Gormin paused to listen, but it was not repeated. The graffas, short-tempered beasts at the best of times, had been worked hard today and should be quick to slumber this night. Great, bullish draft animals, they were more costly than oxen but Gormin had never regretted the expense; their prodigious strength and constitution more than compensated for the additional cost and their irascible natures.

He turned and trudged toward his house. It bore many of the same defenses as the barn, and just past the edge of its roof he could just see the gleaming walls and towers of Keldrin's Landing in the distance. The sun was setting behind the city and a blood-red hue seeped across the intervening land. His was one of the farms nearest the city, and, as far as he knew, the last remaining. The rest of the smallholders in the surrounding lands had abandoned their lands and fled. Between the drop in production and the severe overcrowding in the city, food prices had risen dramatically. As the only grower still tending crops, Gormin knew he was sitting on a fortune.

The financial prospects would have been even better, he thought with a frown, had his family and his hired help not retreated to the city. If they could have cultivated all the fields, what an opportunity! They had borrowed heavily to buy this much land, and in one stroke they could have shaved years from that debt. He swallowed a lump of bitter disappointment. He would not run to Keldrin's Landing with tail tucked to become a penniless beggar on the streets, would not abandon his holding to some infestation of wild pests. There was nothing for it now but to prove them all wrong, and he would do that by riding into town with a mountainous harvest yield.

As he neared the front porch of the house, a large shape rose to its feet in the shadows by the eastern wall. Gormin bit back an oath, his hand going to his hip for a sword he no longer wore before he realized it was just the dog. Other than the two graffas in the barn, the dog was the only animal remaining on the farm. Shaggy and long-limbed, its head reaching nearly to his chest, the beast was far too large for his wife and children to feed and board in the tight quarters of the city, and so they had been forced to leave it behind. What had they named it? Vulf, or Wulf, or something like that? Gormin could not recall. It had a voracious appetite and did no work on the farm, and so to him it was just another mouth to feed. But his family had loved the ugly brute, and so he made no overt efforts to drive it away, though it could also be said that he made no especial efforts to prevent it from leaving, either. He sneered at the dog, and it gave a low growl in return.

Gormin stomped up the steps to the porch and into the house, with the dog several wary steps behind. Once they were both inside, the farmer dropped a heavy bar into place behind the door, lit a lamp, and fell into a broad chair. A few moments of rest, and then he would prepare a meal for himself. And the mutt as well, he thought with some reluctance. He felt the aches and pains of the day fade somewhat as he relaxed, and his gaze settled, as it always did, on the picture tacked over the fireplace. It was a charcoal rendering of the children, done by his wife, Tiri. She had a real talent, he had always thought; she had captured their small faces and impish smiles with a gentle hand. He felt a rising tide of bitter loneliness threaten to engulf him, and he shoved it away, squeezing his eyes shut.

Soon enough he would show them all how they were overreacting. Soon enough, they could be together again…

A steady, rumbling growl woke him some time later, and he sat forward in the chair, blinking away the fog from his senses. The dog was in the middle of the room, hackles raised, staring at the door. Gormin rose to his feet, hushing the dog. He crossed to the door and pressed his ear to it. Faint through the thick wood, he heard a clamor from the barn. The graffas were going berserk, bellowing and throwing their bulks against the stalls. Gormin cursed. The barn was well fortified, but if the scent of some wandering predator drove the graffas to injure themselves, he would be unable to harvest, or to bring his loads to the city afterward.

His triumphant plans threatened to slip from his grasp. He stormed to his room, buckled on his old infantry saber, swept up his pike, and returned to the door. He braced himself to lift the heavy door bolt and paused.

He had heard the tales told by refugees fleeing to the city. Who had not, after all? They told of monstrous creatures and brutal slayings, and he had discounted them as exaggeration, thinking roving packs of wolves a more likely explanation. Graffas were tough beasts and did not frighten easily, however, and the clamor from the barn sounded like panic. He wavered, listening to the beasts bawl and hammer at their containment, feeling all his plans hanging in the balance. He set his jaw and lifted the bar, being as slow and quiet as he could manage. He would at least peek to determine the source of the disturbance, and if it was something as mundane as wolves, he felt confident he could drive them away with shouting and fire.

He set the bar aside and cracked the door an inch, putting his eye to the opening.

The night sky had not fully darkened yet, the hint of an ember glow still lingering on the western horizon. He had not dozed long, then. Straining against the twilight, he could just make out an indistinct upright silhouette at his barn door. He heard hacking and splintering, and saw the figure bow momentarily with the effort of prying at the door. Then it resumed cutting at the door. Anger flared within Gormin. Not wolves, then, but a man! Evidently he was not the last man to brave the wild pests and capitalize on the opportunity, after all. The rogue was doubtless after his draft animals, and that would cripple his plans. He was surprised at the reaction of the graffas, which did not frighten easily, but the sharp chopping sounds in the middle of the night must have unnerved them.

Gormin retrieved his lamp and held it in one hand while taking a firm grip on the pike with the other. This weapon had served him countless times in the infantry, and he had no qualms about using it against a bandit or a thieving neighbor. He pushed open the door and stepped outside onto the porch. He looked back at the dog, which remained in the middle of the room.

"Dog, come with me!" he hissed. "Wulf, with me!"

The dog met his eyes, curled its lip and did not move.

"Worthless cur!" the farmer snarled, shaking his head. He stalked toward the barn.

The hacking sounds had ceased, and the figure was nowhere to be seen. Gormin cast about with his lamp, expecting a sudden attack, but could find no one lying in wait. He approached the barn to inspect the damage. A few yards to the side of the main door, several of the wooden stakes had been pulled from the ground and flung aside, and a hole large enough to admit a man had been hewn through the barn wall. So the scoundrel was still here, had made it inside! A closer examination of the ragged edges showed a great deal of strength had been used, but little precision; there were stray marks and long splinters all about. A burly man, then, with scant experience using an axe, or perhaps in the grips of some kind of a frenzy. He would be cautious, but was undaunted. Strong men and madmen, they all died at the end of a pike just the same.

Struck by inspiration, he retrieved one of the uprooted stakes and propped it against the others still in place, stamping on the end to drive it into the ground and provide a solid brace. He stood back to admire his work. Far from sturdy, but it would suffice for the moment. The stake faced inward at the hole, and with any luck, the villain would flee the barn and impale himself in his haste.

Gormin contemplated the hole once more. He did not relish the notion of entering the barn this way, as the man could be waiting to ambush him. The front door, however, was heavily barricaded and would require several minutes to open, and he did not wish to reveal to the intruder the hidden mechanism he had devised to raise the inner bar from the outside. There was a splintering sound from inside the barn, and one of the graffas roared in anger or pain. Gormin tightened his grip on the iron-shod pike and ducked under his makeshift trap, through the hole and into the barn.

Once inside, he raised the lamp high, illuminating the interior of the building. His draft harness equipment was off to the side: the battered plow, the pull-behind gathering rake and basket, and more. Ahead were

the stalls, many of them empty, while the broad brown backs of the remaining graffas, each as tall as a man, protruded above two of them. At
the back wall was a ladder to the loft, which had served as the living quarters for some of the hired help.

What he did not see, however, was the intruder.

He cast light into the corners near him and peered around the equipment, but saw no movement and nothing out of place. He advanced to the
unoccupied stalls, and lifted his lamp over their edges, but there was no
one concealed within. As he neared the graffas, he heard a soft rattling
sound, but he could not discern the direction and the meager radius of
light revealed nothing. It struck him then that the graffas had fallen silent,
except for labored breathing; they no longer bellowed or crashed against
the walls. Gormin reached one of the graffas, and spoke to it in soft, soothing tones as he shone the lamp over its stall. The graffa was the only occu-
pant, but something in the hay lining its stall caught his eye, glittering
like a shower of rubies. It was blood, he realized with a shock. Tracing its
path up the beast's flanks, he found deep slices crossing its back, and the
animal was shuddering and panting, its eyes rolling in terror. The slices
did not look like axe marks, he judged, but rather were made by something longer and sharper, like a sword or a scythe.

Why would anyone break into his barn to attack his draft animals, rather than steal them?

He looked to the graffa in the next stall. It was not shuddering like
the other. In fact, it was standing still, leaning against the side wall. Too
still. He took slow steps toward it. There were no marks on its back. He
peered over the edge of the stall, and a powerful stench struck him. As he
brought the lamp near, he saw that its entrails and blood soaked the pad of
hay beneath it, and viscous fluid was seeping under the door. The animal
had been disemboweled where it stood and was dead on its feet.

Gormin threw his arm across his lower face to mask the odor. He continued to stare as he went numb inside.

The rattling sound came again, much closer and louder, seemingly
from overhead. Gormin stumbled back a few steps and thrust the lamp
upward. Clinging to the wall, head downward, was a creature the size of a
man, but there the resemblance ended. It was glistening black, folded
tight upon itself, its claws sunk deep into the timbers and its wide yellow
eyes narrowed as it regarded him. It was covered in long, wicked spines
that swept back along its body. As he watched, those spines lifted away

from its sleek body, quivering in a rapid motion that produced the rattling noise he had heard.

Gormin backed away, keeping the pike leveled at the thing. Something nudged him in the back, and he stifled a shout. A quick glance showed it to be one of the handles of his plow. Keeping one eye on the creature, he hung his lamp from the plow handle and wrapped both hands around the haft of his weapon. The rattling noise ceased, and the creature dropped from its perch to land on the dividing wall between the two graffas, leaving bloody prints on the wall. The farmer could see its long black claws, each almost the length of a sword blade, digging deep into the wood on either side as the creature stalked forward. The spines along its body flexed outward and its shoulders rolled like those of a great cat as its low-slung head remained riveted on him. It sprang to the ground and stood on its hind legs like a man, studying him, and began to walk parallel to his position. Gormin felt a chill, seeing it walk upright thus, and he knew it to be the man-like form he had seen assailing the outer wall of the barn.

It suddenly fell to all fours and rushed forward in a blur of motion, and the farmer braced his pike for the impact, but at the last moment it veered away and retreated. It resumed pacing on two legs, and then launched toward him again. This time its claws struck the head of the pike with a metallic clang, knocking it aside. Gormin yanked it back into position, but the creature again withdrew. It was too damned fast, he realized. In this open space, it could sidestep his defense with that unnerving speed. He began to back toward the hole in the barn wall.

In a flurry of motion it came at him again, and he felt the force jar through his arms as the pike was batted aside. He threw himself to the side, frantically swinging the pike around, and he felt contact as the haft struck a solid mass and knocked it aside. He came up into a crouch again and felt a wetness soaking his arm and side. Whatever had scored him, claws or spines, had been so sharp that he was only now feeling the associated pain, but the bleeding was profuse. The creature was near the stalls again, pacing back and forth on all fours as its claws dug long furrows in the hard-packed earth of the barn floor. It made the peculiar rattling noise again with its quivering spines.

Gormin backed another step toward the hole, but as soon as he moved, the black thing hurled itself forward, coming at him in a circular motion to his left. The farmer did not brace the butt of his pike to the ground this time, instead keeping it free and quicker to maneuver into place. The creature swerved at the last moment and launched itself at him from a different angle, and he leaned away, trying to swing the point of the pike into its trajectory. Such speed! Sparks dazzled his eyes as claws struck the pike, and he fought to retain his grip. He fell back as its weight bowled him over, and his leg went numb as the spines pierced through clothing and into his flesh. He shoved with the pike haft, hoping to lever it away from him before it could reach anything vital, but it clung to him. The farmer saw gnashing teeth flash at his face, and he twisted aside—and then suddenly the thing's weight vanished from atop him.

He struggled to his knees to find the dog, Wulf, thrashing on the ground with the creature. The dog had crashed into the thing from the side and worked his muzzle behind the spines to rend and tear with powerful jaws at its neck. The black creature writhed and spun in place, raking at the dog's flanks. Gormin knew that if the creature could bring its deadly claws to bear against Wulf's underbelly, the dog would suffer the same fate as the dead graffa. He lurched to his feet, circled for the right angle, and then plunged his pike through the creature's side and into the ground. The monster convulsed wildly, flinging the dog away from it, and scrabbled at the weapon with its talons. It tried to roll and twist away, but was pinned through to the firmament, and Gormin held resolute to the other end of the pike. The thing turned malevolent yellow slits upon him, and, wrapping its claws around the pike, began to pull itself along the haft toward him.

Gormin stared in disbelief. Retaining his grip on the pike with one hand, he drew his old infantry saber with the other and struck at the thing's neck. The creature lashed out at him with one claw, but being transfixed and trying to climb the shaft, it lacked the freedom of movement to fend him off. His first strike glanced from the spines, but then he slanted beneath them and struck home, hard. The blade bit deep into the creature's neck, and a second blow followed true, all but severing the wedge-shaped head. The monstrosity shuddered, spines clattering in a sharp crescendo, and went still at last. It slid back down the pike to land in a heap on the ground.

The farmer prodded the body with his saber, studying the greenish ichor spilling out, and then turned away. Wulf was a few paces away, panting and lying on his side in a pool of blood. His dark muzzle and ears were torn to ribbons, and one eye was pinched shut while the other was fixed upon the black creature's corpse. Gormin started toward him, but a surge of dizziness reminded him that he was in no better condition. His shirt and pants hung in tatters, and blood flowed down his side in liberal amounts to leave red footprints on the packed ground. He took a steadying breath and went to the dog, falling to his knees at its side. Its eye swung to him.

"Worthless cur," he said in a gentle tone, reaching out to ruffle the thick fur at the dog's neck. Wulf curled his lip in a faint snarl, but his tail gave a few tentative taps on the ground. Gormin blinked away an unaccustomed burning in his eyes. "I cannot lift you now, boy, but the house has clean water and cloth for bandages. I will have you back to your ornery self in no time."

With a last reassuring pat, he pushed himself to his feet and headed for the hole in the barn wall. As he neared it, he heard something outside that froze the blood in his veins: a chorus of dry rattling sounds, many strong. He spun and crossed to his pike, still jutting from the ground, and wrenched it loose. If he could defend the narrow opening, perhaps he could keep them at bay long enough to—what? They were alone out here, far from deliverance of any kind. Anyone with a speck of sense, he realized, had fled to the city.

A sudden, fierce gratitude washed over him that his family was safe within the city walls. His jaw tightened. Perhaps the morning light would scatter these foul creatures. They had only to survive the night to know the answer.

Even as he turned back to make his choke point, however, several of the black creatures crawled through the opening and went skittering up the wall. Their yellow eyes were burning slits in the shadows. Gormin's heart sank as he swung the pike from one to another, and more of the monsters poured in through the hole. The farmer seized his lamp from where it hung on the plow handle and retreated to the dog's side. There he laid aside the lamp and his pike for a moment, and dug his fists into the thick fur to drag Wulf back with him to the corner where the stalls met the outer wall of the barn. He braced his pike there in the corner, and laid his saber within easy reach on the ground, preparing for the rush that would come. The lamp guttered and flickered beside them but held. A detached part of Gormin's mind wondered when the oil would be exhausted, how much light remained to them, but he knew it would not matter.

The dog strained to its feet, crimson beads dripping from its fur, and pressed against the man's side with a rumbling growl at the creatures. Gormin felt a surge of pride at the animal's courage. The farmer heard a distant hacking sound, and surmised that more of the spiny creatures were invading his house. He hoped they would not damage the charcoal picture. He wished he could have seen it once more.

And still the creatures swarmed into the barn, spreading across the walls and ceiling: a dozen, then twenty, then more. Outside, the last of the ember tinge faded from the western horizon, and true night fell.

CHAPTER 5

"Varkhuls. A great many of them."

Amric nodded, though he did not need Bellimar's words to recognize the tracks covering the ravaged floor, or the deep furrows left by their claws in almost every surface of the barn. He and Valkarr were familiar enough with the repulsive creatures.

"They relish digging their prey out from entrenched positions," Bellimar continued, "and they quite excel at it."

Amric knelt in the blackened section of the barn to pluck a mangled knot of metal from the floor with his forefinger and thumb, and he held it up for inspection. An oil lamp, he realized. That explained the meager plume of smoke they had seen from the main road, and the several charred varkhul corpses they had found here in the barn. He pictured the vile fiends running about ablaze, feeling the terror they so relished inflicting on others, and he bared his teeth in a grim smile.

The swordsman turned away, and his gaze slid over a broken pike and an old saber, taking in the scene they framed. Scraps of clothing and fur were scattered about, and splinters of bone and flesh jutted from the deeply churned, blood-soaked mud. From the remains, it was impossible to tell how many creatures the varkhuls had overwhelmed here, but nothing living remained on the farm now. They had already searched the house, and though the spiny creatures had violated that as well, there were no signs of a struggle there.

Bellimar stepped up beside him. "Whoever they were, they did not go quietly," he said, inclining his head toward two more varkhul corpses, hacked apart but untouched by flame. The bodies gave off a sharp putrescent odor that somehow registered above the rest of the stench. It was the ichor, Amric knew; devilish hard to cleanse from one's weapons and armor, as well.

"Died facing the enemy with blade in hand," Valkarr said from the open doorway in a voice like shifting gravel. "All one can ask." The words echoed the Sil'ath ethos, but Amric read the seething anger behind them in the way his comrade's tail lashed and his breath huffed through narrowed nostrils.

"At the risk of sounding greedy, I can think to ask for more," Amric said with a rueful smile. He walked past Valkarr, clapping him on the shoulder as he passed. "Come, my friend. We have learned all we can, and can do no further good here."

The swordsman stepped out into the long daybreak shadow of the barn and kept walking. He drew several deep breaths when he reached the quickening sunlight, allowing the crisp morning air to cleanse and rejuvenate him.

Thirty yards from the barn, Halthak stood with the horses, and Amric watched him as he approached. Despite the pall hanging over the morning, he had to smother a chuckle as Halthak skipped away to avoid a nip from the bay gelding and fixed the animal with a reproachful glare. Amric and Valkarr were only fair riders themselves, for the Sil'ath seldom used mounts for travel or in combat, but the Half-Ork sat the saddle with all the grace of a sack of rocks. Whether indignant at his lack of skill or reacting to his anxiety, more than one of the horses had taken to goading the hapless healer at every opportunity.

Amric sobered. It was a measure of how shaken and saddened Halthak had been by the slaughter within that he had elected to remain outside with the animals.

Amric accepted the bay gelding's reins from a grateful Halthak, speaking soothing words to the horse and patting its neck before vaulting into the saddle. It was a beautiful animal, swift and strong; Bellimar had proven his resourcefulness again by calling in another favor to procure these fine mounts. With a firm hand, Amric guided the gelding in a circle and to a stop again, to continue accustoming it to his control. The time might come very soon when their mutual familiarity and trust would mean the difference between life and death for them both.

Valkarr arrived a moment later, and swung into the saddle of a blue dun gelding. Bellimar approached, and all but one of the horses grew restive. They were no fonder of the old man than they were of Halthak, and it had in fact taken some searching to find a horse that would tolerate him. Bellimar had at last found an elderly sway-backed dun mare, and though Amric was skeptical of its endurance and speed, they had exhausted their available options. In any event, it would outpace their walking speed. Bellimar took the reins for his horse, which stood still, either placid or oblivious, and he mounted as well. Halthak was left with the reins for his chestnut mare, a steadfast creature that endured his fumbling attempts to climb into the saddle without a ripple to its serenity.

"Are you well, Bellimar?" Amric asked. The old man's cheeks held a slight flush and his eyes were fever bright.

"As well as can be expected," Bellimar responded with a tight-lipped smile. "It was stifling in that barn, and I am pondering the implications of what we have just seen. This is not the first reported presence of varkhuls in the region, but it is the closest known occurrence to the city, and in no small numbers. This gives credence to the accounts from the wall-watch of larger things approaching within bow shot of the city at night. Frequency, proximity and numbers; it all portends the city itself under siege within mere weeks."

Amric nodded. "That is how I read the situation as well. And of more immediate import to us, the danger is rumored to increase as one continues east. We have almost three days' ride ahead of us in that direction, and if things have progressed this far, how much worse will they be a day or two hence?"

He squinted to the east, looking into the rising sun as it spread a mantle of gold over the primordial forests that eventually engulfed the main road from the city. It would take a full day's ride without incident to reach the edge of that forest, and their objective lay deep within it. He turned in the saddle to study Keldrin's Landing to the west, lustrous in the morning light and unspoiled, from this distance. The four of them had ridden out in the pre-dawn darkness and past the abandoned cottages outside the city, all silent as the grave. They had crossed a broad bridge spanning a river inlet from the sea, and were on the road past this, the closest farm to the city, when they spotted a thin tendril of smoke from one of its buildings. Amric had decided to check on the residents, since public opinion in the city held that the countryside was entirely deserted. Upon arrival, the riders had been greeted by the bloodshed inside the barn.

"Having second thoughts, warrior?" Bellimar asked.

Amric swung back to his companions and shook his head. "Valkarr and I are resolute on the path ahead, but no one else need be. We have fought varkhuls before, and while they are deadly in numbers, they are far from the most dangerous things we may encounter. We will seek to remain beneath notice and to avoid what we can, but it will not always be possible. The varkhuls and other creatures out there can smell the very blood in our veins, and may well pursue us with such speed and determination that we have to stand and fight. Let us not mince words here; there may well be no more perilous path in all the lands than into the forest ahead."

He paused and met each of their stares in turn, then raised his arm to point at Keldrin's Landing in the distance. "The city still lies within sight, and the ride back is still safe. Past this point, that will not be the case. You see now the least of what we face ahead, but Valkarr and I will not turn back until we are successful, even to escort. Now is the time to reconsider your involvement, and we will take no offense if you wish to return to the city and await us there."

Halthak's gnarled hands knotted about the pommel of his saddle, but he jerked his head to the side in terse negation and murmured, "You will have need of my skills, out there."

"Let us hope not," Amric said, smiling. "But your company is welcome."

Bellimar cleared his throat. "Have you considered that your friends may be dead?"

Valkarr bristled, an angry hiss escaping him.

"Incessantly," Amric said. "But I presume you are courting a point?"

"The party you are following consisted of how many?" the old man pressed.

"Five."

"Tales of Sil'ath battle prowess are legend, and those tales enjoy a strong basis in truth," Bellimar continued. "As skilled as your warriors undoubtedly are, however, they have journeyed into the teeth of what amounts to an advancing dark army. And now you choose to follow them down its gullet."

"I sense that point nearby," the swordsman said in a wry tone, "but I grow weary of the chase."

Bellimar sighed. "A party of five Sil'ath warriors of consummate skill, and they have not returned. You are now two more such warriors. Even with the considerable talents of an old man and a half-breed healer, how can you hope to prevail where they did not?"

"There is something you should understand," Amric said. "The Sil'ath are feared not just for their skill in battle, but also because they cannot be deterred. They will sacrifice themselves to the last man to defend or avenge one of their own, and even rival families or entire tribes will put aside their hostilities to band together over this racial principle. Call it loyalty or call it pragmatism if you wish, but no one wrongs a Sil'ath lightly. I sent my warriors here to determine the source of the corruption that has spread so far as to assail our home to the south as well. Their task needs completing, even if they can no longer do it. Defense alone is a losing strategy, as the spread is increasing unabated. We must find the source."

Amric paused, and when he spoke again, his grey eyes were shards of ice and his words rang with an iron conviction. "I will know what became of my warriors. I will find them alive, or I will avenge their deaths. But with them or without them, I will find the source of this darkness. It must be found and understood, so that forces can be united against it. If it is not stopped, I fear this remote region will be but the first of many to fall. I do not ask you to follow me, but I will not turn aside."

Valkarr grunted assent, his lifted gaze a challenge. Bellimar regarded Amric for a long moment, and then broke into a sudden grin. "I came here to study this mystery as well, so what better way than at its root? And I still wish to unravel the riddle of your aura. After all," he said, spreading his hands, "what have I to fear of death? Let us proceed."

Amric looked over them all, and found each unwavering. Bellimar seemed relaxed and even amused, while Halthak sat taller in his saddle and stared back with increased resolve. Valkarr fidgeted at the reins, impatient to be off. Amric gave a grave nod and swept his gaze over the house and barn one last time before guiding his bay gelding onto the road that joined the farm to the main thoroughfare that ran from the city to the eastern forest. They passed between expanses of fallow field, and Valkarr rode ahead while Halthak fell a dozen paces behind, struggling to provide direction to his mount. Bellimar, appearing well accustomed to riding, guided his sway-backed dun alongside Amric's horse. The old man had raised the cowl of his cloak and kept his head tilted against the morning sun, still cresting the horizon to the east, so that his face was in shadow. Peering back at the healer, he spoke to Amric in a confidential tone.

"You mask it well, swordsman, but every time you turn to check on our hapless Half-Ork rider back there, your eyes linger overlong on the city in the distance. What do you see there?"

Amric chuckled. "Those old eyes miss very little. I thought I saw a lone rider departing the city long after we did, but it vanished from sight in a valley of the road and has not reappeared."

"How curious," Bellimar mused. "Traveling alone out here would be folly."

"My thoughts as well."

"Surely not following us, since the price on your heads has been suspended."

"Hard to unfire a bow," Amric muttered. "It could be that word did not have time to spread before we departed."

"Perhaps it is merely someone retrieving possessions from the abandoned residences outside the city's walls," Bellimar suggested.

"Perhaps," Amric said. "In any event, we have ground to cover, so there is little we can do except continue onward and wait on his intent."

The four travelers reached the wide eastern road and rode into the embrace of the new sun.

Night had long fallen when at last they found a suitable place to camp.

The rolling plains had risen in altitude as they traveled, and finally gave way to a more stern landscape as they neared the forests. From the maps Amric knew that, to the north, great cliffs fell away to the Vellayen Sea. Their destination was more east and southward, however. Here the gradual rise of the plains met the spare and rocky foothills which climbed further into the mountain range cradling the desert to the south. It had been a long, hard day of travel, and Halthak was swaying with fatigue such that Amric feared he would soon tumble from the saddle. Camping in the open was a dangerous proposition, for they would be exposed and visible from a distance, and then a fire would be out of the question.

So they pressed on in the hopes of finding a more defensible location, and at last Valkarr's keen eyes picked out a cave set into a large hillock and high up the slope of the foothills. Its only visible approach was a narrow, winding trail. They scouted the cave and found evidence that it had once been a large animal's burrow, but the faded scent and spoor indicated it was long unused. It had no other entrances, was deep enough to house them all and the horses as well, and the slope of the ceiling would permit the smoke to escape if they built a fire. All in all, Amric decided, a very fortuitous find.

They cooled and watered the horses, and while the animals grazed the travelers gathered dry wood for a fire and cut brush and saplings for the mouth of the cave; this would both mask the glow from the fire and help disperse the smoke rolling from the entrance so that it would be less visible against the night sky. Then they brought the horses up the treacherous trail with great care, and once deep within the cave, gave them their feed bags and hobbled them. Without a word, Valkarr brought his meal with him to the cave entrance to take the first watch, while Amric and Halthak ate around the fire. Bellimar waved off all offers of food, citing delicate digestion and asserting that he had partaken often of his travel rations as they rode. The old man showed no signs of fatigue, and Amric marveled at his constitution despite his age.

They ate in silence for a time, except for the staccato snap and crackle of the fire, and the occasional snort from the horses. Amric sat cross-legged, lost in thought, watching the flames writhe and dance. It was Bellimar's voice that finally roused him from his reverie.

"Valkarr is not much for conversation, is he?" he said.

"He is more comfortable in the Sil'ath language," Amric admitted. "But even then, he will not share much until he knows and trusts you well. I suppose that makes me the talkative one."

Bellimar smiled. "I would know more of the Sil'ath party you seek. What caused you to send them here?"

"You have most of the pieces by now, but I imagine the story bears repeating in order, and in more detail."

Amric sighed and leaned back against his bedroll. "Strange as it may seem, I am the warmaster, the military leader, of a large Sil'ath tribe. They are my family, the only one I have ever known, and I would die for them just as any of them would for me. I would have you know this, so you may understand I did not lightly send them into harm's way. We live to the southwest, near the human city of Lyden. We are allies with the people of Lyden, enjoying a relationship of trade and mutual respect that was built over years, and that both sides now strive to maintain.

"Months ago, the residents of the countryside around Lyden began disappearing. Only a few at first, but more over time, and there was no explanation. Speculation and rumor soon filled that void, and there were some among the citizenry that feared their Sil'ath neighbors were responsible, for vaporous reasons that only made sense to a fearful populace. A number of rural Lydenites were found brutally slaughtered one day, and our carefully wrought alliance was nearly undone in that moment. Tensions exploded, and there were cries for the blood of my tribe as atonement. We were baffled that they would look to us as the source of these atrocities after so many years of peaceful coexistence, but that would not have prevented us from raising our blades to defend ourselves against the attack so many were urging.

"To their credit, the leaders of Lyden remained rational, recognizing that we lacked motivation for the crimes and that the evidence did not support it either; the attacks were too savage, too bestial, and too chaotic to have been done by Sil'ath. We met with their leaders, and agreed to help them patrol outside the city to search for the attackers, though we were further southwest from the city and as yet unaffected by whatever plagued the city's outskirts."

Amric paused, staring into the fire as images rose unbidden in his head.

"It did not take long," he continued after a moment. "Our patrols, and Lyden's as well, encountered dark and unfamiliar creatures hunting the deep countryside at night. For every nightmare we dispatched, another would take its place after a few nights. After a few months of this, it became evident that the number and variety of the creatures was increasing. Our patrols fought skirmishes almost every night by then, against varkhuls and viles, against greels and wights and more. It was costing precious lives to learn the tricks and weaknesses of each new creature. Lyden lost far more, for our warriors were much more capable, but we also had fewer to lose. It did not take a seer to forecast a future when our forces would be too few or too exhausted to protect us all any longer. And it was only a matter of time before something slipped through our patrol net and reached our homes.

"We met again with Lyden's city council. It is not the Sil'ath way to fight a losing defensive battle, and we desired to mount an offensive, if we could but determine the source to target. Lyden, with a standing military that outnumbered ours a hundred to one, was more inclined to debate the matter endlessly while fortifying their defenses."

Amric heard the bitterness behind his own words and took a calming breath before resuming.

"Lyden was helpful in one respect, however. It was through them that we learned of the plight of Keldrin's Landing, and how the countryside here was overrun even as our own was fast becoming. The realm's scholars maintained that the source was in this region somewhere, for here the troubles had been seen first and remained most concentrated. Embattled Lyden could spare no forces to aid in the defense of Keldrin's Landing, however. Neither could we, for that matter, as our tribe was too small to contribute and still protect itself.

"For us, the decision was to withstand and wait, or to abandon our homes and stay ahead of the spreading wave, or to attack the problem at its source. We lacked enough information to make that decision, and the flow of news from Keldrin's Landing was maddeningly slow. As Lyden was mired in indecision, Keldrin's Landing appeared mired in politics and greed. So we sent five of our most capable warriors to this region, to travel quickly and gather what knowledge they could to aid in the larger effort. They were to bring that knowledge back to the tribe, knowledge that would help us select the best course of action."

He glanced up from the fire and found Bellimar and Halthak leaning forward, engrossed, intent on his every word.

"As you know," Amric said, "my warriors did not return. The attacks were increasing, we still needed answers, and we refused to abandon our warriors to unknown fates. I urged the tribal leaders to relocate the tribe further south, out of harm's way for a time. Then Valkarr and I delegated our command duties and traveled here."

"A warmaster is not the tribal leader, then?" Halthak asked.

Amric shook his head. "Among the Sil'ath, the warmaster is the final authority on military matters only. For other matters, the warmaster is but one member of the tribal council."

"Did your tribe leave their homes, as you advised?" Bellimar asked.

"I hope so. The decision was made, but Valkarr and I left before preparations were fully underway. It is no easy thing to leave one's home, even for a people with a nomadic history, like the Sil'ath."

Amric sighed and pushed a hand through his brown-blonde hair. "Come, friends, I am feeling expansive, and we who may be fighting back to back in the coming days should have few secrets. What else would you know?"

Bellimar's response was immediate. "How did you, a human, come to live among the Sil'ath and become their warmaster?"

"Not much to tell there," Amric said with a shrug. "I was too young to remember, but I am told I was found as a child, abandoned and alone, by a Sil'ath hunting party. The tribe gave me a home, and held me to the same standards as any Sil'ath youth. Eventually, I assumed duties in their warrior ranks to contribute to the tribe."

"Bah," Bellimar protested. "You have nothing of the bard in you, swordsman. You could drain all the color from an epic tale, with such a bland retelling."

"As I said, there is not much to tell," Amric said with a shrug.

Bellimar snorted. "I see you would make me work for it. So be it."

He leaned forward until the firelight danced in his eyes and shimmered upon his silver hair, and began firing questions. "Where were you found, just lying about under the open sky somewhere? The Sil'ath are known for their pragmatism, often seen as cold-hearted by other races. Why would they bother to save a helpless human child, given their generally low opinion of that race, much less adopt one? And how did you become warmaster, a rank reserved for the greatest warrior in the tribe, among a people born, bred and renowned for their martial skill?"

Amric chuckled. "You attempt to spin epic drama from nothing. Very well, my friend, I will answer your questions in order. I was found in an otherwise empty dwelling in the forest, many miles from any human city, though members of the hunting party were not able to lead me to it years later. Nay, spare me your theatrical looks, Bellimar; this was many years later, the forests were vast, and that strange cottage may not have stood so long. Why did they take me in? I do not know, but I am eternally grateful. Had they been friendlier with Lyden at the time, I am certain they would have taken me there and been rid of me. Had I proven unworthy, they would have done it anyway, regardless of their distaste for contact with human society. Instead, however, I set myself to vindicating their choice in saving my life. Why did I become warmaster? Every member of Sil'ath society contributes in some way to the greater good, and I was better with weapons than with crafting or other skills."

Bellimar had opened his mouth to object when Valkarr's voice echoed back from the mouth of the cave. His words were low and sibilant, spoken in the Sil'ath language, and followed by a dry chuckle. Amric laughed and, plucking a pebble from the cave floor, threw it at his friend.

"What did he say?" Halthak asked.

Amric grinned. "He said they felt pity for my stupendous ugliness, and that he had been begging his father for a pet anyway. Valkarr's father led the hunting party that found me, and it was Valkarr's parents who gave me a home."

Valkarr rose and padded into the cave on silent feet. He stood above Amric, looking down at him, and put his fists on his hips in a very human gesture. He spoke in the human tongue this time, with frequent halts to enunciate and choose his words.

"Amric is too modest," he said. "We are sword-brothers, closer than blood, raised together. To our tribe's great honor, he became our most skilled warrior. Even new weapons he picks up and they speak to him, and he is fearsome with them. He is a great strategist and leader, finding victory where others see only ruin. *This* is why he is warmaster. It was our fortune to find him in the forest that day, long ago. He will always be my finest friend." He cocked his head down at Amric. "Is 'finest' correct word? What is correct word?"

"Ugliest," Amric replied with a grin. He reached up to clasp wrists with his comrade. Valkarr then turned on his heel and returned to the cave mouth to resume his watch.

Bellimar was tapping one slender finger against his chin. "You raise as many questions as you resolve, swordsman, but it appears you may not know the answers yourself. And it brings me no closer to understanding your peculiar lack of aura."

Amric spread his hands. "Perhaps magic recognizes my aversion for it, and has forsaken me in return."

"I know you jest," Bellimar said, "as I have already explained that it does not work that way. You cannot simply secede from the laws of nature."

"I am confident you will solve the riddle, old man, and we will both be edified in the process."

"Now you mock me," Bellimar accused, a sardonic smile twisting his features. "Your aura may yet show itself, and I will be there to observe it if so. Even if it does not, an explanation will come to me in time."

"I am not certain whether to wish you luck or not," the warrior said with his own smile. "So I will instead wish you enjoyment in the search. In the meantime, given the many faults in my storytelling, perhaps you would favor us with a proper example."

"And what challenge would you lay before me? Am I to spin a fable to speed you to your dreams?"

"Nothing so grandiose," Amric laughed. "I would know the origin of your name. Morland reacted as if it held meaning to him. It seems familiar to me as well, but hangs just beyond my recollection."

"Ah," Bellimar said. "A true telling of that tale would carry us through to the morning light, but I will try to do justice to a drastically shortened version."

He leaned back and the shadows folded about him, leaving only the faint outline of his features and the luminous glow of the firelight from his eyes. His voice, sepulchral of a sudden, slid from the darkness to encircle them, and Amric felt the hair on the back of his neck prickle as he listened.

"Centuries ago, so many centuries ago that written histories of the era are lost to the fogs of time, a mighty human sorcerer walked this world. Obsessed with the arcane from his youth, he advanced his knowledge with single-minded determination. When he surpassed his masters, he abandoned them to find more. Eventually, so rapid was his learning, he exhausted the mentors who were willing to teach him. The few who had knowledge he did not became reluctant to share it, alarmed by his unchecked increase in power and his continual lust for more. But the sorcerer would not be thwarted, and his tenuous grasp on morals fell before his drive. He captured those who would not willingly aid him and wrested away their secrets, and he stole the artifacts others sought to keep from him. When he had reached the boundaries of mortal knowledge, still he was not content. He reached into the dark energies beyond, probing, experimenting, mastering. Other masters panicked at the path he was traversing, but he was beyond reason and had grown too powerful for them to prevent his progress. Some tried to combine their forces against him, but aided by his new dark powers, he repelled them with ease.

"He grew older, and became concerned that he would reach the limit of his mortal lifespan before he had mastered all things arcane, and furthermore became increasingly convinced that he should not be subject at all to that most mundane of limits on lesser beings. His research became focused on this goal above all others, and at any cost, for achieving it would enable an eternity of further advancement. Here his dark mastery offered tantalizing possibilities, and he pursued them with fervor. Eventually he succeeded, and achieved immortality at the cost of his remaining humanity. A bargain price, some would argue, as he had little enough of that to begin with. He supplanted his own spark of life, his very soul if you will, with the wicked energy of Unlife, and became even more formidable as undead than he was when living. And if certain sacrifices were required to sustain his infinite life, well, then such actions were assuredly justified when weighing the fleeting, impotent lives of lesser beings to the needs of a titan such as himself.

"His foul deeds did not go unnoticed, however, and the populace rose against him in increasing numbers. To defend himself the sorcerer reared his own forces, pressing savage races into service and raising his slain foes as undead to swell his ranks. Enraged at the audacity of the common vermin, he unleashed his vengeance in the form of veritable seas of dark forces guided by his potent mind and arcane might. City after city fell before him, razed to the ground, and entire nations followed. Historians hold that at one point his armies had conquered a third or more of all known civilization, and his thirst for blood was still not slaked.

"Putting aside their differences, the remaining lands united against him as one, realizing that he was on the brink of sweeping them all from the map. They called themselves the White Alliance, a pompous name if ever I have heard one, but nevertheless they assembled numbers not seen before or since on this world. The opposing forces amassed to face each other, blackening the earth from horizon to horizon, from the Valley of Souls to the Talus mountain range. The White Alliance pressed its foe on all sides with its greater numbers, but the sorcerer's war magic and necromancy were rapidly turning the tide. The Alliance leaders knew they could not be victorious in a direct clash, when mortal men faced pit creatures and undying troops, and their own dead rose against them under control of the foe. But they had a different strategy from the beginning. In a cunning series of multi-pronged attacks, they coordinated all of their forces to spear deep into the sorcerer's territory, with the goal of severing the head from the snake. It was their fervent hope that his unearthly forces would follow him into oblivion.

"As you may have guessed, the name of the dark sorcerer was Bellimar. Bellimar the Black, the Vile, the Vampire King, Lord of the Night. Branded with countless such epithets, he came nearest to subjugating the known world of any conqueror in history. The holy city of Tar Mora is said to have begun as a desert monument to the fallen in this cataclysm. If, that is, the ancient tales are to be believed."

Bellimar lapsed into silence, his eyes twin pinpoints of amber in the shadows.

"I remember where I have heard the name," Amric said. "I studied military tactics and logistics for a time at the Academy in Lyden, seeking to supplement what I had learned in practice among the Sil'ath. The name 'Bellimar' was associated with some of the military maneuvers we studied; he was considered a brilliant tactical mind, though his origins were obscured."

"I imagine they would be," Bellimar agreed.

"He was defeated by this White Alliance, then?" Halthak asked.

"That depends on how much of the old tales you believe," Bellimar replied. "Legend maintains that the sorcerer trapped and smashed their offensive, but as he moved to wipe them all out and gain unfettered access to all the lands, the gods themselves intervened."

"The gods?" Amric said, cocking an eyebrow.

"They struck him down and dissolved his forces, and his reign of terror was ended." The gleam of Bellimar's smile was visible even in the shadows. "I sense you doubt the story, swordsman?"

"Assuming he ever existed, I find it far more likely that he was slain by this White Alliance, and that some amount of embellishment has bolstered most elements of the story over the many centuries."

"Aye," said Bellimar. "That is the way of such things, to grow in the retelling, and ample enough years have intervened for it to do so."

"That explains why Morland commented on the name being inauspicious," Amric said. "How were you given it?"

Bellimar barked a laugh. "How else? My mother gave it to me. She was no student of history, and it simply held no meaning to her when she bequeathed it."

"You could have changed your name, to avoid the stigma. Why keep it?"

"Discard the first gift I was given after life and breath? How supremely ungrateful that would be," Bellimar chided. "And if, as some believe, one grows into one's given name over a lifetime, at least mine is linked with ambition and accomplishment, however misdirected. Regardless, while it may have once been an appellation spoken only in hushed whispers or used to frighten children, it is all but forgotten now."

They fell silent, and the sputtering fire reigned once more as each dwelled on private thoughts.

"Bellimar," Halthak said at last with a stifled yawn, "I must admit two things. First, you are indeed a captivating storyteller. Second, you may have found the way to prevent me from sleeping tonight, despite my fatigue."

The old man laughed and leaned forward into the ring of light, his face appearing rosy flushed. "No bard could ask for a more rapt audience. Do not let some dusty old fable thwart your sleep, healer, for I suspect tonight we enjoy the calm before the storm."

Amric nodded agreement, studying Bellimar for a long moment before stretching out on his bedroll. He had a few hours to rest before he would relieve Valkarr to take his turn at watch.

Twice when drifting into slumber did he start awake, banishing the wisps of a striking image: a dark and terrible warrior-sorcerer astride a towering nightmare steed, flaming hooves pounding a battlefield thick with twisted corpses as the rider wove foul, colossal magics against his foes. Each time the black horned helm turned toward him and blazing crimson orbs fix upon him, draining his will and drawing him in…. And then his eyes would flare open to find his companions lying undisturbed in the dank cave, their breathing deep and even, as the fire sank to embers. When sleep claimed him at last, it was with one hand curled about his sword hilt.

CHAPTER 6

Amric and company followed the road into the forest as the morning sun crowned the trees with gold. A dark and verdant world closed about them. Mammoth, ancient trees towered above the thick brush and entwined their branches hundreds of feet overhead. Sunlight spilled through that high canopy, dappling the road before the riders. Taut as a bowstring, Amric rode ahead on his bay gelding. The feeling of being watched had been with him since they left the cave in the pre-dawn hour, like a nagging itch between his shoulder blades. It faded from him now, as the foliage walled off the plains behind them, to be replaced by a pervasive sense of *wrongness*. To be sure, a myriad of expected noises enveloped them, the buzz of countless insects and the incessant chatter of birds. The warrior saw no signs of landbound creatures, however; no movement or recent tracks from vermin or game or natural predator, and the voices of the birds echoed down from high overhead. Nothing dares approach the ground, he realized.

Amric cast a backward glance over his shoulder. A short distance behind him rode Halthak and Bellimar, the former appearing to breathe only when he could avoid it no longer, and the latter with a languid air of curiosity. Valkarr brought up the rear of the procession on his blue dun, scanning to either side and behind them. His black eyes met Amric's, and the Sil'ath's expression made it plain that he felt something amiss as well. Facing forward once more, Amric opened his senses to his surroundings, letting the forest whisper its secrets to him. This was his element, and even corrupted as it was, he could read the woods like the worn pages of a familiar book. Moving at a guarded pace, they rode on, following the road as it curved deeper into the wilderness.

It was mid-morning when they came upon a fork in the road. One branch headed eastward and became little more than a trail, so much did the undergrowth encroach upon it. The other branch veered more southward and was as broad as the road in had been, with deep ruts from wagon wheels. Amric consulted the maps given them by Morland, and found that the southern fork led to one of his mines, which explained the higher traffic and the furrows from carts heavily laden with minerals. The mine was a short ride from the fork, according to the map, and Amric led them down that path. Their destination was down the other path, but the detour would cost them little time, and this many weeks later there was no way to tell from the marred surface of the road where the Sil'ath party might have explored and become detained. Or, came the thought before Amric could quell it, if they had even made it this far.

The mine road clove into the forest, arcing further southward for a time until the ground grew rockier and the vegetation began to thin. The path crested a rise, wound around a ridge of boulders jutting upward like the massive knuckles of some behemoth, and then fell away into a large basin. Amric drew rein before the apex of the road, dismounted and tied his horse to a low branch. The others did the same, and then followed him as he left the road. A few quick leaps from boulder to boulder carried him high enough to peer down over the ridgeline without exposing more than the top of his head to the other side. Valkarr followed on his heels, his movements just as nimble, and Halthak and Bellimar joined them both moments later. Together, they studied the scene below.

The clearing was a great bowl in the earth, devoid of any vegetation beyond scattered patches of dry scrub grass, declining gradually on this side and rising more abruptly on the far side into the foothills of the mountain range. The trees parted around this cleft in the earth, standing like silent sentinels on its lip in disapproval of the mortal intrusion here. As a result, the basin was bathed in sunlight, which only made the yawning mine entrance blacker by contrast. The entry was set into the hillside and framed by stout timbers, twice the height of a tall man and forty paces across. Four sets of cart tracks ran into the maw and were swallowed by darkness within a few paces. There were no carts in sight, though there were scattered pieces of broken equipment such as picks and helmets strewn about.

"It is shelter at least," Halthak said. "We could camp here on the return trip."

"I think not," Amric replied. "Look into the shadows within the mine entrance."

Halthak squinted into the distance, and shook his head. "I see nothing."

"Look at the wall at the edge of the light, just past the second timber brace. Be patient and let your eyes adjust."

Amric waited while Halthak stared and strained. Dust motes danced and swirled in the shafts of sunlight before the entrance, and, coupled with the deep shadows behind, did much to mask the interior detail. The longer one looked on, however, the more a portion of the movement seemed incongruous with the idle play of the breeze, and the more evident it became that there was motion on the walls inside the mine. Amric looked aside, watching Halthak's expression, and he knew the moment of recognition because the healer blanched and his eyes bulged.

"What are they?" the Half-Ork whispered.

"Varkhuls. A great many of them," Amric said, quirking a smile at Bellimar as he echoed the old man's words from the previous morning.

"Indeed," said Bellimar. "They are not harmed by sunlight, but they loathe it and become disoriented and half-blind by it. That man-made cave is a perfect abode for them, and there is no way of knowing how many are in that deep network of tunnels, or how fast they are multiplying. Come nightfall, it will be like kicking a nest of hornets; they will issue forth from the mine and carpet the vicinity, seeking prey."

Amric nodded. "Agreed, and given the scarcity of local quarry, we should put a good distance between ourselves and this location before then. Let us be gone from here."

Stealing back to the horses, the mounted up in silence and rode back up the mine road.

Outside the forest, a lone rider approached the cave in the foothills where Amric and his companions had camped the night before. Halting at the foot of the trail that led uphill to the cave, the rider gazed in that direction for a long moment, then downward at the tracks on the road, and finally to where the road pierced the forest in the distance and disappeared. Turning back to the cave, the rider reached up and released the veil that exposed only the eyes, and swept back the traveling cloak's hood. Auburn hair tumbled free to be tugged by the breeze, and the rider drew deep, unhindered breaths as she scented the air. An unadorned silver circlet sat upon her brow and tamed her mane of hair over fierce green eyes. Swinging one leg around, the rider dropped lightly to the ground, using one hand to steady the long quiver bristling with arrows slung across her back. From a sheath tied to the saddle, she slid a recurve bow nearly as tall as she. She braced it against the ground and strung it in one deft motion.

With a whispered word to the black mare, she draped the reins over the saddle horn and ascended the trail.

In her sewn buckskin leathers and oiled cloak, she made little noise as she climbed, bounding up the uneven trail with supple ease. As the mouth of the cave neared, she loosened the knife in its sheath at her side, and one sun-browned hand snaked over her shoulder to draw an arrow with a wicked curve-bladed head and nock it to her bow. From afar, she had seen the riders depart the cave and enter the forest this morning, but precautions were justified given the dangerous nature of her quarry coupled with the other foul creatures crawling about the countryside.

She darted into the cave and dropped into a crouch just inside. The sunlight did not penetrate far, and she gave her eyes time to adjust to the gloom. Once the darkness yielded its secrets to her, she rose and padded further inside. The cave was deep but empty, an ideal location to camp in hostile country. She wondered if they would revisit it on the return trip— if they returned at all. She slid the arrow back into her quiver, and knelt by the remnants of the campfire, sifting through it with the point of her knife. She crept to the back of the cave where horse dung had been swept to its farthest recesses. At last she returned to the mouth of the cave, verifying that her black mare still waited in place below, and she surveyed the broad vista that could be seen from this vantage point.

She frowned. This was not as good a location for an ambush as she had hoped. One could see far from here, and there was little concealment on the spare hillside for a huntress and her horse. It would be difficult to approach unseen from without if they kept any kind of watch. She and Shien could hide here in the cave, striking before they were aware of her presence, but there was no guarantee that her target would be first into the cave, or even that she would have a reasonable shot before she was discovered. The cave was deep, but one could see the full extent of it once one's eyes adjusted, or with the aid of even modest light. She could hope for them to return during the day and be sun-blinded at the mouth of the cave for precious moments, but they were unlikely to make camp until after nightfall.

Her prey was formidable enough, but she was forced to admit that his companions appeared capable as well. They would not give her more than a few seconds of opportunity. She could nock and fire two arrows in the time it took for a man to make one running stride; it was conceivable she could slay them all, with only a touch of luck. Luck favored the prepared, however. She needed one perfect shot before they overwhelmed her.

The huntress reached over her shoulder, and her expert fingers found the fletching of a different type of arrow in her quiver. She drew it forth and studied it, as she had done so many times. Shaft, fletching and tapered head were all obsidian black; the head itself was comprised of an ingenious mechanism ensuring that the four swept-back blades would unfold upon impact to cause additional damage upon entry and untold trauma upon extraction. This was almost incidental, however, to the primary killing power housed within the missiles, and for which she had paid a king's ransom. She rolled the black arrow between her fingertips and the razor edges of the blades spun ravenous fire from the sunlight, as if the arrows themselves were eager to fulfill their grim mission. With an effortless twirl she slid the arrow home into the quiver once more. She had only three of that kind, and she could not afford to waste them. Anything less devastating would not be sufficient for the task.

Pressing her lips into a tight, bloodless line, she started down the trail toward Shien, skipping feather light between rock and hard-packed earth to leave no sign of her passage. She doubtless had some time before they would emerge from the forest, after whatever task they were about, and in that time she would continue to search for the perfect place from which to strike down a fearsome foe. If nowhere else provided a greater advantage, she would return to this cave and lie in wait. She unstrung and sheathed her powerful bow, then stepped into the saddle. With one hand she stroked the mare's glossy neck, and with the other pulled her hood up and refastened the dark veil across her face. Her eyes flashed like emeralds beneath the cowl as she scanned her surroundings once more, and then she swung her mare about and rode toward the forest's edge.

Amric held up one hand, bringing the small column of riders to a halt. He remained thus, unmoving, as the seconds gathered into a minute, then two. His vision strained to pierce the screen of vegetation framing the sinuous trail ahead, and his hearing grasped for the incongruous sounds that had alerted him. He was about to lead his companions into the undergrowth to give a wide berth to whatever was before them, as they had done several times already this day, when he realized that something was different this time. On this occasion, even his keen senses may not have given warning early enough, as whatever it was, it had gone silent and was listening for them in return.

The warrior closed his raised hand into a fist, and the riders behind him guided their mounts into quiet turns, taking slow steps back the way they had come. Once out of hearing, they could seek a way to circumvent the obstacle and be on their way once more. Amric pulled back on the reins, having his bay gelding back-step a few paces before he would turn it, and he whispered soothing words in the tense animal's ear. Just then, a mischievous gust of wind blew toward them, rustling the foliage and carrying the forward scent to the horse's flaring nostrils. The bay shuddered and gave an anxious toss of its head accompanied by a soft snort, and the undergrowth before them exploded.

Dark, wiry forms hurtled through the brush, clawing for him. Amric muttered an oath and one of his swords sang free into his hand while he jerked on the reins with the other fist. Even had the bay been a war horse, inured to the clash of battle and a fearsome weapon in its own right, he was not an expert enough rider to manage the animal with only his knees such that he could wield both blades. And it was evident the gelding was no war horse, as it bleated a shriek and its eyes rolled in terror at the sudden assault. Amric had time to count roughly half a dozen figures of varying sizes, all somewhat humanoid in shape, and he had an impression of rags hanging in tatters over jet-black frames. Then, with blinding speed, they were upon him.

He sent vicious cuts into them, and he felt the force jar back through his shoulder as his blade bit into that black hide, much tougher than bare flesh. They swarmed against his horse, crooked hands clutching at its neck and mane, pulling at its flanks, clawing at the saddle and his flexing leg in its stirrup. His sword described an arcing blur, and a grasping hand spun away from its wrist. He followed with a murderous backhand slash, and the hairless black skull lolled back, attached only by the barest scrap of corrupt hide. Their very flesh seemed to catch at his weapon, and it was an effort to pull it free and to retain his grip at each stroke. He lunged forward and, his thrust propelled by thick cords of muscle, slammed his blade into the chest of a creature with such force that a foot of cold steel burst from its back. To his astonishment, the creature wrapped its hands around the blade skewering it and gave a savage twist of its torso, trying to wrench it from his grasp. Kicking his foot free of its stirrup, he placed his boot against the thing's chest and launched it away even as he pulled savagely back on the hilt of his sword, clearing it.

The creatures surged over the swordsman's horse, ripping at his clothing and seeking to bind his arm. Amric glared in cold fury down into their visages as they writhed up after him. They were deepest black everywhere beneath a swaddling of cloth that hung in shreds from their frames, including even the inside of their gaping mouths, their bared teeth and where the whites of their eyes should have been. He realized with a chill that they shed no blood when struck, and had voiced neither cry of pain nor growl of anger. But for the slap of their bodies and pawing strikes, and the rasp of the rotten cloth about them parting as they scrabbled to climb over their fellows in their haste to reach him, they were utterly silent. Even the ones to whom he had dealt crippling blows were clawing at him with unfaltering vigor; only the one he had all but decapitated had fallen away and not risen again.

The bay's legs began to buckle under the weight as the creatures sought to drag mount and rider to the ground, and then Valkarr was there, crashing into them atop his dun gelding, his blade cleaving right and left. As his horse fell to its knees, Amric rolled from the saddle and away from the bulk of his assailants to land on his feet. His other sword flashed into the air. One of the creatures, a barrel-chested thing that resembled a hairless black version of the beast men he had seen back at the Sleeping Boar, ducked under Valkarr's horse and wrapped its burly limbs about the animal's legs. The dun stumbled and pitched forward, and Valkarr leapt from the saddle as he drew his second sword. The figures pursued the warriors, pawing their way over the downed horses as if they were already forgotten.

"Take the heads!" Amric commanded. "Cut instead of stab!"

Amric hurled himself back into them. The creatures pressed forward in a mass, heedless of their own injuries, seeking to crash over him like a wave. His swords whirled in a glittering net around him as he spun through the knot of bodies. A grasping hand and forearm parted company with the rest of its arm; a slick black skull tumbled to the sward even as its sunken pit eyes still sought its prey; a sharp kick bent an exposed knee the wrong way with a sickly crack, and its owner was propelled to the ground by the force of the blow. All the while, his flickering blades turned aside clutching hands and flailing fists. Then Amric was through the horde. He risked a look at Valkarr to see that his friend had beheaded one of his assailants and sidestepped the other's charge. In that instant, one of the throng he had just cut through swung a wild fist that bounced from Amric's mailed shoulder and struck him across the temple. It hit with the force of a blacksmith's hammer, and for a moment lights burst before his eyes and his vision swam. He back-pedaled as he spun away and fended off their relentless attack.

His sword licked out and its tip passed through an ebon throat, but the creature, unperturbed, came on. Powerful arms sought to encircle him and bind his arms, even as another came in low. As he glanced down, Amric had to blink away the blurriness from his sight to confirm the impossibility of what he was seeing. The creature whose knee he had shattered, rather than crippled, had merely bent each of its limbs at an unnatural angle and was skittering across the ground like some giant, hideous spider, driving at his legs. The warrior lashed out in lightning cuts with each sword, hacking aside a sweeping arm above and cleaving the skull of the crawler below. The latter faltered and sagged, pitching face-first onto the trail.

The standing creature changed tactics and grappled for one of Amric's swords. A whistling arc from the other sword removed its head, and it toppled backward to strike the ground like a felled tree. Amric turned to see Valkarr spin around his last attacker and send it stumbling forward with a thunderous blow to the back. Pouncing after it, the Sil'ath warrior struck the head away, and the body took several more steps before crashing to the earth.

Amric whirled toward the only remaining sound of skirmish, in the direction of Bellimar and Halthak. The old man had retreated a few yards down the trail and was still astride his panicked horse, but the Half-Ork was on foot, facing the last attacker. He swung his heavy staff in a tremendous overhand curve, striking the forehead of his assailant with a resounding crack. It was a blow that would have felled an ox, but the creature merely staggered to regain its balance and then surged forward again. It extended one hammer fist to clout Halthak in the head so hard it lifted him from his feet. As the healer crumpled, the black thing swept his limp form into its arms and raced down the trail as if the listless weight of a man meant nothing to it.

In an instant, Amric and Valkarr were bounding down the trail after it. Bellimar wheeled his mount into its path, but the creature darted to one side, shouldering aside the frightened beast. It was momentarily slowed, however, and that was more than enough for the pursuing warriors. Each struck out at a pumping leg, and the abductor sprawled to the ground, releasing its unmoving burden. The creature sank its black fingers into the earth and wrenched about hard, twisting to face them in a blink. It lurched toward Amric, who struck away its grasping hand, and Valkarr's downward slice sent its gaping head rolling across the trail.

The warriors spun in unison to face outward, chests heaving from the frenzied exertion, swords held low and ready against any new assailants. The impenetrable foliage about them was still but for the idle breeze, and gave no sign of further approach. The birds above had fallen silent, but within scant seconds of the conflict's end below, their prattle ascended to its previous volume. In moments, the only noise out of place was the panicked thrashing of one of the horses where it had plunged into the undergrowth and now sounded thoroughly dismayed by its options. Amric saw Valkarr's blue dun stamping its hooves on the trail as shudders coursed through its flanks, and he realized it was his own mount that had left the path.

"See to Halthak," he told Bellimar. "We will gather and quiet the horses."

Bellimar nodded and slid from his sway-backed mare, which was placid once more. Valkarr collected his own mount and Halthak's, while Amric glided into the thick of the forest on panther's feet to locate his bay gelding. To his great relief, the animal was uninjured and not far from the trail. He did not relish the thought of being on foot as they penetrated further into the forest, or worse, when they needed to leave it. The horse had wandered into a pocket draped with sinuous vines that blocked its progress, and it was as loath to make contact with the web of vines as it was to retrace its steps. Amric sheathed his blades and approached slowly, speaking soft and soothing words to the wild-eyed beast even as he continued to eye his surroundings for new threats. It was the work of several minutes, but he managed to calm the gelding enough to lead it back to his companions.

When he returned with the bay on his heels, Halthak was sitting up with his head resting in his hands. His pebbled flesh looked pallid, and his eyes were unfocused as he glanced up to nod at Amric's approach.

"How are you feeling?" Amric asked, tying his horse to a nearby tree branch with the others.

"Like my skull was used to toll the great bell of some cathedral," Halthak answered in a rueful tone. "But as soon as I can concentrate, I can heal it. I will be fine."

Amric clasped the healer's shoulder as he strode past, and he dropped to one knee near Bellimar, who was examining the corpse of one of their assailants. It looked as if it had once been a man, or was cast in the shape of a man, but all hair had been removed and every exposed inch of its flesh was a glistening black. And black to the core, Amric noted, as he observed the cross-sections where its arm and head had been severed. There was no blood seeping from the wounds, no bone or red flesh visible within. It was swathed in coils of some filthy canvas material that were falling away from it in tatters, as if it had been bound tight in layers of ceremonial cloth at one point. It appeared to be otherwise naked underneath.

Amric's gaze raked over the other bodies, and found them all identically garbed and featured, except that they had not all been of the same race; three were human, two were beast men, one an Ork, and one he could not place, some slender and angular creature with a long beak-like snout. They were all like twisted golems cast in the shape of actual humanoid races.

"I have seen many dark creatures as the corruption touched our homeland," Amric muttered. "But these I have not seen. What are they?"

Bellimar shook his head, his brow furrowed as he ran the cloth between his fingertips. "I do not know. I have never seen these either, and I thought I had seen every misshapen thing wrought of magic this world had to offer."

There was an undercurrent to his statement that gave Amric a fleeting chill. He studied Bellimar a moment before speaking again. "They are strong, fast and impervious to pain. They fought without any regard for their own welfare, ignored the horses in favor of pursuing us instead, and appeared intent on capturing rather than slaying. For what possible purpose, I wonder?"

"We can only guess at this point," Bellimar mused. "Though I would wager Halthak is very fortunate to be pondering that question here with us right now."

The Half-Ork gave a vigorous nod as he pushed himself to his feet. His color had returned, and there was no longer a swelling bruise along the side of his face. He walked past them and bent to retrieve his staff.

"Is anyone injured?" he asked. "I can heal you now."

"Nothing but bruises and scrapes here," Amric said. "All of which can heal on their own without need of magic."

Valkarr nodded at this, and folded his arms.

"Do not be so certain, swordsman," Bellimar warned. "Come, you should see this."

The old man rose and walked from the trail, and Amric followed. The head of the creature which had snatched up Halthak was lying on the grassy sward a few feet from the hard-packed earth of the path, facing away. Bellimar nudged it with one foot, and the head lolled toward them.

Amric growled an oath and had a hand halfway to sword hilt by reflex before he caught himself. The head's grim mouth was still working in a morbid parody of speech, gaping and grimacing at them in soundless fury. Like the rest of its body, it had no hair; there was no beard or stubble, no hair atop the head, and no trace of brows above eyes which rolled to fix upon its intended prey like twin pits of midnight.

"Whatever force powers these creatures appears to be housed in their heads, as you noted during the battle, for the bodies are unmoving," Bellimar said, staring down in pitiless scrutiny. "The skulls you split are inert as well. Any head merely severed, however, is still animated."

Amric stifled a wave of revulsion as the thing leered up at them, still straining to reach them. "Unsettling, but what has this to do with trivial abrasions—"

Even as he said it, he saw what Bellimar meant. The head had come to rest on the grassy sward beside the trail, and the vegetation was dying beneath it in a spreading circle. As Amric watched, several more broad blades of grass bent to the ground in slow curls, brown corruption crawling up the stems to overwhelm the green. On the solid trail, devoid of flora, there had been no visible effect, but here the putrefaction was unmistakable. Amric inspected a scarlet scrape on his forearm, and frowned to himself. There was no hint of corruption yet, but did he imagine a strange itching at the edges of the wound?

"You suggest that the wounds, minor though they might be, could fester if not treated," he said in a quiet tone.

"Worse yet," Bellimar insisted. "Their auras appear similar in signature to Unlife, and I fear their energies will spread through your system in a manner that is more than mere physical infection. If that is true, then no poultice will cleanse it from you."

"I hear more speculation than fact," Amric said.

"I realize you want no part of mysterious forces coursing through you, swordsman, including healing magic such as the Half-Ork possesses." Bellimar leaned close as he spoke, and held Amric's gaze with his own. "But you can no longer prevent it. The decay you see before you may be no less virulent within your body. You cannot choose magic or not. You can only choose between that which you mistrust on principle and that which you mistrust based on evidence."

Amric's jaw clenched, but he knew the truth in Bellimar's words. He stared down at the loathsome object, still wild in its unceasing efforts, and found himself speculating at whether its path to becoming the travesty now before him might have begun with a similar infection of dark energies. He imagined its origins as a mortal man, and his disgust became tempered by pity, followed by an unfamiliar sensation: fear. He would not become like this thing. Amric looked up and found his emotions mirrored in Valkarr's expression. The Sil'ath, like all his kind, had an equally strong aversion to magic, and Amric exhaled in relief when he read in his friend the same resignation he himself felt. He had not relished the prospect of convincing his friend as to what must be done. With an almost imperceptible nod to Amric, Valkarr stepped over to Halthak and bowed his head before him.

The healer reached out and laid one gnarled hand on the bare flesh of the Sil'ath warrior's muscular arm, and he closed his eyes in concentration. Amric knew the Half-Ork had healed himself back at the bandit camp on the night they met, but his view had been obstructed as he approached the camp unseen in the darkness. Now that he was witnessing the healer employ his talent in the daylight and in close proximity, he half expected a glowing nimbus of light to surround Halthak as his magic issued forth, but there was nothing so dramatic. In fact, the only indication of something unseen transpiring was an abrupt stiffening of Valkarr's posture. As for Halthak, his protruding lower lip tightened, and then twisted in apparent distaste. After a few seconds, his hand dropped to his side. Valkarr took a hesitant step back from him, running his fingertips over his skin where a moment before had been a myriad of small scrapes.

"It feels foul, unclean," Halthak said. "I am able to absorb and overcome it at this early stage, and it may be that your body's natural defenses would do the same in time, but I cannot say for certain. I do not know how quickly it will spread."

"One cannot be too cautious," Bellimar insisted.

Amric nodded, took a deep breath and walked to the healer. As before, Halthak raised his hand to contact Amric's arm and closed his eyes. The warrior braced for whatever unpleasant sensation had startled Valkarr and felt... nothing. Well, almost nothing. He sensed an odd stirring within for a fleeting instant, but nothing more. He peered at Halthak's face, watched a frown bloom there, and saw the bushy brows draw down in focus.

"I do not understand," the Half-Ork murmured. "I can feel my magic build, but it goes nowhere, as if it is being turned aside."

Amric did not see Bellimar actually move, but somehow the old man seemed suddenly to be leaning forward with rapt intensity. Halthak's face twisted in determination, his forehead creased and eyes squeezed shut. Still the swordsman felt nothing, save for the insistent clutch of the healer's knobby hand on his arm. Amric glanced at the others. Bellimar was engrossed, flushed with excitement and doubtless viewing the scene with his mysterious Sight; Valkarr looked curious and more than a little alarmed, no more certain what to make of this than Amric.

The swordsman returned his attention to the healer. Sweat beaded Halthak's brow, and there came an audible grinding of teeth as the muscles bunched beneath the furry tufts of hair along his jaw. Amric closed his eyes as well, questing for the slightest sensation around his scratches and bruises, as well as at the point of his contact with the healer.

Ever so slowly, it came. Distant and feeble at first, warmth built at those locations, comforting, inviting, suffusing. After gathering moments it withdrew, drawing his injuries along with it, and it left in its void a cool and bracing sense of revitalization. Before Amric's wondering eyes, the angry welt on his forearm faded, and its twin appeared in the same place on the Half-Ork's arm. There he saw the grey flesh knit over it and close, and within seconds the injury had vanished. Halthak's hand fell away and he sagged, leaning on his staff as he gulped in one lungful of air after another.

"I have never felt the like," he gasped at last.

"Were my injuries so different than Valkarr's, so much harder to heal?" Amric asked, perplexed.

"No, it was as if I was walled away from them. It was like trying to pierce the city wall with a dagger. In the end, as I reached the limits of my endurance, it felt for all the world as if something finally allowed me in. I can find no better words to describe it."

Amric faced Bellimar. "Did your Sight reveal what happened there?" he asked.

"Not with any certainty," Bellimar replied. "I saw Halthak's healing energies gather and finally begin trickling across to you, then grow into a flood as it did with Valkarr. Halthak's aura became vibrant with the exertion, while yours was as absent as ever. There was a bright flash as the transfer began, but it was very brief, and might readily be explained by the healer's forces being pent up as they were. I may have been given a piece of the puzzle, however, if I can but deduce its place in the larger theory."

"Ponder as we ride, then," Valkarr said. "We have tarried here too long, and more things will be drawn to the commotion, may already be coming. We should put some distance between us and this site."

Amric nodded as he stared down at the animate head. "After," he amended quietly, "we ensure none of these things still stir to greet us on the return trip."

He reached over his shoulder to draw forth one gleaming sword, and behind him, a metallic whisper told him Valkarr had done the same. Amric's grey eyes were like thunderclouds as he took a resolute step forward.

Halthak rode through a twilight world of deepening shadows, his hand absently patting the neck of his chestnut mare as his restless eyes roved all about. The setting sun drew lingering crimson talons across the heavens and transformed the canopy above to a blood-red blaze. The fiery display did not reach the ground far below, however, where the riders followed a frail, ephemeral path through the ever thickening murk. Halthak's nerves had been clamoring since they entered this accursed forest, and at a near fever pitch since the encounter with the unnatural black creatures in the morning, but to his immense gratitude they had managed to avoid any further conflicts since then. There had been more moments of acute tension, to be sure, as they led their frightened mounts through the thick, tangling undergrowth, but the preternaturally keen senses of the warriors had allowed the riders to steal through this hellish jungle undetected like so many wraiths.

Bellimar rode ahead of him, slouching relaxed in his saddle as if he traveled through a scenic country estate. Halthak had no idea how the old man could be so serene in the midst of this place, but he envied the man his composure, whether real of affected. Behind Halthak rode Amric, cool as ice on the surface, but the healer knew he was tense as a coiled spring beneath. He had yet to see the warrior truly caught by surprise, even when faced with the blinding rush of the attack earlier; his whirlwind response, the speed and ferocity with which he had cut his way through that tangled mass of jet-black bodies, had stricken Halthak speechless in wonder. At the head of the column, no less fearsome in dealing death earlier, rode Valkarr. His thick scaly tail extended back over both the saddle and his blue dun's rump to mingle there with the horse's black tail. A part of Halthak's mind, hungry for distraction, wondered if the Sil'ath sitting a horse was as uncomfortable for horse and rider as it appeared to an observer.

Valkarr twisted around in his saddle, made a short, chopping motion with his left hand and looked a question at Amric. Halthak looked back in time to see Amric nod in return, and then Valkarr put heels to his horse and sped ahead down the trail to vanish into the gloom. Bellimar glanced back over his shoulder at Amric with one delicate eyebrow arched, and then he lounged forward once more. Halthak slowed his mare and fell into step alongside Amric.

"It is getting dark," Halthak said in a low tone, feeling foolish even as he stated the obvious. "Will we halt soon?"

Amric gave a tight nod, his flint-grey eyes flicking from side to side. "We are looking for a suitable place to stop."

"I—I apologize for the difficulty in healing you this morning," the Half-Ork said. "I have spent much of the day considering its cause, and how I might prevent it in the future."

"Do not fret over it," Amric chuckled. "I am not the most cooperative of patients, given my aversion to magic."

Halthak shook his head. "Valkarr shares that aversion, and administering to him felt no different than a thousand times before. No, your case was somehow different."

"Have you any theories on the matter?" Amric said, craning his neck to search the vegetation enclosing the trail behind them.

"At first I suspected your lack of aura, in which our friend Bellimar shows so much interest, as if you have an unnaturally low affinity for magic in general. No matter how much I mull it over, however, it does not quite fit."

"How so?" Amric asked, sparing him a quick look askance.

Halthak frowned, pensive. "Well, I have treated many people with no inherent ability to speak of, and it has never affected the application of my magic on them. I suspect those individuals had very weak auras, if what Bellimar says is true."

"Bellimar did not say I had a *weak* aura," Amric reminded him. "He said I had *no* aura whatsoever, unlike any person he has encountered before. You should not be troubled that your talent cannot easily reach someone forsaken by magic."

"I have been turning that over in my mind as well, but it does not explain what I felt when it occurred. I could accept it if my magic had seemed to have nowhere to go, as if no vessel existed on the other side of our contact, or even if I had faced a consistent level of resistance. Instead, I was blocked, turned aside as if my best efforts were feeble scratches against a wall of marble. Furthermore, I had the disturbing sense I was being watched, and that I did not break through but rather was *allowed* in after meeting some obscure approval. After that, it felt as it always has. It is beyond my reckoning, but I am glad it succeeded at last."

"And I am grateful for your efforts, Halthak," Amric returned. "This is no place to fall ill, and having faced those mindless things, I dread the thought of where the infections they carry might lead."

Halthak shuddered, for the same thought had occurred to him. They rode on in silence for several minutes, navigating the trail as much by feel as by sight now, in the pressing dusk. Valkarr reappeared on the path ahead, shaking his head at Amric, then tapping a finger below one eye and pointing ahead. He then wheeled his blue dun gelding about and resumed his head position. Halthak turned toward Amric.

"What did—?" he began, but the swordsman interrupted smoothly.

"Healer, I saw a spasm of discomfort cross your face each time when you healed us earlier. Do you feel the full pain of the victim's injury when you draw it into yourself in that manner?"

Halthak paused, confused. "I cannot know for certain, but it seems so, or as nearly as I can judge. Though it is quick to fade once I absorb it, for the wound itself never lasts long. Why do you ask?"

"Curiosity, and regret for having caused you pain," Amric replied. His hawk eyes rested on Halthak for a moment. "And I regret disparaging your use of magic. Taking the hurt from others is a heroic thing indeed."

Halthak flushed, grateful for the mask of twilight, and nodded his thanks. Ahead of them, Bellimar turned and looked at them with luminous eyes that somehow caught the crimson glimmer from above.

"They come, swordsman," he said, sharp warning in his tone.

Halthak's eyes widened as he looked from Bellimar to Amric. He recalled the question he had been about to ask a moment before. "What did Valkarr's signals mean, and why did he ride off at speed like that?" he said. "And what is Bellimar talking about?"

"Valkarr has found a place for us to stop," Amric said. "And he rode ahead in an attempt to draw away whatever has been hunting us for the better part of an hour."

Halthak's tongue clove to the roof of his mouth.

Amric chuckled. "Do not look so accusing, healer. There is nothing you could have done, had you known, except worry yourself into a froth. Valkarr sought to lead them away and lose them in the forest while we broke free in a different direction to take a longer way around, but unfortunately they did not take the bait."

"Then Bellimar meant—"

"Yes, they are closing in. Whatever they are, they initially followed at a great distance, but they are growing bolder as darkness falls."

Halthak turned frantic eyes to the side, straining to pierce the blackness of the forest. At first he saw nothing as before, and then his spine turned to ice. A scarce twenty paces off the trail, he caught a long shadow slinking low to the ground through a gap between two large trees. He gasped, trying in vain to track it further in the gloom, but as swiftly as he had found it, it was lost again. Ten paces behind where he had seen it, another dark shape appeared for a moment, sleek and swift, and then was gone.

"Do not stare!" Amric commanded in a harsh whisper. "They seem content to pace us while we do not focus on them. I think like most night hunters, they are loath to reveal their presence until ready to close the trap, or risk losing their greatest advantage."

"Then they are not the same black things we faced this morning," Halthak said, unsure whether to feel relief or fear at the conclusion. Could the unknown be worse than this morning's horror? It was a question he was very reluctant to answer.

"No, these are something different, and they hunt like a silent pack of wolves. I have my suspicions as to what they might be, but the failing light has kept me from being certain, and they are canny hunters. Ah, there we are, up ahead."

Halthak followed the swordsman's gaze through a cleft in the trees to see a massive square bluff shouldering its way above the forest. Like an anvil of bleached bone surrounded by a mantle of smaller crags and boulders, the monolith reared skyward to be painted crimson by the last sliver of the dying sun.

"When you said we meant to stop, you did not mean to camp," Halthak said.

That steel grey gaze slid across him before returning to monitor their pursuers, but in that brief moment Halthak was taken aback by the fierce, wintry expression on the warrior's visage. The man had entered the void of war, he realized, and was prepared to deal death at any moment.

"We need a good place to make our stand," Amric said. "The day is not yet done, healer."

CHAPTER 7

Eskaras strolled along the battlement atop the eastern city wall of Keldrin's Landing, tapping the butt of his crossbow upon each crenellation as he passed. The night was humid and pressed in close about him, and inwardly, where there was no risk that a superior officer would overhear him, he cursed his patrol assignment.

On the northern wall, he would be enjoying the cooling breeze drifting over the city from the Vellayen Sea. The western wall boasted breathtaking views of the homes of the city's wealthiest residents. Those sprawling, luxurious estates were lit well enough, even at night, to fuel the unlikely dreams of one scraping out a meager existence on the pay of a city guard. His assignment tonight was the southernmost stretch of the eastern wall, however, and it had little to recommend it these days. To be sure, the broad vistas were scenic in the light of day, but they palled to tedium with enough viewings, and after nightfall they dissolved into broad gulfs of impenetrable darkness.

Eskaras dropped his gaze to the flagstone path stretching away before him, fancying he could see a shallow furrow worn into the herringbone pattern from the countless booted feet that had trod this path before him. He wondered how many times he himself had walked this lonely circuit, and his mood darkened. Wall-watch was a duty desired by very few; it was monotonous, too secure to draw additional hazard pay, and too remote to catch the eye of a more generous private employer. Eskaras rapped the next crenellation harder with his crossbow as he wondered what he had done to merit selection for this duty yet again; he had his suspicions that it was guilt by association.

He stopped and peered over the edge to see the stone recede downward into darkness. He could not see to the ground, over one hundred feet below, but he glimpsed the periodic torches in wall sconces, each a tiny nimbus striving to hold back the gloom. There were tales among the city watch of strange and terrible things reaching the walls from time to time, and it seemed every morning a few of the sconces were found torn from their moorings and had to be replaced, but Eskaras had never witnessed such events himself. Even if something did reach the city's perimeter, what primitive forces could dream of scaling or penetrating this sheer stone giant? It was far too high and impregnable to even require a patrol, in his opinion; even one as thin as a mere two guards per wall.

One of the squat bastions punctuating the battlement loomed ahead. He stepped inside, leaning his crossbow against the interior wall to check the oil supply in its hanging lamp. He glanced over the large brass alarm bell hanging from the aperture that overlooked the city. Satisfied, he was reaching for his crossbow when a stealthy shuffling sound upon the flag-stones outside the bastion brought him about with a sharp oath. His fingers curled about the solid wooden stock and he lifted the weapon against him, drawing the string back and latching it into place. He was fumbling for a bolt when a helmed head peered around the edge of the stone doorway. A roguish grin split the bearded face. Eskaras sagged against the bastion wall, exhaling in relief even as he glared at the newcomer.

"Brek, you thick-skulled lummox!" he said. "You could be sucking breath through a new hole right now."

"I have seen you shoot. I had little to fear," the other laughed, stepping forward into full view. "You are as likely to castrate yourself with that thing as you are to hit your target."

"It is *you* I should castrate," Eskaras said with a scowl. Pointing his weapon at Brek's groin, he pulled the trigger. The unloaded crossbow string snapped to with a sharp report, and he took great pleasure in the height of the man's startled jump.

"Do not even jest so," Brek said in mock horror. "Can you imagine the grief-stricken maidens across our fair city, faced with such a cruel twist of fate?"

Eskaras snorted. "I can imagine how many husbands across our fair city would shake my hand in thanks for the deed, not to mention the legions of maidens you've not yet met whose virtue I would be defending."

Brek's grin drooped into his reddish beard, and he hung his head in a passable imitation of injury. "You wound me, my friend, you really do."

Eskaras arched an eyebrow at the other man, and the impish grin emerged once more. Wall duty seemed a perpetual assignment for Brek; he was always getting caught at one mischief or another, and Eskaras knew quite well that for every ill-advised endeavor at which the scoundrel was caught, a dozen more went undiscovered. The rogue's charm was undeniable, however, and his golden tongue had deflected severe punishment and even termination on more than a few occasions. And, Eskaras was forced to admit, he was a fair hand at arms and a competent guard, when he was not distracted by his most recent scheme.

"What are you doing here, Brek? This is my patrol route tonight, may the sergeant's eyes be blasted from his head."

"Can a man not keep his friend company on this dreadfully dull stretch of night?" Brek asked. "By the heavens, there is nothing else going on up here to keep one awake."

Eskaras chuckled and resumed walking along the battlement, and his friend fell into step beside him. He watched Brek from the corner of his eye, feeling a mix of envy and annoyance at the man's jaunty, carefree gait with his own crossbow resting upon his shoulder. Brek somehow seemed utterly at home no matter where he was, and was at ease talking with anyone, regardless of station or appearance. Eskaras had never enjoyed that talent, finding all too often that his tongue became thick and clumsy when he tried to converse with superior officers or attractive women.

They walked together, and though Brek evinced no urge to break his affable silence, Eskaras grew ever more agitated. He could count on his friend for any favor, no matter the size or risk, but Brek was just as quick to make requests of his own, and helping the man seldom came without consequence. And just as old scars sometimes itched before a coming battle, he knew that Brek was after something. At last, Eskaras could take it no more.

"Out with it," he said. "What are you after?"

Brek blinked at him with wide, ice-blue eyes that had unlocked more than a few bedroom doors. "Whatever do you mean, Eskaras?"

"Save your honeyed words for those who do not know you as well. You risk punishment for us both by abandoning your patrol route to join mine."

"Bah," said Brek, lifting his hand from his sword hilt to give a dismissive wave. "Our beloved sergeant favors the guard house by the northeastern corner, since it is nearest the refectory. With his great girth, he can only climb the long stairs to the wall-walk once or twice per night or risk heart failure, and he has already been up to glower at me once tonight. If he achieves the battlement again tonight, he will surely lack the wind to come within sight of your route."

"But if he does, it *will* put him at the end of your route," Eskaras said. "And you can scarcely afford to incur his wrath yet again, just as I would prefer not to share it for knowing you."

"You raise an excellent point, Eskaras," Brek said with sudden gravity. "I am a poor friend indeed for not having considered the reflection upon you should my plans tonight go awry."

"What plans?" Eskaras asked as a sinking sensation developed in the pit of his stomach.

"Well, I had no wish to make you complicit in my own tangled affairs," Brek said, lowering his voice and glancing about as if fearing to be overheard. "There is a certain merchant's wife, forlorn in her plump, sweaty husband's absence only slightly more so than when he is in town…"

Eskaras rolled his eyes. "I should have known."

"I find I cannot be so callous as to abandon her to her plight," Brek said.

"To be sure," Eskaras said, wringing sarcasm from each word.

"So I must slip away from my pointless post this evening for a time, that I might console her," Brek continued, as if his friend had not spoken. Eskaras snorted, and the other ignored that as well.

"As I said, however, I had not considered the potential impact on you, my closest friend, were my absence to be noted. I am resolved to take the compassionate path over treading an empty wall all night, but I could not ask you to cover for me on the lovely lady's behalf."

The man lapsed into silence, furrowing his brow and chewing on his reddish beard as he sought a solution. Eskaras glared at him through narrowed eyes, but Brek was as incapable of shame as ever and continued with his pensive display, seeming unaware of his friend's eyes boring into him as they walked. At long last they reached the point on the wall where their respective patrol routes met. Eskaras sighed and cleared his throat, shrugging aside the familiar feeling of having been maneuvered.

"If we put aside the only sane choice, the one where you do not leave your post," Eskaras said with a pointed look that met only an intent and innocent expression on Brek's part, "I suppose I could walk the full eastern wall tonight. If I encounter the sergeant on your route, I can tell him that we switched routes because you owed me some obscure favor and I preferred the breeze off the sea at the northern edge of each loop."

This last part was true, of course, and Eskaras found himself looking forward to the salty tang of that cooling breath. Brek broke into a broad, triumphant grin.

"I can mention that I saw you quite recently, but I will lie no further if he goes searching for you in earnest," Eskaras warned.

"A sound plan," Brek said, clapping him on the shoulder. "I could ask for no more, and I thank you, Eskaras."

Eskaras waved a hand, dismissing the man and his gratitude at once. "Be gone, you greased eel, before I reconsider."

His friend set off at a jog back the way they had come, heading for the southeastern stairwell. Eskaras sighed again, watching him recede into the distance. Then he shouldered his crossbow and continued the longer route to which he had just agreed. Searching for stars in the hazy night sky, he wondered if Brek's escapades would this time cost them both more than poor watch assignments.

A cool breeze played along his back, carrying with it a strange medley of sounds, and Eskaras halted. He squinted along the battlement in the direction Brek had gone, but he could make out nothing except the distant glow of the lamp in the last bastion. He moved to the interior wall of the battlement and peered down into the city. Even at this late hour, the cobbled city streets in this section were well lit and people moved in miniature along them. He frowned. The wall played tricks with sound, often carrying the faintest of sounds to the heights of the wall-walk, or allowing one guard to overhear another's words over great distance. Eskaras thought he had heard a man's cry and the clang of metal upon stone, but he could see no sign of conflict below. It could have been some shady dealings in an alley below that was screened to his view, but he had an uneasy feeling. It had sounded like his friend Brek, and the draft that carried the sound had come from that direction, when the winds up here tended to run firmly the opposite direction. Most puzzling of all, the breeze had been almost frigid in an otherwise hot and humid night.

Eskaras braced his crossbow, drawing the string back and fitting a bolt into the channel. He held the weapon ready as he stalked back along the battlement in the direction Brek had gone and from whence the sound had seemed to emanate. If it was another of Brek's pranks and he received a bolt in the leg for his efforts, it would serve him right.

The evening hung still and stifling once more. The sound did not repeat, and Eskaras began to think he had imagined it all. Then, as he approached the nearest lamp-lit bastion, the air grew colder with each step, and he noticed a blue tinge mingling with the amber glow spilling through the doorway. Through that arch he saw a crossbow lying in the middle of the floor on its back, as if cast aside. Eskaras hesitated, his breath hanging in a mist before him, when a gurgling moan from ahead galvanized him into action. Uttering a cry meant as much to bolster his own courage as to startle whatever he found within, he plunged through the entry and into the bastion.

Inside was a sight that froze the blood in his veins.

Brek was lying supine in a corner, his sword in one outstretched hand while his other arm was flung up before his averted face, trying in vain to fend off his attacker. He must have been trying to reach the alarm bell, Eskaras thought, as he was but a few feet from it.

Hunched atop Brek was a creature out of nightmare. It was larger than a man but translucent, and its blue radiance filled the small room. It seemed to waver before his eyes, and its lack of definition made it challenging to ascertain its true features, but Eskaras had the impression of a skeletal form swathed in some billowing, gossamer substance. He could not tell if it crouched or floated over the thrashing guard. Its elongated head hung low between bony shoulders, leering close to Brek, and tapered talons seemed to sink into the man's flesh without drawing blood.

At Eskaras's cry, the monstrosity swung its head to face him, and he found himself staring into bottomless eye sockets above a wide, gaping grin that bristled with crooked fangs. It showed no concern at his presence, but instead regarded him with a savage anticipation that made his flesh crawl. *It's a coldwraith*, he thought in shock. His grandmother had scared him with tales of such things when he was a lad, and he had always thought her daft.

Eskaras leveled his crossbow and fired. He felt a surge of satisfaction as the bolt flew true to strike the coldwraith between the eyes, but then he quailed as it passed harmlessly through to shatter on the stone wall beyond. He recalled his grandmother's assertion that iron would discomfit a coldwraith, but only a magical weapon could slay one.

The creature's eyes—or rather the depthless hollows where its eyes should have been—narrowed in anger, and it whirled and swept toward him in one fluid motion. He stumbled back from it as a gaunt arm lashed out at him, trailing that swirling, diaphanous material. He tried to block the strike with his raised arms, but the talons passed through leather, chain and flesh alike without leaving a mark, and left a biting cold behind. His crossbow tumbled from nerveless fingers, his unwilling muscles convulsing as he fell back. The creature flowed over him to perch weightless upon his chest, and its horrid face filled his vision. The aching cold pierced him like daggers of ice, and he went rigid in agony. The wraith inhaled deeply as if savoring the scent of a rich meal. Eskaras's limbs grew heavier, and he watched in horror as the life force was drawn from his body in vaporous strands and wafted into the toothy maw above him.

From the corner of his rolling eyes, Eskaras saw an unsteady Brek regain his feet, his sword still in knotted fist. *Run, you thick-headed lummox,* Eskaras thought fiercely, but he could not force a word past his clenched jaws. Brek lurched forward and sent his sword in a whistling arc through the creature, but as with the crossbow bolt, it passed through without resistance. Eskaras felt the flow of life from him cease as the thing turned its head toward the other man. Brek spun on his heel and left the bastion at an awkward run.

"I will draw it off!" Brek shouted over his shoulder. "Ring the bell, sound the alarm!"

The coldwraith glided after his friend, sinuous and swift, its unnatural grace a mockery of the cold-stiffened movements of its prey. The creature's eerie blue glow went with it, and some of the chill faded from the room. Shivering, Eskaras rolled over and pushed himself to his hands and knees. He tried to rise, but his jerking muscles betrayed him and he fell to the flagstones again. He heaved himself up with curse. He braced himself against the bastion's doorway, and by the time he reached a standing position, he was mastering his wayward limbs once more.

Too long, he thought, frantic. *It is taking much too long!* And, as he raised his eyes, his fears were confirmed.

The coldwraith returned, flowing into the bastion and blocking his path to the alarm bell. A quick glance out onto the battlement showed Brek, fallen not half a dozen paces past the arch, lifeless eyes staring in mute apology.

Eskaras drew his sword and faced the creature. He had seen the awful speed of the thing firsthand; if he tried to escape, it would run him down as it had Brek, and he could not bypass it to reach the bell in this confined space. He set his jaw and tightened his grip on his weapon. It was time to prove Brek wrong about his aim for the second time tonight. In a sudden movement, he twisted and then uncoiled, hurling the sword with all his strength. It spun through the creature without contact and without altering its trajectory, whirling through the air, the polished steel flashing blue and gold fire in turn. The weapon flew true, and it struck the brass bell with a resounding clang, setting up further clamor as the bell rocked and the clapper inside rang against its sides.

Distant shouts erupted from below, and Eskaras smiled in grim satisfaction; it had worked better than he dared hope. His fellow guards would come, and the thing would not be free to make its way into the city.

The coldwraith's eye pits narrowed, as if it understood what he had done. Perhaps it did, he thought. Perhaps there was intelligence behind its relentless malice. He had no way of knowing.

It rushed at him. He tried to spit in its face as it came, but the cold was upon him again, and his jaws were clenched so hard he feared his teeth would shatter. Something struck him hard in the back, and he realized the world had tilted without him realizing, and the floor had risen to meet him. Pain and exhaustion swept over and cut through him, and everything disappeared beneath a tide of darkness.

They attacked as night fell. Amric and Valkarr waited on the slope of the crag, standing just far enough apart that nothing could pass between them without coming within range of their dual blades. Amric breathed, slow and even, his mind clear and his senses extending to embrace this latest battleground. Further up the slope, at the foot of the sheer forward face of the crag, he could hear the snorts and stamping hooves of the frightened horses, and Halthak murmuring low words to soothe them as he held tight to their reins. Of Bellimar he could hear nothing, but he felt the old man's presence up there as well, as still as the rock about him.

He and Valkarr had recognized the bloodbeasts the moment they broke from the trees, having fought their ilk before back home. They would fall before mundane weapons more readily than the infernal black things of the morning, but there were also more of them. They fought in a pack, and were deadly for entirely different reasons. Amric hoped the healer and the old man would prove able to restrain the horses during the impending battle, for the creatures that were coming would not ignore them as the black things had done, and these could rip a defenseless steed to shreds in a matter of moments.

Scrabbling for purchase, the mass of wiry, twisting bodies swarmed up the rocky slope, seeking to crash over the two warriors like a wave clawing at the sand. Confident their quarry was now cornered, the creatures abandoned the wraith-like silence of the hunt and gave voice to snarls and eager mewling. As always, he could not decide if their movements were more reminiscent of a wolf or a great cat, for they had attributes of each and seemed some wretched combination of both. As they neared, he saw their glistening, blood-slicked forms, as if mortal predators had somehow shed their outer hides. By their grisly appearance, they should have left scarlet droplets and paw prints with every step, but none of the moisture, their sustenance, escaped them. The telltale shimmering in the night air above their backs marked the slender tentacles lashing there, sharp at the edges and wickedly efficient at drawing the blood of their prey. Amric waited, head held low and forward to protect his face and eyes.

Then the bloodbeasts were upon them, and there was no more time for study. The one in the lead launched at Amric, slavering jaws open wide. One sword swept up to shear through flesh and bone, dropping the creature without a sound, and the other darted forward to pierce the breast of the next fiend hot on its heels. A dark form hurtled by him as he freed his weapons, and filament-like tentacles caressed his forearm, leaving a stinging wetness in their wake. He felt a familiar surge of revulsion as he saw rivulets of his blood lift away from the wound and drift through the air to join the ghastly coating of his attacker. The bloodbeast emitted a frenzied whine of pleasure. Spinning to one side, he cut it down before it could get behind him, avoiding the lunge of another and hacking the front legs from beneath yet another. Beside him, Valkarr was shifting back and forth, unerring intuition guiding his footing as the press of straining, crimson forms broke against the web of steel he wove before him.

Amric's blades flickered forth, deflecting raking talons and dealing death with every stroke. Instinct and reflex took over as each strike flowed unbroken into the next. Foes fell all about him, crashing to the ground atop one another.

Their footing became treacherous as the hillside ran red about them, and the warriors backed up in unison. A snarling form clambered over its fellows and sprang at him, fangs flashing. His boot lashed out to send it tumbling down the hill. Murderous tentacles writhed against his leggings, and his skin prickled as they penetrated the leather. A sweeping downward cut stilled them, but he felt a spreading wetness there. More tentacles peeled at the chain mail around his chest and shoulder, making contact at last with the bare flesh of his upper arm. Starlight danced on his blade as he parted the appendages from their owner, and he sent a reverse stroke that aborted the resulting howl of rage.

And still they came on. Foot by grudging foot, the warriors gave ground, backing up the hill before the relentless tide. Blood flew wide from their swords as they found their mark time and again, and though

Amric could not spare the attention to watch the cast-off fluid slow in midair and arc back to be absorbed by the ravenous bloodbeasts, he could hear the patter of it alighting on their bodies.

A red haze rose before his eyes, the lifeblood from his many lacerations rising in a fine mist to be consumed by the fiends. A glance aside showed the same cloud before Valkarr. The bloodbeasts did not need to strike a mortal blow; instead they could wear their prey down gradually, draining and weakening it over time until it became too feeble to withstand the rest of the pack. If the battle went on much longer, he and Valkarr would slow and be dragged down. The shriek of a terrified horse at his back told him that they would not be able to retreat much further, either. Very soon, even if the animals did not panic and bolt into the midst of the bloodbeasts, the warriors would lack sufficient maneuvering room to prevent members of the pack from slipping past.

Amric set his jaw, watching for his opportunity. There was a brief lull in the ebb and flow of battle, and he seized the moment. He lunged forward into their midst, a blur of motion as he laid about with demonic ferocity. A bare instant behind him, Valkarr plunged into the thick of the pack as well, a second whirlwind of biting steel. Here at the center of the maelstrom, there was no room for finesse or grace, no precision to the dance of death. Instead there was only force and fury, and a merciless, indomitable will.

The razor-edged kiss of lashing tentacles became a constant pain as the throng closed about them. Amric clove one of the bloodbeasts nearly in half, smashed away slavering jaws with a fisted hilt, shouldered aside a twisting form, and sent a snapping head spinning into the night atop a scarlet fountain. His blades sang in the night air, such was their blinding speed, and he gave rein to his wrath. He felt tireless, unconquerable, but he knew it was the heady illusion of combat. His rage would sustain him only so long. They had to break the charge now, or they were lost.

Suddenly it was over. The snarling creatures faded back from them, and Amric and Valkarr stood alone among the strewn heaps of bodies, gasping for breath. The handful of remaining bloodbeasts gathered down the hill, drawing to themselves the last of the blood from the air and a few long strands from their fallen fellows. The fiends glared up the slope at them with burning eyes, and Amric glared back, his own lip curling. He would show no sign of weakness now, or invite another rush. At last the bloodbeasts turned and loped down the hill, melting into the forest without a backward glance.

Valkarr sank to his haunches, wobbled there for a moment, and then sat down heavily. Amric turned and was relieved to see that all of the horses were still present, and were beginning to subside. Then he noticed Halthak staring open-mouthed at him.

"I–I have never seen the like," he stammered. "Standing fast against such odds…. And the speed! I could not even follow your movements. When you charged into the midst of those dreadful things, I was certain you would be swarmed under."

"There was little choice," Amric said with a rueful chuckle. "And I must admit I was not much more confident of the outcome. It was a close thing, and we were very fortunate."

He flicked his swords to either side to clear the blood from the blades, and sheathed them both. He then peered past the Half-Ork and into the deeper darkness at the base of the cliff.

"Where is Bellimar?" he asked.

Halthak spun around in surprise, his head craning from side to side before he faced Amric again with furrowed brow.

"I do not know," he said. "He never uttered a word once the battle began, and I heard no hint of a struggle behind me. I did not see him slip away either, but I was engrossed in the battle. Where could he have gone, unseen?"

Amric frowned and shook his head as he continued to scan about in vain. "The darkness could have concealed much, and we can certainly claim distraction. At the same time, we can see most of the slope from here, and we are backed by the sheer face of this cliff."

"We are in no condition to chase after him," Valkarr muttered in a thick voice from where he still sat on the ground. "And we do not dare call for him, for fear of attracting more predators. There is nothing we can do for him until the morning's light, and until we rest."

He gave a wet cough as he finished speaking, and Halthak started, hastening forward with wide eyes.

"How stupid of me to prattle on while you sit there, exhausted and bleeding!" the healer said.

Halthak handed the gathered reins of the horses to Amric, and knelt by Valkarr. The Sil'ath, shoulders sagging, made no objection as the healer pressed a hand to the flesh of his arm and closed his eyes. After a moment, those eyes flared open and the look of concern upon the Half-Ork's coarse features was unmistakable. Amric heard his friend's ragged breathing, and realized with a chill that Valkarr had taken more grievous wounds under the veil of night than he himself had.

"Valkarr, listen to me," Halthak said, his tone low and urgent. "Your injuries are severe, and must be treated. By your leave, I wish to heal you now, as I did this morning."

Valkarr looked at him with black eyes that were dull and unfocused, and he slurred something in the Sil'ath tongue that not even Amric could understand. Halthak glanced aside at Amric, who nodded. The healer turned back to Valkarr and continued in a rapid whisper.

"This will make you very tired, warrior, and you may succumb to sleep before I am even finished. This is normal, as your body must give some of its energy to the healing process, and you have precious little to spare just now. Do you understand?"

Valkarr mumbled something else unintelligible, and gave a bubbling chuckle. Halthak bowed his head and squeezed his eyes shut in concentration. He gave a low gasp through clenched teeth, and Amric watched in fascination as a dense, scarlet latticework of stripes sprouted across his grey skin, even as they dwindled from the other's scaly green hide. Valkarr stiffened at first, then relaxed, and when the last of his wounds faded from view his eyelids drooped and his chin fell to his chest. Halthak eased him to his back on the rocky hillside, already asleep. By the time he stood to face Amric, the many lacerations he had assumed had vanished as well.

"It is your turn," Halthak said.

"Not just yet, healer," Amric replied. "We are exposed on this hillside, and must take cover at the base of the crag before I would risk being too fatigued to move."

Passing the reins back to Halthak, he knelt and slid his arms beneath Valkarr, and rose to his feet with a grunt of effort. The Sil'ath people were dense with muscle and always heavier than they appeared, and the loss of blood had sapped Amric's strength. He climbed the hill with legs that burned and quivered, and he was intensely grateful to reach a large cleft in the side of the crag before they gave out beneath him.

The fissure was open to the sky far above, with a tumble of boulders at the back, and it was spacious enough to screen men and horses alike from the forest edge below. Amric laid his unconscious friend down at the back of the cleft, wiping clammy sweat from his brow as he looked around. There was still no sign of Bellimar, but this location was as well hidden and defensible as they were likely to find. They would remain here until morning. He sat with his back to a leaning boulder as Halthak came into sight with the horses in tow. The Half-Ork saw to the horses as Amric had taught him, and the warrior remained seated, resting in silent gratitude.

Halthak brought him a water skin and some salted beef.

"You should eat. Valkarr will be famished when he wakes."

Amric accepted the rations and chewed slowly. His eyelids were growing heavy, and he shook his head to clear the fog. It would be a long night without Valkarr to split the watch duties. They ate in silence for a time before Halthak's gentle voice floated to him.

"Amric, it is time to heal you as well."

"And if you encounter the same resistance as before?" Amric queried.

"Then I will persist until I succeed, as before."

Amric hesitated, and then sighed. "Very well, but I must remain awake to keep watch, so do not reduce me to slumber as you did Valkarr. Perhaps only enough tonight to seal the wounds and staunch the bleeding, and the rest can heal on its own."

"I will do only as much as I think you require," Halthak promised.

"Thank you, healer."

Halthak nodded, little more than a soft silhouette against the starlight as he hovered over him. The healer sat at his side, and Amric felt a warm hand against the corded muscle of his arm. A long moment passed, wherein only the insects, bold in their numbers, spoke into the night.

"I feel nothing, healer," Amric said. "Are you blocked and straining again?"

"No," Halthak responded. "This time I am proceeding very slowly and not trying to force it. This may take some time; will you answer me something as I work?"

"Ask it."

"I would know more about your Sil'ath friends, the members of the party we seek. Tell me of them, their names, their natures, their temperaments. Make them real to someone who has yet to meet them."

There was another long pause, and Amric smiled.

"Halthak, you are without a doubt the most human among us all."

And so Amric told him of the five. Innikar, whipcord-tough and instigator of countless pranks. Beautiful Sariel, who lived for the joy of battle and was graceful as a dancer in its midst. Prakseth, jovial and powerfully built. Sharp-eyed Varek, the most gifted marksman Amric had ever known. And Garlien, sister to Varek and a shrewd strategist, with the potential to be warmaster herself someday.

He spoke of their loves and families, of their mischiefs and maturing. He spoke of them as the friends they had been to him since childhood, and he described their many accomplishments with a swell of pride. With a catch in his throat, he recounted their unwavering support of him as their warmaster, he who was born an outsider and yet proved foremost among them. He spoke at length, and felt something ease deep in his chest, a tightness he had not realized he was carrying. They might have perished out here somewhere in this deadly forest, and he would not stop until he knew their fates for certain. Here and now, however, it felt so good to revel in their lives and triumphs that he rambled on much longer than he intended, grasping at memory after memory.

Somewhere in that time, though he was unaware of the transition, his wounds were healed, his words trailed off, and his memories became dreams.

CHAPTER 8

Halthak sat wrapped in his cloak in the pre-dawn hour, knees drawn up before him and whiskered chin resting upon folded arms. He gazed out from the deep, narrow recess of the cleft and onto a lightening sky, like watching through a door ajar as the darkness yielded in grudging steps to the coming day.

He had dozed several times, he knew, for the night had flown by in passages, and he was not nearly as fatigued as he should have been after concluding the events of yesterday by standing watch all night. The fates had been kind for a turn, and nothing had stumbled across their place of concealment. The only moment of concern had come late in the evening, when he heard noises from down the hill where their battle with the bloodbeasts had taken place. He had listened, striving not to draw breath, as a ponderous tread grew louder, accompanied by snuffling noises that sounded like a great bellows at work. There followed a muffled crunching of bones for a time, and then the lumbering creature departed. Halthak, who had been debating on waking the exhausted warriors, sat back at last with a sigh of relief to resume his watch.

He studied Amric and Valkarr, watched their chests rise and fall in the deep, regular rhythm of slumber. Healing Valkarr had been tiring, given the extent of his wounds, but predictable. With Amric, he had proceeded at a very gradual pace to indicate peaceful intent, just as he would if trying to approach a dangerous wild animal. This tactic had proven successful, for he did not this time encounter the strange, impenetrable barrier that had stopped him short before. Even as he sent his healing magic into the warrior with utmost patience, however, he had the peculiar sensation of being closely monitored, of that same foreign presence hovering all about his efforts and yet remaining just beyond contact. It was perplexing, and while he was relieved to have found a method by which he could heal the swordsman, he was also concerned that the next time might call for more urgency, and he might face that mysterious resistance again.

He pushed it from his mind, as he had already a dozen times over the night. There was nothing for it but to try, when the time came.

He looked skyward, wishing the cleft opened to the east so that he could witness the dawn's full glory as it arrived, when something nagged at the edge of his vision. His eyes fell to the side, and he froze. Standing less than a dozen feet away, so still as to seem a natural part of the crevice's many shadows, was a tall, slender figure folded in a cloak. Halthak clawed for the staff beside him and sprang to his feet as a strangled yelp lodged in his throat.

A throaty chuckle came from the figure, followed by a smooth, familiar voice. "Do you mean to crease my skull for disappearing last night, healer?"

"Bellimar?" Halthak gasped. "By the heavens, man, I think you just shaved years from my life!"

"My apologies for startling you so." Bellimar glided forward, and Halthak glared at him, finding the contrition in the old man's tone did not at all match the twinkle of amusement in his eyes.

"Where have you been all night?" the Half-Ork asked.

"An excellent question," said a low, dangerous voice. Halthak wheeled to see Amric and Valkarr having risen into crouches, silent as ghosts. They had not yet drawn their blades.

Amric spoke again. "I look forward to your answer, Bellimar."

Bellimar met their angry stares with his enigmatic half-smile, and in a slow, deliberate motion, he sat on a nearby rock. The warriors tracked his every movement, but did not ease their postures. Halthak looked between them and winced at the crackling tension.

"Did you think I had abandoned you?" Bellimar inquired.

"It had crossed my mind," Amric said.

"I understand how it appeared," Bellimar said. "I assure you, however, that I did not depart until the conflict was decided."

"Well and good if true, but why did you depart at all?"

"The battle was over and Halthak was offering to see to your wounds," Bellimar said in a soothing tone. "I could not help much in that endeavor, so I set about making myself useful in a different way. I sought a more secure site for us to camp the night, higher in the crag and away from subsequent predators. I departed in haste, hoping to find such a site quickly, before the sounds of the battle drew anything else to us."

"And yet you return instead at the break of dawn, while we spent the night on the ground."

Bellimar nodded, seeming oblivious to the barbed nature of Amric's comments. "Unfortunately, every location I found involved strenuous climbing, which I doubted you and Valkarr could manage in your weakened condition, and which would have meant abandoning the mounts. So instead I assumed a perch well above you, and kept watch from this higher vantage point. I had an unobstructed view of the surrounding area and any approach to this crevice. I regret that I could not shout down to inform you of my whereabouts, for fear of attracting unwanted attention, but I would of course have done so to warn of any approaching threats."

"It all sounds reasonable, if a bit too carefully crafted," Amric said. "And it does not explain why you could not share a word of your plan with Halthak before you left, or how you were able to descend undetected into our midst just now. I have been lying awake for more than an hour, listening to the healer's intermittent snoring, and I was only aware of your presence moments before Halthak discovered you."

Halthak's face burned at Amric's words. He had not realized the man was awake, had never seen him move nor heard his breathing change. Bellimar opened his mouth, but Amric held up a hand to forestall the reply.

"Nay," he said. "I do not doubt that you can supply a ready explanation. Keep your secrets, old man. I already know there is more to you than meets the eye. I respect and even like you, Bellimar, and your aid has been invaluable thus far, but I want you to understand two things."

The swordsman stepped close, pinning Bellimar with a stare. "First, if I judge for a moment that you have goals running contrary to our own, I will not hesitate to take necessary measures. Is that understood?"

The old man tilted his head, searching the warrior's expression for a long moment before giving a grave nod. "Understood. And the second?"

"In the future," the warrior said, his words ringing like cold iron, "if you feel the need to depart in the midst of a crisis without a word to anyone, stay gone."

Bellimar inclined his head again. "Understood on that point as well."

"And you, healer," Amric said, rounding with a scowl on Halthak, who flinched back from him. "You misled me, and broke our agreement by lulling me to sleep."

The Half-Ork, emboldened by Amric's words being more scolding than angry, folded his arms across his chest and thrust out his lower jaw as he faced the other man.

"You needed the rest to recuperate from your injuries," he said in what he hoped was a tone that brooked no argument. "I said I would only do as much as I thought you required, and I did just that. It is the physician's prerogative to ignore the demands of a delirious patient."

Amric glowered at him for a few more moments, before the hint of a grin cracked through. "So it is, healer, so it is. And we would be in dire straits indeed without your expert ministrations." His voice regained its stern edge. "Still, you put us all at risk, and such dishonesty does not fit you well. If we are so unfortunate as to repeat those circumstances, sway me with words rather than deception. Promise me that?"

Halthak exhaled in relief, and nodded. "I would have woken you both had anything threatened."

"Or we you," Amric said with a snort that sounded suspiciously like a mock snore, but a private wink took the sting from his words. Valkarr gave a soft, sibilant laugh and turned away, striding to the entrance of the cleft. He stood silhouetted there, surveying the hillside.

Still seated upon his rock, Bellimar said, "There is something else I must mention."

The old man's half-smile returned as they all turned to face him, expectant.

"In my exploration of the heights above us last night," he said. "I discovered something you should see for yourself."

By the time he reached the safety of the broad stone ledge, Halthak was fighting for breath. Strong hands pulled him over the edge and to his feet, and he peered down into the yawning darkness of the cleft below. He battled a moment of vertigo as he stood with his heels on the precipice; it had not looked so high when he stood at the bottom, staring up the rock face with skepticism as he sought the handholds the others assured him were plentiful. Amric and Valkarr had scampered up before him with infuriating speed and ease, and it was some combination of curiosity, stubbornness, and unease at being left behind with Bellimar that had driven him to follow.

Bellimar stood far below, a distant bit of shadow wrapped in his cloak. He had chosen to remain on the ground, expressing doubt as to whether there was strength enough left in his aging limbs to ascend again by the route he had so recently descended. He claimed to have reached this spot by a less strenuous albeit more circuitous route during the night. Contemplating the return descent now, Halthak felt his chest tighten. He berated himself for following the warriors up here merely to witness Bellimar's reported discovery, but then he raised his face to the sunrise and changed his mind.

The sun's golden light caressed and warmed his face, and he shielded his eyes against its glare to look out upon a living sea of jade. Between the altitude gained from the large hill upon which the crag rested, and the further height of the ledge above the crest of that hill, they were looking out at a level with the tops of the trees. The thick, green canopy spread away from the crag on three sides past the limits of his vision, its surface rippling before the will of the wind. The healer found the ancient forest as beautiful from above as it was treacherous beneath. Here at least there was life, as flocks of birds wheeled and circled high overhead. Halthak felt a sudden, fierce longing to be as free of the evils below as were those birds. He wondered at how magnificent the view must be at the peak of the crag rather than merely partway up, but he could see no way to ascend further from their ledge.

The ledge wrapped around the face of the bluff, and Amric and Valkarr stood at its southernmost edge. They were conversing and pointing at something in the distance, and as Halthak moved toward them he saw the focus of their attention.

On the southern side of the crag, separated from them by a slender swath of trees, the rocky ground gave way to foothills and then rose into a sheer cliff that meandered east like a great stone curtain. Etched into its side was a shelf that ran ribbon-like for many miles above the forest. On its western end, it coiled back upon itself several times before it disappeared into the woodlands behind the crag. Halthak strained to trace its progress to the east, though he lost it eventually to distance and the glare of the rising sun. It seemed to end at or behind a solitary mountain, thrust away from its siblings huddled in the range behind it to reign alone and majestic above the forest. As he continued to stare, however, it dawned upon him that the mountain had too many sharp, angular edges to be the careless artistry of nature, and the myriad shadows upon its face were too uniform as well. Awe crept over him as he realized he was looking upon a mighty fortress, carved from the very top of the mountain. Halthak tried and failed to grasp the enormity of effort required to construct a single structure so massive. It could only be Stronghold, home of the reclusive Wyrgens, and their destination.

Halthak hastened forward to hear the discussion.

"It is not marked on Morland's maps," Amric was saying. "But the maps focus on trade and mining supply routes, and that ridge path looks unsuitable for wagons or large parties, so that could be why. I would wager that four riders on horseback can navigate it in a single column, however, with caution."

"Do you see the bridge Bellimar mentioned?" Valkarr asked.

Halthak peered into the fading distance, and saw no such thing.

"I think so," Amric said, after a moment. "It is difficult to tell for certain at this distance, but I believe I see something connecting the path and the fortress. Damn, but the old man has eyesight a hawk would envy to have seen that far in the poor light."

The swordsman's flat tone seemed at odds with his admiring words, and Halthak puzzled over it before Amric's meaning sank in. Bellimar had startled them on the ground before the morning sun had crested the horizon. What the keen eyes of the warriors could barely discern now in dawn's first light, Bellimar had somehow seen last night in near darkness. Halthak felt a growing chill as he considered the implications.

"If we are mistaken about reaching the fortress from the path, we could lose a day or more to backtracking," Valkarr said.

Amric grunted. "Worth the risk. I find I am open to alternatives to the forest road just now."

"We will be exposed to view," Valkarr noted. "But we will see far as well, and attackers can only come at us one or two at a time on the narrow trail. A better route, if it connects."

"Then let us hope this newfound path is as quiet as it appears," Amric said. "And that Bellimar has indeed found us a way to bypass the last stretch of this infernal forest."

It was late afternoon when the riders reached the end of the high pathway along the cliff wall. At its terminus, the path twisted away from the sheer face and gave way to a broad, tree-studded clearing atop a bluff that jutted over the valley. From its edge, a slender bridge leapt across the intervening chasm in a shallow, graceful arc to the foot of the mountain fortress, Stronghold.

Amric guided his bay gelding onto the plateau, and he felt some of the tension leave the horse's knotted muscles in a brief, shuddering sigh.

The swordsman gave the animal's neck a sympathetic pat. After spending all day navigating the narrow, wind-clawed trail over a precipitous drop, this flat and spacious projection of stone seemed secure indeed. He waited as the others drew rein beside him, relief evident on their faces as well, and together they surveyed the bridge.

"What do you make of it?" Amric asked at last.

"It should not stand," Valkarr replied at once.

Amric was forced to agree. He had been eyeing the structure since it hove into clear view around the curve of the cliff wall. Though the Sil'ath were wondrous crafters on a smaller scale, they seldom built large, elaborate structures. Perhaps it was evidence that their nomadic impulse yet remained. It was just as rare for them to employ siege tactics such as sapping or demolition, but their military training still encompassed something of basic engineering and materials. Furthermore, Amric had taken it upon himself to study at the university in Lyden and bring the additional knowledge back to his people to augment their skills.

And everything he had learned, in direct contradiction to what he was seeing, insisted that the bridge before them simply could not be.

He dismounted and let the reins drop, then approached the edge of the precipice where the bridge began. The structure was wide enough for two horses abreast and composed entirely of some strange alloy, but he could find no seams or bolts demarcating the component pieces. Instead, it appeared to be forged of one unimaginably long, continuous piece of metal. Where the span met the stone at his feet, the two disparate materials merged, and the one flowed into the other without interruption. Ribs of metal looped in high arcs over the walking surface, but there were none of the heavy supports above or below that he expected of a bridge spanning many hundreds of yards. Amric peered down into the gorge, at the dark green treetops far below shot through with bleached veins of rock. If this contraption gave way beneath them, their quest would come to an abrupt and ignominious end down there.

"The Wyrgens are reputed to be unparalleled craftsmen, producers of countless marvels," Bellimar reminded him. "If any could produce a bridge that defies gravity, it is they."

Amric gave a noncommittal grunt. It was also said that the masters of Stronghold guarded their privacy with ferocious zeal, and were known to make examples of unwelcome visitors. This precarious path through the air could collapse by fault of construction or by design to repel invaders, and either way the outcome for Amric and his companions would be the same. Still, the bridge led to an opening in the chiseled wall on the other side, and he did not relish the thought of turning back now to find another approach.

There was no visible activity on the far side, but this was somewhat expected since nothing had been heard from the Wyrgens for many months.

Bellimar had done much on the journey from Keldrin's Landing to fill the gaps left in common knowledge regarding the reclusive Wyrgens of Stronghold. Like their base relatives, the savage Wyrgs of the lowlands, the Wyrgens were powerful and towering in stature, bestial in appearance and capable of rending a man limb from limb. Unlike their more primitive cousins, however, they were extremely intelligent, preferring science and clever manipulation of magical essences to warlike endeavors. Their inventions were highly sought after among the other nations, and with sufficient motivation the Wyrgens sometimes put aside their xenophobic tendencies to enter in trade arrangements with other races. Their feral cunning led to unease in their trade partners, but that discomfort was overlooked to garner the advantage that came with the Wyrgens' technology, particularly in matters of war. As he heard all this, Amric could not help but ponder how selling machines of destruction to other races so they could destroy each other seemed like an arrangement in which the Wyrgens profited in two ways.

Establishing the military fort that would later become Keldrin's Landing may have represented the first foothold of the civilized nations in the region, but as they expanded, men found the Wyrgens and Stronghold already here. No one could say whether the Wyrgens had built Stronghold themselves, or if they had merely appropriated it for their own. For their part, the Wyrgens were tight-lipped on the subject.

Keldrin's Landing had established a trade relationship with Stronghold, and thus enjoyed more efficient mining and research equipment, with a dramatic effect on profits. With the spreading disruption, the city had been pressing for the Wyrgens to produce advanced defensive measures by which the town could protect itself and the surrounding countryside. Then contact with the Wyrgens was lost.

Subsequent envoys to Stronghold had not returned. Morland admitted to having formed his own surreptitious side arrangement with the Wyrgens, for purposes he refused to divulge; Amric was certain it was for some dark purpose, given the merchant's soulless avarice, but even Morland's considerable resources had not enabled him to reach his private contacts.

All of this left Amric facing the bridge and pondering the unknowable. It was possible the Wyrgens were hidden to view inside, unaware or uncaring of their approach, or that no other envoy had made it here or survived the return trip. It was possible, but the alternatives were of more immediate concern. Whether the Wyrgens had fled Stronghold, or remained there but shunned the outside world, the bridge could be a trap to ward off intruders. More sinister yet, if something strong enough to eradicate or drive away the Wyrgens had taken up residence in Stronghold, the riders faced an even more uncertain reception.

Amric gave a mental shrug. There was nothing for it but to try. He would not back down before mere speculation. He strode to his horse and stepped into the saddle. He looked to the others, finding all eyes upon him. Without comment, he turned and guided the bay forward and onto the bridge.

He rode several yards out, and the structure held firm. He paused and glanced back to see his companions gathered at the foot of the bridge, and he resumed crossing. Out over the yawning chasm he rode, steady and unhurried. His horse's hooves rang eerily against the metal frame. Midway across the span, he looked over his shoulder to see the others crossing as well, each spaced a score of yards from the next to distribute the weight. Amric was now confident they need not have bothered, as the bridge made no protest, no creaking or cracking under the weight of horse and rider. In fact, the only indication that he was not on solid ground came in the form of an almost indiscernible swaying with the cross wind.

What seemed an eternity later, he reached the wide stone balcony before the outer wall of the fortress. A huge, square entrance gaped before him, with raised portcullis leading into a sunlit inner courtyard. Amric rode forward to ensure no one lurked within, and then waited for his companions to join him. The level top of the bluff that had seemed so expansive at the other end looked miniscule from this vantage, its thick copse of trees no more than a smudge of green now against a veritable sea of stone.

One by one the riders gained the balcony, and together they passed under the gate and into Stronghold's grounds.

Amric scanned the empty courtyard. It was a large, enclosed grassy area on a slight incline from the thick outer wall to the foot of the fortress. A number of smaller buildings were scattered about, each sizeable in its own right but dwarfed to insignificance by the vastness of the brooding edifice looming above. The swordsman gazed up the disorienting expanse that stretched away above them, perhaps even as far as the mountain's peak itself. Its face was dimpled by many small, shadowed openings starting high above the ground, and when he widened his perspective to take in a larger part of the architecture, he noted strata of epic proportions punctuated by huge, blocky buttresses and other jutting projections. There was no other visible ornamentation, and he saw no seams anywhere to suggest tight-fit ashlar blocks. It appeared as if the entire colossal structure was carved by the same sculptor as the mysterious bridge, and somehow shaped whole from the flesh of the mountain.

At the base of the fortress, he spied a sweeping set of stairs ascending to a recess in the wall, which looked to be the only available path from the courtyard into the fortress.

"This building is a stable," Valkarr said, pointing to one of the smaller buildings.

"And this other looks to be living quarters," Amric put in. "I think we are looking upon support structures for visitors the Wyrgens prefer to keep outside the fortress proper."

Bellimar nodded, his eyes roving over the face of the fortress. "That would be in keeping with the attitude of the Wyrgens. Few are the members of other races who have been within Stronghold itself. I would expect to find concentric layers of increasing restriction inside, with everything truly precious to the Wyrgens found deep within, toward the core."

They allowed the horses to graze on the unkempt grass of the courtyard, and Amric set Halthak and Bellimar to watching the fortress for any sign of life while he and Valkarr searched the out-buildings. They found no evidence of passage by their friends, and Amric was disappointed but not surprised. This seemed a little known entrance to Stronghold and had not been indicated on Morland's maps, which presumably were identical to those given to the Sil'ath party. If not for Bellimar's excursion after the encounter with the bloodbeasts, Amric's party would not have discovered this alternate route either. He wondered how many more obscured entrances could be found around the perimeter of the place, in addition to the heavily fortified main entry to which the forest road led.

The stable proved empty, as had the other satellite buildings, but it was well stocked with feed. They secured the horses there, since they would only be a hindrance within Stronghold, and they gathered at the stairs leading to the recessed entrance they had seen. Wary and watchful, they ascended the steps with Amric in the lead. At the top of the stairway, they found themselves looking into a long, high-ceilinged corridor that ended at a dark set of double doors. Amric stalked down the length of it, and the others followed, with Valkarr trailing behind like a ghost.

Up close, the towering doors shone with a dim, coppery hue, and what little light survived the length of the corridor was cast back in feeble glints from their metal surface. Looking about, Amric could see no handle, knocker or bell anywhere, so he stepped to the door and hammered his fist against it. So heavy and solid was the portal that a muffled series of thumps was all he could elicit. Drawing one of his swords, he slammed the hilt's pommel against the door and was rewarded with hollow booming sounds, but he was still dubious it would carry deep enough into such a vast place to draw its inhabitants to the door. They waited half a minute without response, and then he repeated the maneuver. After a dozen tries, he turned away in frustration.

He was about to suggest they return to the courtyard and attempt to enter one of the lofty windows when a clicking sound spun him around. One of the doors swung outward.

Amric was tall, standing half a head above most men, but the grizzled snout that thrust past the edge of the door was another half a head above him. A long, wolf-like visage followed, with a bristling mane of unruly fur running down a neck corded thick with muscle. The creature wore only a simple tunic belted around its waist, which covered the furry, muscular form from midsection to knees. Dark, liquid eyes glared out at the visitors, taking in each in turn, and the creature's lips peeled back from finger-length fangs.

Amric's scalp prickled in warning as he studied the feral gleam in those eyes. Though he had never before encountered a Wyrgen, he could see the beast was powerfully built, from its heavy shoulders and barrel chest to its long, wicked talons. It was not, however, the Wyrgen's physical presence that alarmed him. Instead it was the gamut of emotions that passed, for a fleeting moment, unguarded in its expression. He knew the Wyrgens came from wilder stock than most civilized races and might well be subject to more turbulent emotions, but still he was certain that in addition to shrewd intelligence, he had also glimpsed covetous scheming and more than a touch of madness.

"Are you real?" it asked in a rumbling, bass growl.

"As real as you are," Amric said, surprised at the query.

The Wyrgen tilted its head to regard him through narrowed eyes before flicking its ears back, evidently finding the answer satisfactory. "Then are you mad to be here, causing a clamor and drawing attention to yourselves?" it demanded, peering back over its shoulder into the interior of the fortress.

Amric frowned, noting the tension manifest in the creature's body language. He shared a glance with Bellimar, whose puzzled expression indicated this made no more sense to him.

"We meant no offense, friend," the swordsman said. "We seek a party of Sil'ath warriors, and we have reason to believe they came here. In addition, the merchant Morland from Keldrin's Landing wishes to ascertain the welfare of a friend here, a leader among your kind by the name of Grelthus."

The Wyrgen turned its stare upon him again. "Morland does not have friends," it snorted. "That one sees others only as tools to be used or obstacles to be removed. But I can assure you that Grelthus still lives, and I can take you to him, if we move quickly."

"Why must we move quickly?" Bellimar asked. "Is Stronghold no longer open to visitors?"

The creature looked past Amric to fix upon the old man. "Stronghold has never been *open* to other races, ancient one. But recent events have made it less tolerant of their presence than ever before."

"What events?" Bellimar returned. "What has happened here?"

The Wyrgen's huge hand tightened on the door, its talons sliding across the metal surface with a faint squeal. A growl roiled in its chest as it darted another glance over its shoulder. "We cannot discuss it here and now. The sounds will have drawn them, and they could be here at any moment. Follow me to safety, if you would live."

"Who do you fear?" Amric asked. "Has Stronghold been seized?"

But the Wyrgen had already vanished from the doorway, leaving it ajar behind him. Amric heard the receding sounds of its padding feet, the talons clicking lightly on the stone floor. He muttered an oath and moved forward to peer through the aperture. A vast antechamber stretched away within, lit by eerie lamps that never flickered against the great stone columns from which they hung. The ceiling was lost to view in the gloom, but layer upon layer of stone balustrades encircled the large chamber, each bordering wide terraces that overlooked the center. A honeycomb of corridors branched from all sides, and at the far end was a stairway rising to the next floor. The Wyrgen was loping at a hurried pace across the middle of the room and toward that stairway, casting furtive glances to either side as it went.

Amric swore again. There was nothing about the Wyrgen or this place that felt right, but they had little choice. The creature was the only uncorrupted life they had encountered since entering the forest, and it was warning them of imminent danger. Moreover, it claimed to know the whereabouts of Morland's contact. Perhaps one or both of them would serve as their advocates within Stronghold, and help ascertain if the Sil'ath party had come this way. If what Bellimar had said about the Wyrgens and Stronghold's construction was accurate, it would be difficult to force an entrance elsewhere. This fellow had admitted them into the interior, and they might not get another such opportunity. Amric just hoped that whatever waited inside would not prove worse than the menaces without.

Amric plunged through the door and into Stronghold, and the others followed close at his heels.

The Wyrgen reached the stairway and bounded up it, taking several steps at a time. It paused halfway up the stairs, tense, listening and scenting the air. Spinning into a crouch, it bared a mouthful of teeth at them in an expression that could have been either hostility or encouragement, for all Amric could tell, and then it beckoned them forward with a frantic wave of one claw. They hurried across the chamber like a chain of wraiths, and by the time they reached the foot of the stairs, the Wyrgen was disappearing from sight at the top. Amric and Valkarr sprinted up the stairway to find the creature darting from corridor to corridor, pausing at each opening with twitching ears and quivering nose. Settling upon one, it again motioned for them to follow. Halthak and Bellimar joined them on the second level terrace, and the companions raced after the Wyrgen.

As it turned to run ahead down the corridor, however, the Wyrgen suddenly drew up short, its head cocked. After a long moment, it whirled and, dropping almost to its belly, slunk on all fours to the bannister. Amric and Valkarr glided to the edge and crouched down, peering into the open chamber below as well.

Snarls and staccato grunts issued from a ground floor corridor beneath the terrace where Amric and the others hid, and seconds later two more Wyrgens burst into view. These wore no clothing at all, and their mien was even more savage than the individual who had answered the door. The pair stalked forward, bent low, talons spread wide at the end of long, powerful arms. Spying the open doorway to the courtyard, one hulking brute gave a roar of fury and lunged forward on all fours. The other was but an instant behind, and they covered the distance with astonishing speed. Sliding to a halt at the metal doors, they stood once more on their hind legs and seized the door, the great muscles bunching in their broad backs as they threw it open. One of the beasts hurtled through the opening and out of sight.

Amric went cold, thinking of the horses, but he did not have long to worry. The other Wyrgen, seeming at first on the verge of following its companion, hesitated in the doorway and then spun back to glare about the chamber. Amric gave a start as he realized the eyes of the beast were glowing crimson, afire with some strange energy that stood stark against the dimness of the chamber. Closer scrutiny revealed that its talons were glowing as well, the same hue, albeit not as brightly.

The Wyrgen lifted its nose and took several uncertain steps into the room, shuffling first one direction and then another, its eyes narrowed to bright scarlet pinpoints of light. It uttered a series of harsh, barking grunts, and within moments the shadow of the departed Wyrgen fell across the open doorway. Amric heaved an inward sigh of relief that the hunter had not gone far enough to hear or scent the horses in the stable building. It came through in a slow prowl, its muzzle held low, and he saw that its eyes and claws radiated an icy blue, rather than matching the strange red of the other.

On the terrace, the first Wyrgen slid back on its belly from the bannister and hunched in silence to all fours. It gave Amric a meaningful look, and then crept toward the hallway it had indicated before. Amric and Valkarr inched back from the terrace edge, rising to their feet only when well out of sight, and they glided after their guide. Halthak and Bellimar followed, making every effort to be just as noiseless.

They had gone a scarce twenty yards when a furious, strident howl reverberated in the chamber behind them.

Their Wyrgen guide hesitated, looking back at its charges with cold calculation. Then it waved them on and sped away down the corridor. Amric and his companions pelted after it, favoring speed over stealth now. Numerous doors blurred by as they ran, and though Amric and Valkarr slowed their pace somewhat so as not to leave Bellimar and Halthak behind, they could not have kept pace with the fleeing Wyrgen even if unhindered. The creature bolted down the stone hallway, sometimes dropping to run on all fours in its haste, and disappeared around a dim corner far ahead of them. When Amric reached that same corner, he gazed down another long hallway with a sporadic assortment of doors on either side. It was unadorned like the last one, crossed by another corridor at its end. Their guide was no longer in sight. How easy it would be to lose one's way, the warrior reflected, in this rabbit's warren of twisting, uniform tunnels. His thoughts darkened further as he wondered if their escort had intended such an outcome from the beginning.

He glanced back the way they had come. Just as Halthak and Bellimar reached the corner, the two Wyrgens from below appeared at the mouth of the corridor. Baying in triumphant rage, the brutes hurtled forward in pursuit, their glowing talons ripping at the stone floor. Amric waved his lagging companions past and into the new hallway, then followed them for several paces before spinning in place to face the corner. Valkarr joined him, and their four blades whispered forth.

The tumult of panting snarls drew near, and Amric braced himself, balanced on the balls of his feet, one sword angled across his body and the other down and away to his side. The familiar icy void of battle settled about him, and he sought his place at its center, aware of everything around him and yet focused on nothing.

The hulking bodies exploded around the corner, a dark hurricane of force and fury. Their eyes, ablaze with eerie energies, went wide with surprise to find the warriors lying in wait and blocking their path. There was no hesitation, however, in their berserk, headlong charge. They launched at the warriors, jaws slavering and talons extended, in a blinding assault almost too quick to follow. As fast as they were, Amric and Valkarr moved faster yet. To meet the irresistible force of those massive forms head on would be instant death. Instead, they spun in mirror images of each other, side-stepping the attacks and hacking aside grasping claws. In blurs of motion, their spins brought their opposite swords to bear in thunderous descending strokes on the thick, outstretched necks. The Wyrgens crashed to the flagstones without another sound, the momentum of their charge carrying them several yards further in a tumbling slide that ended at Halthak's feet. The healer looked down, saucer-eyed, clutching his staff before him with shaking hands. A spreading pool of crimson welled beneath the great, shaggy forms, their heads all but severed. Even in death, their clenched talons and staring eyes smoldered with sinister potency.

Amric looked down. He had felt a slight tug at his oiled mail shirt as his blue-clawed attacker passed, and he was astonished to find the burnished links neatly parted in a long gash, the edges of the incision encased in frost that was already melting in the warm air. He had been prepared and had moved with lightning swiftness, but still the creature had not only come within a fraction of an inch of drawing his blood, but had cut through Sil'ath-crafted mail armor with appalling ease. He inspected Valkarr, and found a similar score upon his friend's scaly hide, slanting across his ribs, from his own scarlet-eyed assailant. That mark was blackened as if by fire, and blood oozed from the wound. Valkarr, of course, behaved as if the injury was utterly beneath notice. Using the tip of one sword, Amric lifted the heavy paw of one of the slain Wyrgens, tilting the appendage this way and that to study the wisps of scarlet flame surrounding the hooked nails.

"What do you make of it?" he asked, glancing at Bellimar.

The old man glided forward, his cheeks flushed and his eyes fever bright in a face that otherwise looked even more drawn and pale than usual. He stared at the fallen beasts for a long moment, seeming transfixed by the scene.

"Fascinating," Bellimar said at last. "I cannot say for certain, but I would hazard a guess that they are infected by some primal force of magic. These individuals appear to have been affected with different elemental symptoms, but otherwise have both regressed to a more savage aspect. The Wyrgens rose above their primitive origins centuries ago, and they bear a strong repugnance now for that part of their heritage. I find it unlikely that any would voluntarily return to this base behavior."

"Perhaps they are not Wyrgens?" Valkarr asked, cocking his head to the side as he studied the bodies.

Amric nodded. "We are not familiar with the Wyrgen races. Could it be these are not Wyrgens at all, and Stronghold has been overrun by a less civilized strain of the Wyrgen race?"

Bellimar gave a slow shake of his head. "I think not. Wyrgens are the tallest and heaviest of the Wyrgen races. These are too large by far to be any of the other variants with which I am familiar. Though, admittedly, none of the races are known to be steeped in radiation, as are these specimens."

A scuffing sound from the corridor far ahead brought them sharply about. Their Wyrgen guide crept into view and froze in place, outlined in the murky light cast by the steady, flameless lamps along the stone walls. It started toward them with halting steps at first, and then picking up speed until it broke into a run. Uncertain of the creature's intent, Amric stepped forward to meet it, blades still in hand. As it neared, the Wyrgen slowed to a shuffle, surveying the scene. It seemed to move in a fog, bewildered, its stricken gaze flitting from its fallen fellows to the naked, blood-smeared steel of the warriors' blades.

"You killed them, you killed my…. Why did you kill them?"

"We had little choice," Amric replied. "They attacked us, and we could find no escape."

Those dark, liquid eyes rose to his, and Amric bore witness to a silent war raging within the Wyrgen. Murderous intent burned its way through the creature's swirling confusion, and the creature tensed, claws convulsing open. Amric measured the distance between them out of reflex, preparing for the vicious rush that was to come. The rage vanished as quickly as it had emerged, however, and the Wyrgen subsided, lowering its head.

"Of course you had to defend yourselves, of course you did," it mumbled. "My people are... not themselves, of late. They are not responsible for their actions, and must be treated as unwell."

"What happened to your people?" Bellimar asked in a smooth, calming tone. "What calamity has befallen proud Stronghold?"

The Wyrgen grunted. "Proud Stronghold, indeed. Too prideful we were, and too confident in our ability to harness the greatest of forces. Our hubris was our downfall. Is it not always thus, with reckless mortal kind ever marching to our own doom?"

The woolly head snapped up as the Wyrgen took a sudden step toward them, causing Amric's swords to flash up and to the ready. The Wyrgen, its expression animated, did not appear to notice in its eagerness.

"But I am not infected, and I will fix it. Am I not Stronghold's head scientist? I will cure my people, bring them back. I just need more time." The creature turned to Amric with a plaintive whine. "So you must not slay any more, do you understand? They understand not their actions."

"I can make no such promise," Amric said. "We will defend ourselves, if attacked again. But perhaps there need be no further conflict, if you can lead us to Grelthus and the place of safety you mentioned."

The Wyrgen's eyes burned with anger, but it dipped its muzzle in a slight nod. "I will lead you. Only I can take you to Grelthus."

The creature gave a mad chuckle and turned away, padding down the corridor. Amric exchanged a look with the others, and they hastened to follow. A faint howl wafted after them. Half a beat later it was joined by a distant chorus of growling voices. Amric's jaw tightened. It seemed more of Stronghold was becoming aware of the intruders.

The Wyrgen glanced over its rounded shoulder, eyes lambent in the lamplight and lips peeled back from long, glistening fangs in a mirthless grin. "It is not far now." It thumped its chest with one hammer-like fist. "Only I, only I can take you to Grelthus."

Their guide swung forward once more, and Amric heard the creature muttering to itself as it loped onward. The remote sounds of pursuit grew steadily louder as the companions made their way toward the forbidden heart of Stronghold, following on the heels of madness.

CHAPTER 9

Amric paced the floor and fought a losing battle with impatience. He stalked back and forth at the narrow end of the long, windowless stone chamber, and each time he passed the door there, he paused to listen.

There were no sounds of pursuit outside, and there had been none for hours. Their Wyrgen guide—Amric had decided he was male—had been as good as his word on that count, leading them through a maze of twisting corridors and chambers separated by solid metal doors. The Wyrgen locked each portal behind them with a small, cube-like device which he was quick to pocket after every use. He explained in a mournful whisper how his people had degenerated too far to recall even the most basic use of their tools, and thus would be unable to reach them through the secured doors.

Even as he knew relief at the frustrated clamor of pursuit growing more distant with each twist and turn, Amric also felt a growing unease at how dependent they were becoming upon their erratic guide. They were at the heart of a hostile labyrinth, and only the Wyrgen possessed map and key.

As he paced, Amric studied the creature from the corner of his eye. The Wyrgen moved around a large table in the center of the room, rummaging through piles of clutter in what seemed an endless, aimless fashion. A walking path had been preserved around that expansive slab, but the rest of the chamber was littered with crates, stacks of parchment, and countless strange devices in various stages of either assembly or dismantling. A number of items caught the warrior's roving eye in the quiet hours of waiting: a fanged skull formed entirely of crystal, a pulsating gem which worked its way through a gamut of different luminous colors, a pair of wicked-looking, clawed black gauntlets cleverly articulated for the movement of each joint, and many more. For every item he recognized or for which he could divine a purpose, there were a dozen more that baffled him. Given the spectacular level of disarray, he could only guess at the additional wonders buried in the room, beyond immediate sight.

The Wyrgen had insisted they wait here, in a room he declared safe, until all was quiet in the fortress once more. He had then rebuffed each subsequent query, even those as basic as inquiring after his name, by stressing the continued need for silence and patience. Their guide's actions, which had at first seemed a reasonable set of precautions, now reeked instead of reticence. Amric ground his teeth with inward exasperation at the delay.

Halthak and Bellimar sat upon wooden crates which had been pinned beneath stacks of debris when they arrived, before the Wyrgen swept them clear. The healer dozed, sitting upright, his head bobbing forward. The old man was wrapped in his cloak, his eyes following every movement of the Wyrgen. Valkarr sat cross-legged on the floor with his back to a wall, one of his swords naked across his knees. His eyes were closed, and even Amric could not tell for certain if he was truly napping. The dried blood caking the side of the Sil'ath's torso was the only remaining indication of his earlier wound, since Halthak had seen to it as soon as their flight permitted.

This had drawn a tremendous amount of interest from the Wyrgen, who had overturned a pile of debris in his haste to cross the room and witness the healer's use of magic. "This is a most wondrous talent," he breathed, regarding the Half-Ork in near rapture. Amric noted a moment of frenzied consideration pass behind the widened eyes, however, before they became guarded once more. Even hours later, as the Wyrgen dug through the chamber's contents, he still cast furtive glances at the nodding healer when he thought no one was watching.

Amric listened at the door again, and again heard nothing. He growled, and wended his way through the clutter to the far end of the long chamber where another door identical to the first was set into that opposite wall. He pressed his ear to the cold metal panel, straining for long minutes to catch any sound. Did he imagine something there, a faint scraping sound, or perhaps a low cough?

"No attack will come from that direction," the Wyrgen said, studying him over his shoulder. "I told you this before."

"We have waited long enough," Amric said. "Your people are no longer pursuing us. We should move while all is quiet."

"We are safest here for now," the Wyrgen grunted. "Stronghold is my home, and I have not survived these many months by being reckless. Have patience, human."

"Why continue to wait?" Amric pressed. But the Wyrgen had already turned back to the table, and did not respond. Amric bit back his frustration and tried another approach.

"What is past this door? I think I heard something moving in whatever chamber lies beyond."

The Wyrgen turned and regarded him with narrowed eyes. "An observation room lies that way, overlooking a grand experiment that stood to change our world. Alas, there are too few of us remaining to complete that work now."

"And what of the movement I heard?" Amric continued. "Is Grelthus in the observation room?"

"No, Grelthus will not be found in there," the Wyrgen replied with a deep, grating chuckle as he turned away once more.

"Is he coming here to us, then?"

The Wyrgen did not reply at once, and the swordsman thought at first he would ignore the question, as he had so many others over the intervening hours. After long seconds, however, he rumbled, "If you meet Grelthus, it will be here."

At that statement, Amric exchanged a look with Bellimar. It seemed their chances of finding Morland's contact were becoming less and less certain. The merchant had indicated that Grelthus held high stature in Stronghold, so Amric had been hoping to find someone more stable than their current guide, with sufficient influence to guarantee them safe passage among the Wyrgens. At least, he amended, among the Wyrgens who were not yet infected with whatever strange ailment coursed through Stronghold. Also, while this fellow claimed to know naught of their Sil'ath friends, Amric held out hope that Grelthus's position of influence would translate to a broader network of information as well. Now that he had their guide talking, however, Amric intended to elicit as much information from him as possible.

"Why should Grelthus come here?" he asked. "I have seen you send no signal. Does he frequent these rooms?"

"Of course he does," the Wyrgen snapped, an irritated snarl slipping into its tone. He lifted a sheaf of parchment papers and thumbed through them before throwing them aside. "These chambers, though currently in disrepair, are dedicated to science and research. And is Grelthus not Stronghold's head scientist? Now be silent, for I must think."

Amric frowned. "Grelthus is head scientist of Stronghold? Back in the corridor, you claimed that *you* were—" He paused as realization dawned. "You! You are Grelthus!"

The Wyrgen froze in the act of pushing aside a stack of relics, then swung slowly about to face him once more. The dark, liquid eyes darted to each of them in turn. Bellimar had not moved, but Halthak sat forward, awake now, and Valkarr, no longer feigning sleep, had slipped into a crouch with bared steel clenched in one fist. The Wyrgen's gaze fell upon Amric once more, and the warrior watched a mad flicker of indecision pass through the wolf-like features. The muzzle curled in an unconscious snarl as the tall, powerful form tensed. Amric shifted his stance and relaxed, measuring his space to maneuver in the surrounding clutter. Just as in the hallway, however, the Wyrgen regained his composure with a concerted effort and the moment fell back from the brink of violence.

"I am Grelthus," he growled.

"Why this damned deception, then?" Amric demanded through clenched teeth. "You could have revealed your identity at any time. Did you not believe that Morland directed us to you?"

"That Morland sent you is no evidence of your good intentions," Grelthus said with a toothy sneer.

Amric found it difficult to argue the point, as the merchant was a snake. Even so, he had agreed to perform a duty, however distasteful. "Morland provided the maps and information that led us here. In exchange, he bade us inquire as to the disposition of your, ah, business arrangement with him, were we successful in locating you."

Grelthus bared his teeth in a mirthless expression. "The merchant and I had an arrangement where the mutual benefit outweighed the mutual distrust, by a very slight margin. It has been superseded by more important matters, however, and our deal is now voided. I owe the man nothing."

"I will carry your answer back to Morland," Amric said in a measured tone. "Our dealings with him were out of necessity rather than choice, whereas our own goal is to determine the whereabouts of our missing friends, the party of Sil'ath I mentioned to you earlier. Now that we are being more truthful with one another, I ask you again: have you seen them?"

The Wyrgen met the warrior's level gaze, head swaying slightly, dark eyes hooded. "No, human," he said at last. "You must seek your friends elsewhere."

Amric swallowed bitter disappointment and gave a tight nod. "Our friends were seeking the source of the disruption plaguing the region. Morland directed them here to Stronghold for answers. Can you tell us aught of this?"

"I wish that I could not," the Wyrgen said with a rumbling sigh. "I wish I could disavow any knowledge of it, but you must understand that it is our nature to study such phenomena. Untold secrets beckoned, seemingly within reach—and with the convergence, and Stronghold so ideally located to study—but little did we realize…"

The Wyrgen's broad shoulders slumped and his hands rose to claw at his head. An agonized groan escaped him. Bellimar leaned forward from his seat on the crate, eyes intent beneath delicate silver brows.

"What did you find, Grelthus?" the old man asked.

"It will be easier to show you," Grelthus whispered, raising his shaggy head from his hands. "Come with me to the observation chamber. It is fitting that you see."

Amric stepped aside as the Wyrgen crossed the room and, procuring the strange cube from the folds of his tunic, unlocked the inner door. The swordsman observed the action from the corner of his eye, noting how the cube was pressed to the metal surface above the door handle and twisted to one side, prompting the muffled click of a mechanism hidden within. Grelthus then swiftly palmed the device before throwing open the door and striding through. He descended into a narrow, darkened stairwell that ran perpendicular to the room, and Amric and his companions followed several paces behind.

The stairs plunged a considerable distance below the floor level of the room they had departed, forty feet or more by Amric's reckoning, and were lit at their nether end by an eerie, flickering glow. Amric peered past the hulking form of the Wyrgen to the doorway below, where a shimmer of multi-hued light danced across the wall in bold relief against the shadows, cast from the chamber beyond. A vague sense of unease stole over him as they neared the bottom, where wispy fingers of light caressed the walls about them and clawed at the stairs beneath their feet.

Sudden vertigo lanced through him, and he almost missed the last step before the landing, reaching out one hurried arm to the wall to brace himself. His vision swam for one disorienting moment, and he glanced over his shoulder at his companions. They did not appear similarly affected. Instead, they looked back at him, their faces streaked with unearthly luminescence and taut with concern.

Amric shook his head to clear it. He took a deep, steadying breath, and passed through the doorway.

A long stone chamber stretched away before them, not unlike the one they had vacated above in terms of size and aspect. There the resemblance ended, however. This room was free of clutter, and had only the one doorway they had come through without a twin on the opposite side. A huge metal cage squatted at the far end of the room. It was capped top and bottom in large iron slabs, with thick supporting posts at each corner. The bars themselves were not metal; instead, crackling bluish beams of energy draped its sides. In the center of the cage was a heaping pile of cloth, and Amric felt the hairs on the back of his neck stir as he saw that bundle of material rustle and flap as if beat by an unseen wind. The cage was large enough to hold several men, if need be, and Amric spied an empty water pitcher lying on its side as well as a chamber pot pushed to the back corner. His nose wrinkled, informing him that the chamber pot had seen recent use.

The cage, with its sinuous bars of fire, was an unsettling sight, but it was not the only source of shimmering light permeating the chamber. The eyes of all in the room were drawn to one long side of the room, which overlooked a scene that dazzled and baffled the senses. At first it appeared the space was enclosed only on three sides and the entire right side opened onto a vast amphitheater. The tight echo of their own footsteps indicated an enclosed area, however, and the dull sheen hanging in midair soon gave the lie to that first impression. The whole of the wall was forged of a single great sheet of glass, or some other transparent material, several feet thick. Amric stepped over to it and brushed his fingers against it to confirm what his eyes doubted. He rapped his knuckles against the unblemished surface, and was rewarded with a feeble tapping sound that was quickly swallowed in the tomb-like silence. Clear as crystal it might be, but the wall seemed as solid and strong as the outer hide of any castle. Grelthus and the others joined him at the wall of glass, and together they looked upon the spectacle below.

The circular amphitheater was enormous, dwarfing even the expansive architecture they had passed through in their harrowing passage into the dark heart of Stronghold. Colossal stone columns stood like a grim ring of sentries, mounting from the floor far below their vantage point to a vaulted ceiling far above. Past the transparent wall, a wide set of stone stairs fell away before them to spill onto a broad terraced landing. Stairways of more modest size flowed downward and away on either side to one of a series of mezzanines encircling the room. The floor itself was comprised of a series of concentric circles, each dropping in elevation from the last to reach the lowest point at the center of the chamber. The entire gigantic coliseum seemed constructed around that center, focusing inward upon some unnamed, anticipated event there.

Looking down, Amric somehow doubted that the builders of this vast chamber had intended for what he was witnessing now.

A ragged fissure gaped at the center, the stone crumbling at its edges. The force which had torn the floor asunder had been sudden and explosive, for huge shards of granite were scattered from the crater to the distant walls in every direction. Adjusting for distance, Amric observed that some of those chunks of rock were better than the size of a cottage, and yet had been hurled hundreds of yards like the toys of a child. Portions of the surrounding pillars and walls had been torn loose in the passing of those ponderous missiles, with a spider's web of cracks radiating from each point of impact.

From that angry wound in the ground rose a titanic geyser of flame, spearing upward almost to the ceiling. They watched, open-mouthed, as the fountain jetted and heaved, writhing like a live thing. It changed colors in fitful bursts, sometimes lingering on a multi-hued arrangement for several seconds and other times strobing through luminous colors in a sequence too rapid for the eye to follow. The fiery display pressed against Amric's senses in a dizzying assault, forcing him to shade his eyes against its brilliance even as a dull roaring filled his ears.

The swordsman shook his head again, averting his gaze from the fountain. In truth, the shimmering, light-filled chamber in which they stood was little better, with their shadows dancing and twisting against the back wall in a mad mockery of their forms. Amric turned to study Grelthus, and found the Wyrgen staring down at the fountain, barrel chest heaving as his breath whistled through bared fangs.

"You are looking upon the remnants of a grand experiment," Grelthus whispered. "It was to be our greatest triumph, and has instead become our darkest chapter."

"What are we looking upon, Grelthus?" Amric asked.

The Wyrgen drew a shuddering breath. "I call it an Essence Fount, and since my people may be the first to have achieved such a thing, I think I can legitimately claim the right to name it."

"The flame does not appear natural," Halthak said, frowning.

"Natural?" Grelthus snorted. "A meaningless distinction. There are only the laws of the cosmos we understand, and those we have yet to decipher. The ancients were far beyond us on this path of comprehension. But I take your meaning, Ork. It is not a flame at all, but raw essence itself. It makes no heat or sound, and yet its power dwarfs any mundane fire—even of this size—to insignificance."

"No sound?" Amric said. "It roars in my ears, within my head, fit to split my skull!"

Grelthus swung to look at him, head tilted to one side. "I hear nothing."

Bellimar too was studying him with a pensive expression as he asked the Wyrgen, "Raw essence? You mean to suggest that we are looking upon a manifestation of pure magical force?"

Grelthus inclined his head. "Indeed, exactly so. But forgive me, you came seeking answers as to the region's disruption, and I should start a few steps closer to the beginning."

"Yes, closer to the beginning," came a new voice from the back of the room. "So that he can form more gradual lies and thus steer you wrong undetected."

They all whirled, and bare steel flashed into Valkarr's hands. Amric gritted his teeth as dizziness washed over him. This place was somehow befuddling his senses, he thought fiercely, for his own swords should have been in hand against any threat with equal speed.

There was movement in the cage at the end of the room. The strange, wind-tugged pile of cloth lurched upward and became the standing form of a man, swathed in flowing robes. He was dirty and unshaven, and both his soiled clothing and grimy shoulder-length hair swirled with that same unfelt wind. He folded his arms across his chest and sky blue eyes raked over them in a baleful glare.

"My name is Syth," he said. "And you are being lied to."

"Pay no heed to this vermin," Grelthus spat. "He is a violent criminal, detained here until he can be returned to face justice in Keldrin's Landing."

Amric looked from the prisoner to the Wyrgen. "What is this man's crime?"

"He is a thief, caught invading Stronghold, and he wounded several of my people in his capture," Grelthus responded.

"He lies, I have not harmed a one of these dogs," Syth responded at once. He fixed the Wyrgen with a level stare as a slow, wintry smile crept onto his features. "But rest assured I will harm at least one when I leave."

Grelthus gave a deep, menacing growl and took half a step toward the cage. "The pest is fortunate that I hold our peaceful relations with the human colony in such high value, for he would otherwise face immediate death under Stronghold's laws for his intrusion."

"Oh, indeed," Syth snarled. "What a kindness you have done me, holding me here these many long weeks as you ponder how best to make use of my nature in your frantic experiments."

"And what exactly is your nature, Syth?" Bellimar asked.

"I am a half-breed," Syth said. "I am half human, and half wind elemental."

"Marvelous," Bellimar breathed. "Of course, I should have seen it."

Amric studied the man anew, astonished. The few elementals he had encountered had been wild and unpredictable, more capricious forces of nature than sentient beings; the only air elemental he had seen before had lacked even a solid form. He tried and failed to imagine how they could produce offspring with humans, or how being infused with such a tempestuous, magical force would affect a man. He realized the man's clothing, which had seemed rustled by a breeze when he was in repose, now whipped and curled about him as he grew agitated.

"This deceitful fool is grasping at any chance, however remote," Syth continued in a heated tone. "He seeks redemption for himself, and for a people he destroyed. I warn you, do not trust him, for if he has brought you this deeply into Stronghold, it is only because he hopes to make use of you as well."

The Wyrgen took another furious step toward the cage, claws flaring open. Then, with a visible effort, he shook himself and turned his back on Syth. "I offer my... apologies for my churlish behavior, friends. I grieve for my people, and have seen very little rest since this all began. I am not myself, and this one provokes me at every opportunity, so that I was forced at last to move his cell down here where he could no longer disrupt my work."

In his cage, Syth made a short, rude noise and rolled his eyes. Grelthus stiffened where he stood, but did not turn. Amric looked from one to the other. He certainly needed no additional reason to mistrust their Wyrgen guide, but the whole exchange had supplied much food for thought. He knew the truth hovered somewhere in between at best, though which direction of center he could not say. He knew as well that the Wyrgen had more yet to reveal. He stepped in front of Grelthus and waited until the shaggy head lifted to meet his gaze.

"You mentioned starting your tale from the proper beginning?" he said.

"Not *the* beginning," Grelthus corrected. "There is much that remains a mystery even to us who sought to study the phenomenon. But certainly it is *a* beginning, and I will share what I do know."

The Wyrgen turned away, and approached the glass wall once more with slow, shuffling strides. He stood there in silence for a time, staring at the blazing fountain as its shifting colors undulated over his thick, unruly fur. He was quiet so long that Amric began to wonder if he had become enthralled with the thing and forgotten their presence entirely. He spoke at last, however, and his low-pitched voice was ragged with sorrow.

"The ley lines are a place to begin. Just as life-giving blood moves through our bodies, so does magical force circulate throughout our world in a network of ley lines. Magic, as you know, has many aspects and manifestations, from elemental to Unlife; but at its most primal, its most fundamental, this force is called Essence. It is neither good nor evil, but instead is merely energy in its purest form, containing the power to create or destroy, to heal or enslave. It becomes tainted and altered by the artisan, the purpose and the vessel through which it is used.

"Essence pulses and flows about our world—and perhaps even between worlds, we know not for certain—through invisible ley lines. Some ley lines are major, like arteries in the body, and can be detected by those sensitive to matters arcane; some are minor, like a web of veins finer than hair, significant only in aggregate. This network of energy, and the field of power it creates, imbues all life on our world and gives rise to all manner of magical creatures. Those that possess sufficient affinity for the energy can learn to manipulate the Essence within them, and about them.

Grelthus threw a glance over his shoulder. "Forgive me if I am covering familiar ground," he said, "but I find it easiest to organize my thoughts if I am thorough."

He drew a deep breath, and exhaled slowly before resuming his lecture.

"This region has always been highly magical because a series of major ley lines pass through it. Stronghold itself was built atop one of these major ley lines, and truly the creation of this fortress was only possible by harnessing a fraction of the line's power to amplify the methods of the builders. We have tried to map the course of these arteries, and we believe they converge somewhere deep within the forest at the eastern end of the bay. What a place of power must be found there, if we could but get close enough to study it—!"

Grelthus paused, a shudder passing through his tall frame. After a moment, he continued. "But I am digressing. The lands to the east have become more and more hazardous, and were impassable by the time we realized their importance. As I was saying, Stronghold stands astride a major ley line, which has enabled rapid advances in our studies. When your kind invaded the region, we met your overtures with some reserve. Certainly, we could have eradicated the interlopers, for Keldrin's Landing was but a paltry fort of twigs and savages at the time. But more would have followed. They always do. Your kind had scented the riches to be obtained, and nothing would forestall their greed. So we let the lesser races have their minerals and shiny baubles, and we entered a restrained trade arrangement with them, all the while making evident our superior technology to curb any imperialistic notions. The true wealth to be had was in studying and harnessing the unique concentration of power here. The merchant Morland, when he came, understood this. He sought a means by which to share in our research, by way of incentive or leverage. Or, as is more commonly his wont, by both methods."

The Wyrgen's muzzle split in a predatory grin. "A fool he was, but useful in his way."

"What went wrong, then?" Amric asked.

The grin faltered, faded. "A handful of years ago, the ley lines in the region grew even stronger, and magical activity rose in proportion. The energy flow continued to intensify, past all expected limits, like stately rivers suddenly overflowing with raging floodwaters, wreaking havoc on the surrounding lands. We cannot explain it, but it is as if something is drawing an unprecedented amount of current from all directions to this region. We, of course, saw this as an opportunity."

"Naturally," sneered Syth, glaring from his cage at the Wyrgen, but the latter did not appear to have heard him.

"We built this chamber like a giant focusing lens to tap into the ley line, to divert a tiny fraction of its force for study, and to contain it within well-shielded confines. But we did not realize to what extent the energy had swollen. So powerful, so concentrated had it become that it took visible form here, bursting past all our carefully constructed restraints. All in the chamber itself were slain in an instant. Those beyond were bathed in a wash of radiant energy that permeated their forms even as they fought to contain it in the chamber below."

Amric stared in horror even as Halthak put it to strangled words, "So all your people, with the fiery eyes...?"

"Infected," Grelthus nodded, his voice tight. "Corrupted by Essence. Many died in the days that followed, retching and bleeding. The ones who survived became what you have seen. The magic affected individuals differently, manifesting as different elemental energies such as fire, or ice, or worse. They have reverted to base savagery, and show no recognition whatsoever when they gaze upon me. I am now an exile, forced to flee my own kind."

"How did you survive the event?" Amric inquired.

"I was in this very viewing chamber," Grelthus said, "perhaps the only one that withstood the eruption, through some stroke of luck or hellish misfortune." The Wyrgen put a tentative hand to the transparent wall. "I know it is a force of nature, no more sentient than a thunderstorm. At times, however, I think it probes at my barriers like a live thing, looking for any weakness, tireless in its pursuit of the one who eluded it..."

"Were there no other survivors, then?" Valkarr interrupted.

Grelthus let his hand drop and gave a barely perceptible, defeated shrug. "I have seen no uncorrupted Wyrgens, save myself. Any who did not succumb to the Essence were probably torn asunder by their erstwhile comrades. By limiting my exposure to compromised chambers and always hiding from my people, I have survived these past months."

Amric felt a chill travel his spine as he envisioned mysterious forces contaminating their flesh as they traversed the halls of Stronghold on their way in, oblivious to the unseen danger. "And you hope yet to cure your people?" He failed to keep a note of skepticism from his voice.

The Wyrgen wheeled on him, snarling. "I must!" he hissed. "What alternative is there? We are a people rightfully proud of our mastery of arcane science, sitting atop what might well be the greatest source of power in our world. If the answer can be found, it must be here!"

"Of course, and it is a noble endeavor," Amric soothed at once. "It is just that I know very little of the intricacies of magic, and would be lost as to how to proceed, were I in your place."

He waited until some of the tension eased from the bristling form, before asking his next question, careful to frame it in a neutral manner. "Is this Essence Fount then responsible for the sudden spread of dark creatures in the region?"

The Wyrgen shook his head. "Nay, the Fount itself is but a sliver of the elevated currents coursing through the lands. It is an effect localized to Stronghold and possibly its grounds, but no further. But its underlying cause, the greatly increased Essence throughout the region, will continue to amplify many things and cause them to strengthen, to swell in numbers."

Amric frowned, absorbing this. "With so much magic in the area, how does it not corrupt all life as it has done your people?"

"You have a sharp mind, warrior," Grelthus said, regarding him with a hint of new respect. "You could do more than swing a blade. As I said, this is a localized reaction. Consider your body's response to an invading infection, how the flesh swells and becomes an angry red in color, discharging unhealthy fluids and scabbing over. The body, a wondrous machine, focuses its defensive efforts on repelling the invader. In our zeal, our hubris, we provoked such a targeted response, and secured our own downfall."

"You sought to study and harness the symptom, then, while the true source remains unknown."

"Regrettably true," Grelthus said. "Though I suspect the answer might lie further east, at the convergence of these major ley lines, if one could but forge a path there and somehow survive whatever forces have congregated."

In silence they turned back to study the blazing fountain, each in the room alone with his own thoughts for a time. Amric's mind raced over their options from this point. It seemed tantamount to suicide to continue further east, but if there was any evidence his Sil'ath friends had gone that way, he would follow. Since they did not appear to have made it even here, however, the logical course was to double back and resume the search. Even if the source of the spreading corruption was far to the east, they would need to join forces with their comrades against this hostile land. And if their friends had perished, there was the requisite matter of avenging their deaths; if necessary, he would attend to that matter before making any further decisions about how best to complete their mission.

Amric felt dizziness wash over him once more, and the roaring sound returned to batter at his ears. He squeezed his eyes shut to block out the sight. Why was the damned thing affecting him so? And why only him?

Grelthus uttered an angry growl, interrupting the warrior's thoughts. The Wyrgen stalked over to the cage and halted several paces from the crackling blue energy bars, bowing his shaggy head before the prisoner.

"I regret the necessity to detain you, thief, but even more so I regret that distress and distraction have made of me a poor host. Pass your water pitcher through the bars, so that I may refill it for you."

Syth folded his arms across his chest and shook his head, glaring at the Wyrgen. "You cannot part your jaws without lies spilling forth, you mangy cur. There is no food or water in this room, and if you depart this chamber alone you will surely betray your guests and imprison them down here, even as you have done to me."

"Very well," Grelthus sighed, spreading his hands and turning to Halthak. "Healer, would you do this mistrustful prisoner the kindness of refilling his water urn, from the barrel by the door in the chamber above? I will prepare his meal later, for that requires travel to another chamber and I would not ask it of you. While you are gone, I will remain here, guarded by your warrior friends."

Halthak looked from the Wyrgen to Amric, and then to the prisoner. He took a step toward the cage, but Grelthus raised one clawed hand to forestall him.

"First kick the jug out of the cage, thief," Grelthus snarled. "The thief moves like lightning, and is too cunning by half."

Syth favored the Wyrgen with a dark scowl, but did as he was bid, toeing the water jug a safe distance from the bars. "What are you playing at, Grelthus?" he asked, brow furrowed. "Why this sudden show of concern for my welfare?"

The Wyrgen ignored him as Halthak retrieved the pitcher and started for the stairs. When the Half-Ork had passed out of view, Grelthus strode back to the glass wall.

"My people sometimes come to the chamber below to gaze upon the Essence Fount," he rumbled. "Once corrupted, they seem no longer troubled by its energies. They treat it with some primitive reverence, almost worship. Perhaps it has become a god to them, in their weakened minds. Sometimes I can see them lurking behind the great columns, or in the far-flung shadows of the chamber, and I try to catalog the energies afflicting them. I know the red is fire, the blue a bitter cold, and there is a sickly green that eats at the flesh about wounds..."

The Wyrgen muttered in a low tone, seemingly more to himself than to any other in the room. He pressed himself against the glass wall, peering downward in search of the self-same subjects of his discourse. He slid back and forth along the wall, seeking various viewing angles as his ongoing chatter became a detailed recounting of his many failed attempts to cure his compatriots. Amric began to tune out the rambling jargon, and he found himself glancing down as well to seek hidden figures below.

Suddenly he realized their mistake.

He had stepped back from the viewing wall in an unconscious movement to allow the Wyrgen to travel its length, and he noted that Valkarr had done the same. Grelthus, in his wanderings, and seemingly intent on the scene below, had put himself closer to the stairwell than either of the warriors by almost a full pace. And the chase earlier had already proven the astonishing speed of the Wyrgens.

Even as awareness struck, the furry figure burst into motion. He crossed the room in a single explosive leap and vanished up the darkened stairwell. The warriors sprinted in immediate pursuit. Amric cursed his weakness as the strange dizziness returned and clutched at his trembling legs, and he forced obedience from his unwilling muscles with an effort of will.

They reached the foot of the stairs with Syth's roar of outrage echoing behind them. From above came a startled cry, the heavy thud of bodies colliding, and the booming crash of the thick metal door slamming shut. Amric and Valkarr vaulted up the stairs, taking several at a time. A clattering sound reached their ears, and the water jug followed, sloshing water as it tumbled end over end down the stone steps.

The warriors gained the landing at the top and hurled themselves against the polished door, but they might as well have been slapping at the base of a mountain for all the good it did them. They hammered at the handle with their sword hilts, and pried at the outline for exposed hinges or other mechanics, but to no avail.

At last they fell back, panting, the acrid taste of defeat rising in their throats like bile. It was no use. Halthak was taken, and the door was impervious to their efforts. They were trapped.

CHAPTER 10

Amric slammed his fist into the metal door and glowered at it, as if the seething intensity of his fury could do what physical efforts had not. There was no sound from the other side. The traitorous Wyrgen had either rendered Halthak unconscious or taken him from the chamber.

At his side, Valkarr lashed out at the door with his sword; an array of sparks flowered in the gloom, but the glinting surface of the door was barely marred. The Sil'ath let out an angry hiss between bared teeth. The warriors exchanged dark looks, and Valkarr stepped back to crouch in the shadows behind the door while Amric turned and stalked down the stairs. As he descended, the swordsman cursed himself for a fool. He had witnessed first-hand the speed of the Wyrgens, and yet had allowed the enemy to separate them and gain the momentary advantage of position.

Now they might all pay for his mistake with their lives.

In the chamber below, Bellimar and the prisoner Syth had not moved. Their faces were drawn with apprehension, but otherwise they were a study in opposites. The old man stood still and straight, cloak wrapped about him, eyes gleaming, a storm roiling beneath a calm surface. In the cage, Syth had his feet planted wide apart and his fists clenched, and his clothing swirled and whipped about his lean frame in a frenzy of motion. Amric stalked across the room and stabbed a finger at the man who claimed to be half wind elemental.

"Did you know aught of this?" he demanded.

"If you could not guess, I am not privy to that demented beast's plans," Syth retorted. "I warned you that Grelthus planned betrayal of some kind, though I did not then know what form it would take."

"A man in a cage does not inspire trust," Amric snapped.

"Remember your words when some other fellow finds *you* here months from now."

Amric sighed, and struggled to rein in his anger. "I apologize, Syth. My worry for my friend, now a captive of that mad creature, has sharpened my tongue."

Syth regarded him a moment, a sneer twisting his lips as his hair swirled before his face. Then he grunted and waved a hand in curt dismissal.

"How did you know Grelthus intended betrayal?" Bellimar asked. "Did he know of our approach, and perhaps speak of his plans?"

Syth shook his head. "No, but I am not the first captive Grelthus has held here. I am merely the last. Grelthus was uncertain as to what use my magical nature could be in his efforts to cure his people, but at the same time he was unwilling to dispense with a potentially useful subject. Others were more clearly valuable—or clearly not so—and thus did not last as long." His jaw clenched and his eyes blazed. "For the first time in my life, I find I am thankful to be an enigma."

Amric studied the unusual man, reading anguish and rage in every line of his bearing. He found himself believing that the fellow had survived a great deal, and his own thoughts darkened as he considered the implications for Halthak.

"Syth, are there any other exits from this chamber?" he said.

"These transparent walls can be raised somehow, if one is insane enough to flee in the direction of the Essence Fount. Doing so requires the same key device as the door above, however, and though the door mechanism seems simple enough, I have not seen how the viewing walls are triggered."

Amric frowned, his gaze raking over the bare room. "And your cage, how is it opened?"

"Again, it requires one of those cube-keys that Grelthus always carries upon his person," Syth responded.

Amric muttered an oath, stalking around the perimeter of the cage. "The trap was well laid; this chamber is devoid of anything we can use to escape. If only we had a heavy table like the one in the upper chamber, we could use it to block these bars of fire long enough for you to leap out, or to force a crack by ramming it into the thick glass wall."

"I like your thinking, swordsman," Syth said with an approving nod. "But while your idea might work on my cage, it would fail to even scratch this strange, clear wall, just as your blades will be useless in that regard. The Wyrgen could be quite garrulous, with just a hint of caress to his ego, and he told me once that the viewing walls are not made of anything so fragile as glass, despite their appearance. Rather, he confided to me with no small degree of pride, they are constructed of some strange material, harder than stone, which is as impervious to physical damage as it is to the radiant energy of that accursed fountain."

"The walls are not as invulnerable as Grelthus would have you believe," Bellimar remarked, "if the Fount's eruption breached so many of the viewing chambers."

"Aye," Amric said, drawing one of his swords. "And perhaps those that remain were weakened in that initial explosion, or by the subsequent months of exposure to the Fount's energies. In any event, I am not inclined to wait here on the Wyrgen's whim without exploring every option. If we can wrest one of those keys from Grelthus, we can return here to free you from that cage."

"I might have an easier way," Syth commented, halting the swordsman in mid-step. The prisoner reached inside the rippling folds of his robes and drew forth an object which he then held high in the air for all to see. Perched on his outstretched fingertips, luminous in the shifting hues of the fountain, was one of the peculiar cube-shaped key devices used by the Wyrgens.

"How did you come by it?" Bellimar asked, arching a silver eyebrow.

Syth gave a harsh laugh and twirled the cube between his fingers before making it dance across the back of his knuckles. "I took it from Grelthus's tunic without him knowing, one time when he passed too close to my cage. At the time, I was kept in the chamber above, though he put an end to that. Oh, how long I practiced for that moment, and when my chance came, it was executed without flaw! Thought I had caught my robes afire for a moment, but nay, it was a clean grab. Grelthus was livid when he discovered it missing, and naturally he turned his suspicion upon me, but in the end I convinced him that I had last seen it amid the clutter of his table. He procured another, but he was, regrettably, much more guarded around me after that."

A hard grin spread across his features. "I invited him to join me in the cage and search my person for the key, but he declined."

"A moment ago you were protesting your innocence," Bellimar chided, the corner of his mouth quirked in a slight smile.

"I said I had harmed none of the Wyrgens in my capture," Syth said. "I never denied being a thief, and a rather accomplished one at that."

"Damn your hide, Syth!" Amric growled. "If you had shared this earlier, we could have pursued Grelthus before he gained such a lead."

He strode toward the cage, but Syth waved his hand in a flourish and the metal cube vanished from sight. "Not just yet, friend," he said, wagging his index finger back and forth. "I had to make certain you would free me first, and while your attitude thus far has been laudable, I will nonetheless require your promise on the matter before I pass the key over to you."

"You have it," Amric said, holding out one hand. "From the moment you spoke, I had no intent of leaving you in the grasp of a madman."

"Noble words. Swear it," Syth gritted.

Amric caught and held the man's gaze with his own. "I swear, if it be within my power, that I will free you from this cage and from Stronghold as well. If I cannot free you, I will end your life if you wish it, rather than leave you as a captive here."

Syth's eyes narrowed, searching the swordsman's, and then he gave a slow nod. A flick of his wrist brought the cube into view once more, and he peeled back a billowing sleeve to thrust one sinewy arm between the bars of the cage, careful not to let the crackling blue fire contact his flesh. Amric lifted the device from the man's palm, finding it lighter than expected, and he studied it as he stepped back from the cage. It was metal, as he had already observed, its outer surface etched with an intricate tracework of fine lines that pulsed faintly with contained energy. He grimaced. Magic and more magic; he was surrounded by that which he sought most to avoid.

"Quickly now, how do I use it to open your cage?" he asked.

"This cage sits atop a glowing pad of some kind, which powers the bars," Syth said. "Look for a metal panel set into the stone of the wall here, it will appear much like the stone but will be glossier and smoother to the touch."

Amric located the panel, smooth and featureless amid the coarser stone of the wall. "Found it. Now what?"

"Press the cube to the panel and give it a twist, and the bars should extinguish."

He did so, and the brilliant blue shafts sizzled and winked out, leaving the brooding metal husk dull and lifeless in their wake. Syth eyed where the barrier had been for a moment, as if disbelieving its absence, then sprang from the cage in one lithe movement. He stretched his hands over his head as high as he could reach, and then leapt into the air in a tight spin before landing cat-like on his feet once more.

"Magnificent!" he exulted. "Many thanks, my friends! At this moment, even the fetid air of this cave of jackals seems sweet indeed. Let us depart this foul place without further delay, for I have not felt the kiss of sunlight upon my face for far too long."

"Soon enough," Amric said, striding for the stairwell. "We are going after our companion first."

Syth darted across the room to halt before him, blocking his path, and Amric felt an accompanying gust of wind brush across his skin.

"Hold a moment," said Syth. "Stronghold is infested with savage, mindless beasts that enjoy nothing more than to dismember intruders. This place is a veritable maze, warrior. I have seen the maps spread across Grelthus's table, and tried to study them without him knowing, against my eventual escape. Even if Grelthus survives to reach whatever destination he has in mind, and even if you can survive wandering the corridors as well, you still have no idea where they have gone and you do not even know the layout of this place. I hate to say it, but your friend is gone."

"We are not leaving him behind," Amric said, stepping to the side to pass around the man, but the latter slid back and to the side to remain before him, standing at the foot of the stairwell and barring its entrance.

"I did not regain my freedom only to exchange it for my very life on a fool's errand," Syth said, an edge of iron to his voice.

"No one is asking it of you, thief. You are free to go your own way," Amric said. "Now move out of my way, or it won't be the Wyrgens who take your life."

Syth's eyes narrowed, and he thrust out one hand, palm up. "Give me back the key, then."

"You know that I need it to pursue Grelthus," Amric returned. "The key stays with me."

"And you know that I cannot escape Stronghold without it," Syth said. He bared his teeth in a cold smile. "Perhaps I take it from you. I have been watching you, swordsman. You are suffering from odd spells of illness in this place, and I am a dangerous man. Can you protect yourself from me, in your condition? Do you trust your body not to betray you at the crucial moment?"

"Yes, on both counts," Amric answered at once, though he spoke with more confidence than he felt, for the unexplained bouts of dizziness continued to gnaw at him. "Furthermore, my companions will help ensure that we waste time on this foolish squabble later."

Syth opened his mouth and then abruptly stiffened, his retort frozen upon his lips. Valkarr appeared behind him like a ghost in the shadowy recesses of the stairwell, the razor tip of his sword pressed against the thief's spine and encouraging him to an attentive posture. Syth's eyes flicked to the side, but whatever reaction he might have had was instantly quelled as a second blade caressed his throat from the front. He sucked in a startled breath, and even the incessant breeze swirling about him fell to a whisper. His gaze traveled up that length of shining steel, to where it projected from Amric's fist, and past that to traverse an arm sheathed in muscle which seemed not plagued at all by illness at the moment, and further yet to find eyes as cold as winter staring back at him.

"You have a choice now, thief, and be thankful for it," Amric said softly. "Your life can end here as a spreading pool of blood on uncaring stone. Or you can find your own way from Stronghold, and I wish you luck on your journey. Or you can accompany us, and help rescue a man who would do the same for you without hesitation, were your situations reversed."

Syth's throat bobbed against the keen edge of the blade as he made to swallow before thinking better of the idea.

"I saw the anguish on your face when you spoke of what the Wyrgen has done to you and other captives," Amric continued. "Would you argue to leave another in his clutches, now that you have won your own freedom?"

"Very well, I will help," Syth said through clenched teeth. "I will delight in seeing to it that Grelthus never claims another victim." Despite his evident care in speaking, a spot of crimson welled at his throat where the blade touched. Amric held his stance a moment longer, then withdrew his sword, though he did not return it to its scabbard upon his back.

"Good," Amric said with a twisting smile. "We can renew our efforts to kill each other after we escape Stronghold alive."

Behind the man, Valkarr let his weapon drop as well. Syth let out a breath and put his hand to his neck. Amric moved past him and bounded up the stairs, while Valkarr waited for the thief and followed close at his heels. Bellimar brought up the rear. By the time the others reached the door, Amric had it unlocked and was stalking through the cluttered chamber beyond.

"A moment, while I reclaim what is mine," Syth murmured, pausing at the long table. He shoved stacks of debris aside, his movements growing almost frantic as he searched for something. With a growl of triumph, he lifted the black metal gauntlets that Amric had seen there earlier. Syth donned them immediately, flexing the cleverly jointed fingers several times and inspecting the ebon-clawed tips. A wicked grin spread across his features.

"Now I am ready," he said.

Amric frowned. A flicker of something—pain, or perhaps relief—had twisted the man's expression when he regained the devices. He turned to scan the chamber. "You mentioned seeing maps of Stronghold here before. Do you see them now?"

Syth shook his head. "I tried to examine them without drawing the attention of Grelthus, but he caught me one day and removed them all from the room. I know not where he hid them."

"How much do you remember of them?" Bellimar asked. The old man carried Halthak's discarded staff, and was circling the table as he studied its contents.

"Some," the thief admitted, "though it has been weeks now since I saw them. And I was more intent on plotting my eventual escape route from the fortress than looking for the bastard's sanctuaries. Still, I recall him marking certain rooms and shading sections of the map to demarcate paths of high and low activity."

"Take us to the nearest," Amric said. He moved to the closed metal door and employed the key once more, then pocketed the device. He glanced back, looking to each of them until he received a nod in return, and then he cracked the door and peered out into the hallway beyond. It was still and silent as a tomb, lit along its length by those unwavering, flameless lamps. He waved the others forward, easing the door fully open and drawing his remaining sword.

"Tell me, thief," he said. "Were your earlier words boastful or true? Are you truly a good hand in a fight?"

"You will find out soon enough," Syth responded with a fierce grin.

They slipped into the empty corridor.

Awareness returned to Halthak in measured stages. First came the throbbing, like a steady, ruthless drum inside his skull. Second, as by reflex he tried to put a hand to his head, he realized his hands were bound behind him. His eyes flared open. He was lying prostrate on a stone floor, and he sighted along the cold flagstones against which his cheek was pressed. Memory began to make a grudging return as well. He recalled entering the darkened stairwell with water pitcher in hand for the prisoner Syth when a bulky silhouette hurtled up the stairs and filled his vision. He had flinched to the side in an effort to avoid the onrushing mass, but it caught him in a grasp like iron and dashed him against the wall behind him. His head struck the unforgiving granite, and the world was torn from him for a time.

Halthak surveyed his surroundings, or at least what little he was able to from his lowly vantage point. He was in another viewing chamber, with the Essence Fount's lurid hues flickering against the stone. At first he thought it was the same chamber he had vacated, and perhaps he had fallen down the stairs, but the contents of the room told him different. The other viewing chamber had been almost empty except for Syth's cage, and this room contained a row of smaller tables hemmed in by stacks of crates and other clutter. He could see no more from his current orientation, as he was facing a corner where the stone and glass walls met. There was a faint shimmer of reflection in the transparent material of the viewing wall, but it was not sufficient to perceive any additional detail in the room at his back.

And he would very much like to see more, as something was moving behind him in the chamber.

He listened to the shuffling sounds of movement, accompanied by bursts of low muttering. There was a pause followed by the clink of metal upon metal, and then the movement resumed. There was nothing for it, Halthak decided; he gained little by remaining in this position, pretending to be unconscious still. He needed to assess his situation, to determine where he was and how many of his companions were present. With a grunt of effort, he heaved himself to a sitting position and fought back a wave of dizziness.

The muttering stopped.

"Excellent, you are awake," said a deep, guttural voice. "We can begin."

The world swam into focus, and Halthak found himself staring into the dark, liquid eyes of Grelthus, as the Wyrgen sank into a crouch before him. A quick scan of the room showed that he was alone with his captor; it also revealed a chamber with a much more functional arrangement than the other viewing chamber had evinced. Several tables were large enough for a man to lie upon, and thick leather straps sprouting from their surfaces confirmed their dark purpose. Interspersed with these were smaller tables, replete with metal implements of various sinister designs. A cylindrical device squatted at the center of the room, rising almost to the ceiling. It bulged outward at its middle, coursing with strange energy, and shiny black cables snaked from it to various points within the room. Looking upon it, Halthak was struck by the impression of some great nest of wasps, teeming inside with obscene life.

Grelthus continued to watch him as he examined the chamber, and the Wyrgen's muzzle began a slow nod as grim realization stole over the Half-Ork.

"Yes, you are apprised of your situation now," Grelthus said. "We will not be disturbed here."

"Where are my companions?" Halthak demanded. "Have you harmed them?"

The Wyrgen's grizzled head tilted to the side, and one tufted ear twitched. He lashed out with one powerful arm in a blur of motion. Halthak found himself on his back, his head ringing from the blow, and the stinging wetness of his own blood running down the side of his face. He blinked a few times and drew in ragged breaths until his vision cleared. Then, with a laborious combination of levering his bound arms and squirming, he sat up again. Grelthus still crouched before him, impassive expression unchanged.

"This will be a conversation only in the sense that I will ask questions and you will answer them," the Wyrgen rumbled. "It is best that you learn this lesson quickly, for we have much to do."

Halthak said nothing, glaring at the creature. Blood trickled down his whiskered jaw and into the neck of his robes. Grelthus nodded and stood, towering over him, and waved one clawed hand in a permissive gesture.

"Good, then we have an understanding. You may heal yourself now, and we will begin again."

Halthak began to do just that; he reached for his magic and was rewarded by its ready surge, an invigorating suffusion of warmth spreading through him. Ridding himself of the infernal pounding ache in his head would enable him to think more clearly, and he would need his wits about him if he hoped to escape the Wyrgen and rejoin his companions. But then, as he was on the verge of directing the gathered healing energy with a familiar effort of will, some instinct made him pause. He could feel the weight of the Wyrgen's gaze upon him still, burning in its intensity, and that very eagerness nagged at him. His addled thoughts congealed into suspicions and struggled to chain together.

Grelthus had isolated him from the others by sending him for the water pitcher while ostensibly remaining under guard in the chamber below. Rather than escape alone, the Wyrgen had instead assaulted him and brought him to this new room, unconscious and bound. If his captor's words were to be believed, the healer was now beyond rescue, and the Wyrgen had plans for him. Upon finding himself captive, Halthak had at first seen himself as the only viable choice; the warriors were far too skilled in combat to subdue easily, and there was something mysterious and unsettling about Bellimar that made him a less likely choice as well, despite his apparent age.

That left Halthak as the most vulnerable. But why take a hostage at all? Grelthus could have used his superior knowledge of Stronghold's labyrinthine layout to evade pursuit and leave them all behind, trapped and lost. For that matter, why draw them deep into the heart of Stronghold in the first place? If his goal from the beginning had been to see them slain, he could have left them to the tender mercies of his corrupted brethren without ever so much as showing himself.

It followed then that Grelthus had thought to make use of them in some way, and now wanted something from Halthak. Admittedly, the conversation could have become adversarial after Halthak left the room to fetch the pitcher, but he had heard no sounds of conflict from below, no voices raised in heated exchange. And if the Wyrgen had meant to trap them all in the chamber below, he could have left Halthak there at the top of the stairwell, sagging to the floor after being hurled against the wall.

Assuming his selection was purposeful, then, Halthak began to work back from there. He recalled Syth's bitter words about Grelthus keeping the thief around until some use could be made of the man's half elemental nature, and his warning that Grelthus would only have led them deep into Stronghold for the same reason, to feature somehow in his experiments. Halthak then thought of when he had healed Valkarr's minor injury after the skirmish with the infected Wyrgens in the corridor, and Grelthus's wide-eyed fascination with the demonstration of healing magic, and suddenly the pieces fell together. Halthak cursed himself for not seeing the obvious earlier.

Grelthus was after his healing magic.

The Wyrgen was desperate to cure his people, and was grasping at any chance to further that effort, no matter how remote that chance, and no matter the cost. He must have felt that fortune had smiled upon him at last when a strange group of intruders fell into his clutches, one of them possessing healing magic. He wanted Halthak to employ his talent now, under observation, in order to study and harness it. Halthak tested the chain of logic, and it held.

And as he looked ahead to where the chain led, he quailed inside.

Feeling the Wyrgen's unwavering stare still upon him, Halthak closed his eyes and furrowed his brow, as if in concentration. After a few seconds he released his gathered magic, letting it dissipate, and donned what he hoped was an expression of frustration.

"I am blocked somehow," he said, looking up at Grelthus. "My magic gathers but I cannot focus it. It might be the blow to my head, or the nearness of the Essence Fount, causing interference."

The Wyrgen's eyes narrowed. "Your magic worked well enough earlier, when you healed your friend. You were not hindered then by proximity to the Fount."

"Then it must be the knock to the head. This has happened before," Halthak lied.

Grelthus growled, and his claws twitched as his long ears folded back against his skull. "Perhaps you merely lack proper motivation."

"I just need a few minutes for my head to clear," the Half-Ork stammered. "Any injury now will only lead to additional delay."

His captor eyed him, disbelief evident upon his wolf-like face. Then he relaxed, and shrugged his massive shoulders. "No matter," he said. "We have time. I have questions to ask that will aid in my study, and so long as you are cooperative in answering them, your head can clear without interference."

The Wyrgen sank into a crouch before him once more, elbows resting on furry knees while wickedly curved claws dangled directly in Halthak's line of sight. This close, the thick, musky scent of the creature was almost overpowering.

"How long have you had your talent?"

"As long as I recall, so I suspect I was born with it," Halthak answered. "I became aware of it as a child."

"Did either of your parents possess any magical ability?"

"My mother did not," the Half-Ork said, his jaw tightening. "I never knew my father, but I found it doubtful he had any such ability."

The Wyrgen studied his expression, and then nodded. "What are the limits to your healing?"

"I can repair any simple injury to the body, though it might take repeated ministrations if the wounds are too severe for me to absorb at one time. There are some progressive diseases I have been unable to affect in any lasting way, and magical afflictions are often difficult or impossible to draw into myself, as they can be resistant to leaving their host." He paused, pondering. "And the dead are entirely beyond my power," he added after a moment.

"This is not surprising," Grelthus said. "There must be some spark of life in your subject with which your magic can interact. You send your magic flowing into your patient, then? And it transfers the wound into you, to be healed there, as I saw earlier?"

The healer nodded.

"What of the other way?"

Halthak blinked. "I do not understand."

"You describe a flow of magic from yourself to another, used to fetch damage. Could you instead send it? How well can you control this flow of energy?"

"You mean—you suggest—to inflict injury instead of heal?" the healer asked, brow furrowing. "Why would I do such a thing?"

"To strike at a foe, of course," Grelthus said, his snout wrinkling to reveal the tips of his fangs.

"I have never attempted it," Halthak whispered, aghast at the very notion. "No, I do not believe it can be done." But even as he said it, he wondered. He recalled how it felt when the magic gathered within him, roiling and eager, and how it responded to his unspoken direction. He considered how even the tools of medicine were double-edged, how a misused scalpel was a weapon and the incorrect dose of an herb could kill instead of cure. These things and more he turned over in his mind, and he wondered.

"What if you do not recall your magic? Would it remain in the other?" the Wyrgen asked.

Halthak shook his head. "There is some current from one to the other, but it bridges between participants during the healing process, and the magic flows across this link. It is shared at that moment, not fully in one or the other. If physical contact is broken, the magic returns immediately to me by means I do not understand, its work unfinished."

Grelthus grunted. "Perhaps. There are means by which to forcibly extract Essence from creatures, just as there are methods to prevent its return."

Halthak felt a chill course through him at both the words and the utter indifference with which they were spoken.

The Wyrgen rose to his full height and turned away in a smooth, unhurried movement. He padded over to a low table, and began sorting through its contents. Halthak could see nothing past the creature's broad back, but the clink of metal floated to his straining ears. When Grelthus swung to face him again, he cradled in his large paws a glinting, metallic device of strange design. It looked something like a long lance point affixed to a heavy handle, with four curved blades projecting from its base above the handle and tapering like talons back to the central shaft. A crystal globe the size of a man's fist was embedded there amid the clutch of blades, and within that sphere a murky green radiance swirled and eddied.

"We have reached the limits of what may be learned from discourse alone, healer," Grelthus said. His hard features were lit from beneath by the emerald glow as he started forward. "Now we must encourage your reticent healing talent to reveal itself in earnest."

Amric knew the instant he entered the chamber that it would be much like the others, and at the same time, very much unlike them.

He tucked away the cube-key device and pushed open the now unlocked door with his free hand, noting with surprise how the door wobbled very slightly on its hinges. He slipped through into the room like a stalking leopard, one sword extended. The others followed him, fanning out into the chamber in silence. They had been exceedingly fortunate thus far, as they stole like ghosts through the winding innards of Stronghold, in that they had not yet run across any of Grelthus's corrupted brethren. They had taken pains to guard this good fortune, using hand signals in place of conversation when possible, and speaking in hushed whispers only when it could no longer be avoided. No amount of quiet on their part, however, could mask the scent of their passage, should the wild occupants of the fortress chance across their trail.

Most of the doors they encountered had been locked. Amric recalled Grelthus's rueful comment about how the infected Wyrgens could no longer manipulate even so rudimentary a tool as the key device, and it seemed Grelthus had used this fact to his advantage in securing entire sections of the place from their intrusion. This room was identical in most ways to the last several they had traversed, dusty and empty but for isolated stacks of mundane clutter, but it was also different in several key respects.

First of all, this room led to a viewing chamber below, as they had not seen since departing the room in which Grelthus had trapped them; Amric knew this by the shimmering hues registering faintly in the gloom through the open door at the far end of the chamber. Second, that thick metal door had yielded to violent stress, for it hung loose on its top hinge, bent and warped as if by some titanic wrathful hand. For the third and final difference, the swordsman was struck as he crossed the threshold by a wave of dizziness and nausea, even more potent than he had felt when looking upon the Essence Fount through the wall of glass. His breath came in labored gasps, hissing between clenched teeth, and his knuckles whitened on his sword hilt as his vision darkened at the edges. He felt like a war horse had kicked him in the midsection, and then sat upon his chest for good measure.

Bellimar appeared at his elbow, his pale forehead creased in expressions that were by turn appraising and concerned. Again, the others seemed unaffected. An icy weight settled in the pit of his stomach as he wondered if his lack of aura somehow made him more vulnerable to the Fount's effects. Would it kill him outright, or would he become savage and twisted like the Wyrgens, turning upon his friends without a glimmer of recognition? Even as his thoughts darkened, the strange affliction receded somewhat, the weight upon him lessening. He dragged in several deep breaths, forcing his weakness behind an inner wall forged of anger and determination. While it did not dissipate entirely, he found he was free to operate once more.

Syth stared at him with one eyebrow raised. "This is madness. We could spend a lifetime within these stone walls and never find the Half-Ork. And in your condition, you will be of no use at all if we blunder into a group of Wyrgens."

"You talk too much, Syth," Amric gritted. "If you want to reconsider your options here and now, you will find I can still muster some strength."

The thief's gaze flickered to each of them in turn before returning to Amric. Then Syth broke into a lopsided grin. "Let it not be said that I took unfair advantage of you in your weakened state, warrior. We will settle our differences when you have recovered." He wagged one finger in the air, sheathed in the black metal of a gauntlet. "But do not think to put off our reckoning forever."

Amric snorted and walked toward the damaged door.

"Do not turn your dead eye on me, you lumbering reptile," Syth said, scowling at Valkarr. "You can take your place in line behind Amric. Just keep it fair, mind you. I will not fight you both at once. I have seen your kind fight recently, and though I am very skilled, I am no fool."

Amric froze in mid-stride, and wheeled about to face the thief.

"What did you just say?" he asked.

Syth's brow furrowed. "I am no coward, but fighting you both at once seems less than—"

"Not that," Amric interrupted with an impatient wave. "You saw Sil'ath fighting recently?"

"Yes," Syth answered, eyes darting between Amric and Valkarr as he took in their sudden interest. "I mentioned earlier that I was far from the only victim of Grelthus's deception. Some weeks ago, the Wyrgen led a small group of lizard folk—like your friend here—into that huge Fount chamber. He brought them through the chamber containing my cage, just as he did with you, and fed them the same story about me being a dangerous criminal and he the compassionate diplomat for sparing my life. I think he meant to capture them, as he did me. But he caught me alone and unawares, and these five Sil'ath were all quite alert and bristling with weapons, just like the two of you. Regardless, the biggest of them seemed suspicious of his tale, and kept measuring me with his eyes."

"That would be Prakseth," Valkarr murmured. "He has a strong sense of justice, and will not be swayed until it is satisfied."

"Go on, Syth," Amric urged.

"Grelthus convinced them to follow him into the amphitheater, insisting that the answers they sought could be obtained by closer examination of the Essence Fount itself. He was lying, of course. That cur cannot move his mouth without lying, but he bolsters his deceit with enough facts to make his words seem sound. The big one gave me a surreptitious nod as they left, though I know not what he meant by it."

"Prakseth meant to return for you," Amric said softly. "He would not have left you here, if it was within his power. What transpired then?"

Syth shifted his feet before continuing. "I surmise that Grelthus intended to trap them in the amphitheater, to study the effects of exposure to the Essence Fount on another race. These plans went awry as well, however. Dozens of infected Wyrgens flooded the chamber and gave chase. Grelthus, slippery eel that he is, escaped with his life, leaving the reptile warriors battling the rabid Wyrgens."

"The Sil'ath, did they perish?" Amric asked. His words, quietly spoken, carried a hard edge and promised death. Syth flinched and cleared his throat.

"I cannot say for certain," he said. "I was trapped in my cage, and though I nearly burned myself on the bars striving for a better vantage, they became obscured from my view by the lip of the terrace below. They were giving a ferocious accounting of themselves, however, for the Wyrgen dead were heaped about them as they fought toward one of the chamber's exits. I saw at least one of the warriors fall in battle, but the others fought against the surge to retrieve his body, and were dragging him as they retreated. Given the numbers they faced, I do not see how they could help but be overwhelmed."

"Many foes of the Sil'ath have made the same assumption," Valkarr grunted. "Much to their later regret."

"Did you ever see their corpses?" Amric said.

Syth shook his head. "No, but Grelthus went looking for them, when everything had grown quiet once more. He returned furious, and when I broached the subject he flew into a rage. He roared at me that the Sil'ath were gone, and he threatened vivisection if I mentioned the episode again. He did not search for them further, so I believe he truly thought them gone. Whether they died or escaped from Stronghold, however, I know not."

"The list of crimes for which Grelthus must answer grows longer and longer," Amric said, exchanging a dark look with Valkarr.

He stalked to the battered door with sword in hand, and peered down the stairwell. As before, colors cavorted along the darkened walls in twisting, maddening arrangements, and a wave of vertigo blasted against him like a tangible thing. Amric kept it at bay this time with the seething heat of his rage, and he started down the narrow stairs. The roaring sound built in his head as he went, and by the time he reached the chamber below he feared his skull must split. As he and the others entered the lower room, they discovered a fourth difference between this viewing chamber and the previous one.

The glass wall was shot through with great cracks, shattered and gaping open over almost half its expanse while large shards of the material were splayed about the chamber. A web of cracks radiated outward on the stone floor and ceiling bordering each section where the clear sheet had failed, and the bottom steps of the staircase were gnawed and crumbled at their edges.

This explained the ravaged doors above, Amric thought. The blast that shattered the wall had channeled up the stairwell with enough force to wrench the thick metal portal from its very hinges as well as weaken even the outer door. It also explained the heightened effect of the Essence Fount upon him here, for they were directly exposed to the deadly geyser here through the breaches in the wall.

And that was not all they were exposed to here, he observed. A throng of hulking, furry forms was gathered outside the broken glass wall, their fiery eyes narrowed to hateful slits as they glared at the chamber's occupants. Amric spat a sulfurous oath under his breath. Whether due to disastrous timing or because the unguarded conversation in the room above had carried far enough to draw them here, the corrupted Wyrgens had found them.

With glowing talons of all hues, the creatures gripped the yawning fissures in the glass wall and pulled themselves through, dropping into feral crouches and crawling forward. Amric and Valkarr both drew their second swords, and Syth flexed his sinister black gauntlets as his robes whipped about him. Bellimar withdrew into the shadows of the stairwell, folded within his cloak.

The shifting, shimmering light of the fountain reflected from bared steel in the ruined chamber as the beasts crept toward them.

CHAPTER **11**

Halthak crashed to his side on the stone floor, the echoes of his last scream chasing each other throughout the chamber. Sweat and blood mingled in rivulets that slid across his face as he lay there, panting. There was a crimson tinge to the froth caking his lips as well, and he tried to muster enough saliva to clear it by spitting, but his throat was too cracked and raw. His vision dimmed dangerously at the edges, and he felt for a long, precarious moment like he was falling down a darkened well and watching the hazy light of the opening recede above him.

He fought to remain conscious. It was too soon, he thought. He was not ready yet. He drew one ragged breath after another until his vision cleared. Then, clenching his teeth, he pushed himself on shaking arms to a sitting position once more as the rope bindings bit into his wrists, and he met the furious gaze of his tormentor.

Grelthus stood a few paces away, glaring down at him, deep chest heaving like a bellows.

"What is this idiocy, healer?" he stormed. "Why endure this pain merely to thwart me?"

Halthak said nothing, striving to compose his ravaged face into a tranquil mask. In truth, he was not certain he could have answered in any case, for his tongue was swollen and dry as parchment.

The Wyrgen spun away with a curse and slammed the blood-slicked weapon down on the table with such force that the other silvery implements there leapt jangling and spinning into the air. The device itself seemed to quiver even at rest, and the inset green orb pulsed hungrily, drawing blood along the blades to vanish into its glowing surface.

Halthak felt his stomach turn with revulsion and fear as he eyed the sinister device. Beyond even the considerable damage Grelthus could inflict with the thing, it seemed to magnify pain to a level he had never before experienced. He was not sure how much longer his will could hold out against that evil instrument.

Grelthus took several deep breaths, and then turned back toward him, outwardly calm once more.

"There is no need for you to suffer so," he said in a voice laden with concern. "Your frail form cannot take so much damage, and you will surely die if you do not repair the wounds. I ask but to observe as you employ your magic, and there need be no further pain inflicted."

Halthak knew it for a lie the instant he heard it. He decided it deserved company.

"My staff," he croaked. "It serves as my focus, and I require it to direct my magic. Perhaps if it was retrieved—"

"Do not toy with me! There was no affinity for magic in that object," Grelthus said, muzzle peeling back to reveal a mouthful of teeth like daggers. "Your friends are back in that room, trapped and alive only at my whim, and I will not return there until I decide what to do with them."

The Wyrgen dropped to all fours and stalked forward until the stink of his hot breath washed over Halthak's face. "It is within your power to save them, healer. Give me what I want, and I will release your friends and aye, even usher them from Stronghold. What say you?"

Halthak felt a stab of temptation, but he knew full well that it was but another of the creature's empty promises. In any event, Amric and Valkarr would never agree to depart at the cost of him remaining captive here. So the Half-Ork grinned and said, through cracked lips, "What say I? I say we postpone this conversation until I can look through a fortress window and see their backsides departing the grounds. Not that I have any reason to doubt your word, you mangy mongrel."

The wolf-like visage twisted with rage, and though Halthak never saw the blow coming, his head rocked back with its force. To his amazement, he managed to retain both consciousness and his upright position, even if he had not the faintest notion how he accomplished either. Woozy, he marveled at the boldness of his words, more than a little shocked they had tumbled from his own mouth. It seemed that time spent around the swordsman had bolstered his courage at the cost of his manners, and perhaps his self-preservation as well.

He glanced down at his torso to assess the damage that Grelthus had done to him thus far, for he was growing too cold and numb to know by feel alone. Some detached part of his mind nagged at him that this was a bad sign in itself, but he waved it away. His robes hung in tatters, as did the flesh beneath, soaked with the blood that was forming a languid pool beneath him. The Wyrgen was truthful in one respect: these wounds would prove fatal soon, if Halthak did not act.

He blinked the sweat from his eyes and regarded his captor, careful to keep his expression neutral.

"Do you still believe your friends will find and rescue you?" Grelthus was saying. He shoved one clawed fist into a tunic pocket and pulled forth the cube device he had used to unlock interior doors in the fortress. He thrust the device before Halthak's weary gaze, pinched between his talons. "There is no way you could know this, Half-Ork, but this is not just any key. As Stronghold's head scientist, I was one of a very few who command- ed a set of master keys which can open any door in the fortress. And that is not all."

The Wyrgen bounded to his feet and leapt across the chamber to stand by a smooth panel on the wall. He placed the cube-key against the panel and looked at Halthak with a mad light in his eyes.

"With the master keys, I can open the viewing walls as well, exposing viewing chambers like this one to the full glory of the Essence Fount. What's more, I can open or close them all at once from any of these pan- els."

Halthak stared in horror as it dawned upon him what the creature was suggesting. Grelthus barked a horrid, cackling laugh, and wrenched the key in a savage twist against the panel. With a dull boom followed by a shuddering grumble of thunder, the glass wall in the chamber began to rise. Air hissed beneath it, and Halthak felt an eerie tingling scamper across his skin, raising bumps across his already pebbled grey flesh.

"What are you doing?" he gasped. "It will kill us both!"

"It will not affect us so quickly," Grelthus said, taking slow strides back toward the healer. "It took several days to poison my people, to trans- form them into savage, mindless monsters. But we have only a few minutes, for a different reason. You see, I know from experience that the sound of the machinery required to lift the walls draws my corrupted brethren to the Fount chamber from all corners of Stronghold. They will be gathering in great numbers soon, and there may even be some lurking in there already, so we haven't much time."

"W-why did you open it?" Halthak said.

"You would have me believe that the Fount's proximity is somehow inhibiting your magic," Grelthus sneered. "But I know that for a lie. The Essence Fount is magic at its most primal. It does not counteract other magic, but rather amplifies it, draws it out, sings to it with inexorable power. In its presence, you could perform feats with your inherent talents which have always before been beyond your reach. It is my theory that your magic will rise to the surface as you are bathed in the Fount's direct radiance, despite your continued attempts to suppress it."

Halthak swallowed. He felt nothing of the sort yet, but the Wyrgen's cold conviction was unnerving. "And if this theory of yours proves false? Are we to be torn limb from limb by your people?"

Grelthus chuckled, a dark and ugly sound. "You should realize by now, Half-Ork, that my ingenuity knows no limits. If you do not employ your healing magic with all due haste, I shall lower our viewing wall here and raise all the others. Your trapped friends will lose the only protective barrier between them and the hundreds of slavering, enraged Wyrgens who will have gathered by then."

The Wyrgen reached down with one long, powerful arm and lifted the cruel, many-bladed device once more from the table. Halthak choked back an involuntary babble of terror before it could escape his throat. He noted with a chill how its glowing green orb and gleaming metal were now clean and free of even a speck of blood; the thing had somehow drank up all that had coated its surface. Grelthus hefted the weapon before him, patting it as he would a cherished pet.

"The cost of your petty defiance will only continue to rise," he said. "Will you be the instrument of demise for your friends, merely to stall the inevitable for a few minutes more?"

Halthak met his bleak stare for a long moment, then his shoulders sagged and he hung his head. He shifted his arms, still crossed behind his back, ignoring the protests of his aching shoulders and chafed wrists. He had no way of knowing how the exposure to the fiery geyser would affect what he was about to do, but he was out of time and out of options. With a mild effort of will, he brought his magic surging forth, invigorating his shaking body with welcome warmth and a brisk jolt of energy.

"Yes, yes!" Grelthus murmured, shuffling forward a pace. "That's it, healer. Magnificent!"

Halthak ignored the Wyrgen, gathering what he needed and then more, continuing to draw upon it until his very veins were afire. His magic filled him to the point of bursting, roiling within like a storm-tossed sea, anticipating his bidding.

And there he held it, pent up behind his will, denying it release.

"Why do you hesitate, healer?" Grelthus demanded, his tone hardening into a harsh snarl.

The Half-Ork continued to slouch there with his head hung low and sweat dripping from his lank, wispy hair. He shook his head back and forth, over and over, repeating something in a mumbling whisper.

"Speak up, fool! What are you babbling about?" Grelthus said as he threw an uneasy glance past the open glass wall and into the vast amphitheater beyond. "We do not have much time, healer. No time for games, if you wish to save yourself, or your friends."

Halthak's head began a vigorous nodding, and his slumped shoulders shook with what might have been laughter. He continued to whisper as his magic flared within him, swirling but contained.

Grelthus spat an oath and dropped to all fours, stalking forward until his bared fangs were no more than a hand's breadth from the face of his captive.

"What are you saying, damn you?" Grelthus snarled. He reached out and, with one huge fist, seized the healer's unruly shock of hair and jerked his hanging head back into an upright position.

Halthak lunged forward like a striking snake, using all the strength remaining in his battered body. His arms, trailing frayed and parted ropes, whipped around to slap clawed hands to the sides of the Wyrgen's shaggy head. His long nails dug into fur and flesh there, holding the startled creature fast.

"I said I have claws too, Grelthus," Halthak hissed into his face, and he sent his magic slamming into the Wyrgen.

He had been anxious about this part, as he planned this desperate gambit. Grelthus's own question about directing the flow of his magic had planted the suggestion, and a seed of wild hope had sprouted. Parting the ropes that bound him had been a laborious process, in part because it had been challenging at first to bring his claws to bear and in part because he had been forced to proceed at a snail's pace to avoid arousing suspicion. Even as the mundane first step of his scheme proved achievable, however, doubts had assailed him about the next stage.

He had only ever used his talent to heal, to form a brief symbiotic connection with another living creature and draw away its hurt. What if his magic found the notion of inflicting damage as repugnant as he did, and would not obey him? What if he could not figure out how to direct it in this way before Grelthus overcame his moment of astonishment and tore away from his weakened grasp?

These misgivings and more vanished in the first instant of contact, burned to cinders by the flood of his released magic.

Just as countless times before, his talent leapt at his bidding, flowing and bridging into Grelthus. The Wyrgen stiffened as the unfamiliar sensation filled him in a sudden burst. Halthak's many wounds began to disappear; bruises lightened and vanished, cuts sealed over like wet clay being molded by some invisible hand. He felt the ache of knitting bone and the itch of new skin nipped by the air. His labored breathing eased, and strength coursed through his limbs once more.

Even as all the wounds faded from Halthak, they appeared on Grelthus. The creature's lips split and oozed blood. His eyes glassed over, seeming to sink into his skull. The massive frame gave a violent shudder at an appalling cracking noise. Several ripping sounds followed, like the tearing of wet cloth, and scarlet spattered to the flagstones. At once sickened and fascinated, the healer watched the entire transformation. A rumbling moan rattled in the Wyrgen's throat, and he sagged in Halthak's grasp.

Halthak released his hold and let the body crash to the floor, where the Wyrgen writhed in pain. Rolling to his feet, he swiftly moved to kneel at the creature's side, where he dug at the thick fabric of the tunic in a frantic search for the cube-key device. Grelthus groaned and twisted, sweeping a claw at him, and he was forced to scramble clear. The Wyrgen had a stronger constitution, and the initial shock of his transferred injuries was wearing off all too quickly. Already Halthak could see the rolling eyes coming into focus and fixing upon him with a wild glare that promised retribution.

He eyed the many-bladed weapon on the table, its soft green glow seeming to pulse a dark invitation to him as his gaze fell upon it, and for a fleeting moment he considered trying to use it to stun or slay the Wyrgen. He was loath to slay, however, and he was no warrior besides. And Grelthus was recovering his wits, gathering his strength, his powerful back and shoulders bunching with muscle as he strove to push himself up from the floor. Halthak had witnessed the terrible speed and savagery of the beasts in combat, and he knew he had little chance if he came within reach of those killing claws.

The healer turned his attention to the raised glass wall and the cavernous amphitheater beyond. A broad set of stairs began at the lip of the viewing chamber, descending to a terrace level below. He had hoped to obtain the cube device in his escape, but there was nothing for it now. His best hope was to find an unlocked door in the amphitheater before the place filled with corrupted Wyrgens or the Fount struck him down, and then find a way to free his trapped friends. He knew it to be a slim hope at best, but at the moment he would take almost any shift in circumstance. If he could just find the others, they would know what to do next.

Halthak swallowed hard, hesitating a bare moment longer as he summoned his courage. Then he raced from the viewing chamber and down the stone steps, bathed in the brilliance of the surging Essence Fount.

Amric ducked under sweeping talons and came up in a whirl of steel. The corrupted Wyrgen's lunge carried it a pace further before it faltered and crashed to the cold stone, its fiery amethyst eyes wide and unseeing. The swordsman wheeled around to help the others, but found it unnecessary. The last of the attackers was down.

Valkarr strode over a floor slick with crimson and littered with corpses to peer through the splintered glass wall. He gave Amric a quick shake of the head; no more approaching at the moment. Amric flicked the blood from his swords and sheathed them, looking next to Syth.

The thief was wending his way between heaps of wooly forms, and though he was breathing heavily, Amric judged it to be more from emotion than exertion. The man had not overstated his martial skills, for he was indeed a formidable fighter. Syth fought without any weapons other than those wicked black gauntlets encasing his hands. He moved like the storm wind itself, sudden, unpredictable and impossible to contain. He delivered blinding strikes with feet as well as hands, but the blows dealt with the gauntlets carried shattering force, and Amric suspected the objects were ensorcelled somehow. For all his evident prowess, however, Syth fought with a reckless frenzy that was altogether unsettling. Amric had taken pains not to expose his back to the man during the battle, in light of both the continued tension between them and the berserker rage that seized the man when they engaged the Wyrgens. Amric recalled the wild-eyed expression, and wondered if the fellow had even been able to distinguish friend from foe in the heat of the moment.

"You fought well, swordsman," Syth called to him.

"And you as well, Syth," Amric returned.

"I did not give you enough credit before. You are as good as your lizard friend there."

Amric inclined his head and said, "A fine compliment, thank you."

He swayed slightly and caught himself, hoping no one noticed. The nearness of the Essence Fount continued to plague him, and more than once a fleeting, ill-timed instant of weakness had almost been his undoing during the battle.

"Were I a lesser fighter, or capable of fear, I would be having second thoughts about facing you," Syth continued in a distracted, conversational tone as he walked, his gaze directed downward. "But of course I am neither of these things. Perhaps we should have a bard present to chronicle our fight. What do you think?"

Amric shook his head in disbelief. Syth stopped, still looking down. A low moan issued from the figure sprawled at his feet. Dropping to one knee, he dealt the Wyrgen a thunderous blow with one gauntleted fist, dispatching the creature in an instant. His eyes were hard as granite as he stood and continued to prowl the room, checking the motionless forms of their assailants.

Amric turned and found Bellimar. The old man stood tall and straight amidst the carnage, like a slender, stately tree somehow untouched in the wake of a hurricane. His pale face was flushed and his eyes shone strangely above a tight smile, but he appeared unharmed. At one point during the battle, Amric was certain he had seen one of the beasts turn its attention to Bellimar, lurking in the corner; it had leapt toward him, powerful arms flung wide to engulf the old man. Amric had started toward him, but a multitude of Wyrgens swarmed at him just then, blocking his view and path to the old man. Even as a desperate shout to the others had gathered in his throat, however, he caught movement from the corner of his eye and found Bellimar on the other side of the room, away from the press of conflict once more. For an instant Amric had doubted his own sight, but as a Sil'ath warrior and warmaster he had developed an innate sense of what transpired in battle around him at all times. No, it was another of the old man's mysterious tricks, then, and well timed at that.

Bellimar picked his way across the room, managing to avoid even a drop of blood on his grey robes.

"What next, warrior?" he asked.

"Onward to the next room," Amric replied. "Grelthus, blast his conniving hide, must be hiding in one of these chambers."

"We were fortunate this time," Syth said. "Stronghold is vast, and it will take days to search just the chambers bordering the Essence Fount. We may not be so lucky in our next brush with the Wyrgens."

"Leave if you wish," Amric growled. "I will not abandon Halthak in this pit of demons, even if I have to turn over every stone in the place."

"Perhaps we need not go to such lengths after all," Valkarr said from his position at the ruined glass wall. He stood before a jagged aperture large enough to walk through, and he leveled one muscular arm to point at something in the amphitheater. Amric and the others joined him and peered in the direction he indicated.

Partway around the circular chamber, on the terraced balcony level just below them, was Halthak.

Made small by the distance, the healer was running for all he was worth. Amric slid his gaze along the path he had traversed and discovered the reason for his haste: the brutish figure of Grelthus surged along on all fours less than a hundred yards behind. The Wyrgen's gait was weaving and unsteady for some reason, but he was nevertheless closing on his prey with frightening ease.

Movement on the immense amphitheater floor drew the swordsman's eye still further down to reveal another new threat. Score upon score of corrupted Wyrgens were flooding into the chamber, their burning gazes upturned and questing. Even as he watched, their dark forms began to swarm up the stairs leading to the next level. As the stairways clogged with the heaving mass of bodies, the enraged creatures clambered over balustrades and over the backs of their own fellows in their frenzy. Halthak and Grelthus were many levels above the floor, but he judged it would take the swelling horde no more than a handful of minutes to reach that height, given the speed of the Wyrgens.

Amric plunged through the breach and into the Fount chamber, bounding down the steps that would take him to the terrace level below even as his swords flashed into his hands.

CHAPTER 12

Halthak sprinted along the terrace, his desperate gaze fixed upon the next ramp of stairs. They were too far away yet to see if they offered any egress, but he had little choice except to try. The damnable Wyrgen had shaken off his imparted injuries with alarming speed, and now the panting snarls of pursuit grew louder with every step. Halthak heard the rasp of claws on stone almost at his heels, and he went cold as he realized he would never make it to those bleak steps before rending talons found his flesh and he was dragged down from behind.

His jaw clenched. He had been passive in the face of violence for all of his life, accepting it as inevitable, and seeking afterward with meek resolve to repair it if the fates allowed. Not this time. No, if death sought to claim him now in the guise of this evil creature, it would find him facing his attacker and fighting on the way down. He wished for the familiar comfort of his stout, gnarled staff, but he knew as well that even were it here now in his hands, it would do little to improve his chances against such a powerful killing machine.

He skidded to a halt and spun to meet Grelthus. Facing back the way he had come, he cursed at just how little distance he had covered since his escape. There was only a fleeting instant for self-reproach, however, before the furious mass of muscle and fur was upon him.

The Wyrgen launched itself at him, grasping claws outstretched. Surprise momentarily displaced rage on the wolf-like visage, however, as the Half-Ork fell backward and Grelthus hurtled through the empty space above him. Lying on his back, the healer lashed out with both feet to send the Wyrgen tumbling past. Halthak could never say afterward with any certainty whether the maneuver was tactical inspiration on his part, or if instead he had fallen backward in abject terror; if he lived to retell the moment, it would doubtless depend on his audience. It bought him precious seconds, however, even if it put his pursuer between him and the stairs he sought to reach.

He scrambled to his feet, hoping to rush past his stunned adversary, but the plan was short-lived. Shaking his great head in a rustle of thick, matted mane, Grelthus rose to all fours and glowered at Halthak once more.

"You are a troublesome creature, Half-Ork," Grelthus said, his eyes eerily luminous in the shifting glow of the Essence Fount. "You have more fire in you than I thought."

"Keep your praise," Halthak called back. "Leave me be, and I will trouble you no more."

The Wyrgen's only reply was a rumbling laugh, and he began to pace forward in a low crouch, his deep chest almost brushing the floor. The healer edged back from him.

"I will die before I yield to you, Grelthus. You must realize that by now."

Grelthus gave a rolling shrug of his immense shoulders as he crept forward. "It is no matter. There are things your body can teach me, even in death. And I must admit that the baser part of my nature hungers to see your blood at the moment, healer."

Halthak felt a chill at the creature's hard, indifferent tone. He wondered if all Wyrgens were so cruel, or if Grelthus had been driven to this state by solitude and what he had witnessed. He stepped to his right as the Wyrgen circled to his left. Maybe he could keep the creature talking, keep him distracted.

"I—" he began, and then Grelthus sprang at him.

He twisted back and to one side, but to no avail. The Wyrgen's weight slammed into him, tearing him from his feet and knocking the wind from him. Halthak writhed and thrashed, but he was clasped in thick, furry arms corded with muscle, and he might as well have been a flailing child for all the effect his struggles had on his captor. Grelthus wrenched him around and threw a mighty forearm across his chest, pinning him tight and facing away, and the other hand rose to clutch at Halthak's throat with curved talons.

"Cease your struggles, Half-Ork," Grelthus hissed in his ear. "Or I will rip out your throat."

Halthak wheezed a laugh, and tightened the grip of his own hand upon the beast's forearm to apprise the Wyrgen of its presence there. His magic swelled within him. "Best hope for a clean kill, Grelthus, or it will be your own throat you open."

The Wyrgen froze. Hot, rank breath washed over the side of the Half-Ork's face as Grelthus panted and considered.

Halthak considered as well, his mind racing. How quickly could he bring his magic to bear, particularly if affected by so grievous an injury? Halthak himself did not know, but he meant to try. Talons tightened on Halthak's throat, and beads of scarlet slid down his neck. Grelthus grunted as his own throat dimpled in response, and tiny rivulets of blood slicked into his fur, but he did not loosen his hold. Halthak felt the Wyrgen's forearm tense, and he braced himself for the release that would come in one form or another.

Suddenly a new voice intruded. "Release him, dog."

Halthak strained his eyes to the side to see Amric and Valkarr stalking toward them along the terrace, bared steel in their fists. Behind them trailed Bellimar, holding Halthak's staff in one pale hand, and Syth, the strange prisoner from the cage of blue flame. The latter wore polished black gauntlets now, clenched at his sides. His clothing rippled about him in fitful swirls, and he made no attempt to mask the burning hatred in the stare he leveled at Grelthus.

"How is your ailment, swordsman?" Grelthus sneered. "You should flee Stronghold before it claims you."

"We have unfinished matters between us first," Amric said, still striding forward. "And they start with our friend you are holding there."

"Then your arrival is well-timed, as I was about to give him a look at his own insides. Keep your distance!"

Amric shook his head. "I think not, Grelthus. I am close enough to cut you down like the murderous jackal that you are, if you are foolish enough to make your strike. The healer's life is the only thing protecting yours at the moment."

"Your kind cannot match my speed," the Wyrgen snarled, but Halthak could feel the great form tensing. Those dark eyes darted back and forth as Amric and Valkarr spread out to either side of him.

"We are prepared this time," Valkarr said, his scaly tail lashing behind him as he crouched. The Sil'ath warrior's gaze raked over them, from the blood soaking both of their clothing and fur to the fresh spatters on the flagstones beneath them. "And you are wounded now. Unsteady."

Grelthus bared his fangs at Valkarr in a rumbling growl.

"And," said Amric, "even if you can escape 'our kind', are you so confident you can escape your own?"

The growl sputtered and died, and Halthak felt the talons twitch at his throat. "What do you mean?"

"Your beloved people are scaling their way up the chamber's levels to reach you as we speak. I would wager we have no more than a minute before they arrive. We cannot spare the time to fence with words."

Even as Amric uttered the words, however, several hunched shapes darted onto the terrace from the lower stairs, back in the direction from which he and the others had come. Eerily silent, the corrupted Wyrgens cast about in a flurry of motion, their muzzles upturned to taste the air. Their glowing gazes fell upon the group across the arc of the balcony wall, a scant two hundred yards away, and they broke into triumphant, strident howls. The call was answered from the depths below as a sudden cacophony of savage cries filled the vast chamber.

More shapes spilled from that distant stairwell and over the stone railing to drop into crouches on the flagstones. The creatures lunged forward into loping runs, bounding toward them.

"You were right, Grelthus," Amric said, his lips pressed into a grim line. "Your kind are indeed fast."

A frantic whine escaped from between the Wyrgen's clenched teeth. Gazing upon the thundering horde that approached, Halthak had to agree; he felt like whimpering himself.

"Release the healer," Amric said. "We run or die, now."

"You said it yourself, human," Grelthus said, his frantic gaze flicking between the approaching Wyrgens and the warriors surrounding him with drawn steel. "The Half-Ork's life is the only thing that ensures mine. Else you will surely cut me down."

"Release him, and we can settle matters between us once we escape your people," Amric commanded. "You cannot outpace them while wounded and carrying a captive. Release him, or we all die here."

Grelthus hurled Halthak from him with a roar of fear and rage, then wheeled and bolted back in the direction from which he had come. The healer stumbled and was caught by Syth.

"Quickly, follow Grelthus!" Halthak shouted. "The glass wall is raised in the room we left, and we can shut out the creatures if we get there before he shuts us out as well!"

They raced after the Wyrgen. Ahead, more hulking lupine shapes were pouring onto the terrace beyond the stairs that led to the viewing chamber they had to reach. Behind, the savage tide hurtled after them.

Amric grimaced as he reached the foot of the narrow stairway. Like its twin on the other side, it led from the terrace to a landing atop a square bulkhead, which then opened onto the much wider steps before the viewing chamber. He had hoped to defend these narrow access points until the wall could be lowered, but he could see now that he needed a new strategy. Several of the beasts crowded up the narrow stairs on the other side, while still more hurled themselves at the bulkhead with prodigious leaps, catching at the edge to haul themselves over the side. One of the corrupted Wyrgens caught Grelthus on the broad upper steps, and the pair fell to grappling, snarling and thrashing back and forth as they tore at each other with claw and tooth.

Amric's mind raced. The lower stairs were already overrun, and could not be held in any event since it was obvious the creatures could scale the bulkhead with relative ease. The open wall of the viewing chamber was too wide by far to hold with their current numbers. The chamber might have a confined stairwell like the other, but the swift Wyrgens would drag them down before they could reach it, and he was loath to gamble their defense on the layout of a room he had not yet seen. The mindless creatures were gathering by the hundreds below in the amphitheater. Any mistake at this point and they would be trapped and crushed beneath the onrushing wave; likewise, any hesitation, and they would be just as quickly overwhelmed in the open.

"Clear the upper stairs!" he shouted to the others. "Valkarr and I will hold them as long as we can. You three help Grelthus, we need him to close the glass wall. When it starts to lower, we will dive under and join you. Now go!"

Amric leapt up to the landing. The Wyrgens there were slinking forward in anticipation, focused upon the combatants on the stairs above, and he was among them before they were aware of his presence. Two went down beneath his blades without a sound, and a third whirled toward him only to pitch forward with a cloven skull. Valkarr plunged into the midst of those crawling over the side of the bulkhead, his dual swords whistling in lethal arcs that sent woolly forms tumbling from the landing.

The Wyrgens recovered quickly, however, and surged after this new threat. Amric ducked under slicing talons, ripping his sword upward in response, and the attacker pitched backward in a crimson spray. His other sword swept out to send a grasping claw spinning away, and reversed in a lightning stroke to open the gaping creature's throat. He hammered a kick into the thing's barrel chest, propelling it backward to crash into its fellows on the narrow stairs. Amric followed, and in the chaos his darting swords silenced each Wyrgen that sought to struggle past the thrashing mass to reach him.

A shout from Valkarr brought him around. The Sil'ath warrior had momentarily cleared the edge of the landing, but the wave of Wyrgens following them had reached the foot of the lower steps. The swarm was building rapidly on all sides of the bulkhead as the creatures sought to ascend but were hindered by their own numbers.

Amric threw a glance upward to see Syth and Halthak cresting the stairs, dragging the stumbling Grelthus between them, leaving two dark forms sprawled in their wake. They passed under the raised glass wall and into the viewing chamber, disappearing from view. Bellimar followed, his grim expression inscrutable as he met Amric's gaze for the briefest of moments.

The warriors backed up the steps, spreading apart to cover as much of the broad passage as they could. The approach was far too wide for two men to hold for long, especially against such numbers, but he hoped they could keep the beasts focused upon them so that none slipped by to pursue the others. If they could purchase a minute or two, it should be sufficient to trigger the mechanism lowering the wall and see it closed.

The heavens help them all if it took longer than that.

The Wyrgens came onward, streaming from the lower stairways and clawing their way over the edge of the bulwark. They filled the landing, the crest of a snarling wave that rose from a sea of pressing bodies on the terrace below. Slavering jaws grinned wide below fiery eyes, and curved talons in a myriad of brilliant hues flexed in anticipation. Howling in rage, they surged up the steps at the waiting warriors.

Amric and Valkarr gave ground in the initial rush, slipping like phantoms away from snapping fangs and raking claws. Steel flickered in the blaze of the Essence Fount, and the charge faltered as the eager howls mixed with shrieks of pain and anger. The front rank of Wyrgens slumped to the stone, and as the next ranks made to hurdle over their fallen fellows, the warriors plunged forward as one to press the attack.

Amric fought like a man possessed, teeth bared in fury, cutting a scarlet swath through his foes. Hulking forms fell back from him on all sides, but more clambered over the heaped corpses to hurl themselves at him.

Valkarr was beside him, a whirlwind of cutting steel, and they drove like a fearsome wedge into the horde.

Then Amric's fear came to pass. Even as the bulk of the host hurled itself into the teeth of their onslaught, some of the creatures began to slip around them on the outside edge of the stairway. The warriors were forced to spread out more to prevent the mass from flowing around and surrounding them, or racing past to the viewing chamber. As they did so, however, several of the Wyrgens thrust themselves between them, isolating and encircling them for a perilous moment. They leapt back up the stairs, fending off the press of bodies as the charge threatened to overwhelm them.

Amric cursed. The two of them could not hold these stairs any longer, and the glass wall had still not begun to close.

A sudden gale of wind erupted at his side. Claws rasped on stone as the attackers in the front line staggered back, and the creatures threw up hairy arms to shield their squinting eyes as the wind ripped at them. Syth slid to a halt beside Amric, and flashed him a fierce grin.

"What is this, thief?" Amric said. "I had the impression that you were not much for a losing cause."

"I am not," Syth admitted. "But you are out here making valor look so good that my common sense has been overwhelmed for a time. Besides, I would not see this mangy pack of dogs cheat the storytellers of the epic fight that you and I will yet have."

With a scream of fury, Syth dove forward into the mass. One metallic black fist slammed into a furry torso with a resounding crack, while another swung in an open-handed blade to shatter an outstretched arm. Dropping into a low spin, he swept the legs from under several Wyrgens and exploded upward into a tremendous uppercut that catapulted one of the creatures into the air to land atop his fellows. Syth barked out short bursts of maniacal laughter as he moved among the creatures like a devastating whirlwind. Taken aback by the sheer ferocity of his attack, the Wyrgens shrank from him for a moment, screaming in frustration. Amric and Valkarr took advantage of the confusion to press the attack, and the three warriors spread out to cover the stairs.

For a long moment, the scene stood thus, like a persistent wave crashing against the stubborn rocks of shore. The charge was repelled, and neither side gave ground. But the enraged Wyrgens kept coming, sometimes hurling the lifeless bodies of their own kind from the stairs in their eagerness to reach the intruders. Blood flew from sword and gauntlet, but glowing talons inevitably found their marks as well, tearing through cloth and armor to sear the flesh beneath with foul energies. The creatures pressed forward with renewed fervor, sensing that their foe teetered on the edge of being overwhelmed. The first strike that did more than graze the agile warriors would end the stalemate.

It happened in an instant.

Bolstered by his battle fury, Amric had managed to put aside the strange illness caused by the Essence Fount through sheer force of will, and he anchored the center of their defensive line behind an impassable wall of steel. Over the heaving sea of Wyrgens, he saw the Fount pulse and swell, its light flaring to a sudden crescendo of brilliance like some impossibly massive stroke of lightning within the amphitheater. Amric staggered, his head swimming and the strength draining from his limbs, and a moment's weakness was all it took.

Grasping claws pulled at his mail shirt, throwing him off balance, and huge hairy fists slammed into him, knocking the breath from him. Jaws gaped at him from a wolfish visage, and he slapped away a clutching arm and lashed out with a return stroke that drew a yelping scream. His vision dimmed and he stumbled back, making weak cuts at the forest of claws that raked at him. Then he fell back on the cold stone steps, the wave crashed over him, and all went black.

Halthak was helping to lift Grelthus to his feet when he saw Amric fall beneath the corrupted Wyrgens on the stairs. He froze in horror, his breath caught in his throat. Bellimar released Grelthus's other arm and took a rapid step toward the stairway.

With an incoherent cry, Valkarr leapt to his fallen friend's defense. Heedless of his own safety, he burst among them like a demon, cleaving through the creatures with a berserk ferocity. A snarling, grizzled head tumbled down the stairs, freed of its body. Another hulking form staggered and fell back, cloven nearly in twain. Syth joined him an instant later in a blast of biting wind, hammering powerful blows into spine and skull until the beasts over Amric retreated or were still. Shoulder to shoulder they fought, driving back the Wyrgens for precious seconds.

"Healer!" Valkarr bellowed. "Pull him free!"

Halthak turned to Grelthus, who was now recuperated enough to stand. "Be ready with that wall!" he ordered as he shoved the Wyrgen toward the panel nestled on the side wall of stone.

Darting out of the chamber and onto the broad stairway, he knelt by Amric. The warrior was unconscious and bleeding from countless minor wounds, but was still breathing. He slid his hands under Amric's arms and heaved, dragging him from beneath the panting combatants. Wicked talons reached for him from amid the press, and Halthak flinched away without relinquishing his grip. They never landed, however, and when the healer looked again the severed arm was rolling on the flagstones nearby, still twitching. With a surge of effort, the Half-Ork pulled the man free and started up the stairs.

Behind him, the vibrating rumble of ponderous machinery began, and the enormous glass wall began its slow descent.

Too early, Halthak thought as panic rose like ice in his chest. After all it had taken to revive the stricken Wyrgen, he had now triggered the wall at the worst possible time. He threw a glance over his shoulder to see Grelthus leaning against the side wall, watching the battle on the stairs with an unreadable expression. Bellimar was behind the lowering portal, standing poised and rigid like he meant to throw himself into the fray. The Half-Ork looked up to the clear sheet of diamond-hard material, several feet thick, rumbling its way downward to the floor. His gut twisted as he realized he was not going to make it. The wall would come down before he could reach the safety of the chamber, burdened as he was, and it would either seal them without or crush them under its weight.

"Hold the wall!" he cried.

Grelthus tore his eyes from the battle to meet the healer's gaze.

A slow, malevolent smile spread across the savage countenance, and the wall continued to descend.

Halthak shouted a warning to Syth and Valkarr, but the warriors were locked in battle and could not turn away to help or even to escape themselves. He gritted his teeth and heaved with all his might, dragging the limp form of the swordsman up the steps. Certain death awaited them out here. He had no choice but to beat the descending wall. He resolved not to look back again, but instead to pull for all he was worth, and he and Amric would either live or die together. He reached the top of the stairs and lunged backward, grunting with the effort. His head struck the edge of the glass wall. He ducked under it and tightened his fists in Amric's chain shirt, sinking his claws into the link to retain his grip. He wrenched back, pulling desperately at the warrior, sick with the knowledge that he had not been fast enough, but unwilling to abandon their only chance.

With a squealing groan of protest, the wall's descent came to a sudden stop.

Halthak's mouth fell open in disbelief, and he turned wide eyes upward. Bellimar stood above him, eyes glowing red like searing pinpoints of flame, pale hands straining under the edge of the wall. The old man's back was bowed and his frame shook with the effort, but somehow, impossibly, he was holding up the titanic weight of the wall.

"This may look easy, healer," Bellimar gasped through clenched teeth. "But I pray you will hurry, nonetheless."

Halthak scrambled into the chamber, dragging his charge behind him. Amric groaned and began to stir. The Half-Ork looked under the wall to where Valkarr and Syth were still locked in combat with the Wyrgens, and he shouted to them, beckoning them on with repeated, frantic gestures.

He saw Valkarr risk a look back and then shout to Syth, "I will turn them back one last time while you run for the wall!"

"I'll not leave you to die in my stead," Syth snarled back, his gauntleted fist smashing out with a cracking report to cave in a grizzled skull.

"There is no time to debate it!" the Sil'ath returned. "Go now, and I will be on your heels."

The warriors locked gazes for a split second, and Halthak witnessed some grim understanding pass between them. Then Valkarr plunged forward in a blinding whirlwind of steel, uttering a battle roar. The horde swayed back from the savagery of his assault.

Syth lashed out to send another Wyrgen reeling, and then hesitated as he watched the swarm close around the frenzied Sil'ath. Then he wheeled and bolted up the stairs. He dove under the massive wall in a rush of air, rolling smoothly to his feet inside the chamber.

The glass wall made a dull grinding sound and dropped another half a foot before Bellimar caught it with a grunt. A violent trembling rocked his slender frame, but the wall hung suspended once more. Syth and Halthak turned their anxious stares to the fight raging below on the stairs.

Valkarr cut his way free in a bloody swath, and for a fleeting instant, he was clear. He leapt up the stairs, grim resolve written in every hard line of his face. A claw raked at his leg, leaving the flesh ragged and blackened in its wake, and he swept away the offending appendage with a terse stroke. A brutish Wyrgen bounded through the air to crash into his back, and he twisted, spinning into a sweeping cut that laid the creature open even as it was thrown from him. Talons caught at his leather baldric, slinging him to the side, and he crossed his arms to thrust behind him, impaling his assailant with both blades.

Halthak's mouth fell open, his breath caught in his throat. The effort was incredible, stunning in its display of swordsmanship and determination, but the speed and power and endless numbers of the corrupted Wyrgens made the conclusion inevitable. More and more claws snaked through to catch at the fleeing Sil'ath, slowing him, staggering him, tearing into his scaly flesh. He went to one knee, still hammering lethal blows all about him, and finally pitched forward beneath the weight as the swarm enveloped him.

Within the chamber, Halthak watched aghast as Valkarr disappeared from sight beneath a surging mass of rending claws and fangs. Bellimar sagged forward, groaning in agony as his grip failed at last.

The massive wall slammed to the ground with a shuddering boom of thunder.

Amric blinked, trying to clear the haze from his vision. Everything swam before his eyes, blurred and washed out, as if he viewed the world through a swirling white mist. Several figures stood above him, their outlines muddled and indistinct, but he could see they were all facing away from him.

He clenched his teeth in pain. His insides burned as if afire, and some dim part of him wondered if the Fount had corrupted him at last. Or perhaps the vicious Wyrgens had torn into him, and he was simply too obstinate to die.

His hands remembered sword hilts, and he groped for them, but his fingers met only cold stone. Something unfamiliar clawed at his clouded awareness; he felt a rush of alien sensations thrust upon him, as if the conflicting emotions of some other being were somehow bursting inside him. It was mercurial, seeming at once insistent, fearful, eager, ashamed and restrained. It raged with fury and clamored for his attention, and then shrank from his scrutiny as he tried to focus upon it.

He pushed himself up to one elbow and concentrated on the strident forms around him. They wavered into focus. Halthak, white-faced and rigid, pressed against the glass wall. Bellimar, slouching exhausted against the wall, one pale hand spread against its clear surface as if trying to touch someone or something on the other side. Syth, shouting and hammering his fist against the wall as his robes whipped violently about his taut frame. Amric squinted past them and through the glass wall, searching for the cause of their distress.

He saw Valkarr, beyond the glass wall, thrashing on the ground beneath the mass of savage Wyrgens. He saw gleaming fangs flecked with crimson froth, and smoldering claws stained with blood as they raked repeatedly at the Sil'ath's body. He saw the mindless fiends ravaging the body of his dying friend, and for Amric, in that instant, everything else ceased to exist.

A scream of anguish was torn from his throat, and all the fire churning inside him rose with it. The thing within him came gibbering to the fore, flaring with power that scorched through his veins and threatened to burn him to ash. Amric sensed a kindred rage in the thing to match his own, and a wild desire to help. Beyond reason, he embraced it, and felt its fierce exultation even as he was filled with the rush of power. Then everything dissolved before his eyes in a blaze of white fire.

Bellimar's hand slid down the glass wall and fell to his lap. He had revealed himself and worse, broken the strictures imposed upon him. He would pay dearly for it, he knew. Already the need worked at the edges of his will, and still it had not been enough. Perhaps if he had acted sooner, he thought; but nay, there were limits he could no longer ignore, no matter how grave the circumstances.

A scream from Amric brought him sharply about. There was an unnatural quality in the timber of the swordsman's voice that sent a chill coursing through him, and he had not thought anything in this world could still have that effect on him. The shout parted the air with a razor edge, beginning as a cry of grief and loss and becoming something else entirely, infused with rage and thrumming with intensity.

Amric rose to his feet, blazing with power. His eyes radiated dazzling white fire like miniature suns, and that terrible gaze was fixed upon the grisly scene outside the chamber. He stretched out one hand toward the glass wall with fingers spread wide, and Bellimar's hair lifted from his head as a strange pressure built there. Sudden instinct warned him to dive aside, and he shouted a warning to the others. Syth grabbed the gaping Halthak and yanked him out of the way.

Seeming unaware of their presence, Amric strode forward. He clenched his hand into a fist, and the wall exploded outward with an ear-splitting report. Massive shards tore ragged swaths through the Wyrgens crowded without, sweeping scores from the terrace. Deafened and taken aback for a moment, the creatures crouched frozen as he approached. Their baleful, unblinking stares were fixed upon him, and their glowing eyes against the sea of hulking forms were like a constellation against a velvet midnight sky. Then they surged forward as one with a throaty roar, hurling themselves at their bold prey.

Amric never broke stride. Crossing his arms before him, he then whipped them apart in a vicious cutting motion, as if he held his swords in both hands and was cleaving into a foe.

The ripple of power tore at Bellimar's robes, even behind the swordsman as he was, but it was nothing compared to the devastation before him. Scything forces swept through the Wyrgens, peeling them from the stairs and hurling them back by the hundreds. Twisting and clawing madly for purchase, the Wyrgens were scattered like dry leaves over the edge of the terrace, where the creatures tumbled through the empty air toward the amphitheater floor far below.

In the blink of an eye, the broad steps before the viewing chamber were clear but for the broken figure of Valkarr, lying in a spreading pool of his own blood, untouched by the reaping forces that had cut through the Wyrgens.

Amric knelt at Valkarr's side, gathered him into his arms, and stood. Those flaming eyes swung back to the viewing chamber.

"He still clings to life," he said, his voice cracking with grief and yet carrying an eerie resonance at the same time. "Help him," he pleaded.

Behind him, in the cavernous amphitheater, one of the great columns burst with a crack of thunder, spewing granite fragments in every direction. Halthak swallowed, his gaze flitting between Amric and the burden he carried.

"I—I do not know if I can heal injuries so severe," he stammered. "I do not even know how he still draws breath. He—or he and I both—may not be strong enough to withstand the process."

Amric climbed the steps, carrying Valkarr. He strode through the shattered portal and into the chamber. Bellimar's eyes narrowed. A faint nimbus of light surrounded both of them. Amric halted before the healer, and Halthak shrank before his fiery scrutiny, but the swordsman's next words were solemn and surprisingly gentle.

"All I ask is that you try, Halthak," he said. "I think that you will find the strength here, in this place." He laid Valkarr on the floor at the Half-Ork's feet.

"Come, Halthak," Bellimar urged. "I have some medical knowledge, and I will assist you however I can. We have very little time, if we are to perform a miracle."

As the two bent over the ravaged form of the Sil'ath, the forgotten Grelthus found his voice from the corner of the viewing chamber.

"What have you done?" he moaned, shuffling out onto the steps and casting his stricken gaze all about. "What have you done to my people?"

He whirled toward Amric, hunching over and spreading his claws wide. Hatred and madness twisted his features as he spat his words through bared fangs. "You have slain them all, human!"

"Not all, Grelthus," Amric said. "Not yet."

The incensed Wyrgen dropped forward into a crouch, bristling and bunching to leap.

"Your traitorous ways have cost the lives of many, Grelthus," Amric continued, his voice a ringing pronouncement of doom. "The time has come for you to join your people."

The Wyrgen sprang at him, launching his powerful form through the air with jaws frothing and curved talons outstretched. Amric lashed out with one hand, palm forward. The brutish creature was struck in midair by some invisible force and swatted aside like an insect. Spinning and twisting, Grelthus was hurled across the terrace edge and out of sight, his howl of rage dwindling away.

The swordsman strode over to where the glass wall had been. He bowed his head and spread his arms. As if in response, the Essence Fount leapt skyward, surging and swelling until it nearly filled the amphitheater. It thrashed violently, spinning like a cyclone of flame and sending tendrils of blazing energy curling about the colossal stone columns in the vast circular chamber.

One by one, the pillars shattered and exploded, crumbling into ruin. As the last of them fell, Stronghold itself shook in protest, quivering in the throes of its agony. With a rumbling roar, the great domed ceiling of the chamber split and fell. Ton after ton of rock poured into the chamber. The Fount was obscured as the avalanche continued and the very heart of Stronghold collapsed in on itself.

Bellimar, still kneeling over Valkarr, gaped in awe. On impulse he brought up his Sight and tried to look upon Amric's aura. His vision filled with intense, flaring white light, and he fell back with a startled cry as his eyes were nearly seared from his head. He dropped his Sight, flinging up one arm to shield his tightly shut eyes.

Long seconds later, when he could see once more, the deluge of rock had ceased. The Essence Fount was lost to sight, and the vast chamber housing the experiment that was the demise of the Wyrgens was filled with stone. A rippling cloud of grit and dust carpeted the viewing chamber, causing everyone to cough, and fragments of stone skittered and danced upon the partially exposed stairway outside as the mighty fortress still trembled.

Syth stood over the men attending to Valkarr, shifting from one foot to the other as his wide-eyed gaze bounced from Amric to the now solid core of Stronghold.

"Remember all that talk of wanting to fight you, swordsman?" he said fervently. "Forget every last word of it."

CHAPTER **13**

Amric stepped into the courtyard under a star-speckled sky. He inhaled deeply, savoring his first breaths of truly clean air in over two days.

Syth brushed past and hurled himself to the grass, rolling back and forth with a gleeful howl. Amric looked back at the brooding fortress out of reflex at the man's careless commotion, but the darkened apertures in the sheer stone face remained as empty and lifeless as the eye sockets of a skull.

In fact, the entirety of the flight from Stronghold had been a study in contrast to their frenzied arrival. On the way in they had been harried and hunted and at the mercy of their deranged guide. On the way out, no other living creature had stirred to obstruct their exit. Before, the hush of the fortress had been like the bated breath of a crouching predator. Now it was instead the cavernous silence of the crypt. Amric did not know whether the Wyrgens had all perished in the collapse of the Fount chamber and the innermost core of Stronghold, or if the survivors had fled to remote corners of the place in the aftermath. In the end, he did not care much which was the case, as long as the foul creatures kept their distance.

Amric drew another deep breath and smiled. Let Syth revel in his regained freedom, anyway. After his months of captivity and his courageous actions during their escape, he had well earned it.

Halthak emerged from the corridor at his back, hollow-eyed and leaning upon his staff. Valkarr appeared beside him, and the pair descended the stairs to the courtyard with slow, deliberate movements. Amric felt a stab of worry at the way the Sil'ath warrior swayed on his feet, but he let none of it show in his tight smile. His friend was too proud and stubborn by far to let the others see the full depths of his fatigue, and any display of concern would only discomfit him.

The warrior's insides twisted as he considered how close he had come to losing them both. It had been a near thing indeed, according to Bellimar; Halthak came so close to following the Sil'ath into the abyss that Amric made to abort the attempt for fear of sacrificing the man on a doomed cause. The Half-Ork was already lost in his efforts, however, and would not abandon the task. Through it all, the power flooding through Amric somehow kept the other two men infused with energy as well. It held them on the precipice while Halthak put forth a feverish, herculean effort. At last the healer's bolstered magic won out, snatching them both back from death's covetous grasp, and they collapsed into well-deserved oblivion.

After hours of slumber, Halthak had awakened to confirm that Valkarr was out of immediate danger, though he was quick to caution that a week or more of rest would be needed for full recuperation. Their provisions were running low, however, as the bulk of them had been left outside with the horses. Furthermore, by unspoken agreement, each of the men wished to put Stronghold behind him as soon as possible. So it was that when everyone was recovered enough to stand, they began the tense, cautious trek through the deserted fortress, aided by their sense of direction and Syth's fading memory of Grelthus's maps.

Last to appear at the mouth of the corridor was Bellimar, materializing from the shadows. He paused at the top of the stairs and turned a bold stare upon Amric, as if daring the unasked questions to fall from his lips. The swordsman met his gaze and said nothing. The time for that conversation would come soon enough.

In a welcome stroke of fortune, their horses were still in the squat stable building, unscathed if also very skittish. As he approached and soothed them, Amric wondered how much of the carnage within the fortress had drifted far enough to reach their keen senses out here.

The party left the courtyard and crossed the arcing metallic bridge on foot, with Amric leading the horses. After many hours traversing the tortuous corridors of Stronghold, Valkarr and Halthak were too tired to sit their saddles over such a precarious drop, and the nervous equines were on the verge of spooking as it was. Once they reached the tree-studded bluff at the other end of the bridge, they hobbled the horses and allowed them to graze. They set up camp for the night there, nestled back beneath a scruffy copse of trees. Partially screened from view by the trees, they built a fire and gathered around it to eat and rest in silence for a time. Halthak and Valkarr lapsed into sleep before even finishing their meals, leaving the other three wrapped in their own thoughts.

Amric gazed across the valley at the fortress, a towering black silhouette cleaving the night sky. He looked forward to being much further from that place of death, but there was nothing for it tonight. The high trail along the cliffs was too treacherous to navigate in the darkness. Perhaps by morning Halthak and Valkarr would be rested enough to attempt it, and if not, they would remain here on the bluff until they were ready. At least there were only two approaches to this location, and both were narrow and difficult to traverse with any measure of stealth.

"What next, Amric?" Bellimar asked, his voice pitched low so as not to wake the sleepers.

The swordsman turned away from Stronghold to find the eyes of both men upon him.

"Back to Keldrin's Landing, for now," he said. "Halthak and Valkarr need a place to rest that is warm, dry and safe."

The old man chuckled. "It is difficult to say just how safe the city will prove for us. Morland may not be satisfied with the news we bring back."

"Morland?" Syth asked, sitting forward. "The merchant?"

"The same," Amric said. "He had some contact with my missing friends, and pointed us in this direction in exchange for our efforts in locating Grelthus. Evidently the two are—were in business of some kind together."

The thief slouched back, a look of distaste twisting his features. "I know that full well. It was Morland who paid me to come here in the first place, to steal back some baubles of his from Grelthus. According to Morland, they had a falling out of some sort, and the Wyrgen then refused to return various items that belonged to the merchant by rights."

"And you took him at his word?" Amric said, lifting an eyebrow.

"Not for a moment," Syth admitted. "But I believed in the color and quantity of his coin. For the king's ransom he offered me for the task, these items must have been very important to him. Unfortunately, I did believe the snake when he said that invoking his name would gain Grelthus's trust. In truth, it had rather the opposite effect." His expression darkened with anger, and then brightened again into a broad, wolfish grin. "Come to think of it, I am certain I saw some of those items on the Wyrgen's table, there above the viewing chamber. Quite a pity that we were unable to retrieve them, is it not?"

Amric barked a laugh. "I'm for thwarting the devil myself, but it occurs to me that we are all returning to Keldrin's Landing having failed in the eyes of a ruthless, powerful man at tasks he had a strong desire to see completed. Bellimar is correct; we are not likely to see the price on our heads lifted when we return."

Syth's eyebrows rose. "A contract out on you, eh? Nothing done in half measures with you, is there?"

"It is safest if we travel together until we near the city," Amric said. "But we can part company before the gate, so that you do not invite a price on your head as well."

The thief looked away and gave a slow shrug, picking at food between his back teeth with one fingernail. "You will have to deal with Morland at some point, or be forever looking over your shoulder," he said. "I might like to be there to have my say as well."

"Regrettably, we do not have an extra mount for you," Amric said, studying the man. "However, we will already be taking a slower pace to accommodate our wounded. We can rotate doubled-up riders among the stronger steeds for some stretches, and walk through others."

"I appreciate the thought, but I can travel on foot faster than most men," Syth remarked as he stifled a yawn. "Besides, horses and I have reached an understanding in the past: neither of us will attempt to ride the other, except in the most unusual of circumstances."

Amric smiled and stood, wincing as he did so. He stepped away from the fire, his attention once more upon the brooding shadow of Stronghold in the distance.

"You should have allowed the Half-Ork to heal you," Bellimar reminded him.

The swordsman realized he was scratching at his crude cloth strip bandages again, and he let his hand drop. "Nothing more than minor cuts and bruises. They can wait, or heal on their own. In any event, you saw him. Any more strain would have done the poor fellow in." He glanced back. "Thank you again for your aid in treating and bandaging my wounds."

Bellimar inclined his head. There was a pause, and then, "Have you felt it again, since?"

There was no need to guess what the old man meant. "No. Not since it left me, just after Halthak saved Valkarr and they both fell unconscious. And my aura?"

"Undetectable to my Sight, as before," Bellimar replied.

Amric exhaled in relief. He recalled the moment in the viewing chamber, when the threat of the Wyrgens had passed and he had turned his attention inward to confront the alien presence that had invaded him. Revulsion and fear swept through him at the thought of becoming corrupted like the Wyrgens, or being fused forever with this burning torrent of magic, unable to force the powerful spirit from him. Its mysterious intervention had saved their lives, he had to admit, and he had sensed nothing malicious about its intent save for a white-hot rage toward their enemies. It had guided him, and yet he had still felt in control of his actions. He supposed that was the insidious allure of such power at work, and one never truly realized loss of self until it was too late to turn back.

A lifetime's aversion to magic had flared then, and he searched for the thing within him, braced to battle for his very soul. There was nothing to contest against in the end, however; a fleeting instant of contact, a tentative brush against his senses, and then it had faded and vanished before his loathing like the early morning mist burned away by the new sun. He was left weary to the bone and wondering if he was truly alone in his flesh once more.

Even though no hint of it had resurfaced in the many hours since, he found himself compulsively focusing inward every so often, dreading its return.

"Do you still believe you were possessed by the Essence Fount?" Bellimar asked.

"Of course," Amric said, frowning. "What alternative is there?"

When Bellimar did not respond, he swung around to face him. The old man's eyes caught and held the lurid glow of the fire as he studied Amric.

"Out with it, man," the swordsman demanded. "Share your theories."

But Bellimar shook his head. "I do not have an explanation yet that would hold up to scrutiny, but there are some theories I can refute."

"Go on," Amric said, his eyes narrowing.

"Well," Bellimar began, seeming to choose his words with care, "the Essence Fount is not a sentient thing, capable of an intrusive manifestation like you describe. It is a pure force of nature, more akin to a tidal wave or forest fire than to a living creature. Its power can harm or even consume those near it, and it might be tapped or directed somehow, but it has no will behind it."

"You know that I have neither affinity for magic nor desire to work it," Amric objected. "I could not have done what I did without something providing the power, and guiding my hand as well. And you said my aura became bright as the sun while I was under its influence."

"I know all this, and yet it could not have been the Fount. It could certainly have affected you over time, changed or sickened you. But it could not come to your aid and then depart as you describe. It possesses no more intelligence than an avalanche, or a tornado."

A sudden gust of wind raked over them, dragging at the flames of the campfire. Both men turned to see a broad grin creasing Syth's face.

"You make your point, thief," Bellimar said with a rueful chuckle. "I am referring to *common* such phenomena, however. And elementals are not capable of possession either, to my knowledge."

Syth shrugged. "If not the Fount itself, then what?"

"That I do not know," the old man said, his expression pensive.

"And what of the rage I felt from it?" Amric put in. "I thought perhaps it was the Fount, furious at the violation of the Wyrgens, seeking some way to retaliate."

Bellimar snorted. "If that was the case, it was already having its revenge in small steps, robbing the surviving offenders first of their intellects and later, I suspect, of their lives. If a force of that magnitude were backed by intent, I doubt it would have needed agents as insignificant as us. No, the phenomenon coincided with your anguish and need. Are you certain it was not merely your own anger you felt, at seeing your friend fall?"

The warrior shook his head, staring into the fire as the memories of those chaotic moments tumbled past. "Whatever it was, it brought its own. It was separate and distinct until I accepted its help, and then it added its fury to mine. We became somehow fused, joined in purpose for a time."

"I can think of many creatures capable of possession," Bellimar said, his eyes boring into the warrior. "But few would wait on your acceptance while you were so vulnerable, and none would so easily relinquish control afterward."

Amric blew out a breath. "I suppose I can live with the mystery, so long as it is gone now, and gone for good." He met the old man's unwavering gaze. "After all, that was not the only unexpected thing to happen back there in the fortress."

A tight smile spread across Bellimar's face. "Is there something you wish to ask me, swordsman?"

The fire snapped and popped as the two men stared at each other, and Syth's eyes flicked between them as the silence stretched out and became brittle.

"There are many questions I would ask of you, Bellimar," said Amric at last. "But only one of import, at least until we are clear of this foul wilderness."

"Ask it, then."

"Are you with us?" the warrior said in a tone edged with steel. He held up a hand to forestall a reply. "A moment, before you answer. No playing at words, no evasion. There is no doubt that your actions saved us in Stronghold, but in the past two days I have had all the treachery I can stomach. The truth of what you are and what you seek can wait, but if you mean any of us harm, I would know it now. I will have your commitment, or we part company tonight. Are you with us, and for us, until we reach the city?"

Bellimar gave a solemn nod. "A fair question," he said. "I mean no harm to anyone here. I am with you, and for you, until the city and beyond."

Amric regarded him over the fire. "Good enough, for tonight," he said. "I will take the first watch."

With that, he turned and disappeared into the night. Bellimar watched him go with an unreadable expression, and Syth in turn watched the old man. For once the thief seemed without comment.

The fire crackled and danced merrily, oblivious to the troubles of men.

Syth sat cross-legged in the darkness, twisting a long blade of grass between his fingers. He savored the feel of it sliding against his bare skin. His eyes darted from time to time to the black outline of his gauntlets lying on the ground beside him, but he resisted the urge to don them.

The scent-laden breeze skirted him, and he cast his gaze upward. The sky had not yet begun to lighten, but it could not be more than an hour or two away, or so he thought. There was a time he would have known such a simple thing with precision, with unshakable certainty, but the internal clock he had always taken for granted seemed to have deserted him during his long months trapped deep within a prison of stone. It was as if nature held him apart as a stranger now, no longer recognizing one of its own, and a twinge of sadness pierced him at the rejection.

A horse whickered somewhere behind him, and he glanced over his shoulder. The fire had burned low in its pit, a dull red ember sunken amid the copse of trees. Its glow warmed the outlines of the men sleeping there, and he considered the companions thrust upon him by circumstance. Shaking his head, he faced forward once more.

He wondered why he had not already slipped away into the night. He was better on his own, had always been better alone. He had insisted on taking the last watch in part to give himself the opportunity to depart unseen. He smiled, remembering the open suspicion on Amric's face when he pleaded to do his part and relieve the man. He suspected that the warrior, if he slept at all, slumbered now with one eye open and affixed to Syth's back.

That alone would not have kept him here, however, and his smile faded as he pondered his own inaction. If he ever owed these men anything, he had repaid it in Stronghold. He had always felt little enough need for the respect or affection of others. Why, then, did he not leave, he who had always chafed in the company of others? There was validity, he thought, in the reasoning that the forest had become too dangerous to travel alone, even for one with his talents, but he was disturbed to find it a partial truth at best. Perhaps being so long in the grasp of his inhuman captor had awakened a deeply buried hunger for companionship. He shuddered. He hoped it was a condition that would pass; in his experience, nothing good ever came of depending on others.

A rustle of grass brought him about, wind coiling beneath him by reflex and lifting him to his feet in a burst. His hands clenched into fists within the black gauntlets, though he did not recall snatching them up when he stood. Syth relaxed. It was the Half-Ork, wending his way between the gaunt trees, leaning on his staff with movements cautious and stiff. He watched the healer's slow approach.

"I did not mean to startle you," Halthak said in a hushed tone as he halted a few paces away.

"I am on watch," Syth responded with a grin. "It is my duty to jump at every sound. Did I not impress you with my vigilance? Or did you expect to find me dozing?"

The healer smiled back, his creased face splitting to display the tusks at the each corner of his wide mouth. Even in the faint light afforded by the glimmering stars overhead, Syth could see the fellow's tired, drawn expression.

"You should be resting, conserving your strength," Syth said.

"I will, soon enough," Halthak replied. "I needed a moment to say something to you."

"Oh?"

Halthak nodded and hesitated, as if uncertain how to proceed. "I wanted to thank you for your part in rescuing me, and for risking your life for us all, in the end. Amric told me you had a choice. You could have fled with your freedom, but you chose to stay. He said without your knowledge of Stronghold's layout, the cause might well have been lost."

Syth stared at him, recalling his heated exchange with Amric over possession of the key device. He flushed, though whether in shame or anger he was not certain, and he found himself grateful for the concealing dark. "Well," he said at last, "your friend Amric can be a persuasive fellow."

"Nonetheless," Halthak pressed, "I owe you my freedom, and probably my life as well."

Syth fidgeted, and then shrugged, flashing his ready grin. "I have stolen much in my lifetime," he said. "I thought it would be a welcome change to be rightfully owed, for once."

Halthak nodded and swung away. Syth watched his silhouette pick its way back toward the camp, and then he sank smoothly to the ground to sit cross-legged once more, facing out into the night. Later, when the sky began to lighten with the coming morn, it found him still seated there, a solitary figure lost in unaccustomed thoughts.

The man in black emerged from the Gate to stand on a broad platform high above the ruins. He glanced behind to see the Gate seal itself, a searing vertical slash of light that frothed and hissed at the edges until it dwindled and finally vanished. Then the portal was tranquil once more, or at least as tranquil as it ever became.

The man cocked his head, regarding its shimmering surface within the great enclosing arch of stone. As always, he could not decide which it resembled more, the iris of some massive eye without a focusing pupil, or a roiling, fibrous mass of clouds. And he shrugged, as ever before. It was a thing of function, not of beauty, though he had always felt there was an ancient splendor to it that transcended mere beauty.

He turned his back on the construct, and took a few cautious steps. His knees quivered but held, and already he could feel strength seeping back into his limbs. Passing through an Essence Gate was always disorienting, but in this case the reward was almost immediate. He tasted of the energies gathered here by the Gate, and he smiled. Nothing compared to the heady rush of power back home, except of course for this, when a Gate was gathering. And this one was doing little more than sipping thus far, he thought with anticipation, trying to imagine the concentration of force it would reach when in full operation.

The black-robed man strolled around the platform, hands clasped behind his back as he took in his surroundings. Tiny, dark shapes wheeled high overhead in a cloud-streaked sky, but they did not approach and he paid them no heed. The mid-morning sun struggled to pierce that high shroud, sending sparse shafts of warmth down to dapple the crumbling ruins, which stretched away in every direction to the limit of his vision. A blanket of mist rolled and curled over the ground, like some turbulent phantom sea. Where the white waves parted, he could see vegetation pushing through shattered paving, and great mounds of wind-worn, sun-bleached stone.

Bent, misshapen forms shuffled and crawled through the mist, but they gave a wide berth to the colossal pedestal and the wide stairs leading up to the Gate. Good, he thought, as it would save him the trouble of dealing with them.

His expression twisted in distaste as he surveyed the ruins, and with long fingers he stroked a neatly trimmed ebon beard shot through with grey. The place was a shambles. He preferred it when the locals kept the Gate locations in a suitably respectful state, but that had obviously not been the case here. There was no longer power enough to spare from the other side for the old ways either, he reflected with some regret. No matter, he supposed; the Essence Gate was the important thing, and it was fully functional and well preserved by magic. On a whim, he tried to recall the name given to this place. It took long seconds, but finally, through the dusty halls of memory: Queln! That was it, he decided, pleased with himself at this small indulgence.

Then his mood darkened as he remembered his purpose in coming here.

Indeed, how could he forget the name of this place, even over the intervening years? Another part of this otherwise insignificant world had played host to a personal failure which had taken him a great deal of time and effort to overcome, ever since. In many ways the echoes of that time haunted him yet today, for he suspected its influence in the treatment he received, in the assignments he was given, and in the galling pace of his advancement.

And now the vanished threat which he had long argued was dead and gone, which he insisted had been swallowed by a primitive and hostile realm, had instead been detected after all these years in a flaring burst of power. He was not sure how it could be, but one thing he did know: this was his chance to wipe away that past failure, once and for all.

After the initial shock, he had insisted it must be him that went. His jaw tightened as he recalled the looks of scathing contempt upon their faces, as all of the old doubts and suspicions were dredged to the fore. How costly that one mistake amid a lifetime of service! But he had been resolute, and in the end, they had relented and sent him.

He closed his eyes and reached out with other, less restricted senses. It was difficult, here in the presence of the Gate. Though it boosted his strength, it also clamored with signals of its own and gave rise to or attracted other disruptive elements, interfering with such delicate efforts. After several minutes he sighed and opened his eyes. Even with the raucous tumult assailing his senses here, he was certain; the force he sought was nowhere to be found, concealed once more. The magnitude and signature of that first bright signal had been unmistakable, however. His quarry was alive, on this world, and somewhere to the west of this very Gate.

He ground his teeth. He refused to return now, abashed, bearing the same inadequate answer as before. His masters had not bothered to state the obvious, that anything less than resounding success this time would be the end of him. In fact, he wondered how long he had before they sent another to assume his mission and dispose of him as well. There was no room for failure in empire. He sighed. He would wait then, here on this pathetic excuse for a world, and pray that this time his quarry could not remain hidden from him for so long.

Magic on that scale always left a trail of some kind. Sooner or later, he would track it to its source.

He gathered power to him, drawing in more and more, holding it until it burned at his core. A fierce, exultant smile spread across his aquiline features. He considered giving reign to his anger and shattering these paltry ruins further, leveling the place—except of course for the Gate and its platform—and scorching its slinking inhabitants. But no, even this petty pleasure was denied him, for he could not be certain how sensitive were the defenses of the one he sought, and he had no wish to alert his quarry to his presence with such a display.

With a pang of regret, he let most of the power slip from him, keeping only a red-hot ember within that burned as hot as his hatred. He strode from the platform and began the long descent down the wide stairs, hoping that some dark creature from the mist below would be foolish enough to linger in his path.

CHAPTER 14

The huntress surged to her feet, her narrowed green gaze striving against the distance and the gloom of late evening. For long seconds she stood thus, poised upon the hillside, camouflaged both by the fading light and the thick outcropping of scrub grasses behind her which matched her buckskin leathers in hue.

Then she whirled away, snatched up her recurve bow and bounded down the slope like a gazelle.

As she went, she was careful to put the rounded ridge of the hillock between her and her quarry so as not to risk being seen, however slight the risk might be at this distance. She hissed a soft whistle, and her black mare dutifully wheeled from where she grazed and trotted to meet her. She stroked Shien's glossy neck and whispered to her as she led her up the steep, shifting trail and into the cave. The animal quivered, and her velvet ears flicked as she sensed the tense excitement in her mistress's words.

When the huntress reappeared at the mouth of the cave, having quieted the mare deep within its recesses, the cowl of her cloak was drawn up and she wore the dark veil across her features, exposing only her eyes. Her knuckles whitened around the handle of her bow as she scanned the hillside. She had been waiting for days, and doubt had become her companion during the long vigil. His party might have perished within the forest, and while she could not believe it would claim one such as him, such an occurrence might free him to travel by less mundane means and thus rob her of the chance to intercept. Or perhaps the party had already emerged by some other route and slipped by her.

Even if they did return the way they had come, as she deemed most likely, this location—while the best she had found—was a poor location for her ambush. The rough foothills around the cave offered some cover, but were too far back from the road to offer a sure shot, and the ground between here and the road was too exposed. If they had returned in the full light of day, they would have no reason to stop here, and she would likely be forced to trail them again and seek another opportunity.

Now, however, all the factors were coming together in her favor. Her prey was returning this way on the verge of nightfall, such that she could still spot them breaking from the trees. Furthermore, it would be fully dark by the time they drew abreast of the cave, and their previous camping spot would beckon against the hazardous prospect of traveling the road under the shroud of night.

She could scarcely credit her good fortune. Perhaps chance favored the just in the end, after all.

Her eyes raked over the cave mouth and the mantle of rock that swept back from it on either side, though in truth she had studied it all so often in the past few days that she had committed every detail to memory. As she had already done a hundred times, she weighed and rejected a dozen perches from which to take the one shot she needed. She cast one more hasty look around, and back again toward the distant tree line, though it was a futile gesture; it had already grown too dark to see such a distance. She melted back into the deep shadows of the cave entrance, partially shielded from view by the dried brush still piled together from when her quarry had camped there a handful of nights ago, and settled in for the wait.

It would have to be a perfect shot, she knew, and it had to be fast. His sight was as keen in utter darkness as that of a mortal man in the comforting illumination of midday. Step from the cave, draw a bead on him and fire, all in one smooth motion. It would be perfect, because it had to be.

The minutes slid by, teasing at the frayed edges of her patience. She stood unmoving, letting her eyes adjust to the gathering dark, and kept her breathing shallow and all but inaudible.

When the first noise came to her from down the hill, she suppressed a start. It seemed too early, unless they had ridden very hard to reach this point, but she knew how lying in wait with pulse pounding in one's ears could distort one's sense of time. She strained for every sound. Several footsteps, a small shower of pebbles, the scuff of foot against stone. There were a handful of them as expected, making little attempt to mask their approach, and they were on the winding trail below the cave. The huntress took slow, shallow breaths, in through the nose and out through the mouth, praying that Shien would not choose this moment to fidget deep within the cave. But no, the mare was well trained, as disciplined as her mistress; she would not betray their trap.

Her fingers brushed the fletching of the black arrow as she reassured herself every few seconds that she had selected the right missile in the darkness. She listened to the sounds drawing near, and tried to gauge her timing; he had a tendency to hang back, to let others risk themselves, and she needed him within range without allowing those in front to interfere with her shot.

As she tensed to leap from the cave, the noises came to a sudden stop.

She froze. Had they spotted her tracks on the rocky trail? It seemed impossible, as she had been so careful. Were their senses impossibly sharp, that they had heard some telltale sign from her? She chewed on silent, sulfurous curses as she wondered what had given her away. Shuffling steps and scrapes floated up to her, receding now but strangely unhurried, as if the group had merely lost interest in the cave for some reason.

She ground her teeth. Every step she allowed now would lengthen her shot. Now was the time, and if his back was turned such that he never had an opportunity to evade the lethal strike, so much the better.

Gliding from the cave, she drew back on the bow until her fingers brushed her cheek. She sighted down the arrow shaft and past the curved blades of the head, shifting from one moving figure to another as she sought her target. Several things dawned upon her in an instant: her target was nowhere on the trail below, and the creatures now whirling to face her were not the men with whom he traveled.

Moreover, the creatures were not even human.

There were six of them arrayed on the crumbling path, the nearest less than ten yards from her. They were clad entirely in tattered strips of cloth, and their black flesh shimmered dully in the meager starlight like unpolished obsidian. Bulging eyes and gaping mouths worked in soundless ferocity as the creatures gazed up at her.

Without hesitation they burst into frenzied motion, bounding and clawing their way up the trail. By reflex, she aimed at the one in the lead before she caught herself; she still had one of her three black arrows nocked, and they were far too valuable to waste on random assailants such as these. Cursing the lost seconds, she returned the deadly projectile to the quiver across her back, and, selecting another, she drew and fired.

The shaft slammed into the creature's chest, staggering it back a step from the sheer force of the blow. To her astonishment, however, it uttered no cry of pain, and instead surged forward with undiminished vigor. In a blur of motion, she sent three more arrows hissing through the air to find their marks. The head of the nearest creature snapped back at an angle no mortal man could survive, and when it hunched forward again a shaft had sprouted from its forehead to match the one in its chest. Its unblinking eyes found her again, and it lurched after her with arms outstretched. The one behind it pawed to get past its cohort on the narrow trail, feathered shafts projecting from both of its legs. The foul thing seemed unaffected, its wounded legs bearing its weight without slowing its progress in the least.

The huntress gave a sharp whistle back into the cave, and then stepped forward to the top of the trail. She set her jaw and took a tight, two-handed grip on the lower limb of her bow. As the first creature reached the crest, she swung the weapon in a vicious arc, hammering it from the path to tumble down the hillside, rolling and clawing for purchase.

She struck at the next figure in line, but it caught at the bow and she was forced to release it. It cast the bow aside and came for her again, and she whipped out her long hunting knife to hack aside its grasping arms. Unflinching beneath the razor-edged blade, the creature grabbed at her first, its crooked black fingers catching at her clothing as she danced back to remain out of reach. She licked out with the blade, and it fumbled for that as well, seeking to grasp the weapon with its bare hands and wrest it from her.

Two more reached the top of the trail and flung themselves at her with the same heedless abandon, and she was forced to leap back into the cave or be surrounded. Yet more of the black things crested the trail, and they closed in, relentless.

So intent were they upon their prey that even the thunder of hooves from within the cave did not distract them until the horse was upon them. Shien slammed into the gathered throng, sending several of the creatures sprawling. The mare lashed out with iron-shod hooves, and another assailant reeled back under the force of the blows. The huntress leapt to the saddle and dug her heels in. Together she and the mare plunged through the press of bodies. At speed, in the dark, the treacherous path might well be the death of them, but they would have to risk it to escape the clutches of these unnatural, undying black monstrosities.

They hit the loose gravel of the trail and began a stomach-lurching slide. Shien dropped her hindquarters and braced all four hooves as the huntress tried in vain to discern the ephemeral ribbon of the path against the darker hillside. A sudden weight crashed into her back, knocking the wind from her. A black arm encircled her neck like a collar of steel as reeking, tattered cloth filled her gasping mouth. She sought to reach her attacker with the hunting knife, raking with desperate strokes. Several strokes found their mark, but the creature made no sound in reply, and the arm encircling her neck did not loosen.

It tried to wrench her from the saddle, and she scrabbled at the saddle horn to keep her seat. Just as she began to slide, the mare lurched forward with a shriek. The huntress strained to peer downward. She saw more of the creatures wrapping themselves about the horse's legs, and in a split second the entire mass was pitching from the tail in a thrashing tangle of limbs.

The sloping, uneven ground and the night sky exchanged places, whirling together in a dizzying dance. The huntress was thrown free, and she screamed in pain as rocks and roots dug into her flesh and crushing weights came down atop her. Somehow she twisted violently in midair as her parasite shifted its grip, and she kicked free from it to tumble alone, end over end, down the hillside. She sprawled at last to a stop, wheezing and spitting blood from smashed lips.

When she raised her head, she saw that Shien still lived, for the moment at least. The mare was kicking and heaving, trying to roll to a standing position once more. Pinned beneath her glossy black bulk, the duller black of several crooked figures swaddled in cloth could be seen clawing at the ground, their unblinking eyes fixed upon the downed huntress.

She cast about for a weapon, but her knife and bow were both lost somewhere on the dark slope. She felt for her quiver, and found it gone. The creature on her back must have torn it away. Faint glimmers in the grass nearby marked where several of her arrows had come to a scattered rest. She crawled toward the nearest, groping as she went for a rock she could pry loose from the ground and use against her attackers. The instant her fingers closed around the missile, she knew it for one of her precious black arrows, and she groaned.

A grip like iron seized her ankle, and she rolled, lashing out with her boot to hammer kick after kick into the gaping creature. It came onward, undeterred, pawing and crawling its way over her like she was a rope to be climbed. Its face drew near to hers and the soulless wells of its eyes fixed upon hers, the mouth opening wide in some hideous, silent parody of mortal speech. An ebon fist drew back, trailing coils of tattered cloth.

She lunged forward with both hands and jammed the black arrow into the yawning mouth and up into the thing's brain.

With a savage flare of satisfaction tinged by regret at the waste, she bore witness to what a small fortune in gold could purchase from a master arcanist, and to the fate she had planned for her malevolent quarry. A crack of thunder split the air, and a brilliant flash of light stole her vision. A rush of heat blistered the skin of her hands and face, and the weight vanished from atop her.

Blinking away the colors popping before her eyes, she cast about and found the mangled remains of the black thing lying in a motionless pile several yards distant. Thick tendrils of noxious smoke rose from where its head had been but moments before.

Rapid footsteps intruded upon the ringing in her ears. She twisted toward the sound, trying to face her attackers, but heavy blows rained down upon her and she knew no more.

Amric reined in his bay gelding, peering into the distance where the flash of light had erupted and then faded just as abruptly.

"Did you see that?" he asked.

"Do you think me blind?" Syth grumbled. "Of course I saw it."

The thief sat astride Valkarr's restive blue dun, and if he scowled down at the horse in distaste, it was no worse than the spiteful glares the beast bestowed upon him in return. The others drew rein behind them, with Halthak and Valkarr riding double on the Half-Ork's chestnut mare and Bellimar on his placid, sturdy old nag.

"What in the heavens was that?" Halthak said.

"I have no idea," Amric replied with a shake of his head. "But it was no more than a few minutes up the road, very near the cave."

"An evoker's magic, from the sharp report," Bellimar said. "Though as to its purpose, I cannot say."

Amric was silent for a moment, looking into the darkness. When he spoke, his voice had become cold and resolute. "It lies in our path. I mean to investigate it."

Syth stared at him. "Do murderous lights hold some newfound fascination for you, after the Fount? Are you a moth, to be drawn so to the flame?"

The swordsman turned wintry grey eyes upon him. "I lost the trail of our missing friends at Stronghold," he said. "If fortune is so kind as to offer me a pointer back onto that trail, I'll not take the risk of circling wide around the sign."

"You would assume that everything is now a possible sign from the fates?" Syth demanded. "How can you pursue every strange occurrence in this land gone mad?"

"One at a time," Amric replied.

The thief threw up his hands in exasperation, then grabbed for the reins once again as the dun gelding shifted in a move that looked suspiciously like it was trying to shrug him out of the saddle.

"But you are correct, Syth," the warrior continued in a mild tone. "It could be dangerous, and perhaps it would be wiser for you to remain here."

Syth ground his teeth, eyes narrowed in an icy glare. "I'll not have it said I took the coward's route," he gritted. "I will be at your shoulder, if I can keep this useless mountain of horse flesh pointed in the right direction."

Amric chuckled and turned to Valkarr. The Sil'ath still looked gaunt and tired, but pushed himself stiffly upright to sit tall on the horse, his chin lifted.

"I know you wish to ride with us on this, my friend, but you have not yet regained your strength. I need you to stay with these two and keep them safe while you all follow at a short distance. Be ready, for as much as I would hate to lose time to a retreat or detour, it may prove necessary."

The Sil'ath sighed and nodded. With a curt nod to Bellimar and Halthak, Amric wheeled his bay and kicked it into a gallop. Behind him, amid a shower of muttered curses, he heard Syth's mount follow.

Minutes later, they slowed as they neared the location from which the burst of light had emanated. All seemed quiet, the only movement being the short scrub grasses of the foothills swaying under the hoary light of the stars. Amric's eyes picked out the winding trail leading up to the cave, and he was guiding his mount off the road and toward that narrow path when a sound further up the main road drew their attention. They cantered ahead and found the source. It was a riderless black horse, a glossy patch of ink against the night, giving a subdued cough and stamping its feet as it backed away from them. Amric studied the trembling animal, taking in the rolling white eyes and the froth of sweat on its coat. It had seen strenuous activity, and quite recently. He scanned about for the rider, but found no sign.

Then another sound drifted to them from ahead and north of the broad road: a muffled scream, almost lost to distance.

Amric spurred his mount to a gallop, leaning low over the bay's muscular neck. The gelding was somewhat tired from the long day of slow travel picking along the base of the rocky foothills bordering the forest, but given its first chance in many days to open up and race, the eager young animal seized the opportunity. Syth fell behind, bouncing awkwardly in the saddle and spewing a steady litany of blasphemous threats at his mount. Amric strained to pierce the gloom as he rode ahead, for he could not triangulate on the sounds over the clatter of his horse's hooves, and at last a flurry of movement north of the highway caught his eye.

At first he thought he was looking upon some many-legged beast, scurrying through the long, waving grasses where the foothills gave grudging way to gently rolling plains. As he stared, however, he realized it was a handful of the repulsive black things dressed in rags that had assaulted them in the forest. The source of the indignant cry became evident as well, for the creatures bore a thrashing captive among them. The group was clustered around their prize, running in unison, cleaving through the undulating sea of grass in headlong, rapid strides.

With a jerk of the reins, the warrior sent his horse leaping from the road. The creatures were fast, moving at the kind of unflagging dead run which a mortal man could not endure for long. All the same, they could not hope to match a fast steed.

As he closed the gap, one of his swords slid gleaming into his hand, and he knotted the reins in his other fist as he leaned from the saddle. He overtook them on a small, rolling rise, sweeping by in a thunderous cloud, and his blade sang in the night air. The rearmost creature pitched forward to the sward, its head bumping along the ground without it for several yards. Another fell with one of its legs shorn almost clean through.

The remaining monstrosities reacted with astonishing speed. The pair in the lead swerved away from the threat, while the one now at the rear of the entourage broke free of the pack to sprint after him. Amric steered his mount wide, outdistancing his pursuer and circling back toward those still fleeing with their hostage.

His bay gelding suddenly reared as something rose before them. It was the one he had injured, dragging its useless leg behind it as it skittered rapidly through the grasses on its remaining crooked limbs like some huge, hideous spider. It gathered and hurled itself at him in an impossible bound, and he lashed out in a vicious cut that sent the grimacing head spinning away into the night even as its limp body crashed into the horse. He dragged on the reins, bringing the terrified bay under control, and surged forward once more just as the creature chasing him tore through a curtain of waving green stalks mere yards behind him. He peered over his shoulder as the fiend pounded after him in untiring pursuit. A tall, bulky shape loomed behind it, and he almost shouted in fierce exultation when the creature suddenly vanished, ridden down from behind by Syth's blue dun. He did not see the thing rise again, and he hoped that iron-shod hooves had found its skull.

The remaining pair whirled to face them, dumping their burden to the ground where it rolled to an unceremonious halt, still writhing. Amric sprang from the saddle, and his other sword was in hand before his boots touched earth. Scant moments later, a gust of wind flattened the grasses around him, and Syth was at his shoulder.

"Aim for the heads," Amric said.

"I will aim for whatever I please," Syth retorted.

Amric grinned, and they leapt to meet their charging foes.

Afterward, Syth prodded with a metal-clad finger at the still form of one of the creatures as Amric wiped his swords clean. The things did not bleed, exactly, but instead left behind a clear, slimy, foul-smelling film on the blades that left him as eager to remove it from the metal as he was to avoid any unnecessary contact between it and his flesh.

"What manner of creature are they?" Syth asked as his lip curled in disgust.

"I do not know, but they seemed once again intent on seizing rather than slaying," Amric mused. "I wonder to what strange destination they were bearing their captured prey."

He gazed in the direction they had been headed, but to his knowledge nothing lay in that southern region for countless miles except rolling hills of prairie.

The thief rose to his feet with a lop-sided grin. "It seems to discover that, we had only to belay our interference for a time and follow them instead. Doubtless this poor fellow could have bided a while longer as we satisfied our curiosity, no?"

Amric studied the figure on the ground, bound tightly in coil upon coil of ragged cloth such that only a few glimpses of leathers and a dark cloak were visible. The captive still drew in deep, rasping breaths, but had otherwise grown still once the sounds of combat ceased.

"I rather think he would disagree with you on the point, Syth," Amric said. "But it is time to let him speak for himself."

He stepped forward, sheathing his swords and drawing his belt knife. "I am going to sever your bonds, friend," he said. "Be very still, if you value your flesh."

The figure froze, and Amric knelt down. The cloth parted beneath his blade and fell away from torso to thigh, and the warrior rose, stepping back. In an instant, slender hands made pale by the starlight were clawing at the remaining bonds, tearing and peeling.

Syth put voice to a realization that had dawned upon Amric as well. "That is no fellow," he breathed.

Those hands reached up and unwound the strips from about the head, and then swept back the hood of the cloak. Auburn hair tumbled free, and startling green eyes regarded them both from an oval face swollen with a myriad of cuts and abrasions. Amric saw a strange mixture of fear and anger pass through her expression as she looked past them to search the darkness beyond. When frantic gaze returned to the two of them, she sagged with relief and seemed to regain a measure of her confidence. The warrior frowned. It appeared that she had expected someone else, had been in fact braced for another attacker of some kind.

"Well?" she demanded. "Which one of you is going to help a lady to her feet?"

They rejoined the others on the road near the cave.

Amric let out a breath he had not even realized he was holding when he saw the three men astride their horses, with no further sign of the foul black creatures. Halthak held the reins of the quivering black mare, and was speaking soothing words to it in a low tone. As they neared, the huntress slid from her seat behind Amric on the bay gelding and gave a sharp whistle. The mare jerked the reins from the Half-Ork's hand with a toss of its head, and trotted to her.

"You are developing a way with horses, healer," Amric said with a laugh, as Halthak gave a rueful shake of the stung hand. "But the horse well knows its mistress."

He watched as the woman ran her hands over the horse and down each of its legs, checking for serious injuries. Amric noted that she kept her back to Halthak, Valkarr and Bellimar as she did this, and when she swung into the saddle a moment later, she kept her head low and looked out at them from under a tangle of tresses such that her features were almost entirely masked.

Amric cleared his throat. "The lady declined to give her name until we were all together, but she was an unwilling guest of the same black man-like creatures we encountered in the forest. Now, if I may introduce—"

The huntress, however, paid no heed to him whatsoever, and instead circled her horse wide around the group and left the road at a canter. She reached the trail leading up to the cave and dismounted, searching the hillside for something. Syth urged his horse forward after her, but Bellimar held up a hand and shook his head.

"Give her a moment, gentlemen," he said with a hint of a smile. "Introductions should resume shortly."

Syth exchanged a puzzled look with Amric, but held his position. For long minutes, the woman clambered over the hillside, thrashing about in the weeds in search of something, casting repeated glances over her shoulder toward the group.

Bellimar rode a few yards away from the others. He had his back to her as he sat relaxed in the saddle, scanning the countryside. At last she returned to her horse with a purposeful stride and rode toward them again. Amric saw that she now held a bow in one hand, and a quiver full of arrows was slung across her back. His eyes narrowed. She was guiding her mare with only her knees, so that both her hands were free. Valkarr nodded at him; he had noticed the same. Amric threw a hard warning look to Syth and then rode forward in a slow, non-threatening walk to meet her. The other men waited, expectant, as she approached. Bellimar guided his horse into a languid turn to face her, the same enigmatic smile playing across his features.

"Madam, I think there may be some misunderstanding—" Amric began.

His words died in midsentence, however, as the huntress suddenly stood tall in her stirrups. She raised the black arrow she had been holding along her thigh, nocked it to her bow, drew back and fired, all in a blinding flicker of practiced motion. Amric muttered a startled oath and jerked to one side, his sword ringing forth. But the shot flew well wide of him, and he realized it was not intended for him at all. He whirled to chart its course and saw Bellimar's pale hand flash up before his face. Vibrating in his clenched fist, its razor point inches from his left eye, was the black arrow.

Amric's mouth fell open. The old man had caught the bloody thing in mid-flight, without even changing expression! He spun back to the woman, only to find her with another black arrow drawn and aimed at

Bellimar, though this one she did not release. Amric knotted his fist on the reins and prepared to charge, but she swung the bow toward him.

"Stay back!" she shouted. "I will feather the first to move toward me."

"Nasty piece of work, this," Bellimar was saying, rolling the missile between bony fingers. "I think it might well have fulfilled its purpose. How did you come by it, my dear?"

The huntress did not respond, except to level the bow at the old man once more. Amric studied her eyes, her expression twisted with hatred, her slender frame shaking with suppressed rage. Seldom had he seen such naked animosity.

Anger of his own flared within him.

"You have a strange way of repaying a courtesy, woman," he snapped.

"And you, man, can be judged by the vile company you keep," she retorted with a sneer. "You travel with an ancient evil: Bellimar the Black, destroyer of nations, the Vampire King himself. I have to assume that every one of you is either under his control or just as dark-hearted as he."

Amric lifted an eyebrow. "You believe this old man to be the conquering sorcerer by the same name from untold centuries ago?"

The woman said nothing, the tip of her arrow tracking Bellimar even as her mare shifted back and forth with nervous steps. Amric opened his mouth to try again, but the old man interrupted with a sigh.

"Your words will not smooth this one over, swordsman. She speaks the truth."

Amric stiffened and turned to stare at him. Bellimar did not spare him a glance, however. His tight-lipped smile parted to bare gleaming teeth at the huntress.

"Greetings, Thalya," Bellimar said. "You are a long way from home."

CHAPTER 15

Thalya crouched within the sloping entrance of the cave, relaxed as a coiled spring.

Her back was to the stone wall, and one sun-browned hand was knotted in her black mare's dangling reins. Her other hand guided the tip of her broad-bladed hunting knife through the dirt caking the floor, making idle patterns which her eye did not follow. Instead her narrowed gaze pierced deeper into the cave, past the roiling haze of smoke that clung to the ceiling on its way to the night sky, to fix upon the men gathered below around a feeble campfire.

Her target sat among them, staring into the tiny remaining flicker of flame amid a bed of glowing embers, looking like nothing more than an ordinary, tired, silver-haired old man. She wondered if he was as vulnerable at the moment as he appeared, and she considered the bow and single black arrow that were meticulously positioned at her side. No, she admonished herself; he was merely goading her to make another attempt just as he was affecting the sad and weary expression he wore like a jester's painted mask. Moreover, he had kept the arrow he caught outside, and that left her with but one remaining that was capable of slaying the fiend. Another wasted shot would be her undoing, leaving her without the means to fulfill her mission as well as putting her at the mercy of the monster. She would have to bide her time, then. When she struck again, she would ensure he could not avoid it.

Thalya forced her eyes from Bellimar and let them rove over the others, disembodied faces floating in the gloom above the banked fire. She had to admit, these were not the dark, soulless men with which she had expected the fiend to surround himself. They seemed stricken by her words and awaiting an explanation, but she reminded herself that evil came in many packages, often wrapped in layer upon layer of deception.

Syth, one of her rescuers, turned to gaze up at her. He was a strange, scruffy fellow somehow wrapped in his own perpetual gust of wind, and unless she had lost her skill at reading such things, there was desire in his eyes when he looked upon her.

"Lass, are you certain you will not join us?" he called. "I can give you a hand down the slope, if you are still unsteady on your feet from your earlier ordeal."

"I have a fine view from here," she returned. She held up the hunting knife. "And I will be removing any hand—or other appendage—directed my way."

Syth let out a guffaw and settled back with a broad grin of admiration.

"Will you not at least reconsider the offer of our skilled friend Halthak here to heal your injuries, then?" he asked, indicating the quiet Half-Ork at his side.

Halthak raised his eyes to meet hers, their wide, childlike innocence incongruous amid a countenance that was so ugly as to be nearly deformed. In truth, she ached and stung all over from the earlier scuffle, but there was no way she would permit a cohort of the Black One to work his magic on her. No, she was in this cave against her better judgment and only long enough to hear what lies the fiend would spin; if these men knew not whom they harbored, perhaps they could be swayed to join her against the monster. She gave a sharp shake of her head, and the Half-Ork dropped his gaze.

Amric, the tall, powerfully built warrior with the storm-grey eyes who had been the other of her rescuers, cleared his throat and the others grew still. This one had a hard look about him, and yet his voice carried at once both the ring of command and a steady underlying current of compassion. It was clear he was the leader of this motley group, but she had yet to puzzle out why a creature such as the Vampire King would pretend to defer to him, even for a time.

"Bellimar," the warrior said. "As you urged, we have withheld all questions while we took shelter from the hazards of the open night. There can be little doubt that you have proven an invaluable companion on this dangerous road, but it is no longer possible to look past the lurking ghosts of your secrets. The time has come to have answers."

Bellimar said nothing for long moments, still staring into the meager campfire. Thalya fidgeted. She was eager to hear the monster's admission of guilt, but she refused to be the one to break the silence, and so she clenched her fist over the hilt of her knife and waited. When at last the old man spoke, it was in a whisper that somehow carried throughout the cave with startling clarity, like a chill breeze through a darkened crypt.

"I will save you the trouble of asking outright," he said. "The lady named me truly. I am indeed Bellimar the Destroyer, the man whose rise and fall I recounted to you a mere handful of nights ago in this very cave. I am the conqueror whose vile deeds were scrawled in the blood of innocents on the dim-shrouded pages of history now long lost to this world, and I am guilty of countless more offenses than were ever chronicled."

His eyes rose from the fire, but drank its flame. Gone was the old man, weary and resigned, shed and discarded like a dried husk. In his place was a man of fierce, primal intensity, his lean face set in ruthless lines and his eyes burning with blood-red power. His voice crowded out the other sounds of the night until even the echo of his words from the stark ribcage of the cave retreated in dread. Thalya felt a chill along her spine. It was as if he were whispering at her very shoulder, his bloodless lips at her ear.

"Know, friends, that in my time I have crushed entire nations under my heel. I turned mortal men, good men as well as bad, into unfeeling killing machines. I raised armies of the dead when there were not enough mortal men at hand to corrupt, and I commanded things of deepest shadow. The world, a more primitive place so many centuries ago, trembled at my very tread. I grasped for power, eternally more power, and dark forces granted my every excess. There was a terrible price to be paid, but I paid it then with nary a second thought. I suspect I have been further over that black precipice than any man in the history of this world, and it embraced me as its own. I became the Lord of Night, the Vampire King, and not even the combined might of nations could stop what I had built, what I had become. I had cheated mortality, abandoned my humanity. Time no longer held sway over me, and nothing remained with the power to stop my undying reign."

He paused, glancing around at their pale faces. "Nothing in this world, at least."

"And yet you *were* struck down, by some force," interjected the Sil'ath, Valkarr. Thalya suppressed a start. Until his words, spoken in a coarse, guttural tone that lingered on the sibilant sounds, she had all but forgotten the presence of the reptilian warrior.

"So I was," Bellimar admitted. "I was struck down at the height of my power, even as I was on the verge of plunging the world into an age of shadow such as it had never before seen. I was struck down by a gathering of forces from beyond that dwarfed even my own strength."

"So the tales were true?" Amric asked, incredulous. "The gods themselves intervened in the mortal arena?"

The old man barked a bitter laugh. "First, tell me your definition of a god. What are the gods, anyway, except beings above us in power, capable of demanding obeisance and inflicting their will upon lesser creatures such as ourselves? By that standard, yes, it was most certainly the gods who struck me down. Whatever you call these beings, they appeared to me as men and women of great power, and were not content to defeat or even destroy me. Instead, they changed me in ways I still do not understand, and then cast me out into the world, even as they dispersed the dark forces I had assembled around me."

"I do not understand," Halthak said. "What did you become after your fall? What are you now?"

Bellimar swung his gaze to the Half-Ork. "In many ways, I am what I was before, an affront to nature by my very existence," he said. "I am an ancient vampire."

Halthak started back from the man as if struck.

"Whatever is the matter, healer?" Bellimar asked, baring his teeth in a blood-chilling smile. "Are you thinking, perhaps, of all those nights I feigned sleep whilst listening to the languid pulse within your senseless, slumbering form only a few tantalizing feet away? Ah, but listen to your heart race now!"

In what Thalya would have deemed a physical impossibility, the Half-Ork whitened even further.

"Enough, Bellimar!" Amric said, slicing his hand through the air in a curt motion. "Leave him be."

Bellimar swung his gaze over to the man.

"And you, warrior," he hissed. "Your pulse remains strong and steady, scarcely rising under threat of violence even though I can smell your fear. A testament to the steel of your nerves, no doubt, but is your composure misplaced? Aura or no, I suspect your blood carries hidden power."

Amric met the vampire's fevered stare, unmoving, unrelenting. "If you were merely some blood-mad fiend," he said, "you have had ample opportunity to strike. Instead you saved us in Stronghold, and you gave me your word you were our ally."

Thalya snorted, but Amric ignored her and pressed on. "What game are you playing at, Bellimar?"

The old man met his iron gaze for a long moment, and then sagged back, looking suddenly aged and weary once more.

"I am no longer certain," he said at last in a low, brooding tone. "At first it was the drive for knowledge. I sought to end this new curse, to understand how I had been changed, to unravel the riddle of what they had done to me so that I could return to my former glory. I realized the obvious from the beginning, that I had somehow been stripped of my sorcerous powers; they eluded my will even though I retained the full extent of my arcane knowledge itself.

"The more subtle aspects of my transformation soon began to settle upon me, however. I still required the blood and life force of living creatures as sustenance, and the infernal craving was with me always, but I could no longer bear to take sentient life as I had so casually done before. In fact, I felt nausea, revulsion and pain whenever I contemplated doing harm to another creature. And so I was consigned to feeding on game and lesser creatures like some depraved scavenger, and even that only in the extremes of my hunger, when necessary to sustain my very existence. Perhaps in exchange, I could once more endure the light of the sun and other things considered anathema to my kind. I felt their searing kiss on my flesh, and yet somehow I was not destroyed. I had been thrust into some half existence, and thus it has been for all these centuries, as I pay penance for my sins."

"Are you living or dead, then?" Syth asked in a hushed voice.

"What does it mean to be living?" Bellimar replied with a shrug. "I have free will, and so by that definition—"

"No more word games," Amric interrupted. "Answer the question or be gone from here."

"I do not mean to equivocate, swordsman," Bellimar said with a sad smile. "In truth, I do not know the answer. I have been altered in ways beyond my understanding, and I suspect I am either none or all of those things at this point. My aura was altered in some way every bit as fundamental as when I passed from mortal life and became a vampire. By strict definition, I am not living, dead or undead now. And since I have been each of them at one time or another, I may be in a unique position to know. No, I am in a purgatory all my own."

He lapsed into silence, and the shadows cast by the sinking flames writhed along the deep lines of his face. When he spoke again, his voice was lower yet, almost inaudible. "I now feel like my quest for this knowledge is—has always been—the final spasm of a dead man, the twitch of limbs that do not realize the spirit has already left the body. I am a hollow shell pursuing a remembered impulse, when the motivation for it is long lost. I no longer know if I seek the knowledge in order to gain release from my constraints, as I once did, or to prevent an accidental reversion to my former self. Perhaps I seek the knowledge simply to put an end to my wretched existence, once and for all."

Thalya scowled and reached out to brush her fingertips against the black arrow. If he truly desired an end to his existence, she was more than ready to assist. As if reading her mind, Bellimar glanced toward her. The firelight performed a lurid dance in his eyes as he regarded her for an instant with an unreadable expression. Then his gaze slid away.

"Your interest in the unusual auras of others," Amric was saying. "You hope to find in them the key to your own."

The old man gave an approving nod. "Very good, swordsman."

"And your extensive knowledge of them comes in part from your years feeding upon the life force of others, as the monster you were," the warrior continued in a cold tone.

Bellimar flinched as if struck, and gave an almost imperceptible nod. "Regrettably true as well," he whispered.

"I have seen your face become flushed when you are in the presence of spilt blood," Amric pressed. "The farm, the bloodbeasts, the Wyrgens. I mistook it for an aversion to violence, but now I realize it was the strain of controlling your hunger. And what of the night you disappeared, after the fight with the bloodbeasts in the forest?"

Bellimar looked away. "There was so much blood, everywhere. So much of your blood, and Valkarr's, and it had been so long since I fed...." He raised his eyes, lifted his chin. "I did not trust myself around you in your weakened state. My hunger threatened to overwhelm my imposed constraints and my willpower both, and I was left with only one course."

Amric studied him over the campfire. "Did you feed that night?"

"No, there was no suitable prey to be found nearby, and I was loath to range beyond earshot for fear of more creatures finding you while I was gone. The forest is tainted to such a degree now that few natural creatures remain within its confines, I fear. I merely kept my distance until I could regain my composure."

The warrior rubbed at the stubble on his chin, seeming to mull this over. "And yet you returned, to later be exposed to more bloodshed within the fortress of the Wyrgens."

Bellimar sighed. "You must understand that there are three primary factors that drive my hunger," he said, raising his hand and beginning to tick off points on his slender fingers. "First, exposure to mortal blood or to a particularly tantalizing life force. Second, heightened emotion such as being in the frenzy of combat or other life-threatening situations. And third, intense physical exertion such as tapping into the unnatural strength I possess as a centuries-old vampire."

His hand fell to his lap again, and he shook his head with a rueful smile. "It has been no easy thing, warrior, being in your company."

Amric leaned back, frowning. "I confess that I do not know what to make of you, Bellimar," he said. "It would seem that you put our lives at risk by your very presence, yet your knowledge has been invaluable and you have given no evidence of wrongdoing in our presence. I am left to wonder if you are truly friend or foe, and further, if you can be trusted to know which, yourself."

"Perhaps the results are the same," she snarled, causing the men around the fire to glance up toward her. "His enmity is boundless, as we know from the tales. Lesser known by history is how his purported friendship is no prize to covet either. Is that not true, foul one?"

"Ah good, we come to it at last," Bellimar said. "How fares your father, dear girl? You were but a wisp of a child when last I saw you, in that light green cotton dress of yours."

Thalya reeled as his words churned to the surface a flood of images from a more joyful time she had thought long and well buried. She clenched her fists until the knuckles whitened to conceal the sudden trembling. When she was certain she could speak without tremors in her voice as well, she said, "He died years ago, demon."

The vampire studied her, his eyes searching her enraged expression. "He was a good man, Thalya. I am greatly aggrieved to hear of his death."

"Empty words," she said as she turned her head and spat in the dust of the cave floor. "You know nothing of grief, or loss, or guilt. To you, he was just another pawn to be used and then discarded, and his death lies at your feet just as surely as if you had slain him with your own hand."

Bellimar gave a slow shake of his head. "I can see that my familiarity with this tale is incomplete, but I will begin it nonetheless, with the hope that the young lady will supply the ending."

The huntress said nothing in reply, maintaining a level glare at the old man. Bellimar sighed and began speaking.

"Over twenty years ago, my wanderings brought me once more to the beautiful city of Hyaxus. I trusted that enough time had passed since my last disastrous visit there, and no one would recognize my face, unaltered by the years as it was. One can only lose oneself in the remote corners of the world for so long, after all, before the need to return to true civilization becomes unbearable. It was in that elegant city's academy that I met

Thalya's father, a jovial fellow with an honest face by the name of Drothis. He was a devoted scholar of the arcane and a middling talent at alchemy, as well as being a recent widower with an infant daughter."

"He was a renowned professor of the academy," Thalya gritted, "and a *gifted* alchemist."

"He had an unusual aura," Bellimar said, continuing as if she had not spoken. "Erratic, unsteady, somehow incomplete. Having learned of the recent loss of his beloved wife, I had a clinical curiosity as to whether profound grief and depression might be the cause of his flawed essence. My studies were hampered, of course, by my not having had the chance to observe him before the loss."

"How dare you speak of my father thus?" Thalya demanded, rising to her feet. Behind her, Shien shifted and gave a nervous whicker. "He was a good man, not some specimen in a jar!"

The old man favored her with a look of mild reproach. "I have already admitted that he was a good man, Thalya, but these are my memories, given forth unembellished. It may not be flattering to you or to me, but these were my initial motivations for making your father's acquaintance. Now, please sit down and lower your voice, as the countryside out there is veritably crawling with things that would like nothing more than to find so many beating hearts trapped in this small cavern."

Thalya paled, throwing a glance over her shoulder and out into the darkness. She knew his words to be true, for in the days of lying in wait for the return of her prey she had witnessed a multitude of things skulking through the night, misshapen things that turned her flesh to ice. Always she had been able to give them a wide berth, at least until earlier that night when she stumbled across the strange black man-creatures on the trail outside. No, it would be foolhardy in the extreme to remain out in the open night, or to draw its denizens to them now. And since she refused to allow her target from her sight now that she had tracked him down, she was forced to share this cave with him until she determined how he could be slain.

It was some small consolation, she had to admit, that she found herself hungering for every new word of her father, even if the vampire's words stirred as much rage as recollection. She patted Shien's neck and sank to her haunches with a scathing glare at her nemesis.

"Drothis and I became friends," Bellimar continued. "We shared some common interests in the field of arcane studies, and I presented myself as a traveling scholar, though I was always careful to mask the true extent of the knowledge I had gained over many centuries as well as through my, shall we say, former preoccupation with certain subject matters."

He paused, staring into the fire. "I stayed too long," he said. "I had made the same mistake in the past, and so I knew better, but I had come to value his company. For Drothis, I seemed to fill some of the companionship void that his wife, a highly intelligent scholar herself and a shrewd foil for his theories, had left behind. As the years passed, I knew I should move on, for the peculiarities of my nature cannot be concealed forever. But I hesitated to leave him alone and bereft again. I had become convinced that his broken nature would never fully mend after the loss of his bosom companion, and somehow my presence soothed his pain for a time.

"I grew too comfortable, or perhaps the buried part of me that knew I had overstayed was trying to force my hand. Whatever the reason, I began to make mistakes. I let slip references to things from the distant past, and glimpses of my dark side peeked through cracks in my carefully constructed façade. Mayhap I meant to scare him away, but my actions seemed to have no effect. I should have known better. Drothis was hardly a fool, and his intellectual curiosity was ever more ravenous than one would know from his affable outward manner."

Bellimar lapsed into silence then, and as the seconds slid by it seemed he had entirely forgotten his audience. At last, Thalya spoke into the stillness.

"The night of the attack," she prodded.

The old man glanced up from his reverie, meeting her narrowed gaze and flashing a wan smile in return. "Indeed so," he said. "Thank you, dear girl. Everything changed that night. We were returning home from the academy, having stayed long past nightfall debating some dusty topic or another in its great library. Drothis was fretting about how the family hosting young Thalya here would be angry at the late hour, when we both knew this to be false, since she was all but a member of their family by that point. A band of brigands set upon us, emboldened by the late hour and the richness of our attire. They did not even demand the handful of coins in our purses, for they made clear their intent to leave no wagging tongues behind that might betray them to the city authorities. Corpses seldom make objections to parting with their possessions, after all."

Bellimar sighed, shaking his head. "Even these murderous cutpurses, more akin to rats than true men, I could not bring myself to harm. Of course, they did not know that. It was an easy thing indeed to part for a few moments the mortal veil I maintain about myself, to bring forth the shade of my former self, to give these cutthroats a glimpse of the fearsome sorcerous warlord who had scattered legions of terror-stricken foes before him on one bloody battlefield after another. For a fleeting few seconds, my dark presence expanded to fill that deserted street in Hyaxus, sucking the very light from the torches in their quavering sconces, and I was once again Bellimar the Black, the Vampire King of old. The brigands screamed and scattered as if a host of demons were nipping at their heels, and though I quickly shrank back into myself, I knew I had gone too far. I had tried to shield Drothis from it, to direct it only toward our attackers, but I had failed; he had seen my past, my other side, and he stared at me, open-mouthed and dumbstruck.

"I tried to explain it away, offering up feeble stories of possessing a modest talent at spinning illusions even though I had never displayed such ability to him before. He believed none of it. He confronted me right then and there in the street with an astonishing amount of evidence he had collected against me over time, and though he had been astute enough to piece together much of the truth about me, he had not wished to credit the possibility that his friend could be such a monster. He even deduced my real name, as I had labeled myself with a derivative form of it, in my boundless arrogance. Unwilling to insult him with further lies, I admitted to it all.

"He became furious, no doubt due in large part to my deceit, but also because his reasoning had already taken him in directions I had not foreseen. He accused me of befriending him to gain unfettered access to the academy and its resources, which was, of course, initially quite true. He further believed that I had arranged that access for some nefarious purpose, that I was planning some new effort to shroud the world in darkness as I had come so close to doing before. He was incensed and no longer heard my protestations. He flung himself at me, soft and kind at heart though he was, and I vanished into the night rather than see him injured. I was gone from Hyaxus by the morn, and have never returned."

Bellimar fell silent once more, and his last words hung quivering in the air like strained notes. The campfire sputtered, casting a strobing, fitful glow across the faces of the men seated around it. Thalya sat frozen, stunned and lost in her thoughts. Damn the fiend, but he sounded so bloody sincere! She still managed a venomous glare at him, but inwardly it felt as if he had stolen the very breath from her chest.

"Thalya," Bellimar prompted gently. "I would hear the rest of your father's tale now."

The huntress took a steadying breath and began speaking, her voice thin at first but gaining heat as the words tumbled out, one atop the other.

"My father would brook no discussion of that night. He would only say that you were gone, and that we were well rid of you. He became obsessed with new research, neglecting his obligations at the academy and locking himself away for days on end. Sometimes he was away for months at a time as well, traveling to some remote corner of the lands to meet with obscure experts. About what, he would not say at first. Only when the heads of the academy threatened to cast him out for dereliction of duty did he reveal what he had discovered.

"He believed he had borne witness to the return of a great evil, and he felt compelled to take action against its rise. He said that he had foreseen the world being swallowed by darkness, and that the end of all we know would be accompanied by the return of the ancient conqueror, Bellimar the Unholy. Further, he claimed that the kindly old man that had wormed his way into our family's trust was no less than the bloodthirsty tyrant himself. He was ridiculed for his statements, and his fervor to warn others was dismissed as the ravings of a madman. My father would not be swayed from his convictions, however. In the end, he was cast out of the academy and branded a lunatic. He left the city, taking me with him, and we withdrew from all we had known."

Thalya stared at the old man across the cave. "My young life became a living hell, demon. My father was convinced that I must be prepared for war, for whatever cataclysm was to come. If he were to fail in his mission to find and destroy you, I was to carry out this all-important task. He impressed upon me the consequences our world would suffer if we failed in this. We were always on the move, never remaining anywhere long enough to put down roots, always seeking signs of your passage. We learned the use of weapons, and the bow in particular. Picture it, devil: we trained endlessly, a little girl and a man who should have remained a scholar, so that we would have the skill to slay the monster when our chance came. Years passed as we continued this nomadic existence, and I became far more acquainted with the harsher ways of this world than I would wish on anyone.

"My father grew frustrated, despairing, for he had long lost the trail. He withered under the long years of fear, obsession and self-imposed isolation. His health finally failed such that we could no longer travel freely, and we were forced to settle into a village near Velnium that boasted all the charm of a cesspool. I had begun to think it was over, that despite my unflagging faith in him he was after all just a deluded old man obsessed with nothing more than feverish visions and vaporous fears.

"Then word came to us of the corruption of the land's magic to the north, of a desolate wasteland spreading to engulf the lush plains at the foot of the Hoarfang mountain range, of dark and twisted creatures spilling from the forest at night to prey on the countryside. My father was convinced this was the inception of the dark vision he had feared for so long, and he was certain that the Vampire King was at the black heart of it all."

The huntress paused, her gaze locked to Bellimar's with an expectant air, as if awaiting a confession. The old man sat as still as a marble statue, offering nothing in return.

"My father was too frail to continue his quest, demon," she said. "He sickened and died in that miserable village. Grief-stricken and alone, I came north. I owed him that much more at least. I was skeptical that I would find anything to support his predictions, but much to my amazement I discovered that you had indeed been lurking about Keldrin's Landing for some time, and I had only just missed your departure. And here I find you, run to ground at last, having aged not a day in twenty years."

Thalya rose slowly to her feet, her recurve bow in one hand and the black arrow in the other.

"Bellimar," she intoned. "I hold you responsible for the death of my father. You poisoned his soul back in Hyaxus, though it may have taken twenty years to claim him. You took my life from me as well on that same night. And I accuse you now of all that he foresaw, of being at the root of the upheaval which threatens to destroy our world."

The other men stared at the vampire, their expressions ranging from calculating to stricken as they waited for his response. Bellimar, for his part, did not permit his gaze to waver from the huntress.

"I accept your accusations on all points but the last one," Bellimar said in a solemn tone. "I now hold myself responsible for the downfall and demise of Drothis, even as you do. I conceal my nature in part because exposing it never leads to anything but fear and suffering in others. Whatever remains of my soul is blighted by your father's death, though I suspect it can be blackened no further. I deny, however, being the cause of the spreading corruption. I am tempted to admit to involvement, if only to honor your father and give you the closure you seek, but I cannot do this. I have enough sins for which I must atone without laying false claim to others."

Thalya eyed him, her face a frozen mask as she rolled the arrow back and forth between her fingertips.

"No one can fault you if you choose to fire that arrow," Bellimar said. "But it appears to be your last, and understand that I am not prepared to perish in that fashion."

The huntress said nothing. The glow from the bed of coals glinted from the curved blades of the arrowhead as it spun in her hand. Amric rose to his feet in a swift, lithe motion and stepped between them.

"Enough!" he commanded. "We have heard from both of you. Now, if you wish to slay each other, depart the cave first so that the rest of us can get some sleep."

"I'll not be sharing a camp with this devil," Thalya growled.

"You cannot survive out there," Syth objected.

Bellimar flowed to his feet like a long, slender shadow cast against the stone wall. "She will not have to," he said. "I am long overdue to feed, and this is an opportune time to find game, away from both the corruption of the forest and the sweaty confines of the city. If you will step aside and let me pass, dear girl, I will depart. If Amric wishes to send me away for good when I return in the morning, I will accept his judgment."

Amric turned to face him, but the old man shook his head. "Do not fear for me, warrior," he said with a tight-lipped smile. "The night has ever been my element. I will be safe enough in its embrace."

Thalya guided her mare down the sloping floor to where the cave widened enough to permit the vampire's passage at greater than arm's length away. Her emerald eyes followed him warily until he glided from the cave and disappeared into the yawning darkness beyond. Ignoring the other men, Thalya left Shien with the other horses at the back of the cavern and stalked back to the entrance, where she slid to a seat against the rock wall with bow in hand and black arrow nocked. Only then did she address them, without a backward glance, as she stared out into the night.

"The first watch is mine."

Thalya awoke with a start as a chill breeze played across her cheek, and her hand tightened convulsively on her bow. Her frantic eyes raked the darkness beyond the mouth of the cave, and then darted to the deeper blackness of the cave's interior. Outside, nothing moved except the lazy, star-stroked grasses on the hillside, waving in the capricious wind. Inside, nothing stirred either, and her straining ears picked out the soft, rhythmic breathing of the men sleeping against the larger humming backdrop of the night. Her fingertips brushed the fletching of the arrow, still resting at the string of her bow, and the cool press of the stone at her back brought her comfort.

Her momentary waking panic gave way to relief, which then evaporated before the advancing heat of her anger. What a fool she was to have dozed off, she chided herself savagely. The night was swarming with dangers, her vile nemesis foremost among them, and here she was napping like a babe in arms, as if she could afford to be without a care. That she was worn down from her days and nights of constant, solitary vigilance in the midst of a hostile countryside was little excuse; her foe could exercise the cold, calculating patience of the immortal killing machine that he was, and so she simply could not make such mistakes.

The huntress cast another swift glance around, assuring herself that nothing approached the cave. She laid her bow across her legs and made to set the arrow aside on the ground so that she could rub her eyes to force herself further awake. Suddenly she froze in mid-motion, the blood congealing in her veins.

Lying neatly beside her leg on the rocky ground was the other of her black arrows, identical to the one in her hand.

The first of her priceless enchanted missiles had been destroyed in slaying one of the foul man-like creatures which had attacked her at dusk. The last of the three was still in her possession. This, then, was the one she had fired at Bellimar, which he had caught and kept.

She lifted the arrow and inspected it closely in the dim light. There was no trick that she could see; the fiend had returned the arrow undamaged, leaving her once again with two chances to slay him. She grimaced as she pondered the implications. The monster had slipped into the cave while she dozed, swift and soundless, and had come within inches of her to set the shaft at her side. Had he wished her dead, he could have torn out her throat with ease and been lost again to the darkness before her gurgling cry could bring the others running. Instead, he had restored a deadly weapon capable of ending his existence to someone who wished exactly that, though for what reason she could not begin to fathom. Was it a show of confidence, meant to intimidate her, indicating that he would swat aside any future attack as contemptuously as he had her first? Or did he truly wish to die?

Thalya recognized her fatigue and knew she should get someone to relieve her and take the next watch, but sleep was suddenly far from her thoughts. She made certain her quiver remained within reach, leaning against the cave wall beside her, and then she settled back as well and gazed out into the darkness. All around her the night stole onward in a hushed whisper as life struggled to endure beneath the spreading mantle of death.

The first breach of the mighty city wall surrounding Keldrin's Landing came that night.

In the somber hours preceding the dawn, the cry rang out even as the city was preparing to release the collective breath it had held throughout the night. The wall-walk guards, having raised the initial alarm, watched in stunned silence as a seething wave of motion swept toward the city from the east. What had appeared at a distance to be a vast ripple of vegetation before a forceful wind soon resolved into something much more sinister: an advancing tide of dark, twisted creatures clawing their way over and past each other in their eagerness to reach the city and its people.

Huge, bulky things drew themselves up from the very ground and shambled forward amid the smaller forms, scattering them with spiteful blows when they got underfoot. Long, sinuous shapes carved through the mass, preying indiscriminately on the smaller spiked creatures even as the entire heaving mass crashed toward Keldrin's Landing.

City guards gathered at the eastern gate, their faces and knuckles white as they clutched shaking swords, spears and halberds. The heavy gate doors stood closed and barred. These days, after the sun fell, they parted only to permit the occasional caravan or group of travelers bold enough—or foolish enough—to brave the landscape at night. In recent days, rumors had spread with greater and greater frequency from the guards patrolling the city wall. There were tales of strange things sighted beyond, sometimes approaching the wall to scrabble at its surface and shriek in outrage, or to gaze upward at the guards in hateful silence. There were also rumors of wall-walk guards and gate watchmen vanishing or being slain in gruesome fashion, but most people dismissed all these stories as fear-mongering, at least in the comforting warmth of the morning light.

Even if a portion of the tales were true, others reasoned, the perimeter of Keldrin's Landing had been built to withstand a siege. What was there to fear?

There was no denying the approaching horde or its numbers, however, and now even the towering gate doors looked vulnerable. City guards with longbows raced to the wall-walk, sending volley after volley into the charging mass as it drew near, but they were unprepared for such a sudden onslaught and their initial numbers were few.

The horde struck the eastern wall with shrieking fury, clawing for purchase against the sheer wall and hammering into the gate. The great gates shuddered under the weight, and the captain of the guard, a square-jawed man named Borric, started at the sound. He knew the gates would have splintered under that first assault had the force been organized enough to concentrate on that point alone rather than spreading across the entire wall in haphazard fashion.

He raised his sword above his head and bellowed, drawing the eyes of his dumbfounded men to him. Borric shouted orders, shoving and cuffing the frozen men nearest him to get them moving. In a widening circle from his center, the guards sprang into action. Men carried forth huge timbers at a run, bracing the creaking gate doors. Barrels of oil arrived by cart and were swiftly unloaded beneath the gateway portico. Additional archers raced up the stairs to the crest of the wall, while those inside the courtyard below formed defensive squares that could move quickly as a unit in case the wall was breached at any point.

Atop the wall, longbows and crossbows thrummed in a frantic, disjointed symphony. Huge, heavy forms battered at the base of the wall, while the smaller spiked creatures swarmed over and around them to climb the wall like spiders. Blazing yellow eyes glared up at the guards as the creatures sank long, tapered talons into the stone and wormed their way upward. Their grip seemed precarious on the smooth stone, however, and a direct hit with arrow or bolt usually proved sufficient to dislodge one, even if it did not kill it outright. But the archers were few while the spiked creatures were many, and the attackers came onward with chilling determination.

In the courtyard, the gates shuddered under a steady rain of titanic blows. Captain Borric shook his head in disbelief. Stout hardwood doors as thick as a man's arm was long, bound by iron, and still they threatened to fracture. He ordered his men back from the gate's outer arch and directed them to lower the portcullis recessed in the inner arch. A massive curtain of iron bars, it may not hold when the doors had not, but it was another line of defense against which the attackers would have to hurl themselves.

As the portcullis rumbled down, a great splinter of the wood door shot into the courtyard, leaving a gaping hole through which the starry night sky beyond could be seen. A face out of nightmare filled the gap, leering through at the men behind a long muzzle that bristled with crooked fangs. The guards gasped and fell back, raising their weapons. The thing shot through the hole in the door, wriggling and undulating its way past the narrow aperture and under the descending portcullis like some great, hideous eel. Its legless mass struck the flagstones with a slap, and in a flash it was among the men. It thrashed about, its flailing bulk sending several men sprawling, and then it lunged forward like a striking snake and one of the men disappeared into its gaping maw. The hapless man's scream was cut horribly short as the jagged jaws snapped shut, and the creature whirled and tucked its head back into its coils, gliding and flexing in some rapidly spinning complex knot formed of its own sinuous body.

The guards rushed forward, hacking and stabbing at the creature, and it keened in pain and fury. Whipping free of the knot it had formed, it lunged in a new direction, sliding out from under the sharp blades. Another guard vanished into its gullet, and again the vile creature convulsed into its eye-baffling knot of twisting flesh. The remaining guards converged on it with a vengeance, and in moments the creature sagged quivering to the ground beneath their attack before it could claim another victim.

High above, the spiked creatures clawed their way over the crenellations to drop among the guards like drops of ink spattering to the floor. More and more archers were forced to cast aside their bows and draw the swords at their hips to defend themselves against the slavering fiends. In turn, without the hail of missiles to suppress their advance, more and more of the bristling shadows worked their methodical way up the sheer outer surface of the wall. The men drew together into defensive islands against the encircling tide, fighting almost back to back as the creatures slunk toward them, shaking the glistening spikes on their bodies in an eerie, rattling chorus.

At the gates, huge misshapen claws tore at the ragged edges of the holes in the doors, widening them one cracking shard of wood at a time. The smaller spiked creatures poured through the fissures, crawling down the door and along the walls of the arch, their amber gazes fixed upon the men clustered beyond the iron grating.

Borric shouted an order, and his men fired hammer-nosed arrows into the barrels of oil, shattering the plank sides and spilling their viscous contents upon the flagstones just inside the door. Another shout, and several torches spun in unison between the bars of the portcullis. The oil ignited with a roar, and the resulting wall of flames licked hungrily skyward. A number of the spiked creatures were engulfed in the sudden blaze. They perished, shrieking and thrashing. The rest shrieked in frustration and clawed their way back through the gaps in the gateway doors, disappearing out into the night.

Captain Borric smiled in grim satisfaction. He ordered his men into position for the next wave that would likely burst the battered doors asunder. All together they waited with eyes wide and weapons clenched in fists slicked with sweat, but the next assault never came. The towering doors of the gate no longer shuddered under dread impact from outside.

Suspicious of the abrupt stillness, Borric tilted his head upward. The sky was beginning its slow brightening with the coming morn. He heard the faint shouts of the men high atop the wall, and he could see them waving down to him and pointing into the distance, outside the city. The enemy horde had retreated, fading back from the city as suddenly as it had come. By the time slow, pink fingers of light were reaching across the heavens, the twisted creatures had all disappeared like wraiths into the pre-dawn gloom. All that remained to give testimony to the brief, fierce struggle that had transpired were the scorched and ravaged doors of the eastern gate and the scattered bodies of the slain from both sides.

The men of the city guard gave a weary shout of victory, but their captain did not join in the cheer. Borric looked about and saw only the vestiges of an attack by an unknown, implacable enemy turned aside more by the looming approach of day than by the efforts of his men. Keldrin's Landing would require a great deal of preparation if it was to withstand the next such assault, and nightfall would be on the heels of the coming day all too soon.

CHAPTER **16**

Amric drew rein before the eastern gate of Keldrin's Landing and studied the flurry of activity taking place there beneath the damaged archway. He took in the scorched and blackened stone, the shattered remnants of the great ironbound doors, and the deep, raking marks that scored the length of the massive city wall. A veritable legion of sappers scrambled here and there under the bellowed direction of a stout, red-faced man who must have been the combat engineer in charge.

With a practiced eye, Amric assessed the fortifications the men were constructing: rows of outward-facing spikes jutting from the ground, deadweight drops suspended in the archway, staggered trenches carved through the paving and waiting to be filled by the precisely placed barrels of oil, an archer's wall in the courtyard beyond.

The city had suffered a concerted attack, and was preparing for war. From the frantic pace of the sappers, they expected the next assault to come at any time. Amric noted the way the setting sun ahead painted the top of the city wall a burnished red-gold hue, and he decided they might have good reason indeed to make haste. He wheeled his bay gelding about to face the others. Valkarr and Syth looked upon the preparations with stony expressions, comprehension plain upon their features. Halthak's eyes were wide, and he divided his attention between the gate and the road that stretched out behind them, winding like a ribbon over the rolling hills as the deepening dusk gnawed steadily at its distant end. Bellimar sat his old nag with his usual composure, but his eyes devoured every detail as they approached.

Few words had been exchanged that morning when the party emerged from the cave with the horses and found the old man standing in the road, his cloak drawn tight around him. Amric had met the vampire's gaze and held it for a long moment, waiting until he was certain that Bellimar read the warning and the promise contained therein. When understanding passed between them, Amric handed him the reins to his sway-backed mare and they both mounted without another word.

The warrior had elected not to comment on the fact that Bellimar's silver hair was now streaked with dark grey, and some of the fine wrinkles on his ancient visage had faded over the course of the night. He preferred not to dwell overlong on the implications such changes raised for how Bellimar had passed the hours alone until morning.

Thalya sat with a stiff back upon her glossy black mare. She looked as if she had swallowed that broad-bladed hunting knife of hers sideways, an expression she had worn since Bellimar rejoined them in the morn. Her narrowed eyes never strayed far from the man who, for his part, affected not to notice her icy glares.

"Valkarr, come with me," Amric said. "The rest of you, wait here."

The two warriors rode to the gate, keeping to an unhurried pace. Guards watched every step of their approach, hands resting on weapons and arrows nocked to bows. Amric smiled grimly to himself. Gone was the blithe indifference among the city's forces, replaced by a much more vigilant mien. Two soldiers strode out to meet them, and Amric hailed the men as they drew near.

"This gate is closed to travelers," shouted one of the men, a tall, bearded fellow with a barrel chest. "You and your party will have to circle around to the southern gate."

His companion, a lean, hawk-faced man with a scar running from forehead to chin, eyed the newcomers but said nothing.

"What happened here?" Amric asked, nodding toward the ravaged entrance. "What force inflicted this damage?"

The larger man glowered at him. "Does it look like we have time to trade idle chatter with every fool straying from the city?" he demanded. He waved one meaty hand in a curt gesture. "Be on your way, and let us return to our work. We have much to do yet before nightfall."

Amric bit back his first response. He was road-weary and caked with dirt and dried blood, and he intended to be within the city wall before the sun fell below the horizon. All the same, there was no reason to vent his temper on a man who was merely doing his duty. He took a breath and tried again.

"We are travelers," he said. "We have been away for almost a week to the east, into the forest and back. I would speak with your commander, to share the things we have seen on the road back to the city. It may well have some bearing on what has taken place here, and what comes next."

"You would have us believe that you and your motley handful here have been wandering about the countryside, day and night, and that you even ventured into that accursed forest? And somehow you all survived to make your return?" The guard boomed out a harsh laugh. "If we were swapping tales in a tavern, I'd toss a copper your way for your creativity, but I have no time for this folly just now."

"Very well," Amric said. "Then do me the kindness of pointing me to your superior, who hopefully puts his skull to better use than simply keeping his helm from clattering to the ground."

The burly guard's expression darkened and his beard bristled as he thrust out his jaw. "You'll not be staying on my good side, lad, with talk like that."

"Imagine my dismay," Amric replied. "Now run along."

The guard's hand tightened on the sword hilt at his hip, but his eyes roved over the warriors as if seeing them for the first time, taking in their weaponry and their relaxed manner. His gaze lingered on Valkarr, who was regarding him as he would a struggling insect of no particular interest, and finally the guard relaxed his grip, drumming his fingers upon the pommel once before letting his hand fall to his side. "A signal from me," he growled, "and those archers back there will feather you with arrows."

Amric shook his head. "Not in time to save you, my friend. Now, as you pointed out, you and I have nothing left to discuss. Fetch your commander, and leave your friend here. Surely not every member of the city guard is so poor at making conversation."

The barrel-chested guard glowered at his companion, and then at Amric. Muttering into his beard, he turned and stalked back toward the gate.

"Do not judge him too harshly," said the hawk-faced guard as he watched the fellow's retreating back. "He is a good man in a scrape, and everyone's nerves are frayed at the moment. He is right that we do not have much time."

"It is already forgotten," Amric replied. "And I will not waste your commander's time. Now, tell me all you know of the attack."

By the time the lean, scar-faced guard had recounted the events of the previous night, a dozen soldiers on horseback were picking their way past the fortifications and riding out from the gate. The warriors shifted their mounts to facing the approaching contingent. The man in the lead, a powerfully built fellow whose irritation showed in the firm set of his square jaw, began shouting as he drew near.

"What in blazes is this idiocy? I do not have time for—"

Amric interrupted in a clear, carrying voice. "The spiked creatures are called varkhuls. They attack in swarms and cannot tolerate light, and though they have not the cunning to form strategies, they are tenacious and will flow like water around any obstacle. They can scale almost any surface and their talons secrete a mild venom that induces lethargy in their victims. You will need many more torches atop the city wall if you are going to prevent them from overrunning it. Flaming arrows in their midst will also sow chaos among them, sometimes even making them turn on one another in the confusion. Once established, varkhuls multiply like mad around any food source, and you have hordes of them infesting nearly every farmhouse and other shade-providing structure between here and the heart of the forest. The forest mines alone must contain thousands of them. You may be able to blunt the attacks at night by sending forces during the day to raze every structure and burn out every cave."

The leader slowed his mount, his eyes narrowing as he fell silent, and his men slowed with him.

"The huge creatures that battered down your gates are known as shamblers," Amric continued. "They seem to be primitive elementals driven somehow mad by the twisting of the land's magic. They draw a coating of armor about themselves from nearby rock, dirt and vegetation. You must tear that shell apart and fracture it into pieces too small to operate on their own, to force the animating spirit to abandon it and flee. The serpent creatures are greels. They usually dwell deep underground in damp caverns, and no one knows what has driven them to the surface. Just as no one knows why these disparate creatures and many others, who bear no love for each other, are growing ever stronger in numbers and attacking human outposts in a blind rage."

The commander drew his mount to a halt, and his men fanned out to form a line behind him.

Amric jerked his chin toward the eastern gate. "You have a good start on fortifications. You might consider soaking the spikes or sheathing them in iron so that the burning oil does not destroy them too quickly. Also, if you mount enough torches and spikes high along the archway wall and angle your rows of ground spikes more to funnel the varkhuls toward a center path, their own numbers will inhibit them and your archers can concentrate all their fire there. The same trick might work with torches projecting from the wall crenellations to direct the focus of the varkhuls, so that your men need not spread too thin up there."

The commander stared at him. "Who *are* you?" he asked.

"I am Amric, a warmaster of the Sil'ath," the warrior replied. "I and my party have just traversed the full length of the eastern road. When we left the city days ago, we saw scattered tracks around the abandoned farms. Today, I doubt you could enter any building out there without encountering them. They are moving in droves at night, spreading from the forest."

The commander cleared his throat, and gave a solemn nod. "I am Captain Borric, commander of the Keldrin's Landing city guard. You bear grim news, Amric, but I thank you for every scrap of it. At least we are forewarned." He ran an appraising look over the warriors. "When the next attack comes, I could use every available sword in defending this city. If it is gold you are after, the wealthy here may prefer to finance their own private armies, but they are finding sudden cause to contribute more generously to funding the public defense."

Amric laughed. "If the attack comes tonight, Captain, rest assured that we will join in the defense of the city. At the moment, however, I am after the first hot meal we have had in almost a week. And if I do not wash away all this grime soon, I may be mistaken for a shambler myself."

Borric chuckled and waved him away. "Be on your way then, Amric, and fare you well."

"You as well, Captain," Amric said, wheeling his mount about. He and Valkarr rode back to the others as the sounds followed them of Borric shouting new orders to his men. The party wended its way around to the northern gate as the sun sank behind the eastern horizon.

The massive fortress of Stronghold leered down, as lifeless and empty as a grinning skull, upon the forest crowded around it. The setting sun was impaling itself upon the towering, primordial trees to the east, bathing one side of the mountain structure in deepest crimson even as the other side blackened into shadow. The place was silent, like dust settling in a crypt, and yet a distant, steady power still pulsed and thrummed somewhere far beneath its broken core.

In the sprawling courtyard within the innermost defensive wall, before the titanic main doors of the fortress, the evening air began to crackle. Light gathered there, a multitude of swirling motes drawing together to form a wavering, brilliant weal against the deepening gloom. The rift parted, torn open with a hiss, and the man in black robes stepped through. He cast a swift glance about, probing the long shadows thrown by constructs of pitted stone as the air hummed with the power gathered about him. He found nothing, and the tension eased from his tall form as he released some of that power. The rift closed behind him with a sizzling sigh, its luminance fading after it like a dying candle flame, and the man began to walk.

He had not really expected an ambush. Everything he had sensed thus far suggested a foe that was clumsy and inexperienced. Otherwise he would not have risked opening a Way directly here. It had been easy enough to orient upon the site of the event, given some time, and it was always liberating to be on a world where such travel was unknown and therefore not warded against. Tearing open a temporary Way was still a draining effort, however, and could leave one vulnerable to ready resistance on the other end. As he had surmised, there was nothing of the kind awaiting him. Still, a phenomenal amount of power had been employed here, more than enough to give him pause, and he had not survived so many years doing such dangerous work by being careless.

There were also, of course, the savage denizens of this world to consider. They should not pose too great a risk to one of his abilities, provided he employed reasonable cautions. As the Essence Gate in the ruins of Queln continued to operate, however, the magic of this world grew more and more unstable. The magical elements here, then, would swell in number and become increasingly maddened. They would do a marvelous job of keeping the more civilized occupants busy, but at the same time they would also make it more challenging for him to travel unmolested. All the more reason to complete this unpleasant business and be gone before it all began to crumble. This ripe world would descend into madness on its path to becoming a lifeless, desiccated husk, and he did not care to be present to witness any of it first-hand.

He considered for a moment whether he would prefer to remain here as the end approached or return empty-handed again, and the sting of a chill sweat broke out on his brow. It must not come to that.

The black-robed man climbed broad steps and stepped onto the sweeping terrace level that girded the imposing front of the fortress. He knelt there, placing one splayed hand upon the stone beneath his feet. The pain of this place ran very deep, like black rot devouring the heart of a great tree all the way down to its roots. It went down well into the earth. Those fingers of corruption had found fire there in the very veins of the world, and even that cleansing flame had not been sufficient to scour this place of its disease. He was always mesmerized at the ways in which primal essence could twist the weakness of flesh and structure both, seizing that which was thought buried and bringing it unwilling to the fore, quickening it in impossible, exquisite agony.

He found the signature of the one he sought, of course, a blazing brand smoking against a still quivering hide. From there, however, the signs tapered off again, albeit slowly, as if that other had been almost reluctant to resume masking himself.

The man rose to his feet once more. If he could trace his quarry's steps, he might well be able to discern a faint auric trail, and then it was but a matter of time. Few enough could mask this much power effectively, and fewer still could hide thus from a trained tracker such as he. Yes, it would be but a matter of time, now.

He strode toward the immense marble arch that marked the imposing front entrance to Stronghold. The metal doors cast back dull gleams from within the shadows of the archway, as if the fortress itself bared its teeth at his presence. He began to draw in power, a predator's grin stretching tight across his face. It was time to give a polite knock.

Amric pushed away the empty plate and drained the last of the mug of ale. Beside him, Valkarr tore into a third heaping plate of food with feverish abandon, shoveling each new bite between wedge-shaped jaws as if his meal would evaporate before him at any moment. Amric smiled, feeling a wash of relief. It was the most enthusiasm his old friend had shown since he had nearly perished in Stronghold, and though his hands still shook slightly with each rapid movement, it was still a good sign that his recovery was gaining momentum. And he had to admit, whatever else one might say about the Sleeping Boar inn and its gruff owner, the Duergar Olekk, it served food of surpassing quality.

He glanced around to the others at the table, and burst out laughing. Halthak, Syth and Thalya, having finished their own meals, were staring at the ravenous Sil'ath warrior with wide eyes, and their expressions ranged from incredulous to appalled. The healer had been explicit that Valkarr's body would require a great deal of extra rest and nourishment to replenish the enormous amount of energy taken from it by such an intense healing. Although Amric had long ceased to marvel at the ability of the Sil'ath to gorge themselves and then go without sustenance for much longer than a human could, he sometimes forgot that not everyone had grown up with it.

His laughter elicited a gimlet-eyed glower from the Traug, but at least the hulking creature managed not to growl at him as when he had walked through the door an hour before. Evidently forgiveness would be a long time in coming for his baring steel against the Elvaren within the confines of the inn. He gave the Traug a cheery wave, and earned in return a curl of thick upper lip that bared a jagged row of teeth. Amric chuckled.

"Winning hearts and minds wherever you go, eh, swordsman?" Syth asked with a grin.

Amric shrugged. "Mayhap all this road dust is inhibiting my natural charm."

"Mayhap there is nothing beneath that road dust except more of it," Thalya said with a snort. "Speaking on behalf of all fellow occupants of the room, when will you be taking that bath you mentioned?"

Amric flashed her a rogue's grin. "Soon enough," he said. "There is one more odious task left to complete the evening, and then soft bed and hot bath can duel for my attention. Ah, here we are, then."

Thalya turned to follow his stare and stiffened in her seat. Bellimar had appeared at the inn's front door, his gaze sliding around the crowded common room before he entered. As he glided toward them, Amric noted how the patrons sitting at the tables to either side of his path unconsciously leaned away from his passing presence. The warrior shook his head. He had known from that first meeting that there was something unusual about the old man, but he had attributed it to the fellow's past association with sorcery. Little had he suspected at the time that his wildest suspicions would prove but pale wisps next to the truth of Bellimar's nature. He recalled the reluctance with which he had decided to endure the man's company as a necessary evil, tainted by his history of magic as he was. Since then, it seemed as if every step of the journey had been steeped in magic from all sides, and Bellimar had somehow proven to be the least of it so far despite his dark origins. Amric gave an inward sigh; he was not certain whether to be pleased or alarmed at having made such personal strides against his aversion. In a land increasingly ravaged by magic, he could not afford to be paralyzed by its proximity if he was to succeed in his mission. Still, it was discomfiting to realize he was becoming more accustomed to such forces than he would ever have thought possible.

Bellimar reached their table and slid into an empty oaken chair with a perfunctory nod to everyone. If he took note of the huntress's hateful stare, he gave no outward sign. The serving girl passed by, giving Bellimar a questioning look, but he responded only with a warm smile, ordering no food. Amric recalled the untouched meal sitting before the old man when they first met, and realized there was little need for further pretense on such matters now, with this group.

"My contacts report that no other Sil'ath have been observed entering or leaving the city since our departure," he told Amric. "This includes the harbor as well as the gates, though it is getting increasingly difficult to monitor the traffic at the quays. The number of people desperate to secure any available passage away from Keldrin's Landing has increased greatly in the wake of last night's attack. My contacts will remain vigilant, however. They will raise your name to any Sil'ath sighted, as you have requested."

Amric nodded his gratitude, disappointed but not surprised. He knew by this point that his friends would not be so easily found. "And the other matter?"

"It is arranged," Bellimar replied. "Morland is waiting for us."

"You mean to return to that serpent's lair?" Halthak blurted.

"I mean to keep my word," Amric said. "We would not have found Stronghold so easily without his maps, and he put us on the right trail, even if not out of altruism. I will pay his price by delivering news of Grelthus's fate, though doubtless he will not be pleased by the outcome. We shall see if the serpent then keeps his word and lifts the price on our heads."

Valkarr sat back from his empty plate, drawing one forearm across his mouth. "I am ready," he announced with a belch.

"No, my friend," Amric said. "Bellimar and I will go. You and Halthak still require rest. We both know that black-hearted devil's estate is very heavily guarded, and I cannot have you infiltrating it again until you are more recovered. There is no need for Morland to know this, however. I ask that you both remain in your rooms while we are gone. If you are out of sight, then we do not have to test whether Morland ever truly bothered to suspend the price on our heads, and he still has to worry about a stealthy blade prowling somewhere about his mansion."

Valkarr grunted and rolled his eyes in a very human gesture, but finally nodded. Halthak gave his own reluctant agreement as well.

"What of me?" Syth asked.

"Morland may already know that you are with us, if he has been watching for your return," Amric admitted. "You are welcome to accompany us to see the merchant, if you wish. He will no doubt be eager to determine if you brought anything he seeks in your return from Stronghold. Nonetheless, I am not your keeper, and you are also free to vanish."

The thief pondered a moment before breaking into an impish grin. "I find myself wanting to be there when that shriveled mask he calls a face cracks with disappointment."

"And I will come as well," Thalya put in, with a cold sidelong look at Bellimar.

"No, you will not," Amric said. Her head snapped toward him, green eyes flashing with outrage. Her lips twisted with the beginnings of an angry objection, but he cut through it in a tone that brooked no further argument. "I can say nothing as to the right or wrong of your vendetta with Bellimar, as I can only speak to how he has conducted himself in my presence. I can, however, choose not to allow your conflict to land in my lap at a time and place that could get us all killed. We are heading into a viper's den where cool heads must prevail, and no good will come of inviting upon yourself the attention of a powerful and soulless man like Morland. You are not going."

The two locked gazes for a long moment, but Amric did not waver, his grey eyes dispassionate under her withering glare. At last she sat back with a dark scowl directed alternately at the warrior and the old man.

"Cool heads, eh?" Bellimar remarked with a sly grin. "The heavens forbid we do anything in his presence to fan the flames of his wrath."

Amric flushed, but his expression remained resolute. "Much as I despise the man and his disdain for the lives of others, one power-hungry lordling is too far down the list to concern ourselves with at the moment. He certainly has the means to interfere with our more important goals, however, so we should make every effort to avoid incurring any more of his ire than is strictly necessary. If all goes well, we will conclude our business with the man tonight and be rid of his involvement for good. Valkarr is recovering rapidly, and it is my hope that after two nights of rest here in the city we will be ready to depart again on the following morn. Any who wish to accompany us, meet us here at dawn of that day. Any who do not, I wish you well in your travels."

Halthak's brow furrowed. "Depart? To where?"

"To follow a suspicion," Amric said. He sat back and took in their puzzled expressions. Only Bellimar straightened in his chair, eyes glittering with prognostication. The swordsman took a breath and continued. "As you know, we lost the trail of our Sil'ath friends at Stronghold. If Grelthus is to be believed, they were fighting their way from the fortress, likely wounded and weakened but still alive when last seen. I have been trying to reason where they would have gone if they did manage to win free, and what might have befallen them from there."

"What makes you think they did not simply die there?" Thalya demanded.

Amric turned flint-hard eyes upon her. "They are Sil'ath," he said. "We do not die easily." At his side, Valkarr lifted his chin and hissed a note of assent.

The huntress raised an eyebrow but said nothing. He let out a breath, and the edge faded from his voice. "I know nothing for certain, but I have seen no evidence of their demise, and until I know their fate I must consider all avenues. These are some of the best warriors of a people born into battle, who have fought together since childhood. They may not have had the advantage of Halthak's miraculous healing ability, but five such warriors can cross hostile terrain like so many ghosts. I will grant you that they might have fallen prey to the hideous perils of the forest, or were entombed in the fortress, but somehow it does not ring true. No, I believe they survived Stronghold, just as we did."

"We survived by seeing the very heart of the place, along with its rabid inhabitants, crushed in a strange surge of power unlike any I have seen," Bellimar reminded him. "I am not so certain one can draw parallels to our own experience."

Amric shook his head. "I can offer no better explanation, and I have no proof one way or the other. All I have is my intuition, and I intend to follow it. I cannot ask anyone else to do the same."

He fell silent, glancing around the table at expressions that were by turns skeptical and pensive. He noted that Bellimar was studying each of them as well, his dark eyes making a slow circuit of the table beneath iron grey brows. A half smile brushed at the vampire's lips, and broadened slightly when Halthak cleared his throat to speak.

"Tell us of your suspicion, Amric," the Half-Ork said. "Where are you going, two days hence?"

"I believe," Amric said, "that there is more than one force in operation here, possibly working at different purposes. We have seen creatures brought from the depths and barrows of the land, driven mad by the raging essence swelling in the region. Most are like rabid beasts, mindless in their fury, slaying indiscriminately and assaulting mortal life wherever they find it. This is what we faced in Lyden, the distant ripples of the same spreading wave that is engulfing Keldrin's Landing. Here and in the forest, we are much closer to the source. This wave emanates from the east somewhere, from something so powerful that the Essence Fount at Stronghold was but a symptom, as Grelthus admitted. Whether it lies in the forest or beyond it, we have not found that source, that center, yet. We only know that the magical essence is being drawn that way, becoming more potent the further east we go, and that the corruption of the land and its creatures worsens as well. And while most of those creatures hunger for flesh or life force, there is one type that seems to have a different purpose: the man-like, cloth-wrapped black creatures."

"They capture rather than kill," Valkarr murmured.

Amric nodded. "We have faced most of these creatures back home as the attacks worsened," he said. "These are something we have not seen, something new. And they have fled in the same direction each time, with their prey."

Thalya and Halthak each shifted in their seats, exchanging an uneasy glance. For both, it was all too easy to recall being borne helplessly along in the clutches of the implacable creatures, before these very warriors had saved them from an unknown fate.

"Yes, you are correct," Bellimar hissed, sitting forward as he grew more animated. "They are not corrupted spirits or elementals, not dwellers in the dark or enraged beasts. They bear the remnants of clothing or wrappings, as if they have been made by the hand of another, rather than formed of or mutated by magic. Yes! I should have seen it before now."

"Our friends were wounded," Amric continued. "Regardless of whether they believed the Essence Fount to be the source of the corruption or understood the source to be further east, they would have been forced to retreat for a time to recuperate. On the way, they may have encountered the same strange man-like creatures and chosen to investigate, or some of them could have been captured in their weakened state and the rest set out to recover them. We have not found any of their bodies or equipment, which implies some or all of them were not taken, since the black creatures have shown no interest in anything but living captives."

"Your analysis of these peculiar creatures is perceptive, swordsman," Bellimar said with a slow shake of his head. "The thread of logic concerning your friends, however, is tenuous at best."

Amric sat back and folded his arms across his chest. "A suspicion, as I said. And it is all I have, so I will pursue it. I intend to trace these black creatures back to their source."

Syth stared, disbelief and admiration warring in his expression as his brown hair swirled about his shoulders in subdued eddies. "Swordsman, have you ever passed a hornet's nest without wanting to wear it as a hat?"

Amric barked a laugh. "Well, there you have it," he said. "We leave after two nights, if the fates allow it. I will not blame you if you want no part of this mad scheme. You owe me nothing."

"I will be ready tomorrow," Valkarr asserted, hammering a fist onto the thick oaken table and causing the plates to jump and rattle. "Already I feel the strength returning to my limbs."

"Then you will be even more ready the following morning," Amric said with a smile. "You have come a long way from death's door, my friend, but I need you back at your best. You saw how hard those unnatural things were to kill. In any event, the extra day gives us time to gather supplies and rest the horses as well. After all, the next leg of the journey may well prove as strenuous as the last."

He pushed back from the table and stood, drawing another suspicious glare from the Traug towering in the far corner of the room. Showing what he felt was remarkable restraint, he elected not to bait the surly creature again.

"It is time to conclude our business with Morland," he said, with a final glance around the table. Bellimar and Syth rose with him and together they headed across the raucous common room of the inn and made for the doors.

"If you are meeting with a nobleman, perhaps you should take that bath first," Thalya called after him.

"Not a chance," Amric said over his shoulder. "There is nothing noble about this man, and I fully intend to leave muddy footprints all over those priceless rugs of his. Besides, I would only need another after we met with him."

Syth chortled to himself as he and Bellimar followed Amric from the inn and into the night.

Morland sat in the high-backed chair, drumming his jeweled fingers on the table. His cold eyes shifted, sliding over each of them in turn with deliberate indolence.

Without looking away from the merchant's cadaverous visage, Amric studied the glowering guards flanking the man. The one on the left was too bulky to possess much speed, and the one on the right was a touch soft. Even unarmed as he was, the warrior felt reasonably certain he could down them both before Morland was more than a few steps from his chair. He sensed the presence of the guards several paces behind him as well, heard the periodic creak of leather as they shifted with nervous tension. The merchant had seated his guests farther away from him this time, as well as increasing the number of guards in the room, and he seemed to think himself safe.

Amric let a slow smile play across his lips and a brash invitation creep into his gaze. *Break your word, merchant,* he thought, *and we will discover together if that confidence is misplaced.* If Morland took any note of the goading, however, he was betrayed only by an almost imperceptible tightening at the corner of his eye.

"Let me see if I have the right of this tale," Morland rasped at last, tapping his index finger twice more on the table before his fingers became still. He looked at Amric. "You, who were to return with word of my business contact, instead slew him." He turned then to Syth. "And you, who were to return with my misappropriated belongings, instead left them all behind."

"You left out the part where we collapsed the place, in all likelihood burying or destroying your belongings in the process," Syth put in helpfully. "I am quite certain we mentioned that part."

Morland's face twisted in sudden fury, but Bellimar interrupted before he could respond.

"The Wyrgens tapped into primal forces they could not hope to control," the old man said. "The consequences drove Grelthus and his people to bestial madness, even as it weakened the very structure of Stronghold itself. We were fortunate indeed to escape that place of death, so that we could return to you with this news, as was our agreement."

His tone was level and eminently rational, and he placed a subtle emphasis on the last words. Morland's angry gaze flicked over to him, and it was evident that the reminder had registered.

"Despite the embellishment of our friend Syth here," Bellimar continued, "only a central portion of the fortress actually collapsed. While it is indeed impassable, much of the structure was unaffected. Once travel to the east becomes less hazardous, a man of your considerable resources could no doubt mount an expedition to Stronghold. It may yet be possible for you to retrieve the artifacts you seek."

"Perhaps," Morland said, letting the word escape through clenched teeth.

As Bellimar resumed speaking, the soothing quality of his voice deepened to embrace an almost mesmerizing quality. Amric, not even the target of it, nonetheless felt the liquid timbre slide beneath his skin with a numbing and almost hypnotic effect.

"We regret, my lord, that we bring unfortunate tidings. We can only hope that the regrettable fate of your ally will not prove too disastrous to your business endeavors. But even as I utter the words, I know them for a foolish worry! A man of your shrewd nature will have readied a way to achieve the necessary ends despite this minor setback. You are no doubt already cultivating alternate plans."

"Of course I am," Morland snapped. "Your incompetence on this matter pains me, but I have designs of greater significance in motion as well, so no matter." He blinked as if surprised at his own words, and his lips tightened into a bloodless line as he glared at Bellimar with sudden suspicion.

"Then, since we have fulfilled our obligation to you, the price on our heads can now be removed," Amric said. He gauged the distance to the guards again. If treachery was afoot, now was the time. He hoped Syth was ready as well. The merchant stared at them with half-lidded eyes for long seconds. His fingers, as if of their own volition, resumed their rhythmic drumming upon the table.

"It would seem so," he finally grated.

Amric nodded, studying the man for any twitch of betrayal, and then rose from the chair in a deliberate movement. Despite the care he took to move slowly, he heard a momentary shuffle of boots behind him accompanied by the telltale rasp of several inches of steel being bared.

Morland's gaze never wavered, but he flicked a finger in a dismissive motion, and the guards fell back.

Syth and Bellimar stood as well, and the three of them turned toward the exit at the far end of the long room. A handful of the guards fell into step behind them, but on sudden impulse, Amric stopped and turned back to Morland.

"Merchant, have you heard any word of peculiar man-like creatures in tattered cloth wrappings, black inside and out, roving in packs intent on capturing rather than slaying?"

Morland sat motionless, regarding him steadily. When he spoke, his voice was cold, impatient. "I have not heard of such things. Why do you ask?"

"We encountered these creatures deep in the forest and on the road back to Keldrin's Landing," the warrior replied. "These black things are very hard to kill. We were only able to stop them each time by severing their heads. If you send your men into the countryside, they should be forewarned."

The merchant's hawkish countenance tilted in a sardonic nod. "Very thoughtful of you to consider my welfare."

"It was not for you, but for your men," Amric said evenly. "After all, it seems the city can expect to be under siege soon, and we are all in this together, are we not?"

"The refrain of the helpless and needful," Morland sneered. "Do not seek to draw parallels between your fate and mine. Now take your banalities and be gone."

Amric gave him a wintry smile and spun away, striding from the room with the others on his heel.

It was a short time later, as they sat in the carriage clattering its way across the bridge leaving Morland's estate, that Bellimar leaned toward him.

"He was lying," the old man said.

"I know," Amric said.

"What made you test his awareness of the black things?"

"I do not know," the warrior admitted. "Nor do I know yet why he would conceal his knowledge."

Bellimar nodded, frowning in thought. "The man is involved in something he does not want known," he mused. "He has found some way to profit from the suffering of others."

"Do the wealthy do aught else?" Syth remarked. "And what of the subtle spell you wove back there? He was drawn to reveal more of his plans than he meant to. The man parts with nothing unless he can sell it dearly."

The vampire turned to him, lips peeling back into a smile. His eyes were scarlet embers in the shadowed interior of the carriage. "My curse is not without its benefits, thief."

Late the following night, the same carriage rumbled away from the southern gate of Keldrin's Landing. A score of soldiers on horseback surrounded the vehicle, and the torches they held aloft formed a flickering halo against the pressing blackness as the procession snaked its way along the southbound road.

Within the carriage, Morland stroked his clean-shaven chin as he stared out the window into the night. Beside him sat the mercenary Vorenius, scratching his dark, unkempt beard like a boorish reflection of his urbane relative. On the opposite bench sat the twin Elvaren assassins, Nyar and Nylien, lounging with an insolent air of boredom. One of the twins—Nyar, thought Morland, though he could never be certain—appeared to be dozing sitting upright, while the other seemed engrossed in the study of his fingernails on one pale hand. Vorenius shifted in his seat, casting surreptitious looks from the merchant to the assassins. Morland ground his teeth, striving to ignore the man's irksome presence. Vorenius leaned forward to peer out the window, chewing his lip. Morland flicked an irritated sidelong glance at him, and unfortunately the man noticed and took it for an invitation to air his vapid thoughts.

"Since when does one have to ply the gate guards with a pouch of gold merely to exit the city?" he demanded, scratching again at his beard.

Morland sighed, mourning the broken quiet. "Since I do not want them sharing news of my comings and goings," he said. "You saw their reactions when I dismissed their warnings about venturing out after dark."

"So I did," Vorenius muttered. "And I have to admit, I heard merit in their arguments. I do not understand what could be important enough to draw us out here. There was no attack on the city last night, but there is nothing to say it will not come tonight, nor that the next assault will be restricted to the eastern wall."

"Do not seek to question my decisions," the merchant snapped. "The reward will warrant the risk, and that is all you need know for now."

The man sat back, raking his lower lip with his teeth. Opposite him, the assassin looked on with evident amusement, twirling locks of his white hair between his fingers.

"It is quite agitated, is it not?" the Elvar murmured.

The mercenary leaned forward, coarse features twisting in anger as he jabbed one thick finger at the assassin. "No one asked you, you pasty—"

"Vorenius," Morland said in a sharp tone. "Let your tongue be still, for once."

Vorenius flinched at the rebuke. "I am sorry, uncle. I—"

"And do not call me uncle," Morland interrupted, his lip curling. "I am a distant cousin at best, and it strains my belief at the best of times that we share blood at all."

"Of course, u—Morland," the mercenary stammered. "I do not mean to be ungrateful. You are gracious to give me this chance to redeem myself in your eyes."

"You handpicked your best men for this trip, as I asked?"

"Yes, all except for the handful which are from your personal guard."

"Good. Fear not, Vorenius, you will prove your worth yet."

Morland watched the man's twitching movements in throwing another look outside the carriage. How did the fool think himself a leader of men, when he had a spine of water?

"What is my role to be in this venture, then?" Vorenius asked. He swallowed and hastened to add, "So that I may serve you better."

"I reached out to powerful allies, and they have accepted my overtures," Morland replied. "You will be an instrumental part of securing their trust. This alliance is an important step toward achieving the loftiest of my goals, Vorenius. Tonight's meeting will be a pivotal point in my plans."

Vorenius eyed him and gave a rapid, earnest nod. "I will not fail you, Morland."

"I trust you will not," the merchant said with a brittle smile.

They traveled in silence for a time, the carriage rocking over the rutted road. At last it slowed and lurched to a halt, and the languid demeanor of the Elvaren changed in an instant. The eyes of the dozing assassin snapped open, and he curled forward and slipped through the door in one liquid movement. His twin vanished out the other side with equal alacrity, leaving Vorenius craning his neck back and forth in a vain effort to see what was transpiring outside. Morland sat with hands folded neatly in his lap, eyes closed and head tilted back to rest against the carriage wall behind him.

Voices carried to them, men's voices and something else, something deep and rough like granite boulders colliding. Minutes later the assassin Nylien reappeared at the carriage door, holding it open. The merchant climbed down and his mercenary cousin followed, with the assassin close behind.

Morland looked back at Keldrin's Landing. Good, the city was little more than a glow in the distance. His men's torches might be seen faintly from the city walls, if the guards there happened to look in this direction, but it was too great a distance to distinguish more than that. He strode forward, passing the front of the carriage where the driver struggled to calm the team of horses. All the soldiers' mounts were tethered at the rear of the carriage, and they were nervous as well, snorting and prancing in place. A handful of men remained there with them, a hard-bitten lot with torches held high and scarred faces set in grim, impassive silence. None of them sought to make eye contact with the merchant.

Ahead, the remainder of the men formed two standing lines across the road, facing something further down the road. Morland approached with Vorenius at his heels, and the guards parted to allow their passage. As they passed through, a strangled gasp escaped the mercenary.

A large shape waited in the center of the road, a dozen yards away. What little light reached it from the ring of torches was all but absorbed by its dark hide, but Morland was able to discern a hint of its outline. It was a huge form, squatting or perhaps kneeling, with long, thick arms that reached down to knuckle the ground. Its front was smooth and matte black, though a forest of protrusions jutted from its back and shoulders; whether they were spikes or tentacles of some kind, Morland could not tell without getting closer, and he had no intent of doing that. Just being out here was a show of faith on his part, but past a certain point promises and alliances were just empty words without actions to prove them.

Nyar stood several paces ahead of the wide-eyed array of guards, and Morland drew abreast of him. Vorenius halted a pace behind, his face drawn and pale. Nylien stood at the man's elbow with a smirk twisting his fine Elvaren features.

"I am here," Morland announced.

An elongated head shifted toward him. He tried to pick out its eyes amid that nightmare countenance, but it was a futile effort. Every bit of the thing was black, just as the previous representatives had been. An eerie, grating sound emanated from the thing in a grotesque parody of human speech.

"A Nar'ath queen speaks through me," it said.

"Very well," Morland said. "What has your queen decided of the arrangement I proposed?"

A murmur ran through the men, but the merchant ignored it.

"The arrangement is agreeable," the creature rumbled.

"And I shall have all that I was promised?" Morland asked, eyes narrowing.

The creature dipped its head and its bulk shifted. "The arrangement is agreeable," it repeated. "All your conditions shall be met."

The merchant suppressed a fierce surge of exultation, keeping his tone level. "Then tell your queen that the Nar'ath have an agreement. When is it to be?"

"Tonight," it responded.

A momentary chill played along Morland's spine. "I need more time to prepare," he said. "Can it instead be two nights hence?"

The creature shifted again, torchlight playing along the low ridges that ran along its black skull. The seconds ticked by and Morland quailed inside, though he let not a ripple of his fear show on the surface. They needed him, he reminded himself, just as much as he needed them. Each side would achieve its goals much faster, this way. And so he waited, outwardly calm, though the hands laced before him tightened painfully to keep them from shaking.

"Two nights hence is agreeable," the thing finally said.

"It shall be done," Morland said. He heard the faint quaver of relief in his own voice, but he dared not glance around to see if anyone else had noticed. "I bear a word of warning for your queen, however. I spoke with men in the city yesterday who showed knowledge of the Nar'ath. They have seen your kind and somehow survived."

"It matters not," came the rumbling reply. "We grow strong now, and the time for concealment is almost done."

"As you say. I wished only to share the information I had gained, in the spirit of maintaining no secrets between allies. These men are few but dangerous, and if I am not mistaken they have command of some modest magic as well."

The hulking thing rocked back and forth, but did not respond.

"Very well, is our business concluded, then?" Morland asked.

The creature gave a rolling shrug and leaned forward, the protrusions on its back flexing in some odd movement that was lost to the darkness. The light thrown by the torches caught on a lighter hue against the thing's hide: strips of tattered cloth, caught amid those protrusions and draping across its back. Morland caught the flinch his body tried to make, and gave an inward sneer at the almost-weakness.

"There is one more matter," that unnatural voice grated in a basso drone. "The queen requests a demonstration of commitment, now, tonight."

"I expected as much," the merchant replied with a humorless smile. He turned to Vorenius, who swallowed hard and tore his round-eyed gaze from the creature. "Cousin, it is time for you and your men to prove your worth. Give our new ally what he requires."

Morland turned on his heel, Nyar and Nylien fell in behind him as he strode toward the carriage. The thin, stammering voice of Vorenius floated after him.

"W-What does it want? What am I to give it?"

The merchant paused at the carriage door, lifting the richly embroider hem of his robes in preparation to step up into it. He glanced at the handful of men clustered around the vehicle. Their eyes were forward and resolute, and their features might as well have been carved from solid stone for all the emotion they betrayed. He then turned his gaze back toward Vorenius and his dozen or so hand-picked men, standing on the road with torches clutched in white-knuckled fists.

"Do not worry, cousin," he called. "This is one job you cannot fail."

Even as he said the words, a chorus of rustling sounds arose all around them. Scores of man-like figures rose from the tall grasses on either side of the road, black as jet and swathed in ragged cloth. They scuttled forward like converging waves of chitinous black scarabs, encircling the cluster of men in the road with silent and implacable efficiency.

"Morland!" cried Vorenius, ripping his sword from its sheath at his side. "It is an ambush, we are betrayed!"

The merchant did not reply, but instead took an unhurried step onto the rail of the carriage, still staring at the mercenary. Vorenius cast a bewildered look around as his men turned their blades outward at the foe. His frantic gaze shifted from the approaching Nar'ath to Morland, and then to the small cluster of men about the carriage who were making no move to draw their own blades. Comprehension dawned, and shock and disbelief gave way quickly to rage.

"You black-hearted devil spawn!" he screamed, his voice cracking. "You would sell out your own kind, your own *blood*, in some unholy pact with fiends such as this?"

A steady string of epithets followed as Morland looked on, his face a frozen mask. The Nar'ath gathered around the trapped men, and like a swarm with a single mind, they pounced as one.

Blades rose and hacked as wiry limbs struck and enfolded the men. Vorenius ran one of the creatures through the chest, but though his sword jutted from its back, the thing was not slowed. It lunged toward him, pinning the mercenary's arm between them, and wrapped steel-strong limbs about him. Morland's last view of the man as he disappeared under the seething mass showed him screaming in fury toward the carriage, his teeth gleaming in the torchlight amid his dark beard. Then a black hand covered his mouth and most of his face, and drew him to the ground, and he was lost to sight.

The battle lasted only moments, for the Nar'ath greatly outnumbered the unprepared men. One by one, the torches tumbled to the hard-packed road and were snuffed out below the press of bodies. Cries of pain and anger echoed through the chill night air, but swiftly dwindled in number until only the sound of scuffling remained. The horses, which had been shrieking and jerking against their bindings throughout, were at last brought under control by the remaining guards around the carriage.

On the road, the Nar'ath wasted no time in hoisting their unconscious prey to black shoulders and threading away like a chain of otherworldly insects, moving at a dead run.

The Nar'ath lieutenant, as Morland had come to think of the larger ones that could speak, faded back into the blackness and was gone. Aside from the brutish lieutenant, the Nar'ath had made no sound whatsoever during the encounter. Morland suppressed a shudder as he watched them disappear into the darkness. In mere moments, the only signs of what had transpired were the unlit torches strewn about like charred bones. The merchant considered the agreement he had made and felt an odd twinge, but he quelled it savagely. A man of his refinement and station should not be engaging in such base activities, that was all. In the future, he would leave such visceral deeds to lesser men.

He turned and ducked into the carriage.

"What of the extra mounts?" one of his men asked in a hushed tone.

"Bring them along," he replied. "There is no reason to waste good horses."

Nyar and Nylien joined him in the cabin and shut the door behind them. The carriage wheeled into a turn, and soon was trundling on the road back to the city. Morland leaned his shaved pate back against the carriage wall and closed his eyes. It was several minutes into the ride before the silence in the cabin was broken by a quiet voice.

"My lord," murmured one of the Elvaren. "We will return to the city with fewer men and a number of riderless horses. The guards at the gate may raise questions."

"Tell them whatever you wish," the merchant said without opening his eyes. "Remember their faces, however, for you will then seek them at their shift change later in the night and make sure their tongues do not wag to anyone else."

"Yes, lord," the assassins whispered together.

Morland allowed his mind to wander, lulled by the rocking motion of the carriage. He had many preparations to make and not much time in which to make them. Fortunately, in sharp contrast to the ride from the city, the return trip was quite pleasantly free of annoying chatter.

CHAPTER 17

Amric sat his bay gelding in the courtyard by the southern city gate. High above him, brooding clouds scudded across an iron sky. The mantle of night had been peeled away, but the new dawn had brought nothing of its usual comforting warmth or color. In fact, he mused, it looked as if the cordial revolving arrangement between night and day had ended at last and they had fought each other to a standstill, leaving the land caught somewhere in between. He gave a rueful shake of his head; such peculiar thoughts did not become a warrior, and he should instead be focused upon the coming journey. In any event, the stormy skies were a blessing in the sense that they would not have to endure the crushing heat, and their supply of water would last all the longer.

The bay snorted and tossed its head, prancing back a few steps, and Amric kept a firm hand while allowing the horse to work off some of its nervous energy. It was a spirited animal, eager to be off after its time confined to the Sleeping Boar's stables. *Would that I shared your carefree enthusiasm*, he thought with a smile as he patted the glossy neck, *but then, I know more of where we are heading.*

All about, the city was shaking itself awake. More and more of the citizenry seeped into the shadowed streets with each passing moment, and the guards at the gate welcomed the next shift with bleary-eyed gratitude. Amric watched as the heavily laden carts of a portly baker and a short, furry stonemason almost collided. He winced, waiting for the inevitable shouting match as to which was more at fault, but instead the two merely exchanged a tight nod before hastening past each other on their respective errands. They were not alone in their demeanor, he noted. The subdued manner evinced by the residents of Keldrin's Landing owed something to the cold, early hour, but there was of course a larger pall hanging over everyone. Two nights had passed since the abrupt morning attack that shattered the eastern gate, and the city was still holding its breath for the next.

Amric absorbed it all, the sights, the sounds and smells of a city in the vise-like grip of fear. He took it in with eyes the same hue as the unforgiving sky above, the eyes of a man raised in battle. The city—nay, the very land, and perhaps the world as well—was being slowly strangled. He wondered if the city would enjoy another unhindered breath. For that matter, he wondered if anyone would.

The crisp clatter of hooves approaching on the cobbled courtyard shook him from his reverie. Valkarr rode toward him on his black dun and drew rein alongside. Amric gave his old friend a broad, warm smile, and in return the Sil'ath warrior inclined his wedge-shaped head in a salute overdone with mock formality.

"Quit needling me, you great oaf!" Amric laughed. "I am no longer your warmaster, if you will recall. Out here, we are merely friends, as we have been since before either of us could hold a blade."

Valkarr snorted. "Perhaps before *you* could hold a blade, with those useless pink paws of yours. As for me, I am quite certain I held my first breath upon entering this world until my hand curled around a hilt. There is a proper order to be observed, after all."

Amric grinned. It was a vast relief to have his friend hale and hearty again.

"It is a fine joke the fates play on us, is it not?" Valkarr said.

"How do you mean?"

"Putting two friends who wish nothing of magic on a path to try to put the world's magic aright," the Sil'ath said with a chortling hiss.

"A fine joke indeed," Amric said with a laugh, though he found himself quickly sobering. He realized with some discomfort that his viewpoint on magic had begun to alter of late, and he sought to trace the source of that unwelcome change. Was it a sense of gratitude for whatever force had intervened on their behalf at Stronghold? There had certainly been plenty of evidence of the catastrophic effects of magic to counterbalance one beneficial event. Had he been swayed by Bellimar's description of Essence being intrinsic to life, being everywhere and an irrevocable part of all living things? Or was it perhaps Bellimar's own struggle for redemption after an unmatched descent into evil, where magic played a key role in both parts of the tale? Whatever it was, he no longer viewed magic with the simple conviction he had enjoyed before.

He also found a new flicker of empathy within himself for the creatures whose magical natures were twisting in pain along with the land, for he had to entertain the possibility that they were somehow driven to their hostile actions. Some of them might be much the same as the mountain cats back home; those predators were wild and dangerous, to be sure, but only when wounded or cornered did they lash out without discrimination, in a berserk rage.

He frowned. Of course, he thought darkly, it could be that he had become tainted from prolonged exposure to the corruptive influence of Essence, and his own aversion was a defense that had been overrun.

"We are ready, yes?" Valkarr asked after a moment. His friend regarded him askance, seeming to sense the shift in his mood.

"Yes, we are ready," Amric said with a lop-sided grin that he hoped would reassure.

"Not just yet," called a voice from across the courtyard. Bellimar rode toward them on his sway-backed dun mare, with Halthak beside him on his own chestnut mare. "You will not be rid of us so easily, swordsman."

"You are late," Amric returned. "I promised to leave with the dawn, and you'll not convince me that you, of all people, overslept."

Bellimar barked a laugh, but his gaze darted about the courtyard. No one paid their conversation any heed, however. Amric felt the reference was too obscure to cause worry, but then he supposed the layered cautions of keeping such a secret for centuries would easily stir to the surface. It was a revelation of Bellimar's strange situation that, freed of both the mortal need to rest and the vampire's need to hide from the sun during the day, the old man never slept. It must be a relief for the vampire, he thought, that he need no longer maintain the ruse of sleeping at night and eating sparingly with claims of delicate digestion.

"Indeed not," the old man said. "Most of the stabled horses did not welcome my presence, and I required some assistance from the good healer here in retrieving my mount so as not to cause a panic among the irritable beasts. At least there is one regal lady among the swine who is a more astute judge of character." He gave his placid mare a soothing pat on the neck.

A shrill whinnying turned their heads in a new direction. Syth entered the courtyard from a cobbled side lane, wrestling with the reins of a spirited smoke grey horse. Thalya followed on her black mare, her expression caught between alarm and amusement as she watched the thief and his mount dance in every direction except a straight line. Syth wore a broad grin, and the excited breeze swirling around him fluttered both his clothing and the horse's flowing mane.

"Is he not magnificent?" he crowed. "I found a trader willing to part with this fine young stallion for a song! I think it only fitting that a warrior of my caliber should possess a mighty steed of war such as this one."

Thalya burst into rich, genuine laughter, doubling over in her saddle. "That is no war stallion," she gasped. "It is a mare, though I will grant you it is a tall one, and it would be generous to call it broken to the saddle. I thought you knew since the evidence was, ah, plain to see." She cast a meaningful glance at the underside of the horse.

Syth's face fell. "Not a war stallion, eh? So that fat fool of a tradesman took advantage of me." Then he shrugged, and the grin reappeared in a flash as he raised his eyebrows at the huntress. "I thought perhaps it was a kindred warrior spirit that caused the animal to be so unquestionably drawn to me, but now that I know it is female its attraction is, of course, less of a mystery."

Thalya wiped away mirthful tears. "Better keep your charms in reserve for now, thief, at least until you can tell the difference between stallion and mare. One never knows where the next such mistake will lead you. And I will ignore, for now, your unwise implication that a woman cannot possess the spirit of a warrior."

The pair quieted as they drew rein before Amric, Syth looking somewhat abashed and Thalya's face becoming a frozen mask as her emerald gaze fell upon Bellimar. Amric noted that the huntress had never allowed Halthak to heal her, but the bruising and abrasions had subsided enough now that her features were more evident. She was a stunningly beautiful woman, even with her features settled into lines of anger and suspicion, as they were at the moment.

"I must admit, I am surprised to see you all," Amric said. "Unless you are here to see us off?"

The others exchanged glances, but Bellimar spoke first, the intensity of the old man's gaze like a physical thing pressing against him. "There are questions yet to be answered, swordsman," he said. "I will be there when the mysteries are solved."

"I go where the fiend goes," Thalya said immediately through clenched teeth.

Amric turned to Syth. The man drew himself up in his saddle, and his words simmered as he spoke. "I spent months in a cell, waiting for an inglorious death at the hands of a madman. I had nothing of freedom, excitement or change in scenery, and no chance to strike out at a deserving foe." This time when his grin returned, it was a slow, wolfish thing. "At least this madman offers those things."

Amric looked finally to Halthak, who flushed and gave a sheepish shrug. "Someone has to keep all you mad fools alive," he said.

The warrior considered making another attempt to dissuade them, but as he looked around at each of their faces he read defiance and quiet determination, and he bit down upon the words before they could form. Who was he to impugn their courage, anyway? They had each made their decisions with full knowledge of what they faced. For their own reasons, each had chosen to accompany him to aid his missing friends and, with luck, all of the lands. He and Valkarr were well accustomed to the battlefield, and Bellimar had certainly seen his share of death, but the others were not so inured. All in all, he decided, he could think of no more valorous act.

He nodded his thanks to them and wheeled his bay gelding toward the city's southern gate. The riders fell into line behind him, and they rode from the city under the gathering sky.

Twin pairs of eyes, pale and sharp as the hard frost before the first driving winter snowfall, watched from high atop the southern wall of Keldrin's Landing. As Amric and company disappeared over the first distant rise where the winding thread of road split the rolling green sward, the Elvar assassin Nyar turned to his brother Nylien.

"They depart the city," he remarked.

"Our lord predicted as much," Nylien said.

"Our lord is wise, as ever."

"The Nar'ath will no doubt ensure they do not return," Nylien said in a sorrowful tone.

"But our lord prefers to take few chances," Nyar pointed out.

The other brightened. "Just so, brother, just so."

"There will be many Nar'ath on the move."

"But we are shadows," Nylien said with confidence.

"So we are, brother. We are indeed shadows."

"I believe our lord will wish us to follow, and ensure they cannot affect his plans."

"We should prepare for travel," Nyar said with an eager nod.

"Ho there!" bellowed a voice from further down the wall-walk. A heavyset guard strode toward them, slightly favoring a bandaged left leg, and a crossbow dangled from one hand at his side. "What are you two doing there? Citizens are not allowed upon the wall-walk."

The Elvaren blinked at each other and broke into slow smirks.

"It addresses us, brother. It demands to know our purpose."

"So it does. It would be rude not to respond, despite our hurry."

"I had the same thought, my brother."

Pushing themselves lazily from the wall, they spread out and began to stroll toward the guard on either side of the walkway.

The guard slowed and faltered, his brow clouding as his gaze darted between them. "Wait, what are you doing?" he stammered. "You cannot be up here."

The assassins continued to advance at a leisurely pace, vulpine smiles splitting their features. Their pale faces and shocks of white hair seemed to float disconnected above their dark, leather-clad forms. The guard raised his crossbow, bracing it with his other hand and leveling it at first one and then the other. The Elvaren took no apparent notice of the weapon. The man searched their expressions and blanched. He began to take shuffling steps backward.

"You cannot be up here," he repeated in an overloud voice. "Do not come any closer, or I'll raise the alarm!"

Nyar slowed to a halt and put a slender finger to his lips, tapping them in thought. "It raises a worthy point, brother."

"How do you mean?" asked Nylien, stopping as well and turning to face him.

"It occurs that if our conversation proceeds with this one, the aftermath may serve to draw additional unwanted attention to the southern wall and gate, today and tonight. And our lord would certainly not wish this."

"Ah," sighed Nylien. "As ever, brother, your adherence to duty does you credit. Of course you are correct."

"Regrettably, the pleasures of conversing with this one will have to wait until we return," Nyar agreed with a sigh of his own.

"If it still remains within the city," Nylien said, raising one delicate eyebrow.

"It is the price of pursuing larger game, and doing our lord's will. We will not be so constrained, when he rises to power."

"But until then..."

"Yes, until then."

The assassins turned to the guard once more. The man stood facing them, bewildered, the point of the loaded crossbow bolt wavering between the two figures. His finger tightened upon the trigger as the pair regarded him with all the detached interest one might show an intrusive, uncommon insect. Then, in unison, they spun on their heels and began to walk the other way with identical sauntering gaits. The guard let out a long breath and watched them go, tracking their progress until they disappeared into the stairwell leaving the wall-walk. They did not once look back.

Amric kicked free of the saddle and slid to the ground. He knelt there, brushing his fingertips over the parched earth and then digging in to withdraw a fistful of sand. It poured from his hand and was caught by the breeze, swirling away like a gossamer veil. He squinted back the way they had come. A mere twenty yards away the soil was dark, rich and moist, giving rise to the lush green sward that undulated away behind them.

"What do you make of this?" he asked.

"Something is leeching the life from the very land here," Bellimar responded at once, nudging his steed closer. "There has long been a desolate region at the southern foot of the Hoarfang mountain range, but it was isolated, ringed in by crags and fertile plains."

"It is the same, the spreading wasteland my father heard about," Thalya said with quiet conviction. "It must be."

Bellimar's expression was grave. "If this extends all the way to the mountains, then its expansion has been rapid indeed," he said. "Too rapid."

Amric nodded and stood, brushing the sand from his palms. He turned and sighted along the ragged line where the vegetation gave grudging way to the advancing desert. Along that line, the grasses browned and grew thin, and the scattered copses of trees withered into weak, skeletal things. The transition was far too abrupt to be natural.

That the land was dying was plain to see. The questions that had to be answered now were how, and why.

"Could this be another way the disruption of Essence in the region manifests itself?" Halthak asked.

"I do not know, but I doubt it," Amric said with a slow shake of his head. "These symptoms do not match those of the forest, where life is maddened and twisted but not drained like this."

"I must concur," Bellimar said. "The magic in the region is rising out of control, strengthening magical effects and causing chaos through the agitation of all things that are linked to Essence. This would seem to represent the opposite. It does not match the pattern."

Valkarr grunted, frowning down from the saddle at the barren ground beneath his mount's hooves. "The earth dies," he said. "Just as it did beneath the flesh of the black things we fought in the forest."

Amric felt a chill, recalling how the flora had wilted and died wherever even a severed piece of the creatures came to rest for any length of time. It strained coincidence to believe that there was no connection between nearing the source of the foul creatures and encountering this widespread effect.

Syth was scanning the bleak horizon with a look of dismay upon his face. "Even if the flesh of these creatures is toxic, could they have done all this merely by walking around?" he asked in a dubious tone.

Bellimar shook his head. "I do not see how, unless there are unimaginably vast multitudes of them. To cause devastation at this level by tread alone would take more than seems possible, more than could be concealed. But we still do not know their source yet, and I think that might yield the answer."

Thalya sat her restive mare with a drawn expression, her green eyes roving from Bellimar to the seemingly boundless wasteland ahead. Amric tried to guess at her thoughts, but her stony expression yielded no hints. He swung into the saddle of his bay gelding and wheeled it about to face the group.

"Either way, we must be getting close. We continue south."

They rode on into the wasteland with the somber afternoon sky turning slowly above them. The terrain grew even more bleak, the remaining signs of plant and animal life becoming rarer with each passing hour. Stark outcroppings of sun-bleached rock knuckled their way through the sweeping dunes, and the ground around them seemed to peel back in aversion. The southern road became an ephemeral thing, a tentative strand of hard-packed earth winding through the parched land; it would come and go in glimpses, swept under by the wind-blown sands as often as not. Amric had begun to believe they would see no other creature in this desolate sea when they crested a ridge and caught the first distant signs of motion. At first he thought the shimmering waves of heat clinging to the ground were playing tricks upon his vision, but the more he stared, the more he realized what he was seeing. He brought the column of riders to a halt and pointed.

A group of a dozen or so dark figures was running over a faraway swell of sand, moving together with tireless purpose. As they watched, a second group of tiny, indistinct figures appeared over another hill, and then a third. The creatures were all headed north, toward them. Amric turned and led the way back behind the ridgeline. They left the remains of the highway and rode west for a time. As they threaded along the hills, the terrain offered occasional views of the progress of those they sought to avoid. The creatures did not appear to have noticed them over the yawning distance, as they continued on their respective paths to the north as if on a shared mission. Amric turned the group and headed south once again, deeper into the wasteland.

Over the next several hours, they were forced to change course many more times. Each time they reached a summit, they were greeted by the sight of more and larger packs of the black creatures skittering across the hills. It became an increasing challenge to avoid them, requiring the riders to weave back and forth in an ever more erratic pattern. On several occasions, the creatures passed close enough to the riders that Amric, lying flat upon the hill separating them, could pick out details of their ebon flesh and the tattered cloth wrappings dangling from their limbs. As with the ones they had faced before, these seemed to be modeled after various races, like animate statues cast of some lightless material in the mold of the peoples from far-flung lands. He saw the forms of humans and slender El-varen, stout Duergen and heavyset beast-men, the bird-beaked men from some deep southern clime whose nation he could not recall, and even an occasional Traug. He saw countless others too far away to discern, but their shapes and sizes proclaimed their diversity. At one point he was convinced he saw the tail and lean, broad-shouldered build of a Sil'ath, but it was too far away to be certain and the figure was quickly lost to sight behind the hills.

Amric ground his teeth in frustration at the pace of their progress. It seemed for every mile they struck further south, they spent as much or more effort in backtracking and sidestepping to avoid detection. Sooner or later they would be unable to avoid a conflict, and if the creatures had any way to signal each other over even moderate distance, the riders would soon find themselves thoroughly overwhelmed. Even if they did manage to win free, the creatures would be alerted to their presence, which would only make it more difficult to traverse this harsh wasteland unmolested. Casting a scathing look at the darkening heavens, he began to search for a suitable place to camp and wait out the night.

There had been precious few candidate locations on the journey here. Little more was offered than the lee of a coved hill or a scraggly copse of trees here and there. He preferred something far less visible and exposed to attack, here in the midst of hostile territory. They could turn west and head out of the desert and toward the coastal road, the same road that had brought him and Valkarr to this region, but it was a good half day's ride in that direction and would of course cost them the same amount of time on the morrow to return to this point. No, it had to be something close, and soon.

They veered to the southeast, avoiding two more groups of the black creatures running north with mile-eating strides. The ground became harder in vast, bare patches, as if the capricious winds had worn enough of the sand away to expose the ribcage of the land. The obscured sun began its preamble to setting, tinting with a rosy glow the whole of the sky to the southwest, where the cloud cover was most thin.

As they cautiously peered over another rise, Amric saw a huge, conical structure rising from the earth and forming a sharp silhouette against the pale sands in the distance. His skin prickled the instant his eyes fell upon it. It did not look man-made, and yet its shape was too symmetrical, too purposeful, to have been crafted by nature's hand. His eyes narrowed, straining against the fading light and the blur of the miles that separated them from the edifice. Tiny shapes scurried up and down the sloping sides of the thing like a swarm of black ants.

Amric clenched his jaw. They had found the hive of the black creatures at last.

Valkarr gave a low hiss and pointed eastward. With an effort, Amric tore his gaze from the nest and followed the Sil'ath warrior's gesture to see a huge tumble of rock jutting up from a rolling hill to the east. A narrow, chiseled path ascended to the top, and the ground fell away almost vertically on the other sides. Amric nodded his satisfaction; this would do very well. He took another sweeping look over the dunes, checking the movement and positions of the scattered packs of black creatures, and his eyes lingered again on the upraised nest. Then he swung his bay gelding back down the hill and around its base, wending toward the peak Valkarr had spotted.

It took the better part of an hour to reach it without exposing their profile along a ridgeline. Amric and Valkarr dismounted at the foot of the crag and, leaving the reins of their mounts with the others, began to climb the crumbling path up its side. The carved channel looked water-worn, which seemed incongruous with their desert surroundings, but Amric had to remind himself that this area had not always been so arid. The horses could be led up this path, he decided, but it would be a slow and noisy ascent. Anything lurking at the summit would be alerted by the clamor, and it would be best to ferret out such surprises beforehand.

The warriors worked their way up the path, silent as ghosts, until the soft rasp of metal on stone behind them caused both to glance back. Syth was following, one steel-sheathed hand braced against a squat boulder as he ascended. At their stern looks he flushed and hastily withdrew the offending gauntlet from the rock, but from the set of his jaw the man would not be turned back. Amric and Valkarr exchanged a look and continued up the path.

At the top of the escarpment, the warriors slipped over a raised lip and into a large crown of rock. They clung like shadows to the encircling wall, scanning their surroundings. Here, nestled within this giant bowl, was a marvel of vibrant greenery. A beard of ferns and thick bushes surrounded a strip of trees, and a carpet of fine grass led down to the jewel at the center of the crown, a clear, rippling pool. The waters curled and bubbled, fed from below by some brook or geyser that managed to force its way up through the heart of the crag. Amric shook his head in wonder. Life persevered, even amid such desolation. This explained the smoothing of the stone along the pathway, then. Rainfall and water pressure from below must couple to periodically flow over that lip, the lowest escape point, and over the centuries had carved a channel to the ground.

Amric dropped into a crouch, cocking his head to one side. There was no enemy in sight, but he knew with sudden certainty that they were not alone. One of his swords whispered free of its scabbard along his back, and he turned and melted into the bushes. Valkarr did the same in the other direction, and the warriors began gliding in a slow circuit of the place.

When Syth arrived at the summit, his mouth fell open at the sight that greeted him. He stepped forward onto the grass and took three quick strides toward the pool, grinning in delight.

"What heavenly place is this? I—" he began, and then he stiffened. The cold steel that appeared at his throat brought startling focus to several things in rapid succession. The first was that the scaly, muscular arm holding the weapon and the reptilian visage regarding him belonged to a Sil'ath, without a doubt, but it was not Valkarr. The second was that neither Valkarr nor Amric were anywhere to be seen. The last was that his senses had dulled considerably during his long months as an unwilling guest within Stronghold; he should never have allowed himself to be caught so blithely unaware.

Syth met the dispassionate eyes of his assailant and wondered if this Sil'ath could match Valkarr's blinding speed. He knew himself to be swift as well, and with one quick twist he could bat that blade aside with a gauntleted hand—

"Do not try," the Sil'ath said in a sibilant whisper. "I have no wish to take your head."

"Tis an empty prize you would be claiming there," called a nearby voice. Amric stepped from the undergrowth, and Valkarr rose like a wraith at his side. "And I must advise against making that strike, for fear of dulling your blade on his thick skull."

Syth scowled at the grinning swordsman even as the blade at his throat fell away.

"Warmaster! Valkarr!" the Sil'ath exclaimed, striding forward to clasp forearms with Amric.

"Well met, Innikar," Amric responded, clapping the newcomer on the shoulder as the fellow clasped forearms with Valkarr in turn. Another figure rose to its feet from a tall cluster of ferns a few yards away, and Syth jumped at its sudden proximity. It was another Sil'ath, more slender and wiry than Innikar or Valkarr, but no less formidable in appearance. The figure took a sinuous stride forward, and Syth realized with a start that it was a female of the species. Another round of the oddly formal greetings followed as she traded forearm grips with both Amric and Valkarr, and then she stepped back with a sly smile.

"You have both been away from home too long, if your senses have dulled so far as to permit a concealed potential enemy so near," she said. "Valkarr, were you not the one who instructed me in the ways of stealth?"

"So I was," Valkarr said with a grunt. He reached around and drew a small knife from his belt at the small of his back, reversed his grip on it with a flick of his wrist, and offered it to her hilt first. "Just remember that as long as I have been gone, Sariel, you have been gone longer still."

Sariel burst into musical laughter and accepted the knife, returning it to an empty sheath at her hip. She ran an appraising look up and down Syth, who realized the swirling winds around him had increased with his tension. He took several slow, deliberate breaths, and the air calmed with him. Sariel quirked a delicate brow ridge at him, and he flushed.

"It warms my heart to see you both," Amric said. "We lost your trail at Stronghold, and I feared the worst. Now I find myself hoping that my senses are indeed dulled, however, as I was able to detect only the two of you. Where are the others?"

Innikar slammed his swords home into the scabbards crossed upon his back. Syth noted that he was not as powerfully built as Valkarr, but he was a lean mass of corded muscle and moved with the same fluid ease. The Sil'ath warrior lifted his chin and met Amric's gaze. His tail lashed behind him and then grew still with a spasm of effort, the only outward sign of his agitation.

"We have much to tell you, warmaster," Innikar said in a bleak tone.

Amric nodded and clasped his shoulder again. "The two of you are well, and it is a start," he said. "Syth, let the others know it is safe to bring the horses up here. This peak is well sheltered from below, with a defensible path. We will stay the night here. I can only hope that Halthak has kept the other two from killing each other in our absence."

Syth nodded, and for once he had no retort. As he left, he rubbed at his throat where the caress of the blade's edge still lingered. He found himself hurrying more than was necessary, and he glared down at his own feet as if in reproach. He sifted through his discomfort, seeking the cause. Was he angry that Innikar had surprised him so easily? No, that was little more than a pinprick to his rather durable ego, and was soon forgotten. Had the undeniable femininity of the Sil'ath woman roused surprising feelings in him? No. Well, yes, if he was being honest, but he found no shame in admitting it. He could appreciate beauty in another race, and Sariel was indeed beautiful in an exotic and somewhat frightening way. The huntress Thalya was more stunning by far, however, and perhaps a degree less likely to gut him for making an advance. At least he hoped she was less likely to respond that way.

Soft laughter echoed behind him. The warmth of the reunion was an almost tangible thing at his back, and he felt a hollow pang in his chest in response as he started down the path. He could lay claim to no such future reunion of his own, he knew. No one would have come for him in Stronghold; if chance had not led a group of strangers to him, he would still be there, either dead or wasting away in that dreadful cage. Why did it bother him all of a sudden that no one awaited him with warm smile and firm grasp, eager to touch his flesh and, in so doing, reaffirm his well-being? It never had before. Trudging across the world and into the teeth of danger for the sake of lost friends was a grand gesture, if a bit dramatic for his tastes. And there was the rub, was it not? To be worthy of such gestures, one had to be willing to commit them on behalf of another. The air spun around him and tugged a persistent lock of hair across his eyes. Annoyed, he batted it away.

The rocky path curved and brought the trio below into sight. They turned away from the darkening wasteland to watch him as he descended. His gaze caught on the oval of Thalya's upturned face, and at that instant his heel slipped on a smooth, water-worn patch of stone. He bit back an oath as he caught himself. The green eyes of the huntress, still upon him, sparkled with amusement as a small smile played across her lips. His breath caught, and that strange pang lanced through his chest again. He shook himself and dragged his attention downward to focus upon his footing as he navigated the last portion of the path.

Thalya sat upon a flat-topped rock and dangled her bare feet in the cold water. Having seen the pool in the day's fading light, she knew it was shallow and held no mysteries, but it was easy to imagine different now as she stared into the black, rippling surface made depthless by the night. She looked up, searching again for the glimmer of stars across the roiling tapestry above her, but there were none to be found. The only light came from the insistent silver glow of the moon, pressed tight against the back of the clouds.

Her eyes fell to the men, still gathered around a small fire nestled back against the trees on the far side of the pool. Their conversation was too low to overhear at this distance, but even from here she could read the determination in every gesture made by the Sil'ath warriors. She watched Amric in particular, asking questions and inhaling the answers. The burning intensity in his features both drew and repelled her. Her father had developed such unrelenting focus later in his life, when he became convinced that the fate of the world rested upon his actions, and the change had confused and frightened her as a child. In later years, it had merely saddened her. So she studied Amric with an involuntary tightening of her skin, waiting for the signs she should have seen earlier in Drothis.

Syth glanced over at her many times, as he had been doing since she left the campfire in silence to sit here, alone by the water. She smiled and pretended not to see. Now and again she felt the weight of Bellimar's eyes upon her, but each time she snapped up to meet that unholy gaze with her own promise and hatred, she found him instead with head turned, seemingly engrossed by the conversation at hand, and the sensation faded. She glared a few extra seconds at him each time, but somehow she doubted he found her stare quite as unnerving. Irritated, she reached up in response to the nagging itch of the scabs and welts upon her face and then caught herself. She let her hand drop once more; they would heal in good time, and she would only make it worse and risk infection by scratching at the wounds.

At the fire, Halthak pushed himself to his feet and stretched. She knew in an instant that it was more than the nonchalant gesture he would have it seem. Sure enough, his craggy countenance lifted to send a tentative smile in her direction. He started toward her, picking his way over the rocks at the edge of the pool. When he reached her, he shifted from one foot to the other, his gnarled hand kneading upon the equally gnarled ironwood staff he always bore with him.

"May I join you?" he asked.

"Well, this rock is mine," she responded. "But I am still saving to purchase the others."

He blinked at her, and she sighed. She tried again, this time simply giving an encouraging smile and gesturing for him to take a seat. He settled cross-legged next to her, cradling one end of the staff in the crook of his arm while he swirled the tapered end in the water. He did not say anything, seeming content to sit in silence.

She cleared her throat. "So I see you grew bored of the strategy talk as well."

"They lost me early on," he admitted. "I really only wanted to hear what became of the other Sil'ath. They were all wounded in their escape from Stronghold, and one of them, Varek, succumbed to his injuries shortly thereafter. They were set upon by those black creatures, and only these two were able to fight their way free. Prakseth and Garlien were taken to that strange hive we saw in the distance, and Innikar and Sariel have been recuperating and trying to get close enough to the hive to rescue them."

"I know," Thalya said. "I was at the campfire as the tale was recounted." She winced at the unintended impatience in her tone.

"Oh," the Half-Ork mumbled. "Of course you were. I am sorry."

"No," she said, putting a hand on his arm. "The need for apology is mine. I am not very good with people. I am afraid it was not among my father's priorities when he trained me to hunt Bellimar."

He responded with a pinched smile, his tusks protruding at the corners of his broad mouth. "It is not a skill of mine, either. Too many see my features and reach conclusions that cannot be undone by mere words."

"You are certainly unlike any other Ork that I have seen," she remarked.

"I am *not* an Ork," he said with quiet heat. Then he flashed her a sheepish look. "But I know I owe more of my appearance to that part of my lineage than to my human side, even if I have no taste for war."

"If you have no taste for war, I'd say that makes you uncommon as either Ork *or* human, Halthak. From my experience, civilization is a thin veneer at best for either race."

Halthak chuckled, drawing the tip of his staff through the damp sand at the water's edge. "Perhaps you are right. Still, I would prefer to be normal like the rest of you, and not caught between two unwelcome halves."

Thalya burst out laughing and clapped a hand over her own mouth to stifle the sound, lest she draw unwanted attention to their perch from the denizens of the desert below. The baffled look in the Half-Ork's eyes only made her shake with laughter all the harder.

"Which of us normal folk would you be like, Halthak?" she said when she could safely speak again. "Syth, who is half human like yourself and yet also has a volatile pure elemental half to his nature? Perhaps Amric, born human but a Sil'ath in all but flesh? Would you trade fates with Bellimar the Damned, caught between the worlds of life and death? Even I, raised among my kind, was held apart by circumstance. Those two Sil'ath warriors over there are probably the most normal among us, and they follow a human warmaster despite their kind's fabled aversion to other races. None of us truly belong, for one reason or another. We are all misfits. And yet here we are, striving for what is in each of our hearts. What's more, if Amric is to be believed, this group of misfits might well save this undeserving world."

Halthak stared at her with wide eyes, and snapped his mouth shut after a moment.

"I think you are better with people than you are aware, Thalya," he said in a soft voice. He held out one knobby hand. "May I?"

She cocked her head at him, uncertain what he meant. In truth, her own words had shaken her a bit; the revelation still resonated in her mind, plucking at deep-rooted threads of pain within her like a hand brushing at the strings of some dusty instrument and marveling to find it still in perfect tune. Distracted, she slipped her hand into his, feeling the creases and calluses of his pebbled flesh. The suffusion of warmth that followed stole her breath in a gasp.

The Half-Ork's earnest expression cracked and darkened before her astonished eyes. His thick lip split in several places, and various welts and bruises sprang into existence on his whiskered face. With a start, she recognized them as mirrors to her own injuries. Even as the realization dawned, the marks shrunk and vanished from his features, and in seconds they were gone as if they had never been. Thalya felt the heat subside in her own face, and her free hand rose of its own volition to explore the now unbroken skin of her face. The wounds were gone, the sting and itch no more than a memory. The blooming warmth of Halthak's magic withdrew, and he released her hand with a gentle squeeze. Rising to his feet, he walked back to the others, leaving her sitting there with her hand on her cheek.

Syth stood before Halthak reached the guttering campfire, and he passed the healer with a speculative look. He hopped lightly from rock to rock, and then spun to a seat beside her in a cool wash of air. He wore a boyish grin as he turned to her, seemingly prepared to share some latest bit of mischief, when suddenly he froze.

"What are you gawking at?" she demanded, raising an eyebrow at him.

He closed his mouth with a snap. "Your face—the wounds—" he breathed.

She gave a snort. "You can add poet after horse trader on your list of unlikely professions."

Even in the faint silver light she could see the color rise to his cheeks, but it was quickly masked over by a rogue's grin. "It took me by surprise, is all," he said. "I meant to say that you look lovely this evening."

"How goes the reunion over there?" she asked in a flat tone. He took the hint to change the subject and followed her gaze toward the campfire.

"I believe they have discussed every last detail of the terrain for a hundred miles in any direction. There is no angle of approach that will allow us near the hive unseen, however, especially with the marked increase in activity around it in recent days. They are all looking to Amric to concoct some magic scheme—" his face wrinkled as he seemed to regret his own choice of words "—that will enable a ragtag band of blades to snatch their friends from under the noses of an army of undying creatures. It seems he has a history of pulling off strategic miracles."

"He does seem a man for miracles at times," Thalya mused, studying the warmaster and the Sil'ath warriors gathered around him, hanging on his every word and gesture. "There is something about him that inspires confidence. I only hope it is justified, if we are to leave this wasteland alive."

When she received no response, she turned her head to find Syth's eyes upon her in the dark, his expression carefully neutral. A brittle smile spread across her features.

"Whatever is the matter, Syth?" she asked in a sweet and dangerous tone. "Does it bother you that I might admire the swordsman?"

"No, of course—"

"Will you duel for my affections, then?" she pressed, anger seeping into her voice. "Or did I miss the part where you already staked your claim to me? I hope you struck a better trade than when you bought your horse earlier."

He looked bewildered now, taken aback at her hostility. "No, that's not it at all. I—"

She leaned in toward him. "Are we to rut like animals here and now?" she breathed, putting a new kind of heat into her words. "Or wait until the others are asleep?"

"You don't understand," he said, raising his hands before him to fend her off. "I did not mean—I only wanted—" His shoulders slumped and he shook his head as the ever-present wind whirled about him in fitful gusts. "I am afraid I am not very good with people."

She stiffened as the words stung her. Her own words to Halthak, spoken mere minutes ago, and she had proven their veracity again.

"Since we rescued you, I have been seeking every opportunity to be near you," he said softly. "Every time I resolve not to make a fool of myself before you, and every time I prove myself a liar."

She wanted to mouth a scathing reply, to insist that he did not know her, could not know her, that this pathetic act of devotion did not suit him and was but a poor mask for his baser intentions. Anything to make him leave. But the words lodged in her throat, and in the end she forced her eyes back to the fire reflected in the ripples of the pond. Syth sat a few feet away, not looking at her, seeming uncertain whether to leave or try again to explain.

She cleared her throat at last. "They seem very happy to be together again," she said, nodding toward Amric and the Sil'ath warriors. Between periods of intense discussion across the campfire, there were warm smiles and low laughter, and on occasion one figure would give another a playful shove in response to some jest.

"There is sorrow for the deceased, and worry for those still lost, as well as tension for the morrow," Syth said, appearing grateful for the change of subject. "But yes, there is an abiding joy as well. They are family, and in all honesty, it made me feel uncomfortable to be over there, an outsider among them. It gave me the opportunity to...." He trailed off and looked away.

"To come over here and instead be attacked by a stranger?" she prompted with a wry smile. "It was unfair of me, Syth, I am sorry. But you do not know me, and I have been desired solely for my appearance before."

His face swung back toward her in the silvery light. "Then tell me of yourself. And let me tell you of myself. I have a sense that you grow tired of being an outsider as well."

Her eyes narrowed. "I keep expecting the brash fellow who has been trying to impress me these past few days to make a sudden return."

"Oh, he is still in here, clamoring to slip his bonds," he assured her with a sly wink. "Or perhaps he is scouring the night for some jeweled bauble he is hoping to trade for your affections. We had best talk quickly, before he returns."

She laughed and shook her head. "I think you are better with people than you are aware, Syth."

"That is a kind thing to say," he remarked, drawing his knees up and wrapping his arms around them.

She smiled. "A friend told me that recently, when I needed to hear it."

CHAPTER 18

Through the velvet folds of the dream, grasping hands reached for him. He spun away, trying as he did so to discern their owner, but the phantom figure faded back from him like smoke before the wind. Alert for the next attack, he strove to bring the distorted milieu of the dream into focus, but focus was elusive as well; reality wavered and shuddered, but refused to converge. Angry now, he sought identity instead, and this at least came more readily. His name, he knew upon reflection, was Amric. He was warrior and warmaster, and he would not be denied. With identity came purpose, and he peeled at the intervening layers of the subconscious. Hazy at the forward fringe of his vision, the figure whirled and fled. His swords flashed into his hands, and he leapt in pursuit.

He sped after the darting shadow, racing through a realm of mist. Obstacles reared from the fog, forcing him to hurdle and dodge, and his quarry, seeming more familiar with the terrain, drew steadily away from him. He redoubled his efforts, but still the figure dwindled in the distance. Grinding his teeth in frustration, he pressed on. Sentinel shapes pressed forth from the mist, resolving into huge trees, and sunlight pierced the grey ceiling above to speckle the matted ground before him. A thick, verdant forest coalesced about him as he ran, and its appearance tugged at his memory. It bore a striking resemblance, he realized after a moment, to the sprawling woodlands surrounding Lyden where he had spent his youth among the Sil'ath, hunting and exploring.

The sights and smells slipped easily about him, familiar and comforting as a long-worn glove. It was like returning home, and he could see why he might have summoned these remembered environs in a dream, but the forest seemed determined to prove a hindrance to his progress. Every rock tilted beneath his boot heel, every upturned root caught at his passing foot, every wind-waved branch swayed into his path. At the same time, his quarry seemed to suffer no such difficulties, and even as he struggled past he wondered at how the land he loved could so favor another.

The shadow melted from sight far ahead, and Amric ran on, following on pure instinct. The towering trees whipped by as he ran, and several times he would have sworn they shifted somehow to shoulder him from his path. Twisting and darting, he wound his way among them, his fury undiminished.

He slid to a halt in a sunlit clearing, his skin prickling with warning. His eyes narrowed. He tightened his grips on the swords until the muscles of his arms stood corded in sharp relief, and he began a slow circuit of the clearing, moving with a panther's stride. He reached his arrival point and stopped, frowning. Something was amiss here, he could feel it. He scanned the ring of trees and saw nothing out of place. His gaze fell then upon the grassy center of the clearing, and he froze. He saw his trampled path circumscribing the glade, except for one side where it veered gently inward, away from the perimeter. He had not meant to do that, and did not remember altering his path in that manner. He stalked toward it, and found himself abruptly at the edge of the clearing. He whirled and saw that he had swerved again, away from that spot.

Setting his jaw, he took slow steps in that direction, pausing after each stride to assess his progress. Resistance rose against him, as if he walked against a river's steady current. He concentrated upon the forest ahead, refusing to allow his eyes to slide to either side. He thought at first he was looking at a portion of the forest draped in deepest shadow, and then it seemed that it must instead be a looming, amorphous wedge of rock. His mind struggled to fill the void in his perception. He growled to himself. Damn it all, but this was his forest, in his dream, and he would not be deceived. He concentrated, reaching for what he could not see, and like a parting veil it finally yielded its secrets to him in halting stages.

It was no natural structure, but a cottage or small house of some kind, nestled back amid the trees and sheltered in the lee of the hill behind it. He could not place the architecture, with its strange, almost delicate flowing lines, and yet somehow it struck him as oddly familiar. Revealed at last, it stood in solitude there at the edge of the glade, blending and not blending, as beautiful and out of place as a sparkling jewel lying in a field of grass. Before him was a door, hanging ajar in its graceful, high-peaked arch. A muffled noise echoed within, and Amric's puzzlement and caution dissolved in the heat of remembered purpose. He shouldered the door aside and plunged into the cottage, one sword crossed before him and one held low and away.

The interior of the place was no less otherworldly, and the décor baffled his eye as he tried to place its origins. It was not from any of the western nations. Pakhrian then, or perhaps Illirian? Somewhere remote, certainly, but again he had an overwhelming sense from the instant he crossed the threshold that he should know this place. He had little time to ponder the matter, however; the figure he sought was ahead, crouching over something in a shadowed alcove with its back to him.

Amric leapt forward, raising his blades to cut down this ghostly predator before it could complete its sinister objective. The figure spun to meet him with appalling speed, those grasping hands reaching for him once more—and Amric froze in shock. The figure was wholly human, and its features were his own.

The figure offered no resistance, and its features—his features—were settled into unfamiliar lines of sorrow and resignation. Determination flickered there, and his double took a sliding step to interpose his body before the alcove at his back, blocking Amric's view. There was a dizzying moment as Amric was wrenched from his own body, and he saw as if through the eyes of his double. From there he beheld himself, a hard, frightening, vengeful man in dark leather and oiled mail, standing with wicked blades upraised to deal the killing blow. He saw his own face twisted into a mask of rage and hatred, with that mask cracked in places to reveal confusion. He reached out with open hands toward the other, not grasping or threatening at all, but rather beseeching. And hopeful, ever hopeful.

He watched suspicion cross the battle-hardened visage, watched the raptor gaze of the warrior dart from his face to his outstretched hands, and from there to the shadowed recess behind him. He could not tell if it was the light of comprehension he saw there, or merely the split second decision in battle of the warrior born, but either way the features closed like ironbound doors and walled away the last of his hope. Hatred and fury blazed in those grey eyes that were mirrors of his own, and the swords flashed toward him.

Amric's eyes flared open and his fist tightened convulsively on the hilt of the sword lying at his side. He did not otherwise move or make a noise, but instead took shallow, controlled breaths as he drank in his surroundings. The chill night air of the desert washed over him in a questing breeze, and the lean trees of their elevated campsite swayed overhead. The dry whisper of rustling ferns and the slow bubbling of the spring-fed pool reached his ears, punctuated by the occasional grumbling snort from one of the horses.

Rolling his head slightly to the side, he could see Innikar standing watch near the downward trail. The Sil'ath warrior sat cross-legged on a flat rock with one sword bared across his knees; he was motionless except for the occasional swivel of his head. He kept glancing in one direction, and Amric tilted his head to follow the stare. Bellimar stood there, perched on the outer edge of the crown of rock like some great bird of prey, cloak wrapped tightly around him as he gazed down at the wasteland far below. From below, Amric thought, he must look like just another patch of midnight against the scowling peak of rock. He gave a grim smile; he wondered who was more discomfited by the nighttime watch arrangement, Innikar at discovering that the old man never needed to sleep, or Bellimar at Amric's insistence that an additional person always keep watch with him. The vampire had given no sign that his word—or his self-control—could not be trusted, but even a relaxed tiger was still a tiger.

Amric let the tension drain from him, and he released his white-knuckled grip on the sword. With all quiet at the camp, his thoughts turned to the strange dream. For a fleeting instant upon awakening he had felt near to some burgeoning understanding of what he had seen, but now it escaped him. He struggled to recall the details, which only moments ago had seemed so vivid, before his conscious mind could bury them further. The pursuit over familiar ground, the elusive foe with his features, the alien and yet somehow familiar hidden structure, the jarring shift in perspective at the end; he turned it all over and over in his mind.

There were many troubling aspects to the dream, but most troubling to him were his own actions at the end, when he had clearly seen his quarry to be unarmed and reaching out to him, and yet he had still chosen to attack. He had slain many in battle, but he had never killed in cold blood, and the depth of the hatred marring his expression nagged at him. And what was striking down himself, in essence, meant to signify? Some unsatisfied hostility toward a blood-family he had never known? He had dwelled on such matters as a child, as was to be expected, but in all honesty he could not remember considering the subject for many years now.

He frowned and shook his head, chiding himself for a fool. The morrow would be draining enough without losing sleep to mull over some silly dream. The others were waiting on him to produce a strategy that would get them all safely to and from the hive with their rescued friends in tow, and he had no idea as of yet how he was going to manage that particular feat. He closed his eyes, firmly pushed the lingering remnants of the dream from his mind, and he began sifting once more through all he knew of the hive and the bleak terrain surrounding it.

An hour later, when Valkarr rose from his bedroll to relieve Innikar at watch, Amric was still lying awake as his mind chewed relentless circles around the problem.

"Is it a trap?" Sariel whispered in the Sil'ath tongue.

Amric gave a slow shake of his head without glancing at her. They were lying prone, pressed to the stones like a coating of moss as they peered over the edge and onto the wasteland below.

"It is an unnecessary ruse," Innikar replied in a low tone from the other side of Sariel. "If they knew we were here, they could have swarmed up even that narrow path and overwhelmed us by sheer force of numbers by now."

"Still, the timing is suspect," Sariel mused.

Innikar grunted assent. The trio fell silent, squinting into the gritty, biting wind blowing at them from the north. In the distance, the last of the cloth-wrapped black creatures were disappearing into that swirling haze of sand.

Innikar cleared his throat with an oblique glance toward Amric. "The old man was awake throughout the night," he said.

"I know," Amric responded.

"He said that he requires no sleep. Is he truly a...?"

"Yes. Is or was, and not even he knows which anymore."

Innikar rested his chin on his fist and pondered that for a moment.

"Then," put in Sariel, "he is likely telling the truth about the rest, about what he saw last night."

"Yes, I believe him on that count as well."

"I can think of only one destination to the north for them to march against in force," Innikar said after a moment.

Amric met the Sil'ath warrior's eyes with a grim nod: Keldrin's Landing. A veritable army of the creatures had swept over the wasteland in the hours since dawn's first light, issuing forth from the hive in determined batches ranging in size from a handful to as many as twenty. The sun hung directly overhead now, struggling to pierce the tempestuous haze, and he estimated that more than three hundred of the strange creatures had passed within sight of their perch over the course of the morning. Even more troubling was Bellimar's report after a long night's vigil that the exodus had been going for many hours before daybreak, such that they had seen only the trailing portion of it, and the lesser portion at that. The creatures all seemed to be headed due north, and there was not much in that direction to offer as a target save the city itself. If indeed their path went so far, then Keldrin's Landing was likely in for a concerted attack, and that assault could come as early as nightfall.

"We cannot know the minds of such alien creatures," Amric said. "They might be abandoning one nest to create another elsewhere. We should not draw conclusions until we see inside this hive for ourselves."

Sariel nodded, her expression tight. Amric placed a hand on her arm and smiled gently.

"You are right to think the city is in jeopardy," he said. "It is still the most likely explanation. But there is little we can do from here. We cannot get ahead of that ragged army of fiends in time to warn the city's people. There are now far too many foes between here and there, and even though a good horse can outrun those things for a time, they never seem to tire." It was true; they had seen it before, and every group that had burst forth from the hive that morning had traveled at a dead run, soundless and unflagging, until disappearing over the horizon.

"You misunderstand," she said. "I am indeed concerned for Keldrin's Landing and its people, but I am troubled by something else as well. The creatures bore no captives in their departure."

"Yes, I noted that as well."

Sariel turned a stony gaze upon him. "This implies that sufficient forces remain behind to restrain the captives," she said. "Or that the captives no longer require restraining."

Amric's jaw clenched. "We shall know which is the case soon enough."

He narrowed his gaze against the stinging wind. The black creatures were lost to view, leaving the rippling dunes as unblemished as a vast, crumpled sheet of canvas. He lowered his head and slithered down and backward until he was safely out of sight from below, then sprang to his feet and padded to the other side of the grassy bowl, skirting the pool as he went. He slid into place beside Valkarr and looked down upon the wasteland from the southwestern edge of the tall crag's crown of rock.

The hive was quiet, with nothing more than a black, yawning hole atop a massive dome of sand to reveal its presence. At first glance the structure could almost blend with the more natural landscape surrounding it, but its height and the odd uniformity of its conical shape soon exposed its subterfuge. Upon further observation, it became evident that this eerie monarch of the dunes was the only one among its brethren seemingly immune to the capricious, clawing wind that frayed the mounds around it. Here the wasteland shifted and remade itself continuously; only the hive remained unchanged.

Amric watched the hive for long, crawling minutes, and then made his decision. He sprang to his feet and strode for the horses, tethered and hooded against the blowing sand.

"Mount up, everyone," he said.

Gone was his waking plan to send the stealthiest among them on foot to the entrance of the hive in order to get an undetected glimpse inside. That plan had never satisfied him, but it was the best the situation had offered. The Sil'ath were renowned for their ability to fade like ghosts past enemy fortifications, and he and his warriors were some of the best among a race who excelled at such things, but the terrain offered precious little cover and he doubted even their odds of getting close enough against the swarm of activity around the hive. The circumstances had changed, however, and trap or not, coincidental timing or not, he would have that closer look at their enemy now.

The riders left the crag and picked their way down the treacherous trail. They rode instead of leading the horses, as the prospect of being thrown by a stumbling horse seemed preferable to being beneath one, tugging at its reins. Sariel rode with Amric on his bay gelding, and Innikar sat behind Valkarr on his blue dun. If they were forced to outrun an ambush, the horses would still offer far more speed over a short distance than being on foot, even with the extra weight. Amric's mount lost its footing and began to slide, dropping its haunches and bracing all four hooves on the rocky path. The warrior's stomach took a sickening plunge, but he kept a steady hand on the reins and the beast recovered.

When they reached the sands below, he exhaled slowly and wheeled about to await the others. He patted the bay's shuddering neck and murmured into its flicking ear. He realized with a mild start that the horse had no name; he had not asked after any existing name when he bought it, and he had never given it one. He had not expected to spend so much time on horseback. The animal had a courageous heart, and he decided it deserved a good name as soon as one came to him.

It took the better part of an hour to reach the base of the hive. Looking up its sloping height, Amric was struck by the sheer size of the structure. He had known it was huge in comparison to the more ordinary mounds around it, but here, at its foot, it seemed to stab at the very sky. The surface was hard and unnaturally smooth. It was not the slickness of water-worn stone, or the polish of a cut gemstone, but rather an unbroken, unblemished expanse of sand somehow welded together into a curved surface as hard as granite. There was an abrasive tooth to it, such that even the iron-shod hooves of the horses were able to find purchase on its steep slope.

Amric scanned the rolling hills again, finding them still devoid of life. He motioned for the others to spread out, and then he took the lead up the slope. The incline proved too steep for the horses to make a direct ascent, but he was able to guide his bay gelding in a more gradual circuit of the thing, making a slow spiral to its peak. From its towering height, he was afforded a panoramic view of the surrounding desert, and he stopped more than once to survey the land. The swirling winds still limited sight distance, but nothing stirred in any direction aside from the shambling dunes themselves.

They reached the peak and found that the outer lip marked the outline of a broad crater with a gaping hole at its center. Descending from the edges of the maw were numerous crude stairways which appeared to be carved from the interior wall of the structure. They twisted away into the darkness far below. The entire thing was hollow, Amric realized; given its mammoth size, there was no telling how many more of the creatures might still be contained below.

Amric slid from his horse, and Valkarr did the same. They left the reins with the others and crept forward to the edge of the opening, crawling in silence for the last dozen paces. They peered over the rim, tilting their heads at an angle such that only the barest sliver of silhouette would show to any observers below.

It was afternoon and the sun was no longer at its zenith. Skewed now in the sky, it sent a slanted shaft of thick, muddled light into the hive to pool off center on the floor of the cavern far below. Thus it was that, as Amric's eyes adjusted to the darkness inside, he was able to pick out details of the room's perimeter there first.

The place was huge and circular, and far from deserted.

Scores of large openings were cut into the wall at ground level along the outside arc of the room, and hulking black creatures vanished into or emerged from their depths, moving with industrious speed. Amric noted that the floor of the place was well below the wasteland's ground level. His jaw clenched as he wondered how far that network of tunnels extended beneath the desert. Not terribly far, he decided, or the mass exodus they had witnessed earlier need not have taken place above ground.

The creatures were larger than the humanoid forms he had seen from these fiends thus far, perhaps half again the height of a tall man, with elongated heads pulled in tight to their chests. They were heavyset, at least twice as broad at the shoulders as a man, and they moved with ponderous strength. Their arms were overlong, ending in strange appendages that were not hands, and several thick, sinuous tentacles sprouted from either side of a ridge of spikes that ran down their hunched backs. Even so, there were some obvious similarities; many of the creatures trailed the same strips of tattered cloth, and their flesh was the same dull black as the others had been. It was evident that they shared a common nature.

All this he absorbed in the first few instants of observation, and then a cluster of activity at the heart of the chamber drew his eye. He focused upon the shadowy movement there. The uncertain light from above was not the only illumination, he realized with a chill. Murky pools of some green, viscous liquid shimmered in an array around the upraised center of the room, like sinister spokes radiating from the axle of some great wheel. The fluid gave off a spectral light that bathed the cavern from the underside in a subdued greenish hue. Unidentifiable objects were floating half submerged in those pools. The dark, hulking shapes moved tirelessly between the pools, using both their limbs and their tentacles to push the objects below the surface, or to roll them in the fluid over and over, as if they were basting meat on a spit.

The center of the chamber rose like a cone in a smaller scale imitation of the outer shell of the hive. Even dwarfed as it was by the rest of the hollow structure, it was still quite large, as Amric noted when he saw one of the black creatures scurry up the side of it. His eyes traveled to the peak of the cone, positioned directly below its larger counterpart above, and he squinted, trying to discern the movement he saw there.

Then the details of the grisly scene emerged from the gloom, and the blood congealed in his veins. A sharp, strained intake of breath at his side told him that Valkarr was seeing the same thing.

A towering creature jutted from the opening in the cone. Only its grotesque torso was visible above the stone, but that upper portion alone was twice the height of a man. It was the same obsidian hue as the other creatures, but it appeared to be covered by the overlapping plates of a thick carapace. It had an elongated, triangular head and a broad, protruding, under-slung jaw. Unlike the others, it had eyes that were not black within black, but instead glowed the same luminous green as the pools.

As Amric watched, one of the hulking creatures hurried up the cone with a squirming bundle enfolded tightly in its thick arms and tentacles. The monstrosity reached out with its four long, many-jointed limbs to accept the offering, and Amric saw in speechless horror that the prize was a half-naked man. The hapless fellow seemed barely conscious, but he thrashed and managed a thin scream as the huge thing raised him to its mouth. Amric tensed in futile rage, certain the man was to be consumed alive, but what followed proved far worse.

The monster's huge jaws flared open and separated, revealing features beneath that were almost human in shape, if not in color. Full, curved lips that were uncomfortably female in appearance parted to reveal rows of gleaming fangs. The thing brought their faces together, but rather than tear into his flesh, it pressed its wicked mouth to his in a revolting parody of a kiss. The splayed appendages of its jaw closed upon the man's head, wrapping around it to hold him fast. Its spine arched backward and its chest swelled, and Amric realized it was inhaling deeply, as if drawing the breath from the lungs of its victim. The struggling man stiffened and convulsed, his eyes bulging and fixed upon nothing. The color drained from his exposed flesh, and he grew paler and paler until he reached a ghostly white hue that was striking against the darkness. The creature's glowing green eyes brightened, and an eerie purr of pleasure reverberated throughout the cavern.

Then, without breaking contact, the monster began to exhale. The man's body shook and shuddered as his flesh darkened. Black tendrils writhed along the skin, spreading from his head down his arms and torso and to his lower limbs. Amric's stomach turned. It was like watching a vessel being filled with dark, noxious liquid. The exhale lasted impossibly long, like a single slow pump of some massive bellows. When it ceased, the man had gone limp and his flesh was a deep, dull and uniform black from head to toe.

The monster severed its kiss, and began to spin the body. From somewhere in its gaping maw it produced a thick, sticky cord of some pale material, which it wound about the still form with each circuit. In seconds the body was wrapped so completely that not even a hint of black flesh showed through.

The jointed arms released the cocooned form to be caught in the waiting arms of the servant creature. The latter turned without hesitation and bore this new burden down the slope and away. It lumbered to one of the green pools and slid the stiff figure into the viscous liquid, pushing it carefully beneath the surface.

From its encasing throne at the center of the chamber, the huge monstrosity turned to look expectantly into the shadows. Amric followed its imperious gaze to see a handful of men huddled together in that direction, beyond the pools. One of the heavyset creatures approached, and its tentacles snaked out to grasp another victim. It lifted the thrashing fellow from the ground and caged him within its iron arms, and then wheeled back toward the center at a shambling run.

A white-hot fury rose in Amric, burning away the shreds of his paralyzing horror. He spread his hands to push himself to his feet, but his vision grew bright at the edges and a crippling dizziness washed over him. A sharp sense of vertigo struck him as he considered the fact that he was within mere inches of a plummet that would take him over a hundred feet to the unyielding floor of the cavern below. It was the same troubling spell of weakness that had plagued him within Stronghold, except there was no Essence Fount to blame here. He pushed it from his mind; it was a matter for another time. He pressed his cheek against the abrasive stone and sucked in a steadying breath through clenched teeth.

Valkarr's head spun toward him, fixing him with a worried stare. Amric shook his head in frustration, the sweat beading on his forehead as he fought against the encroaching brilliant white light that threatened to steal his sight. The world around him shrank to a dull echo, enclosing him. With a guttural snarl and an effort of will, he hurled it back and surged to his feet. He stood there a moment, shaking and swaying as the blood roared in his ears. He glanced at the others, intending to make a reassuring gesture, and was surprised to see that they were all swaying as well. He blinked the sweat from his eyes as his vision and hearing returned, and he realized the dome was shuddering beneath their feet with a rumbling sound of thunder. As quickly as it had come, however, the ground tremor faded and was gone, leaving them all shaken.

Amric spun toward the crater just as the monstrosity below cast its baleful gaze upward. Alien green eyes fixed upon his silhouette standing stark against the roiling sky, and narrowed in malevolent regard.

He tensed, bracing himself for the rush of enraged minions that would come storming up the twisting stairs. The martial strategist in him insisted they should flee; he had too few warriors to hold so many exit ramps against the number of hulking creatures he had seen below. But the wolf in him had its fangs bared now, and had no intent of leaving those captives behind to their fates.

To his great surprise, however, the giant fiend in the chamber below did not order an assault. Instead, it turned to its minions and made curt motions with its long, jointed arms. The creatures withdrew in obedient silence, backing into the tunnels that honeycombed the perimeter of the cavern. The one which had been bearing forth a new captive simply peeled back its writhing tentacles and dumped the man unceremoniously to the ground before shambling from the room. The man lay where he fell, groaning but otherwise motionless.

The towering monster turned its gaze skyward once more. It spoke in a voice that was alien and yet decidedly female, a lilting and buzzing harmonic that grated at his ears.

"I had not thought to find your kind again on this world," she said. "Not yet, at least."

Amric exchanged a puzzled look with Valkarr. He did not know what response to make, so he made none. The creature tilted her savage head at him and writhed in her enclosure.

"Come ahead then, Adept," she called with a note of impatience. "We have much to discuss."

Adept? Amric did not recognize the appellation. He glanced back at Bellimar, but the old man was unmoving and expressionless, standing tall and straight with his cloak wrapped about him. The vampire's eyes burned at him from beneath iron grey brows. The warrior looked to the others. He read anger and determination in the Sil'ath warriors; Sariel in particular appeared ready to leap from the edge at a moment's suggestion. Halthak looked pale and uncertain, but his white-knuckled hands were steady upon his ironwood staff. Thalya had an arrow nocked to her bow and her veil drawn across her face, revealing nothing but her emerald eyes. Syth's expression flickered between resolve when he looked at the hive entrance ahead and a protective concern when he glanced to Thalya at his side.

Amric returned his gaze to the pit below, studying the foul creature shifting in place as she glared up at him. He looked again at the prisoners, bent and huddled on the stone floor in that hellish cavern. He could not see any Sil'ath among them, but the distance and the poor light made it impossible to be certain. Regardless of race, they were mortal men, his kind. Soon to become her kind.

He spun on his heel and strode over to the group. He relayed in brief everything that he and Valkarr had seen in the void below. He described the towering creature and the numbers it commanded, and he watched their expressions tighten as he told of the captives and the horrifying transformation one had undergone before their eyes.

"So," Sariel muttered. "It may not have been a trap before, but it is almost certainly one now."

"Without a doubt," Amric replied. His storm-grey eyes were cold and hard, holding an iron promise as they shifted back to the gaping maw in the crater that led into shadow below. "And I am going in anyway."

A wolfish smile spread across Sariel's face.

CHAPTER 19

The black-robed man sat, cross-legged on a high parapet, with eyes closed and mind far away. Wan sunlight spilled across his upturned face, giving his dark beard a tinge of gold, but he did not feel its meager warmth. At his back, the colossal fortress hummed with the power that coursed beneath it like a winter river swelling against its ceiling of ice, but he took no note of this either. If not for the shallow rise and fall of his chest and the occasional furrowing of his brow, he could have been one with the stone.

The clouds crawled above him as time passed, and the sun fell slowly in the sky as if it sought a better look at his still features.

At last his eyes fluttered open as he returned to himself, and his face settled once more into hard lines. He drew a deep breath and spat a sulfurous string of oaths. Slamming a palm to the stone, he pushed himself to his feet. He looked out over the walled courtyards surrounding the fortress, and past there to the spreading mantle of forest. He stood rigid, fists clenched, and then his shoulders slumped.

Almost three days he had spent in this wretched place that reeked of musk and death, and the trail was cold. The marks of his quarry's power were in ample evidence at the core of the fortress, but the lack of guile and restraint employed there was in sharp contrast to the thoroughness of the vanishing afterward. It was a maddening mystery; the cunning and skill required to evade one with his considerable tracking skills bespoke an astonishing discipline, a long practice at the art of concealment that did not match the hasty, brutish splash of power used inside.

Worse, no matter how far he extended his senses, he could detect no further signs of his quarry exercising that power, to any degree. What Adept could go so long without embracing so much as a hint of his potential on this pathetic world? He could be a veritable god among the primitives here.

He sighed and looked down, digging through a pouch at his belt. He brought forth a small, dense loaf of travel bread and a sheaf of dried meat, eyed them both for a moment, and then returned them to the pouch and tucked it beneath his robes. He had hoped to be done with this mission by now, and his supplies were running low. Much longer, and he would have to seek food among the indigenous races here. He frowned in distaste. The fortress still held considerable stores of clean water, for which he was grateful, but what food he had found was either spoiled or revolting in nature. The stench of the lifeless place had grown to such an extent that he dreaded venturing within to scavenge for stores.

For the hundredth time that day, he considered simply striking out to the west in the hopes of following a more mundane trail. He was skilled in such methods, but he would be forced to exercise his power repeatedly to fend off the creatures being driven mad by the draw of magic. Such outbursts could mask the subtle and remote magical signs of his true prey. Worse, they would eventually alert his quarry to his own presence.

He shook his head in frustration. For a mad, impulsive moment he considered returning to Queln and activating the Essence Gate in full. He had the knowledge, as an agent of the Council in a remote and hostile land. No amount of clever hiding would save his quarry from the consequences. Let him go to ground on a sundered world, he thought with savage satisfaction. It beckoned invitingly as the solution to his quandary, but at the same time he knew he would be a fool to do it. It would rather undermine his efforts at redemption, he decided with a regretful sigh, if in the process he committed such an unsanctioned act. In fact, tampering with the Gate without the Council's express orders would make their fury at his previous blunder seem like nothing more than a frown of disapproval; his life would almost certainly be forfeit.

No, as much as he was galled by the delay, patience was still the key. And until his quarry gave himself away by using his power, he was just another grain of sand lost in a desert.

A sudden itch tickled at the fringe of his awareness. He stiffened and immediately squeezed his eyes shut as he reached out with his senses to seek its source. He found only echoes of a single tantalizing pulse of power, fading before he could ascertain more than a general direction: west, as he had surmised, and a bit south as well. Somewhere in the wasteland, then. He looked at the heavy clouds thickening the sky in that direction, and he fought down the wild urge to rip open a Way and leap closer to the one he sought. The pulse had not lasted long enough for him to get a location with any accuracy, however, and so if another signal followed it would likely force him to open yet another Way in rapid succession. If the awaited confrontation was near at last, it would be rash to tire himself without need.

He dropped to his seat upon the high parapet and waited, his eyes closed and his mind searching far away. Patience was the key.

Amric stalked down the crude stairs, and the gloom of the cavern closed over him like dark waters over a sinking stone. Bellimar followed a few paces behind him, a cold, soundless presence at his back. More twisting stairways ran like veins down the interior wall of the great chamber. On three of them, the other Sil'ath warriors mirrored his progress.

He did not glance up; he had to trust that Thalya, Syth and Halthak were following his orders and staying out of sight as well as possible. Given the way the creature's narrowed gaze remained riveted upon his every step, it seemed unlikely she was even aware yet of their presence up top. Amric smiled in grim satisfaction. If things became chaotic down in the chamber, Thalya's skill with the bow could prove useful from her high perch. By her own admission, her normal arrows had proven ineffective when she was attacked by the black creatures, but she still had two of her ensorcelled arrows remaining. Halthak and Syth were charged with watching the surrounding dunes for an ambush, and with protecting the huntress if they came to grips with returning black creatures. Syth had uttered weak protestations at having to remain behind, but from the sidelong glances he stole at Thalya, it was evident that he was relieved to have an excuse to remain with her.

The plan was a simple one. The fiend had fixated upon Amric, and evidently she thought he was something he was not. Perhaps she attributed to him the strange tremor that had shaken the hive and given away their presence. Regardless, whatever manner of creature an Adept was and whatever had caused her to label him as one, it seemed a sufficient threat to force a grudging degree of fear or respect from her. He knew an opening when he saw it. He would keep her attention focused upon him, then, long enough for the others to secure the release of the prisoners. What would transpire after that was anyone's guess, and might well depend on how convincing he was in his assumed role.

It was a dangerous game he was playing, he knew. He had to be convincing as something about which he had not a shred of information, and somehow manage to get both the prisoners and his warriors out of here alive. For a brief window of opportunity, however, the monstrosity was without her army of minions and had even dismissed those closest to her. At any other time it would require a much larger force to have a hope of successfully assaulting this place. He glanced at the prisoners, huddled and sprawled in the shadows. For these men, and perhaps for his own missing warriors as well, it had to be now. He tried not to think about the fact that he had not caught a glimpse of a Sil'ath among their numbers. The light was poor, and hope was not yet lost.

His gaze drifted to the nondescript shapes submerged in the viscous pools of green fluid, and he dragged it back to the creature at the center of the chamber.

Concentrate on the task at hand, he chided himself. Free the living before thinking to avenge the dead.

"Name yourself, Adept," the towering creature called up to him in a grating tone. "We would know our enemy."

It was confirmation that she viewed an Adept as an enemy, at least. His mind raced. Would she recognize a false name? And who else did she include in we?

"Names hold power, foul one," he shouted back. "You may continue to call me Adept for now."

She hissed and shifted in her stand, but gave no sign that she found his response suspect.

"What of you?" he asked. "By what name would you be known?"

"Nar'ath queens have no name," she spat. "Only purpose."

Nar'ath? He frowned at the term, even as he heard a soft intake of breath from Bellimar behind him. He glanced back at the old man.

"Nar'ath means 'of the sands'," Bellimar whispered. "Just as Sil'ath means 'of the scales', very loosely translated. Both names come from a tongue long lost to this world, and it implies these creatures have chosen a name from another time, or were given it very long ago." He stared at the creature below. "It implies they may not be new to this world after all."

Despite the low pitch of his voice, the Nar'ath queen overheard him.

"This fleshling speaks true," she said with an odd mingling of anger and pride in her voice. "But of course the Adept knows this already, for it was his kind that named us. A dismissive, scornful name it was meant to be, given in arrogance. But still we have kept it all this time, and we have made it our own. We have grown strong, and you will not dismiss us again."

The queen watched him with an air of expectancy, but he did not know what reply to make and so made none rather than risk giving himself away. She hissed in dissatisfaction, grasping with long black claws at the stone formed about her. Amric heard a grating noise from within that enclosure, and he wondered at the size and shape of the concealed portion of her form. From the harsh, heavy nature of the sounds, he guessed that there was more of her hidden than showing.

He reached the bottom step and his boot heel sank slightly into the firm sand of the cavern floor. He strode toward her, his manner confident and unhurried, hoping to emulate the being that was fearsome enough to give her pause. Without glancing aside, he was aware of the others stealing like shadows around the edge of the room. The queen paid them no heed, as if they were utterly beneath her notice. Instead she continued to track him and him alone, her alien features an expressionless mask, her eyes a simmering green.

He stopped at the outer edge of one of the pools and looked down. The waters gave off a soft, pulsing glow that seemed to emanate from everywhere and nowhere. It was impossible to tell the depth of the pool, as it was packed near to overflowing with tightly wrapped bodies. Some unseen current tugged at those cocooned forms, rippling the top of the pool as the pods rolled and churned beneath the surface. The sickly green glow peeked through gaps in the moving clusters, cupping them with spectral, possessive fingers of light. It was a disorienting display, a sinister and graceful dance in slow motion.

Amric's stomach turned as he realized that not all the motion came from the current. Some of the shapes were writhing and straining against their bonds. He fought the urge to draw his sword and cut the folds of cloth-like material. Grim instinct warned him that he was not witnessing natural creatures struggling to survive, but rather the awakening of new fiends, subservient to the queen.

"Cunning Adept," the Nar'ath queen murmured, breaking the brief silence. "Have you come to make me pay for my overconfidence in sending forth nearly all of my forces?"

Amric noted her change in reference from plural to individual; another oddity that would hopefully become clear soon.

"Perhaps," Amric replied with a noncommittal shrug. He began a slow circuit of the chamber, circling her from outside the pools. "For now, I am more interested in discussion. For example, I wonder at why you would leave yourself so exposed. What goal could be worth the risk to one such as you?"

"What risk was there?" she sneered. "The fleshlings of this world are weak, and they wield weak magics as well. They are divided and fearful, huddled in their walled city, oblivious to the wracking cries of the land. Oblivious to our presence and to the true threat against their world as well. There is nothing we need fear from these trifling creatures."

"But now I am here," Amric said.

"Yes," the queen said softly, hunching low in her cone of rock. "Now you are here. But we did not know this when I sent my forces against the city. How did you learn of our presence?"

He ignored her question because he had no answer to give, hoping that she would interpret the omission as a mortal foe refusing to divulge such information. "So you will hurl your minions against the city to the north? You said yourself it was no threat to you, and yet you are willing to lose many, battering against their high walls." He decided to venture a guess. "You may lose more numbers than you gain, and then where will you be?"

"Arrogant Adept!" she snapped with indignant rage. "Think you we know nothing of tactics? Our numbers will swell tonight, for the city will be yielded up, ripe for the harvest, by one of its own."

Amric paused. "One of its own?"

Her laugh was lilting and harsh. "Indeed, Adept. We have not faced your kind in centuries, but we remember well your tactics with the lesser races. One of the primitives encountered our strength, and sought to curry favor for himself by making an alliance with us, claiming to be a man of some power among his people. He believed our assurances that we have no wish to rule this world, as well as our promises that he would be made supreme among his kind once we have what we need. As if there will be anyone or anything left to rule." She gave a dark, ugly chuckle. "He knows so much of what is happening, and yet understands so little."

Amric felt a chill at the casual certainty of her words, but he did not allow any interruption in his casual stride as he continued to make a wide circle around her. "This ally of yours sounds too gullible to be a man of influence here," he scoffed. "By what name is this pretender known?"

"I think not," The Nar'ath queen snarled, her distended jaw twitching and flaring slightly open to reveal a glimpse of the human face beneath, contorted in anger. "I have use for him yet, and I will not have you interfering in our deception. The Adepts, above all, know well how credulous these creatures are, but do not think to treat us the same way."

"Naturally not," he said in a dry tone.

"Do not mock us, Adept!" she hissed. There was a sharp report as the edge of the stone rim encasing her cracked beneath her clenched claws. He stopped walking and turned to face her. At the corners of his vision, he saw her hulking minions appear at the mouths of several tunnels, shouldering their way partially from the shadows. Their dull, hateful eyes fixed upon him, their ponderous heads swaying back and forth in response to their queen's agitation. Without taking his own eyes from the queen, Amric mentally marked the positions of his warriors and waited for her to give the command to attack. His hands tingled, aching to reach for his swords, but he held himself utterly motionless. For a long, tense moment they stood thus, gazes locked together at the core of a brittle silence, and then the queen relaxed and settled back with a speculative look. Her minions shuffled back with a sulking reluctance and were swallowed once more by the dark maws of the tunnels.

Releasing a pent breath, he resumed his slow stroll around the chamber. He noted that the Sil'ath warriors had stolen around the cavern perimeter and reached the captives. Valkarr knelt among them in hushed discussion while Innikar and Sariel stood over them. It would be several minutes before his unhurried pace brought him near enough to them to exchange quiet words. It took Amric long seconds to locate Bellimar, as he did not want to crane his neck back and forth searching for him and thus risk drawing undue attention to his position. He finally discerned the vampire standing at the edge of a pool further around the room. He stood tall and straight with his cloak folded tightly about him, little more than a sliver of night in the cavern's gloom. His attention appeared to be absorbed by something in the glowing waters.

"The city will fall this night," the Nar'ath queen assured him. Though she had to be aware of the presence of the others within the chamber, she still seemed to pay them no heed whatsoever.

"You sound very certain of that."

"Even now my forces gather there," she said. "When night falls, the city will bare itself to us, and by morning's light my minions will have harvested them all."

He glanced upward through the opening far above and onto the tortured sky. The oppressive blanket of clouds had walled off the sun at last, and the light that poured down now into the chamber was a dim grey shroud. He wondered how long remained until nightfall. Under normal circumstances there would be several hours of daylight remaining, but if this cloud cover rolled over Keldrin's Landing as well, a serviceable darkness—and the accompanying assault—might come all the sooner.

"Why bother with the city at all?" he asked. "If, as you say, conquering this world is truly not your goal."

She gave a long and sibilant hiss, but he could not decipher whether the sound indicated pleasure or annoyance. "We are after bigger game, as you must realize by now. But we must build our forces, and maneuver them into proper position."

"Again you speak of 'we', and yet all I see here is you."

She uttered a keening, triumphant shriek that he realized was a laugh. "Then you have only begun to look, arrogant one. My sisters and I have grown in strength slowly over the centuries, recovering in secret from the blow you dealt us so long ago. And had you not activated the Gate and begun to draw upon this world, it might have taken many more centuries before we were ready to strike at yours. Now our hives fill the wasteland, draining the land dry of life, and we build our forces to hurl against you. The time for hiding and preparing is almost done."

He paused, reeling with the implications of her words. He quailed at the thought of many more monstrosities like this one, each building its own army of black creatures, their sinister hives pockmarking the land like a spreading disease. They were stealing the beings of this world and converting them into their own blasphemous parody of life, and growing stronger all the time. Very soon, if it had not come to pass already, they would need fear nothing on this world. The Nar'ath queen leaned forward, her long black claws rasping against the stone, as she mistook his partial comprehension for something more.

"Did you truly think that you had eradicated our kind? You, whose avarice granted our existence in the first place? We are a growing cancer on the ley lines that feed your world. We know your addiction. You cannot survive without it, and yet the more you draw upon it, the stronger we continue to grow."

Her tone grew more heated with every word, and he could see her huge form tensing and swelling.

"We have adapted, Adept, evolved over these many centuries that we might more perfectly hunt your race. In your arrogance and greed, you have given us the means to strike at you in more ways than you even realize."

"Calm yourself, foul one," he said quickly, striving for a dismissive tone. "You are not ready to pit yourself against the might of the Adepts."

She gave a deep, grating chuckle, still poised on the verge of action. "I hear 'we', and yet see only you," she said, twisting his own words and casting them back at him.

He threw back his head and boomed a laugh that echoed eerily around the vast chamber, warping the sound until he did not recognize it as his own. "And did you truly think that I came alone?"

It had the desired effect. The Nar'ath queen hesitated, eyes widening to dart suspiciously around the cavern. Her malevolent gaze slid over the Sil'ath warriors, whose position he was nearing now, and dismissed them as inconsequential. She tilted her head upward and froze. Thalya stood upon the rim of the opening high above, silhouetted against the silver sky, her bow drawn and leveled at the creature. Amric hoped she had nocked one of her ensorcelled arrows, as he had a strong suspicion that nothing less would suffice. Another head peered over the edge; Syth's, by the shape of it, though the height was too great to pick out his features.

The queen's ridged skull swung back toward him. "That is no Adept. You bring the fleshlings of this world against me? What game are you playing at?" The last was almost a murmur, more to herself than to him. Good, he had her confused, and she was suspending action against him once more, at least for the moment.

His circuit of the room had finally brought him to the cluster of captives. His heart sank when he saw that all seven of them were human, not a Sil'ath form among them. Valkarr rose and stole to his side with a shake of his head. He stood so close that the words that followed were more breath against Amric's ear than actual sound.

"The men say they are the last to survive," he whispered. "They have seen no other Sil'ath, and no prisoners have been removed from this chamber."

"Can they all walk?" Amric whispered back, barely moving his lips as he spoke from the side of his mouth.

"Some were injured in the taking," Valkarr said. His dark eyes glittered with barely restrained fury. "But they do not lack for motivation. They are ready."

"Good. I will continue around. Take them swiftly up the stairs when the moment allows."

The Sil'ath warrior inclined his head in the barest of nods and stepped away to hold a hushed conversation with Sariel. Amric resumed walking, looking over the captives as he went. They had the look of soldiers, hard and rough-hewn, but they were also pale, haggard, haunted. Their sunken eyes met his as he passed, and he saw reflected there the specters of what the men had been through since their capture. *I can promise you only the chance to live or die on your feet, as men, fighting for your lives*, he thought. *Nothing more, but let it be enough.*

"Adept."

It was Bellimar's voice, the timbre of it hollow and strained. The vampire was staring at him from the edge of the pool he had been studying, the soft green glow writhing along the underside of his features. Amric moved toward him, holding himself to an unhurried stride. The Nar'ath queen, hissing to herself, twisted within her enclosure to follow his progress around the room.

Bellimar thrust out a hand as he approached. "Your knife."

Amric eyed him, but drew his knife from his belt and passed it over without comment. The old man knelt by the side of the pool, watching the dark forms churning within its viscous, luminescent depths.

"Do not touch the waters," he warned. "They are anathema to living flesh."

His hand darted out with lightning speed, fastening to one of the cocooned forms and dragging it toward him.

"Tell me," Bellimar said, "does not the shape of this one strike you as familiar?"

Amric felt a tightening sensation in his chest as he gazed upon the wrapped figure. At first it looked no different to him than the others, just another long, amorphous shape twisting and heaving with corrupted vigor. Then he saw it. Against the folds of soaked cloth-like material, he could pick out broad shoulders and powerful arms pushing at the silken bonds, a narrow waist flaring to flexing legs that were not quite jointed correctly for a man, and behind that a thrashing appendage that suggested nothing so much as a Sil'ath tail. There was understanding and pity in Bellimar's eyes as he held the knife poised, looking a question at him.

"Do it," Amric said between gritted teeth.

With a flick of his wrist, Bellimar swept the knife through the coils around the head. A glistening black wedge-shaped visage thrust its way clear, ebon eyes rolling against the sudden bite of the air. Amric's breath caught in his throat, lodged there, and became stone. Prakseth. Burly Prakseth, jovial and honorable to the last fiber of his being. First to defend, first to comfort. *Oh my friend, what have these monsters done to you?*

Those malignant orbs darted from Bellimar to Amric. There was recognition there, of a sort, but not the kind he would wish. That glimmer was not a greeting for a familiar friend, but rather a sighting of prey. The jaws parted, and the mouth began to work furiously, open and shut, open and shut, as if shrieking without sound. Amric closed his eyes, sickened. When he opened them again, an unspoken agreement passed between him and Bellimar.

The vampire tightened his fist in the folds of material and raised the body partway from the waters as easily as if that hand had been empty. Amric slid backward a step and spun on his heel. One of his swords rang free with a sound like the chime of a bell. In a blur of motion he whirled, and his blade hammered down in a gleaming arc, cleaving through the black skull and into the chest. With one jerking spasm, the figure went still. Amric dragged his sword clear, and Bellimar laid the body gently at the edge of the pool.

Amric panted, struggling to rein in the rage that threatened to overwhelm him. He had known what to expect, he reminded himself. He had seen it happen to that hapless man when they arrived, and from that instant he had feared the worst for his own. In point of fact, he had known for weeks that death might be all he found on this mission. Soldiers die in battle, the rational part of his mind insisted, and it was, after all, far from the first time he had lost friends to the callous whims of war. It was never easy, would never be easy. His teeth ground in helpless fury. So why did it feel so different this time?

A wave of heat washed through him, and his vision went white at the edges. He fought it back, trembling and shaking his head to clear it. This was no time to succumb to whatever strange illness was plaguing him. He needed to retain control, as there were still lives to save. And lives to avenge. His fist tightened around the hilt of his sword until his knuckles creaked.

He threw his head back, gasping for breath, and found the captives climbing the stairs. Some moved under their own power, scrambling weakly up the twisting steps. Others were pushed or half-carried by his Sil'ath warriors. He had to buy them a few more minutes. Whatever he chose to do with his own life, he could not commit theirs to the reckless act of vengeance that was burning at him from the inside. He met Valkarr's stricken gaze as the Sil'ath hesitated, then ducked under the outstretched arm of one of the men to hasten him up the crude steps. *He saw,* Amric realized. *He knows, and yet he does what must be done. I can do no less.*

"What desecration is this?" the Nar'ath queen screeched. "Have the Adepts grown so craven that they cannot face us directly now, but instead resort to preying upon our young?"

He whirled toward her, baring his teeth. "They are not your young," he spat. "They are not *yours* at all. They are *my* people."

Her head drew back in confusion. "Your people? What matter to the Adepts if we harvest them before you harvest their very world? And what matter to such inconsequential beings? They are like blades of dry grass before the spreading flame. Their tiny lives are not their own, either way. At least we offer them existence, and purpose, where you offer only annihilation."

The queen leaned forward once more, her eyes narrowing to burning slits. She swept out one arm in a violent gesture toward the retreating captives. "And when did the Adepts become concerned with the fates of such lesser beings?"

As before, he was not certain what reply to make and so he stood, seething with anger, and made none. This time it gave him away.

"False Adept!" she hissed in sudden accusation. Then she paused, cocking her head to the side. "No, you are indeed an Adept, for I can taste your power from here, and it stands apart from the weak magics of this world's inhabitants as clearly as the full silver moon from the flickering stars. But you do not react as an Adept should, and you hesitate when no Adept would."

He stood motionless, staring back at her. From the corner of his eye he watched the painstaking progress of the Sil'ath warriors ushering the weakened, stumbling captives up the stairs. His mind raced, trying to think of what sufficiently cryptic statements he could make that would buy them the time they needed to reach the top.

"You would test your strength against the Adepts?" he asked again, putting a measure of disdain in his tone when a fierce part of him wanted only to hurl himself against her. "Tread with care, dark one."

"Perhaps you are a youngling," she mused as if she had not heard him, "still uncertain of your powers. Whatever the reason, you seem unable or unwilling to use them. Long have the Nar'ath wished for the day we would test our newfound strength against the Adepts, and long have I wished for the day I would taste the peerless life force of your kind."

The shoulders of the Nar'ath queen bulged as her body bowed and tensed, and a spider's web of cracks shot through the stone surrounding her. Her eyes were narrowed to a painfully bright razor's edge of eldritch green as her head slowly lowered and extended toward him.

"I think, Adept," she said, "that this will be that day."

With a scream of primal fury, she surged upward and burst from her containment. A sound like a peal of thunder tore through the cavern as huge shards of rock exploded outward. Amric threw up an arm to shelter his vision against flying debris. He had a split second in which to see the retreating group on the stairs high overhead, staring downward and frozen in shock. Through the rain of rock and the billowing cloud of dust, he had a fleeting moment to glimpse a mammoth serpentine form fringed with countless angular, grasping arms, writhing free of the gaping hole in the ground. Then the Nar'ath queen was hurtling toward him, and he had time for nothing else.

CHAPTER 20

"I'm telling you, there has to be something guiding them."

Horek paused with his fork midway to his mouth. "What's that you say, lad?"

The younger guard shot a glance at him over one shoulder before returning his attention to the narrow window. "They were all wild, fierce creatures. What else would possess such a horde to attack in unison? Something is organizing their efforts, it has to be."

Horek groaned and shoveled the meat into his mouth, chewing noisily as he drew the back of his other hand across his bearded chin. "Not this again, lad," he said. "Can we not share a single watch without flogging the same old discussion?"

At the window, Sivrin's square, clean-shaven jaw tightened. "It can't be that old a topic," he muttered. "The attack came only a few days ago, and there has not been another since. Do you not find it strange?"

"A swarm of maddened, magical creatures throwing themselves at the city walls? Of course it is strange. Hell's breath, the whole business is strange. But you'll not find me complaining that they have not returned."

"They *will* return," Sivrin insisted. "And mark my words, I will wet my blade in their foul flesh, if I am not stuck on watch again here at the southern gate instead of the eastern one on that night as well."

"The southern gate is every bit as important an assignment, lad. The next attack could come from any direction, not necessarily the east."

"Bah, you don't believe that any more than I do," Sivrin said. "The eastern gate is where the action will be. The Captain knows it as well. He has over thirty men at the eastern gate, and just a few of us here."

"Six of us," Horek corrected him. "Two at the gate, two in the room below, and the two of us up here to man the portcullis. That is more than a few. You saw what those fiends did to the great wooden doors of the gate itself. Quick action on the inner portcullis may be all that keeps them out of the city streets next time." He gestured at the huge, squat winding gear affixed to the stone floor on the other end of the room, its thick system of chains trailing upward into slots in the wall. "It is an important duty, lad, whether you enjoy it or not."

Sivrin heaved a sigh and shook his head. "Do not remind me, Horek. Even on the off chance an attack does come to the southern gate, we must man the device and cannot even respond directly. I am doubly cursed. Is the Captain determined to keep me from proving myself?"

The older guard tapped the fork against his lips as he regarded the other fellow. He was supposed to be training the lad, taking him under his wing and sharing the benefit of his long years of experience. He could not look upon that earnest, boyish countenance, however, without feeling dismay at how much like children the new recruits looked to him these days. So young, and so eager to prove themselves, one and all. Sivrin devoured every old story Horek had to tell, and hungered for more. It did not seem to matter that some tales held only meager scraps of truth; the lad had ears only for glory and bravery, and seemed not to hear at all the horrors, the pain, the warnings that laced each retelling.

Horek sighed, scratching at his chin with the tines of the fork. He kept his own beard and scalp shorn close to the skin to conceal just how much grey had shot through the sandy brown. He wondered if the youth standing before him could even sprout a whisker of his own. He dropped the utensil upon the tin plate with a clatter.

"No attack since the first," Horek grunted, raising the familiar argument. "Does that not suggest more a freak occurrence than a calculating mind behind it?"

Sivrin spun away from the window, his clear blue eyes wide and grateful. "What else could draw such a mix of creatures together with a single purpose?"

"Who knows what drives such beasts?" Horek said with a wave of one callused hand. "The Captain says all the fancy scholars would have us believe the magic deep within the land is being stirred by something, and it is having unpredictable effects on creatures more mystical in nature. I can tell from his tone that the Captain thinks they are guessing as much as we are."

Sivrin folded his arms across his chest, unconvinced. "Why did the creatures all come against the city, then?" he demanded. "It suggests organization, a method to it all."

"That much is easily explained," Horek said with a grim laugh. "Those damned things are growing in numbers out there, overrunning the countryside. Now the livestock are gone from the farms, and doubtless there is precious little wild game remaining as well. That leaves us, lad, sitting behind our walls and lighting our torches until the city glows like a beacon in the night. We must look like a giant cattle pen to their sort. It takes no hidden strategic mind to drive animals to fill their bellies."

"Perhaps not, but they retreated in unison."

"And fought amongst themselves, coming and going."

"They were testing our strength," Sivrin insisted. "Now that they have taken our measure, they will return in earnest."

Horek snorted. "Testing our strength? Lad, they had our measure all right. They caught us unawares, and they broke right through. They had only to press the attack and the city would have been gutted. No, they fled before the light of day, not from any fear of us. Everyone knows such creatures abhor the sun's pure light."

"And who tells us this? The same scholars who a moment ago were just guessing?" Sivrin said in a scornful tone, but there was a tinge of grudging acceptance as well. Horek chuckled to himself; the same conversation each time, clothed in slightly different words.

"These creatures did not leave themselves enough time to finish the assault, Sivrin. That suggests impulse, not forethought."

"Perhaps so," the younger man admitted. He turned back to the narrow window and crossed his forearms on the ashlar blocks of the sill. "But I still say—"

He fell silent so abruptly that Horek was caught for a long moment, waiting upon his next words. Sivrin remained frozen in place, however, peering out at the gently rolling lands south of the city wall. Horek opened his mouth to tease the lad, but in the sudden silence he heard a noise from the room below. It was a faint sound, muffled by the distance and by the thick stone construction of the guard house, but something about it struck him amiss. He hesitated, listening for the sound to repeat, but it did not. Realizing his mouth still hung open, he snapped it shut, irritated by his own foolishness. He knew the two men below, veteran soldiers both, and if they weren't accusing each other of cheating at dice they were probably just engaged in some other meaningless argument similar to the one he and Sivrin were having.

"What is it, lad?" he snapped, returning his attention to the younger guard.

"I can't be certain," Sivrin said in a distracted near-whisper, "but I thought I saw something moving out there. Many things, actually."

"It's probably just some merchant's caravan," Horek said with a dismissive wave. "Fool merchants have more greed than sense, to be traveling overland at this hour. Bloody vultures, anyway! I can't decide if I more want to strangle them or admire them, as prices continue to rise and they all grow fat off the profits of us trapped here—"

"It was *not* a caravan," Sivrin interrupted. "It was in the grasses, away from the road. Besides, the trade caravans all come by the western coastal road these days. No one tries the wasteland any more. There is something skulking about out there, like a host of shadows—There! I saw it again!"

Horek rolled his eyes and pushed to his feet, shifting his sword belt as the scabbard rattled against his chair. "What's this, then, lad? Some kind of joke at my expense, because I have an answer for each of your foolish theories?"

"Just get over here and look for yourself," Sivrin urged.

The grizzled guard heaved a sigh and crossed the room. He stood shoulder to shoulder with the younger man, craning his neck to stare out the window. The grey of evening had settled over the countryside, made thick and oppressive by the low-hanging storm clouds. The tall grasses rippled and swirled beneath fitful breezes, and the sea of motion served to baffle his vision as he squinted into the twilight gloom. He saw nothing out of the ordinary, though he had to admit that his sight was not what it had once been, for he found a blurring in the distant detail that owed as much to his eyes as to the gathering shroud without.

"There, did you see it?" Sivrin exclaimed.

"I saw nothing," Horek replied with a frown.

"Keep watching, it will happen again."

He stared, his eyes beginning to water as he strove to keep them open for fear of missing anything. He kept expecting the youthful guard to elbow him and burst into laughter at his expense, but Sivrin's attention was focused outside with an unwavering intensity. If this was a joke, the lad was carrying it much too far. He was about to tell him so, in fact, when he saw it.

His gaze caught on a small ripple of the grasses within a larger one, like a riptide moving counter to the crashing waves surrounding it. At first he thought it nothing more than some strange whim of the wind, but then he saw that it was accompanied by a score of shadowy, man-like figures rising from the grass to dart toward the city and then disappear again into the thrashing sward. His breath caught in his throat.

"What are they?" he breathed.

"I do not know," Sivrin said, vindication and resolve tight in his voice. "But we need to tell the Captain at once."

"Tell the Cap'n what?" came a raspy drawl.

Both guards whirled, their hands flying to the hilts of their swords. Two men stood casually framed in the doorway. Horek relaxed when he saw that the attire of the newcomers matched that of himself and Sivrin, the armor and tabard of the city guard, but he frowned when he realized he did not recognize either of them. New mercenaries still arrived at Keldrin's Landing from time to time, and he made a concerted effort to know all the experienced ones by sight. These men looked more hard-edged than most, and yet he was certain he had never met them before.

"Who are you lads?" he asked, his gaze narrowing as he regarded them.

"Funny you should mention the Cap'n," the fellow in front drawled in a voice that was almost hoarse. The man had an angry scar running from forehead to jawline, just missing his left eye. He stepped into the room, glancing about with a bored expression. "Cap'n wants to see you both. We're here to relieve you."

Horek hesitated. "It is not yet time for change of shift. Do you bear anything in Captain Borric's hand? Or can the men below vouch for you?"

The scar-faced man shrugged. "They were relieved as well. Cap'n said it's urgent."

"Why would he send you?" Horek demanded. "You cannot have been with the guard long, or I would know you both. Something is amiss here."

"We should go, Horek," Sivrin urged. "Maybe the Captain knows about whatever is out there, and wants to know what we have seen."

The newcomers exchanged a glance, and the second fellow moved into the room. He was a heavyset man with arms as thick as a blacksmith's, and his dark, deep-set eyes darted to each of them before settling upon the plate of uneaten food upon the table.

"He's right, Horek," the first man rasped. "You risk Borric's wrath upon all our heads by tarrying overlong, and none of us want that. The Cap'n could flay the bark from a tree at twenty paces with that razor tongue of his, am I right?"

The man's face split into a lop-sided grin, and Horek found himself relaxing into an answering smile. Borric's scoldings were indeed things of legend, and it was true that he wanted no part of one directed at him.

"Hell's breath, but that is true enough," he said with a chuckle. "Perhaps we had better go at that, lad." He walked toward the door, and noticed the burly second newcomer still eyeing his plate.

"You are welcome to the food, if you've a mind," Horek told him. "I'll not have time to finish it, it seems."

"That's a good fellow," the scar-faced man said. He slipped around Horek and strode toward the window. "Before you go, however, can you show me what you saw out there? The Cap'n sure enough was saying something about it, now you mention it, and I'd like to see what all the fuss is about."

Sivrin turned back toward the window, chattering and pointing. Horek watched them, frowning once more. The nape of his neck prickled with apprehension; the feeling that something was terribly amiss had returned, even more urgent than before. He watched the scar-faced man looking over Sivrin's shoulder and out the window, heard his friendly murmuring as he conversed with the excited lad. His gaze roved over the man, looking for something out of place, and fell to a bright scarlet dot on the floor by his boot heel.

Horek froze. He found another teardrop of crimson gathered at the bottom of the man's scabbard, and his eyes traced the rivulet of red up the length of the scabbard to where a thin line of crimson welled from the top, just below the cross-guard of the sword's hilt. The sound he had heard earlier from below suddenly echoed in his head, the sound that might have been the end of a brief scuffle, the sound that just might have been a well-muffled cry.

"Sivrin, on your guard!" he shouted.

A searing pain ripped through his chest, and he looked down in shock to see a foot of gleaming steel protruding from his chest, streaked with his own blood. As he stared, gaping, the blade slithered back into his chest and was gone. The floor tilted crazily and rose to meet him with a cold, stinging slap. He lay with his check pressed against the stone, amazed at the crushing force that bound him there.

He had landed facing the window, and thus was rewarded with a view of Sivrin's actions. The lad reacted with remarkable speed, spinning away from the scar-faced man and batting away a dagger thrust. Sivrin drew his blade and lunged to engage the man. The scar-faced man's bloody sword leapt from its scabbard, and steel rang on steel. Horek felt a thrill of fatherly pride at the young man's skill; he had trained the lad well.

His vision was momentarily obscured as the heavy tread of the second intruder—his killer—passed over his inert form. He cursed inwardly at being screened thus from the action. The man was so big that he was blocking the very light and casting the room into shadow. No, he realized as a slow chill spread throughout his limbs, that was not the case. Rather, it was his own vision growing dimmer by the second, and this time it was not his aging eyes to blame.

He hoped the lad was giving them hell. By then, his sight had narrowed into a hazy tunnel such that all he could discern was the blurred shuffle of booted feet back and forth across the floor, punctuated by the clash of steel and pants of effort. A sudden sharp cry brought silence in its wake, and another form tumbled heavily to the floor. Wide, clear blue eyes stared back at him, unblinking amid their youthful countenance, and beads of blood trailed across Sivrin's unwhiskered cheek.

The action came to you at last, lad, Horek thought sadly. Was it all that you wished?

His vision darkened even more, at once both cruel and merciful in that he could no longer see Sivrin's face. So much like children, the new recruits. So much...

The scar-faced man spat an oath as he ran his fingers across his bleeding brow.

"Burn my soul, but the pup had fangs after all," he muttered, examining his wet fingertips. "Damn near took my head off, and even so I think I'll have another scar to show for it."

He glanced up to find his brooding, heavyset companion watching him with veiled eyes.

"What are you staring at, you ugly oaf?" he snarled. "Get on with the job and foul those gears while the others and I see to the gate doors. We must return to the estate. This is no night to linger in the open."

The lumbering fellow's nostrils flared, and his lip curled in a loud sniff. He sheathed the red-stained sword and reached behind his back to produce the heavy iron mallet he had tethered there. Clutching it in one huge ham fist, he started toward the winding gear, casting a lingering look at the plate of food upon the table. With a wicked grin, the scar-faced man drew his dagger and impaled the last remaining piece of meat on the tin plate, raising it quickly to his mouth. He chewed with exaggerated motions, meeting the larger man's narrowed gaze. Then his face twisted in disgust.

"Ugh," he said, spitting it noisily back onto the table. "If you ever need confirmation you made the right choice in employment, there it is. Morland would not give food that bad to his livestock, let alone to his men."

He stabbed a finger at the winding mechanism. "Make certain that gear will not turn before you join us below," he commanded. He stalked from the room, and the thunderous peal of striking iron followed him down the steep stairwell.

He returned to the chamber below and strode through without stopping. A pair of lean, wolfish men rose to their feet and fell into step behind him. They wore the attire of the city guard as well, but not one of them spared a glance for the two guards slumped over their table with a crimson pool slowly surrounding the tumbled dice in the center.

The trio left the guard house, turning sharply in the street to pass under the towering archway leading to the southern gate doors. The scarfaced man glanced back, scanning the empty courtyard. The citizenry tended to shun the vicinity of the gates as evening approached, and this night was no exception. Good; fewer bodies, fewer delays. Tonight's task was best done quickly.

Eight more of his men stood before the doors. They each gave him a tight nod, and he nodded back without comment. It took him a moment to find the pair of real gate guards, hidden behind several barrels of oil against the wall. He smiled to himself with grim satisfaction. It was good work. He likely would not have even spotted the faint crimson drag marks on the cobblestones had he not been specifically searching for them. Not that it would matter for long, if their timing was right.

He looked up, regarding the great ironbound doors for a long moment. They were solid and imposing. Comforting. He took a deep breath and gave the signal.

The men sprang into action, moving with ruthless efficiency. The enormous bar was lifted from the door and set aside, the doors pushed open wide. Two of the men lifted stout pails of the noxious foaming substance they had brought, and they drew forth long brushes to quickly paint the lower hinges of the doors, careful to let none of it touch their flesh. The metal began to hiss and bubble upon contact with the slimy fluid, and the men soon tossed the pails aside.

The scar-faced man looked on, expressionless. The heavens alone knew where Morland had procured the foul stuff, but if it worked as he said, it would fuse the metal of the hinges together, forcing the doors to remain open.

The men stood there in the shadow of the southern gate, darting nervous glances between the gathering darkness outside and the torch-lit courtyard behind them. The scar-faced man looked out upon the dark, shimmering sea of grass broken only by the departing ribbon of the city road, and he rolled his shoulders to ease the tension there. This was the part of the evening's plan that he had dreaded the most. He and his men were to defend the gate until Morland's new allies came, and if the city guard discovered their duplicity before the arrival of those forces, it would not go well for any of them.

Those fears proved groundless, however, as they had not long to wait at all.

The doors had been open mere seconds when a vast black shadow appeared upon the rolling hills, darker even than the encroaching night. No, not a single shadow, the scar-faced man realized, but rather many thousands of black shapes, rising in unison from their positions concealed in the tall grasses. As one they surged forward, silent and swift, sweeping toward the city like an ebon tide.

The scar-faced man swallowed hard. He tore his gaze from the onrushing Nar'ath and studied the thick doors yawning open, offering the soft underbelly of Keldrin's Landing to the approaching predator. A splinter of panic lanced through him, and against his will his eyes sought the heavy beam he and his men had cast aside, then darted back to the ruined hinges, and once more out at the advancing horde. The Nar'ath were all moving at the same tireless, flat-out sprint, and they were drawing near with such speed that he could already begin to make out the tattered strips of cloth flapping behind their forms as they ran. An icy weight settled in his stomach. He had thought he feared displeasing Morland more than any alternative, but his conviction seemed to have taken flight all of a sudden.

Just as we should be doing, he thought fiercely to himself. What's done is done. There's nothing for it now but to let the merchant's plan play out, and pray it brings us all the wealth and power he has promised.

"Time to be elsewhere, men," he hissed. "There is only one safe place in the city tonight, and I mean to be there before the screaming begins."

He looked around to see a ring of pale, wide-eyed faces staring back at him. At any other time he would have laughed to see this group of cut-throats looking so shaken, but somehow the humor palled at the moment.

"Unless, of course, you'd rather remain behind to greet our new allies when they arrive," he said, forcing a grim smile. He wheeled and ran back into the city, and the men wasted no time in following him.

The cloud of dust and sand washed over Amric, and behind it came the Nar'ath queen.

The blast of grit blinded him momentarily, and he threw himself to the side on pure instinct. The huge serpentine form hurtled past with an explosive hiss of rage, the black claws scraping the ground. The force of the creature's passage was a hot breath across his skin as he rolled to his feet and drew his second sword. Blinking the sand from his eyes, he whirled and crouched in time to meet the next charge.

The Nar'ath queen burst from the haze, coming at him from a new di-rection. He ducked low beneath the sweep of her long forelimbs and spun away in a flurry of glittering steel arcs. His blades bit into some part of her massive torso, and the resulting shriek of outrage pummeled at his ears, disorienting him. Her sinuous tail whipped at him as she passed, and he ducked. The tail's fringe of small, sharp claws raked along his mail shirt and bit into the flesh of his arm, pulling him off balance for a dangerous moment before tearing free. Then she vanished again into the swirling dust.

Amric dropped to one knee, panting as he listened. His ears were still ringing from her unearthly cries, however, and the heavy scraping sounds seemed to be coming from everywhere at once. The queen was out there somewhere, planning her next attack.

The sand continued to swirl and eddy in the air, like dark thunder-clouds furious at their imprisonment within the vast chamber, and the eerie green light from the pools danced in their midst like flickers of lightning. It was obscuring all vision; even the opening far above was nothing more than a faint grey halo through the haze. The sand was hang-ing in the air far too long, he realized as he squinted against its bite. It should have been settling to earth again, but it showed no signs of doing so. The Nar'ath queen must have some sorcerous control over it. For that matter, the entire hive might well owe its unnatural construction to that same control over the wasteland.

Not just control, he corrected himself; the Nar'ath also seemed to be *causing* the spread of desolation. They were quite literally draining the life from the land somehow, and making use of that stolen vigor to spread their infection to the land's peoples as well. Perhaps most troubling of all, the queen had been vehement in her accusations against the Adepts, insisting that they were no better than the Nar'ath. Who were these Adepts, then, and what were their designs on his world?

Amric shook his head. Now was not the time for such ruminations.

He rose into a low crouch and glided through the haze on noiseless feet, careful to skirt wide around the edge of a nearby pool, lest its light betray his location. The game of cat and mouse had moved past words, and had begun in earnest.

The Nar'ath forces passed through the southern gate of Keldrin's Landing, and flowed into the city like a black river.

The invasion was eerily quiet at the outset. There were none of the exulting cries one might expect of an attacking force gaining entrance to their prize; none of the fierce, startling sounds made to frighten the defenders into fleeing or freezing for precious seconds. There was no clash of metal or clink of armor, no crackling flame or rumbling machines of war. There was not even the harsh, labored breathing of mortal men charging into the teeth of their enemy with their nerves keyed to the breaking point, incensed to the very precipice of a crimson frenzy. Instead, there were only the torrential, rapid-fire slaps of tens of thousands of bare black feet upon the cobblestones, and the whisper of tattered cloth fluttering behind sprinting forms.

The imposter guards had performed their task well. There was no one to bar the passage of the creatures or even to raise an alarm until the broad southern courtyard was filled to overflowing. The Nar'ath did not hesitate for an instant. Without visible communication, they divided their forces evenly and drove into the city's streets and alleyways, infiltrating further and further, pumping like the blood of midnight into empty veins.

The silence could not last for long. Darkness was falling and, consciously or not, the city's inhabitants had sought to distance themselves from the outer walls and whatever might be lurking beyond them. Most had moved indoors for the evening, wherever they had chosen to weather the coming night. The city was crowded, however, and the Nar'ath had come with a purpose. Dark forces continued to stream through the southern gate, and the creatures had penetrated deep into the city when contact was made at last.

Then, just as the scar-faced man had predicted, the screams began.

"My forces have moved upon the city, Adept," the queen's voice came sliding through the murk. "Even now they are within its walls, coursing through its streets, falling upon its inhabitants."

Amric ground his teeth, but he knew better than to reply. She had proven capable of honing in upon the slightest sound he made, and each such mistake provoked a vicious, lightning-swift charge. She was too large and powerful for him to meet head-on thus; he needed to focus on stealth and guile over a direct confrontation, and continue to seek out a weakness. He just hoped something clever occurred to him soon, as he was playing a losing game.

He sidestepped a pile of rubble, careful to disturb nothing. Briefly he considered hurling a piece of it to one side in the hopes that it would draw her into another blind assault that might bring her within reach of his blades again, but he dismissed the idea. She had fallen for the trick once, but not again after that. He kept moving.

"The city will fall," the queen continued after a moment, her sibilant tones echoing from a different direction this time. "Many lives will be lost, but many more will be salvaged and given new purpose. By the morning light, my minions will return with your pets, and I will make those who have lived my own. Does this disturb you, Adept? Does it fill you with impotent rage?"

Amric said nothing, picking his way carefully through the center of the room where the queen's emergence had left a ravaged crater. A rumbling slither from across the chamber told him she was on the move again. A tall shape suddenly appeared out of the swirling sand, looming above him, and black tentacles shot toward him. One of the hulking minions the queen had dismissed earlier. He struck the grasping appendages aside, severing one to fall writhing to the ground at his feet. The Nar'ath minion bulled toward him, seeking to bring its powerful forelimbs to bear, but he darted under the sweep of its arms and ran by it, aiming a terrific cut at a thick leg as he did so. Once past, he did not glance back, but instead continued his run, hurdling a jagged piece of rubble and losing himself in the churning sand once more.

Behind him came the thunderous charge as the queen oriented upon the sounds of the momentary scuffle. He heard a thud as heavy bodies collided. There was a keening snarl from the queen, followed by the skidding tumble of the minion being cast to the ground. Amric chuckled to himself. Perhaps he could force the queen to destroy her own minions out of sheer frustration.

"Why do you not employ your magic?" she hissed. "The stink of it fills this place, and yet you do not unleash it."

Amric frowned. What did she mean? Had he brought contagion from the Essence Fount in Stronghold with him, and she was somehow detecting its taint here? As if on cue with his thoughts, a burning sensation blossomed in his chest and a wave of dizziness swept over him. He staggered, gritting his teeth, and forced it back. She gave a low, harsh laugh, evidently mistaking his silence for some greater comprehension.

"Oh yes, it is well masked, but I was born to scent your kind. The Adepts have never before feared to abuse their power, so why hesitate now?"

Amric crept between pools that glowed through the haze like huge green embers buried in the ground. He worked his way toward the outer wall of the chamber. He froze as one of the Nar'ath minions shambled across his path. It was a short distance ahead and facing away from him. It stalked by, unseeing, a dim outline that faded back into the storm. He waited the span of several slow breaths, and then moved on.

The queen let out an explosive growl, and he flinched to hear how close she was. It was a discordant, dissatisfied sound, and he could not tell above the subdued howl of the sandstorm whether she was drawing closer or moving further away.

"Keep your secrets then," she snapped. "But if you think to catch me in some ruse, know that we have developed certain defenses against your powers. Indeed, you will find us much more capable opponents this time around."

Something in her tone rang hollow, and it occurred to him then why she maintained the obscuring clouds even though they seemed to hinder her as much as they did him. She feared him still. Despite her seething hatred, her awesome physical power and the scornful challenge of her words, she still felt he was a very real threat to her. Or rather, she feared

the thing she thought he was. She was stalking him with the same caution, and guarding against being caught vulnerable in the open.

A trio of shadowy figures appeared ahead of him, and he tensed before
he recognized the outlines of his Sil'ath warriors. The captives must have
reached the top, and his friends had returned. They recognized him at the
same instant, unwinding from their crouches. Valkarr drew near with a
questioning look and mouthed a single word.

Plan?

They eyed him, expressions determined and expectant, eyes slitted
against the blinding dust and sand.

Amric grinned back at them. It was time to bait a trap.

CHAPTER 21

Captain Borric strode into the cobbled street, while behind him his men hacked at the last of another pack of the black creatures. When it had ceased to move, the men wearily reformed their protective ring around him.

Borric raised a forearm to wipe the sweat from his brow, winced at the sharp flare of pain in his shoulder, and used the other arm instead with a rueful shake of his head. Every corner they rounded brought a new skirmish with the infernal creatures, and in this last encounter one of them had seized his arm in a grip like iron and nearly wrenched it from its socket in a frenzied attempt to drag him to the ground. Thankfully it had not been his sword arm injured; from the screams echoing up and down the streets of Keldrin's Landing, he had not seen the end of his need to swing a blade this night.

He glanced around, using the pretext of scanning the area to take the measure of the fifteen men surrounding him. Their faces were drawn, haggard, frightened. They had cause to be. When the fighting began, there had been three times as many in Borric's contingent. The men who remained had seen their comrades overwhelmed and carried away with appalling speed and ferocity. There was not a weak spine in the lot, he knew; every one of these men would face a mortal foe without hesitation. These strange, unliving black creatures that could ignore all but the most crippling of wounds, however, had unnerved them to the core.

They had learned at last that one had to take the heads of these creatures, had to be certain to cleave it or sever it from the body entirely, to put one down. Otherwise the damned things were nigh unstoppable. The Captain's fist tightened around his sword hilt. That knowledge had been won at a very dear cost indeed.

"What now, Captain?" asked one of the men, a narrow-faced fellow the others had taken to calling Mouse for some reason he could no longer remember. Mouse's dark eyes darted toward Borric and then back to the still forms of the black creatures they had just fought, lying headless and bloodless mere yards away. The lean man's nose wrinkled in a sudden twitch, curling his lip slightly. It looked like nothing so much as a rodent with upturned nose questing into the wind, and Borric smiled to himself in sudden recollection.

The smile was a fleeting thing, however, fading like a spark in the darkness.

What now, indeed?

Somehow a large enemy force had infiltrated the city—his city— without any warning from the wall or gate guards. Had his men all been slain, wherever the breach had occurred? Were more of these creatures streaming into Keldrin's Landing even now, hopelessly outnumbering the defenders? It was difficult to know. Borric and his men had been exiting the central barracks to investigate the uproar when they were set upon by a small pack of the creatures, and there had been several clashes since then. They had been fortunate, however, for he had seen much larger hordes running past the far mouth of the street. Facing such overwhelming odds, he and his band would have been swept away before the advancing tide in mere moments. As it was, they could not take many more skirmishes with the smaller groups either, for with each one their own numbers dwindled dangerously.

His jaw clenched as he recalled the fury of the fighting, their silent and implacable foes hurling themselves upon the guards, raining bone-crushing blows down upon the men and bearing many to the ground through sheer weight of numbers. The guards who lost consciousness had then been quickly hoisted into the air and carried off at that same uncanny run, their bearers appearing no more troubled by the weight than if they were carrying a sack of feed rather than a full-grown, fully armored man. He shuddered. He hoped that a sack of feed was not too apt a comparison. It was only because the attackers had thinned their own numbers by carrying off the fallen men that Borric and his remaining soldiers had managed to overcome the last few creatures.

He realized Mouse and the others were staring at him. He owed them an answer.

"We make for the eastern gate," he said. "We have the most men there at the gate and the eastern barracks. If we start there, gathering forces as we go, we can organize the defense of the city."

He said the words with more confidence than he felt, infusing his firm tone with a ring of command that brought immediate comfort to the men. He could see the tension ease from them ever so slightly, and he caught a few quick nods. What he left unsaid was that they were no longer defending the city at all, but instead resisting an enemy who was already within its walls in great numbers. If the cause proved hopeless, they would be forced to head for the docks and try to save as many people as they could with the ships that were available there. If they survived that long.

Borric set off at a rapid march down the street, and his men followed. He resisted the urge to run; he knew that every moment counted, but at the same time they could not afford to be winded when the next skirmish came. The black fiends were as quick as lightning, and had so far shown no indication of fatigue or pain. He and his men would need everything they could muster to face them again.

They passed between the squat shadows of empty buildings, tensed against a sudden attack from any direction. A high-pitched scream from the cross street ahead brought them up short.

A woman and two children rounded the corner ahead, running and stumbling as they cast fearful glances over their shoulders. A few paces behind came a portly, red-faced man in a smudged canvas apron, carrying a small wood axe in one hand and some type of square mallet in the other. Borric squinted; a baker of some kind, unless he missed his guess, though where the man had found a wood axe in the city was something of a mystery. What was no mystery, however, was how ineffective the pitiful tools he was carrying would prove against the dozen black creatures bounding eagerly after him and his family. The mob was forty paces or better behind them, but the creatures were intent on their prey. Given their unnatural speed, it would be over soon enough.

Borric raised his sword to give the order to charge, but one of the men stepped in front of him with one hand held out to forestall him. It was Mouse, and he stepped close to speak in a hurried whisper.

"They are as good as lost, Captain," Mouse said with a grimace. "We cannot take another brush with a pack that size if we are to get through this night ourselves. You saw how many of those things are in the city already. We might be better off lying low in one of these darkened buildings until the creatures claim what they will out here, and then make for the docks and use every able ship there to flee this cursed land."

Borric hesitated, meeting the man's eyes. There was a cold pragmatism in Mouse's words, and the mention of a seaward escape rang uncomfortably close to his own thoughts from moments before. Several of the men tore their attention from the fleeing family, and turned wide eyes upon him. They may not have caught every word spoken by Mouse in hushed tones, but they knew all too well the decision the Captain now had to make.

The captain had always considered himself a practical soldier. He was no longer afflicted with the kind of irrational idealism that had long ago been honed from his character in the forge of duty. So it surprised him nearly as much as Mouse when his hand shot out and seized the top of the fellow's breastplate to drag him face to face.

"You do not need that blade in your hand to hide in some hole and hope this all passes you over," he said through clenched teeth. "For that, you need only be willing to live with yourself afterward, pretending you no longer hear the cries of those you abandoned to their fates. In my estimation, that is too high a price by far."

With a shove, he released his grip on Mouse's breastplate and swept his gaze over the others.

"We did not accept the city's coin only to flee at the first sign of real trouble," he said. "That coin, regardless of how many velvet pockets it has passed through since, came from the likes of those people right there. Tonight we earn it, or give our lives trying."

Borric set off at a run, sword clenched in one fist and a chill settling deep into his stomach at the prospect of another clash with the foul black creatures. He did not look back; nothing he saw there would change his own course. Even so, he was immensely gratified to hear a throaty roar behind him and the staccato drum of boots on the cobbled streets as his men joined the charge.

Amric stood, alone once again in a swirling cocoon of sand.

He closed his eyes, calming his breathing as he opened his senses to the vastness of the clouded chamber. Sight, hearing, touch, smell; he could rely on none of them here as he usually did in battle. The Nar'ath queen had ripped them all away from him with ruthless efficiency, using her sorcerous storm to bombard or mask each of his physical senses until they were all but useless. And yet, as he stood amid the howling, biting winds, it seemed as if the clamor fell away and the chamber itself whispered its secrets to him.

He felt, rather than saw, the Sil'ath warriors lying in wait. He sensed the massive Nar'ath queen sliding through the center of the chamber, and he noted as well the smaller masses of her brutish minions as they groped blindly in the murk, seeking him. He frowned. No, that wasn't quite true. It was more accurate to say that the Nar'ath were each voids in his perception, rather than felt directly. They were roving holes in what should have been.

A distant part of him was bewildered at the clarity with which he knew all this. The positions of the Nar'ath were all so obvious to him suddenly that he could throw a rock and strike any one of them. Another part of him insisted that there could be nothing more natural, that this and more was at his fingertips, and he had only to embrace it…

A burning sensation fought its way up through his chest and all of a sudden his head felt like it would split asunder. He gasped, staggering to the side before he caught himself. The strange clarity faded along with the pain, but not before he sensed the sinuous form of the queen hesitate at the sound and spin in his direction.

Perfect, he thought. Let us give her another whiff of the bait she has been anticipating.

Amric coughed.

He pitched it low, made it muffled as if he meant to conceal it. At the same time, he lightly dragged the tip of one sword along the coarse stone of the floor at his feet to make a gentle rasping sound. With luck, it would sound to her as if he had stumbled for the briefest of moments, grown careless or distracted.

She came at him like a lightning bolt, hurtling across the intervening ground with a speed that was stunning. Amric had a few seconds to crouch and brace himself, and then the Nar'ath queen burst through the churning wall of sand and was upon him.

He waited until the last moment, holding his ground with his blades crossed before him, and then he threw himself to the side. He had been hoping that she, in her eagerness to reach him, would be unable to slow her great bulk before colliding with the sheer wall of the chamber a pace and a half behind him. In this he was disappointed, however, as she evidently knew the bounds of the chamber she had created too well to fall for the simple trick. The countless small, clawed appendages that fringed her serpentine body dug into the ground, slowing her with a high-pitched grinding noise. She slid to a stop, almost brushing the wall.

Quick on the heels of that disappointment came another: he had waited an instant too long to evade her charge.

Her black talons lashed out at him. One set scored the sandstone, leaving angry furrows behind him as he rolled away, while the other raked across his mail shirt and caught. The force of the blow lifted him from the ground and slung him against the wall, wringing all the air from his lungs in one explosive grunt. Amric slid to the ground and struggled to draw a breath. Huge hands seized him immediately, wrapping around his torso and constricting until he thought his ribs would surely crack. Darkness washed over him and was peeled back just as quickly, and he knew that he had lost consciousness for a fleeting instant. His hands closed on empty air, and his stomach plummeted as he realized that his swords had fallen away from nerveless fingers. He began prying at the claws that held him tight, even as he felt himself being lifted through the air.

Amric gasped, trying desperately to fill his burning lungs. His entire body felt as if it was on fire, and the world spun around him in a dizzying cyclone. He craned his neck to see the triumphant visage of the Nar'ath queen drawing closer and closer. As he watched, the huge outer jaws began to flare open and separate.

In unison, Innikar and Sariel attacked from either side of the queen. Appearing out of the swirling sand, they each lunged forward to ram a single blade into her body, all the way to the hilt. The queen's expression twisted from gloating to furious in a single spasm. With a shriek to freeze the blood, she swept her lower set of forelimbs at them without relinquishing her grasp on Amric with the upper arms. The warriors darted back from her attacks, withdrawing their swords from the bloodless wounds. Such minor injuries could not have greatly troubled a creature of her size, and yet she issued a roar of raw hatred as she whirled first one way and then the other, indecisive as to which of the troublesome pests to pursue.

A shadow appeared overhead, indistinct amid the churning clouds of sand, and plummeted down to land astride the thick, curved neck of the Nar'ath queen. It was Valkarr, leaping from the stairway above them in a strike afforded by the distraction of the others. The Sil'ath warrior landed with a grunt and grasped at the overlapping armored scales that ran up the queen's spine with one hand while the other brandished bare steel. He aimed a tremendous cut at her exposed throat, looking to put a decisive end to the battle, but as quick as he was, the Nar'ath queen was quicker. She twisted about like a dervish, coiling her torso forward and then surging upward in place as her long, serpentine form thrashed behind her. Valkarr's blow struck a shower of sparks from the plates of armor but failed to bite into the more vulnerable flesh in front. He was nearly dislodged, forced to scrabble wildly at her scales with his free hand in an effort to keep his perch. One of her lower arms shot across her torso to seize his exposed lower leg. She tore him loose with a single sharp jerk and then flung her arm wide to hurl him away. Spinning out of control, he vanished into the murk like a stone from a sling.

Innikar and Sariel appeared at her sides again, charging in with swords raised, but the queen was ready this time. Her serpentine form lashed back and forth, and the fringe of claws raked at Innikar, trying to pull him down under a crushing coil. He was forced to backpedal, swatting away the hooked appendages. Sariel darted in, and then threw herself flat as the tail end whipped past her, missing by less than a hand's breadth. She was on her feet again in an instant, spinning with an almost weightless grace away from the return stroke of the tail that hammered down upon the place she had been.

Sariel danced back, bracing to attack again, when black tentacles snaked out of the murk behind her and sought to draw her in. Drawn by the rage of their queen, the lumbering forms of several Nar'ath minions emerged from the swirling sand, and Sariel's blades licked out to deflect grasping limbs as she was forced to retreat further or be surrounded.

On the other side, the queen sent her tail lunging around Innikar, encircling him. The coils spun, tightening like some huge fist in an effort to crush him, but Innikar was no longer there. Vaulting high in the air, he leapt for the queen's scaly back. Once more the monstrosity moved with astonishing speed, lashing out with her tail to strike him from midair. The Sil'ath warrior was propelled to the ground, tumbling end over end as he disappeared from sight. The dark, hulking shapes of more minions converged there and vanished after him in pursuit.

Amric struggled to retain consciousness in the crushing grip of the Nar'ath queen. He pried weakly at the talons that dug into his flesh even through his oiled mail shirt, trying in vain to loosen them enough that he might draw a full breath.

"Now, Adept," she said with obvious relish. "Where were we?"

The thick, protruding structures of her outer jaws flared wide, exposing the cold and eerily feminine countenance beneath. A blood-red mouth parted to reveal rows of glistening fangs, grinning in wicked triumph. Amric bared his own teeth and glared his hatred back at her. He fixed upon the slanted, glowing green eyes, and resolved to cling to awareness long enough to strike out at those orbs when she brought him close. Perhaps he could blind the fiend before she destroyed him. His vision darkened dangerously, a descending blackness threaded through with veins of white fire, and he blinked it back with a groan.

Fighting for consciousness, he cursed himself for underestimating the sheer power and ferocity of the Nar'ath queen. Sometimes the most difficult part of a trap was not in the catching, but in dealing with what one caught.

"Well?" Morland demanded. "Tell me what you see, farseer."

"A moment more, my lord," Lorenth murmured. He was a young man with a thin brown beard that matched the hue of his unassuming robes. He peered out the tower window into the night with unfocused eyes. "It is dark outside and the grounds of your estate are quite extensive. I am still finding my range."

"Be quick about it then," Morland snapped. "It is imperative that I know what transpires in the city tonight, and I am not a patient man."

"Yes, my lord," said Lorenth. "You have made your point."

"Have I? I wonder. I can usually tell when I have succeeded in making my point, as I either achieve the results I desire, or the person who has failed me provides a highly motivating example for others. Which will be the case with you, farseer?"

The young man shivered without blinking. Even without the merchant's ruthless reputation, there was the ice in his tone and the ominous leather creak and metal rasp of his guards to lend credence to his words. Lorenth kept his breathing even and clung to his focus with an effort. Whatever else might be said of the man, he paid well for results, and Lorenth desperately needed the coin.

"I will not fail you, my lord."

"See that you do not, farseer."

"I must remind my lord that my farsight cannot penetrate solid barriers—" Lorenth began.

"I am well aware of your limitations, farseer," Morland interrupted. "And I would not have hired you if they would be an issue for this task. Now, we are in the tallest tower of my mansion to provide you the least obstructed view over the bluff's edge and into the heart of the city. I suggest you make use of it, before my patience wears any thinner."

Lorenth bit back his frustration, all too aware that ill-chosen words with this man could prove fatal. A severed hand collected no coins, after all. "Perhaps if my lord would indicate what he seeks to find—"

"And have you merely echo whatever I wish to hear?" Morland snorted. "I think not. I am paying a sum greater than you would see in half a year or more, and I am paying it for the talents of a *true* farseer, not some charlatan fortune teller who would twist the gleanings from my own words into false pearls of wisdom. I would be most disappointed to find that you had misrepresented your skills."

Lorenth's mouth went dry. The room had gone a deadly kind of quiet, but he resisted the urge to retract his sight from the far-flung darkness in order to glance about him. It was a nervous reflex, difficult to suppress under the circumstances, but he steeled himself with the knowledge that it would not help him anyway. He was no warrior; he could not evade the blades of the scowling guards and win his way to freedom even if he could see his immediate surroundings. Also, the additional delay might in fact prove his undoing. No, his welfare depended solely upon his abilities now, and he had best start providing results.

Perhaps if he provided a few meaningful details, Morland would trust him enough to reveal the true requirements for Lorenth's work this evening.

His eyes focused on a distant point, thousands of yards away. He almost slumped with relief to find the outer wall of Morland's estate, bathed in amber pools of light cast by wall-set torches. Finally, some light to work with! He focused over the wall and onto the manicured lane beyond, and from there over the bluff's edge. He could not follow the slope from that point, as the angle from his current vantage point did not allow it. He would be forced to make another leap in focus, but at least this time he had his general bearings.

There was at least one element of truth to the merchant's words, Lorenth reflected as he extended his sight again. The man had offered a considerable amount for what seemed a simple enough job, even if the details were lacking in advance. But then, that was not unusual in itself. Lorenth expected that a portion of the fee was to buy his silence afterward about whatever he would see tonight. He was probably meant to confirm a lover's indiscretions, or perhaps spy on the clandestine dealings of some business competitor. Lorenth sighed to himself. It was usually something terribly tedious like that, some trivial personal or civic matter that was well beneath the scope of his talents, and a far cry from the valorous uses to which he had planned to put them when he first came to Keldrin's Landing.

The darkened top of a building swam into focus, interrupting his roaming thoughts. Somewhere in the trade district, it appeared.

"I have reached the trade district, my lord," Lorenth said. "Where am I to look?"

"Look to the streets," Morland replied, eagerness seeping into his tone. "Anywhere should suffice."

"Certainly, my lord, but if I know not where to look or what to—"

"Just look, you fool!"

Anywhere? It made no sense. Was the merchant not looking for something specific after all? Perhaps this was an extended interview of sorts, to verify his abilities in advance of a more important job that would come later. Lorenth felt a chill. How would he prove the veracity of what he saw if Morland was looking for nothing in particular? He had to find some convincing detail, something that would allay the suspicions of a powerful and vengeful man.

He shifted his gaze ever so slightly. This required a finer degree of control than most people realized, to move his sight only a few feet over such a distance. It was all too easy to jump wildly around and be forced to reestablish his frame of reference entirely. He had managed it over much greater lengths before, however, and the merchant did not seem the type to be impressed with the control Lorenth had practiced so hard to earn, so he swallowed the boastful words he was tempted to utter and resumed his efforts.

A street scene materialized before him. Dark, deserted. Lorenth bit his lip.

"What is it? What do you see?" the merchant's tone was oddly neutral for all its urgency.

"Nothing yet, my lord," the young man responded. "The streets nearby are empty."

"Empty?" Morland exclaimed. He sounded disappointed, disbelieving. "Keep searching."

"Yes, my lord."

The scene was just fading out of focus as Lorenth began to move his farsight again, when a flicker of movement in the distance caught his attention.

"One moment, lord," Lorenth said. "I may have something for you after all. There is something moving further up the lane."

"Tell me."

The young farseer pushed his sight up the cobbled street. A large group of shadowy figures sharpened into detail, running with long, bounding strides. Something about the way they moved struck him as wrong, unnatural, as if they were somehow lighter upon the earth than the size of their forms suggested. The foremost among them leapt high and hurled themselves upon another group, this one of wide-eyed men—soldiers, by the look of them—brandishing swords and spears. Even with the glow of rocking firelamps held high in the clenched fists of the men, the dark attackers were barely visible against the night. The feeble light cast by the lamps formed a faint golden frost upon the creatures, as if their black flesh greedily drank in all illumination.

Steel flashed and bodies collided, and Lorenth gasped at the ferocity of the clash. Then the breath caught in his throat with a dry rattle. He saw a spear ram through the abdomen of one of the black figures, but the creature did not falter; instead it grabbed the haft with both hands and wrenched it from the grasp of its shocked owner. The transfixed creature then hurled itself upon the man and bore him to the ground. Another man stepped toward his fallen comrade with sword upraised, but naked black hands wrapped around the blade, heedless of its cutting edge, holding it fast. Two more attackers leapt at the hapless fellow, binding his limbs. It was the same elsewhere, and the battle, if it could even be called such, was over in seconds. Every one of the men was down, and their unflinching foes bent over them with sinister intent.

Lorenth shifted his farsight in a panic, flinching away from whatever grisly end was to come. Another scene swam into focus, and the young man watched in horror as a different horde of the black creatures smashed in a shop door and poured into the building. The light pressing against the windows from the inside guttered, masked by twisting shadows within for a moment, and then went dark.

The farseer flinched, casting his sight elsewhere in the city, and found a large, embattled knot of the city guard. They were fighting in a protective ring around several huddled families while the black creatures came at them from all sides, constricting around the ring of soldiers in dark waves. With the startling clarity of his magical vision, Lorenth took in the drawn but resolute faces of the guards as they fought, the tear-streaked faces of the children clinging to their parents, and the depthless eyes and gaping maws of the attackers. There was no sound, of course, but all the mouths stretched taut in silent screams was almost worse, somehow; the unheard screams seemed to batter impossibly at his senses, clawing at him for supplication.

Lorenth convulsed, jerking his sight away again and again, only to land on scenes of similar mayhem all over the city. At last he dropped his farsight and fell back with a moaning cry, staggering for a moment as he returned to himself. The lavish interior of the chamber at Morland's estate drew in close about him, cradling him with its warmth. He felt a rush of relief mingled with guilt that he was here in the tower and not down below in the city streets. He sucked in a shuddering breath.

"M-My lord!" he gasped. "The city is besieged, overrun by some strange force!"

Morland stood a short distance away, regarding him with a hooded gaze. The man made no immediate reply, but instead turned away from the farseer and strode to a tall chair, where he sank into its red velvet cushions. Morland placed his hands in his lap and laced his fingers loosely together. "Go on," he said.

"There are thousands upon thousands of these strange creatures within the city walls, like black statues of twisted men come to life!" The young man gesticulated wildly at the tower window, as if the others could somehow bear witness to the same things that his farsight had allowed him to see.

Morland studied him with dark, deep-set eyes. "And how fare the city's defenders against these invaders?" he asked quietly.

"The creatures show no pain and shrug off what should be mortal blows," Lorenth said. "They are overwhelming soldier and citizen alike!"

The merchant nodded, pursing his lips. "The outcome is decided, then?"

Lorenth blinked, darting a glance to the tower window and then back again. Did the man not hear what he was saying? Did he not comprehend the danger that faced them all? "I-I do not know, my lord," he said. "The battle rages on, and though I am no military expert, I do not see how the defenders can—"

The words froze on his tongue as he watched a cruel smile spread across the hard, aquiline planes of Morland's face. Lorenth's eyes widened. The man *knew!* He had somehow anticipated this evening's events, and had brought the farseer here tonight to confirm them from the remote safety of his estate. He stared at the merchant in shock. Morland, for his part, simply watched the young man for a long moment as he sifted through the implications that came with the awareness.

"Do we continue to have an understanding, farseer?" the merchant asked with the cold smile still twisting at his lips. "I would hate to think that you had reached the end of your value to me."

Lorenth opened his mouth to reply, but no sound came out. His eyes flicked to the powerfully built guards standing in the shadows on either side of the chamber's only door. Their hands did not stray near the sword hilts at their hips, but they regarded him with pitiless, clinical stares. Lorenth snapped his mouth shut and looked back to the merchant. At last, he gave a tight nod.

"Excellent," Morland said. "You will monitor the events in the city tonight, and you will inform me immediately of any occurrences that might change the outcome."

With that, the man laid his head back on the high-backed, blood-red velvet chair and closed his eyes. His slender hands remained clasped comfortably before him in his lap. Lorenth swallowed a lump in his throat. Numb inside, he turned back to the tower window and stared out into the night, his eyes going unfocused.

Captain Borric shook his head to clear the sweat from his eyes. His vision remained blurry, however; a glancing blow from an ebon fist had left his head ringing and his left eye nearly swollen shut. How long ago had that been? It seemed like hours, but he knew how the chaos of battle could wreak havoc on a man's sense of time; it had probably been only minutes.

He looked around at his remaining men. Brave men all, they fought like tigers against their implacable foe, but one by one they were disappearing. Even as he watched, one stout soldier raised his shield against a rain of blows and clove the skull of an attacker. A score of strong black fingers snaked around the edge of his shield, however, ripping it away and staggering him off balance. In the blink of an eye, the man was pulled from his feet and dragged on his back across the cobblestones and into the dark wave of creatures. The man to his left, exposed by his comrade's sudden absence, gave a muffled cry as dark limbs wrapped about his head and shoulders. His neck broke with a sharp crack as he was jerked from his feet, and his struggling form sagged in their grasp. A pair of creatures pulled him several more feet before slowing, evidently noticing his condition. They released their hold, and he slid to the ground in a limp pile.

They stepped upon him as they returned to the fray, taking no more notice of his discarded corpse than they would a loose stone in the roadway.

These blasted things want to take us alive, Borric thought. He shouted orders, and two more guards closed the gap immediately with blades flashing, but their protective ring was thinning by the moment.

Borric shot a glance inward at the huddled citizens. It was mostly children now. The able-bodied men and women had already taken up the weapons of the fallen and thrown themselves into aiding the defense. They were not soldiers, however, and had been even quicker to fall before their tireless foes than the members of the city guard. To Borric's blurred vision, the children were one big indistinct mass of shape and color, clinging tightly together. He felt a traitorous flash of gratitude that he could no longer see their frightened expressions.

He had a sudden irrational thought for his own son, the boy he had not seen in the years since Borric had taken this job, the boy who would be a tall young man by now. He remembered wiping away the boy's tears at his departure, his assurances that it would not be as long as it seemed. He remembered his confident promises that he would return one day, laden with his earnings. He had only to accept this important position in a remote outpost for a few years, where the pay was many times what he could earn at home, in a land of untold riches beyond the frayed edges of known civilization...

Someone was shouting at him. Borric blinked, breaking from his reverie and straining to hear the words over the persistent ringing in his ears. He looked around. The ring of guards had thinned to the point of breaking.

"Tighten the ring!" he shouted. "Fall back three steps and tighten the ring!"

The men were quick to obey, their boots stomping and scraping as they backed into a tighter defensive circle. *If the ring shrinks much further*, Borric thought with a rueful grimace, *the men will be tripping over that cluster of children.*

A hole opened in the ranks before him as several of the fiends tried to force their way through in a wedge. Dead eyes stared at him above soundless, gaping mouths, and his men struggled to hold them back. With a roar of defiance, the captain of the guard raised his sword and plunged back into the fray.

Someone was shouting at him. A strident voice, somehow both distant and yet uncomfortably near, was gibbering at him to wake up, to fight back and, in a seeming contradiction, to give in and let go. *Release me,* the voice urged. *Join me,* so *that we may fight together as we were meant to!*

Amric's eyes flared open, and he realized with a chill that he had lost consciousness for a fleeting instant.

The huge visage of the Nar'ath queen loomed before him, and the stench of putrefaction washed over him with her hot breath. Her outer jaws were flared wide, reaching toward him with the hooked prongs that would keep his head frozen in place for the killing kiss. Her ruby lips peeled back to reveal row upon row of tiny glistening fangs that were eager to receive him.

Something slammed into the queen from the side, eliciting a shriek of pain from the monster. Amric gasped as the claws encircling his torso convulsed from the blow and nearly crushed him. She whirled in the direction from which the attack had come, but all Amric could see were the swirling sands obscuring all. Seconds later came another blow from the other side, and she shuddered, spinning in that direction and sweeping her claws in a blind, furious arc.

A phantom laughed echoed back to them, seeming to come from all directions at once. It was a rich, smooth voice, mocking as it slid through the murk and circled them.

Bellimar! Amric realized. The vampire was taking a direct hand in affairs once more, as he had in Stronghold.

A third blow shook the Nar'ath queen with a sound like muted thunder. She lunged in a new direction, roaring in rage and frustration. Shaking Amric like a child's doll, she slithered into a wide, rapid turn back toward the center of the vast chamber, prowling after this troublesome new prey.

Borric recognized his mistake the instant he made the attack that undid him.

The guard to his right stumbled and went to his knees, and half a dozen black hands seized him in an instant and pulled him headfirst from view. One of the fiends stepped into the gap and lunged at Borric, and the battle-forged reflexes of countless hard-fought campaigns took over. The captain of the guard stepped into a smooth lunge and drove the point of his sword into the throat of the attacker. It was perfectly executed, a lethal blow to any mortal assailant, but Borric knew in an instant that he was undone.

Before he could withdraw, the gaping fiend seized his wrist in a vise-like grip. It drew itself forward, surging along his blade until the hilt rested against its throat and the full length of shining steel projected from the back of its neck. With a wrench, the creature snapped the bones of his forearm, and his sword tumbled from useless fingers. He was jerked forward, the sheer force of it causing his feet to leave the ground. Something slammed into the back of his skull like an iron sledge, and all was darkness.

Black hands caught him before he hit the ground.

Morland cracked an eye and watched the farseer at work. The young man shuddered and flinched from time to time, but his eyes remained wide open and twitched between distant targets that only he could see. Tears ran openly across his face and into his beard.

What a fool, thought Morland with a curl of his lip. It was not as if this show of weakness would have any effect on the outcome down there. The city was lost. His Nar'ath allies were doing just as they had promised by demonstrating the inevitability of their conquest. Morland felt a surge of pride. The Nar'ath had skulked about for centuries, hiding and evading notice, building their strength slowly; the time for such subterfuge was at an end.

Not for the first time, he congratulated himself for turning a minor setback into the promise of success. He had been furious when the Nar'ath attacked his trade caravan so many months ago; even though they had left the goods untouched, it had cost him no small amount of time and trouble to replace the men that had disappeared. It had cost him many more after that to track down the culprits, to gauge their strength, and to make careful advances to establish contact with their leader.

It was all worth it in the end, however. The Nar'ath forces would continue to grow, fueled by this victory, and he would be remembered for his part in accelerating their eventual triumph. He swelled with pride. And of course, once they had taken what they needed, they would establish him as the undisputed ruler over the survivors, just as they had promised. He would at last achieve the power that had long been his goal, but on a scale to which even he had not dared aspire.

He frowned. Something nagged at the fringes of his thoughts, a tattered edge to an otherwise perfect picture. How many survivors would be left when the Nar'ath were sated? What proof had they offered of their assertion that they had no long-term interest in this world? Where were they going? These seemed like questions he would have asked, being a shrewd negotiator and a calculating businessman. In fact, he recalled going to his initial meetings with the Nar'ath queen with every intention of learning the answers to these questions and more. Now, however, when he looked back, his memories of that meeting were a fog, and he could not produce the answers to any of these queries. He tried to call forth the details—any details—from those fateful encounters, but they slid away like raindrops down a slate roof.

He forced himself to concentrate harder. The towering image of the Nar'ath queen appeared before his mind's eye, and he found his thoughts dulling, laced with a strange sense of loyalty that bordered on complacency. He frowned again. These thoughts fit him poorly, as if he was awakening to find himself wearing another man's clothing.

He sat forward. He had no qualms about what was transpiring in Keldrin's Landing; after all, conquest on the scale he required was never accomplished without some amount of bloodshed. It was unlike him, however, to enter into such a crucial arrangement without an ironclad set of safeguards in place. How had he—

"My lord?" Lorenth interrupted his thoughts in a quavering tone.

"What is it?" Morland snapped.

"Y-you are certain that the creatures will pass over your estate?"

The merchant opened his mouth to snarl an affirmative, and then paused. He had been given that assurance, at least. Indeed, the Nar'ath had demonstrated their commitment to their arrangement by ensuring that his trade caravans were no longer molested, while those of his rivals suffered the fate with alarming frequency. Even with that promise, however, he found himself facing sudden gnawing doubts. "Why do you ask, farseer?"

"The creatures have torn your gates asunder, and a great many of them have just entered your grounds."

Morland shot to his feet. "Are they coming here?" he demanded.

The farseer turned toward him, and Morland gave a start. The man's eyes had no pupils! Then, as if bobbing to the surface of a calm lake,

Lorenth's pupils reappeared within his pale blue eyes. Of course, the merchant admonished himself; it was just some effect of his strange abilities. Lorenth blinked several times, and the semblance of calm was broken. The blue eyes focused upon Morland.

"I cannot say for certain, my lord," the young man said in a voice barely above a whisper. "They appeared to be headed this way, but once past the braziers at the gate, they passed into darkness and I could no longer see them."

Morland stared at him for a long moment, frozen. Then he cursed and spun on his heel, making a curt motion to the guards. The soldiers snapped to attention and pulled the doors open as he approached.

Lulled and betrayed! He ground his teeth in fury as his mind raced over his options. However he had been ensorcelled by the Nar'ath, he was comforted by the fact that he had at least demonstrated some semblance of his customary caution in establishing certain contingent plans. He had a ship at anchor well away from the docks that was waiting for him to signal it in. He could be away from this gods-forsaken land for good. This, however, was not the time to attempt to reach the sea. No, the Nar'ath were too strong and too many; he would have to weather the night in a safe place and make his escape when the opportunity presented itself, after the chaos had subsided. He had a fortified armory at the center of his massive keep, well stocked with provisions. It would serve his needs nicely. A man with means and foresight such as he possessed *always* had a backup plan.

"M-my lord?"

The thin, tremulous voice of the farseer brought Morland sharply about. He had all but forgotten the meek fellow. His eyes narrowed as he regarded Lorenth.

"What of me, my lord?"

Morland gave him an icy smile. "It seems our business is concluded, farseer. Guards, please see him out the main doors. I believe he can find his way from there."

Lorenth paled. "My lord, please—!" he stammered as the soldiers took heavy steps toward him.

The merchant turned to go. Lorenth's voice, rising several octaves and into the shrill range, followed him through the doorway.

"My lord, wait! Wait! I can still be of use to you!"

Morland paused, half turning. "Make it quick and compelling, or you will exit by means of that window instead."

Lorenth stumbled forward, wringing his hands. "You will need a safe route from the city, my lord," he said in a rush. "I can help, especially if you wait until daylight. I can use my farsight to reveal which roads lead to safety, and which to certain death."

Morland regarded him for a long moment, and then a slow, vulpine smile spread across his features. "How very enterprising of you, farseer. I may just make a savvy businessman of you yet."

Another thunderous blow shook the Nar'ath queen. From the corner of his eye, Amric caught a blur of motion passing by him with inhuman speed before disappearing once more into the swirling sand. An instant later it came again, accompanied by a sharp, cracking report and a keening cry of agony from the queen. One of the claws gripping Amric loosened and fell away from him, and the limb dangled at a broken, useless angle at her side.

Amric took the opportunity to fill his lungs as the crushing grip on his chest slackened enough to allow unrestricted breath. He was rewarded with a mouthful of choking sand, but his tenuous hold on consciousness firmed and new energy flooded his body. As the queen spat her outrage at her unseen assailant, he expanded his chest and flexed his arms outward, straining against the remaining talons. Then, in a sudden movement, he let all his air out in a whoosh and brought his arms together tightly over his head, making himself as narrow as possible. He fell through and plunged to the ground.

He struck the ground and rolled, pushing himself to his feet. He began to run on shaky legs away from the towering shape behind him. Trying to clear his head, he wondered if he could find one or both of his swords in this damnable sandstorm.

With an incoherent scream, the Nar'ath queen swept her remaining limbs wide in a cutting gesture, and the unnatural storm responded to her fury. A concussive blast rippled outward from her, scything throughout the chamber. The sheer force of it slammed into Amric's back, lifting him from his feet and catapulting him through the air. He landed with jarring force, tumbling end over end before settling into a long skid. A sickly green glow beckoned ahead, and he gritted his teeth as he realized he was sliding toward the edge of one of the pools. The howling wind washed over him, pulling at his flesh and clothing with a savage hand, dragging

332 | MICHAEL J. ARNQUIST

him toward the toxic fluids. He dug in to slow his approach, using the edges of his boot soles and the naked flesh of his clawing hands. At last the force of the blast gave out, the wind subsided, and he came to rest within inches of the pool's edge. The viscous green liquid wicked at the stone rim that contained it, as if hungry to reach his flesh. Amric let out the breath he had been holding captive, and spun to look back toward the Nar'ath queen.

The monster stood near the center of the vast chamber. The eerie storm she had raised was gone, its remnants still crawling away from her across the stone floor in wisps and tendrils. Several shapes were revealed as the last of the sand washed over them, emerging like water-worn rocks through receding floodwaters. Some were the hulking Nar'ath minions, thrown to the ground by the blast. One was the figure of a man in gray robes, kneeling low with his cloak flung over his head in a shielding gesture. Bellimar!

The Nar'ath queen was upon him in an instant, even before the raking wind had subsided. Massive claws swept the old man from his feet, drawing him into a crushing embrace. Bellimar thrashed about, prying at her talons, and a frenzied struggle ensued. He writhed and struck over and over, loosening her hold as she fought to tighten it. At last she used all three of her remaining claws to clamp his flailing limbs in place. Her head darted forward, and her outer jaws flared and snapped shut upon his head, locking him into place. She began to inhale—and then she recoiled with a shrill cry.

"What is this?" she hissed in disgust. "Your life force is powerful indeed, but it is tainted and unusable. You are a troublesome, worthless creature!"

Rising to her full height, she hunched forward and drove the vampire into the ground with such force that the very floor of the chamber shook. A ragged cry echoed through the cavernous hive, and Amric realized it was his own. He began to run at the Nar'ath queen.

She reared back, still holding Bellimar. His gray form was limp in her claws. Even as he sprinted toward her, Amric hoped that it was but a ruse on Bellimar's part. The Nar'ath queen might have had the same suspicion, however, as she uncoiled in a sudden whipping motion to send him hurtling away through the air. Bellimar's body flew like a stone from a sling to strike the wall of the chamber with a sharp crack, and then it slid to the ground to lie in a crumpled heap.

The Nar'ath queen was still facing in that direction, eyeing Bellimar's motionless form as if expecting him to rise and attack her again, when Amric reached her. Leaping high, he vaulted onto her back. Catching at the coarse edges of the armored plates along her spine, he clambered up toward her head. She whirled with a startled shriek, but he clung fast. A youth spent among the Sil'ath climbing ancient trees and rocky crags had prepared him well for this task; he was at the nape of her neck even as she started to reach around and claw at him. Her outraged visage swung toward him. He leapt, drawing the knife at his belt, all his attention focused upon plunging the weapon into one of her glowing green eyes.

He never made it.

Moving with impossible speed, she struck him from the air. The world exploded into colors as Amric slammed into the ground: encroaching blackness, scarlet pain, and an eruption of white fire that threatened to engulf him. Something inside him was screaming to be let out. Confusing images pounded at his dazed mind. He saw Bellimar's face, frozen in final death; he saw Valkarr's features melt from worry to horror and revulsion; he saw his own face, flickering between rage, fear and scorn. These images shattered into slivers of glass as a new countenance pushed through them all. It was hate-filled and exulting, with slitted green eyes burning at him above a many-fanged mouth. It was the Nar'ath queen, and she would have him at last.

He was dimly aware, as if it was happening to someone else entirely, of being held in a crushing grip, of his ribs threatening to crack and his lungs burning once more for precious breath. The queen's expression was avid, incensed as she drew him to her. She was speaking to him, but he could not make out the words.

His eyes rolled skyward, drawn by some unknown instinct. Cold, gray clouds churned overhead, showing their disdain for the trivial affairs of the mortals below. A figure rose to stand at the stone rim high above, silhouetted against that steel sky. His vision was fading, but he felt he should recognize that figure. All he could discern was a flash of her auburn hair, the polished gleam of a bent bow, and the murderous glint thrown by the dark missile she had nocked. Then the glint was gone, and the bow was being lowered. A fleeting whistle greeted his ears, rising sharply at the end like an unanswered question.

The queen's glowing eyes were still fixed upon him when everything erupted into heat and thunder. His vision went fiery white, and he had the strangest sensation that he was pushing the heat away from him with his bare hands. He realized he was tumbling through the air, no longer in the iron grip of the Nar'ath queen. He struck the ground hard. As the darkness rose to claim him, it felt as if a portal of white fire opened beneath him instead, and he continued to fall.

CHAPTER 22

He stood in the formless landscape of the dream, surrounded by crawling white mists. It was the material of his will, waiting to be wrought, and yet he suppressed his every instinct to do so.

Amric began to walk.

The mists curled about him, cloaking and embracing, somehow both warm and chill at once. He glanced at his hands. They were empty, and he had no weapon on his person; he was unarmed. As quick as the thought came to him, he was clothed in dark armor, and the well-worn grips of his swords rested against his palms with familiar weight. He hesitated, frowning, and then banished it all. They were the trappings of war, and though the warrior felt a strong desire for the comfort of their presence, they ran counter to his purpose here, this time.

He continued to walk. He was headed neither to nor from any particular destination, and no such landmark offered itself from out of the mists. It was the simple movement he sought, and in particular an almost complete *lack* of focus, for if he was correct it would eventually bring—

Yes, there it was; a feather-light touch at the fringe of his awareness, an extra presence here at the core of a domain that should have, by all rights, been his and his alone. He slowed to a halt, and though the presence shrank, it did not withdraw.

"You may as well show yourself," he called. "For reasons I do not yet fully understand, this is your dream as much as it is mine."

There was a wavering there at the periphery of his senses, a flickering indecision as of something wild and frightened poised to flee. Then it stiffened into a fragile resolve, and there was movement. A shadow appeared in the hanging mists ahead and solidified into the shape of a man as it approached. Amric waited.

When it stepped from the mists to stand before him, it wore his face, as before. Amric studied the other, and he watched it study him in return with searching eyes. There was concern and resignation there that he felt he should understand. He wondered what the other read in his own countenance as it looked upon him. The other began to fidget beneath the intensity of his gaze, so he gave a strained smile and turned to walk once more. He found it disconcerting to be staring into a mirror of his own visage, anyway. After a moment's hesitation, the other joined him, falling into step at his side, but a long pace away.

They strode this way for a time, directionless and unhurried, in a tense but companionable silence. At last Amric cleared his voice and spoke.

"You are—" he began, and then paused with a frown. "You are inside me?"

The other glanced at him, and then quickly away. It gave a shallow nod. Amric closed his eyes, going cold inside, but otherwise kept his reaction from showing. It was the response he dreaded, the very thing he had been adamant in denying to himself, but he did not want to drive this entity back into hiding until he had more answers. Despite his effort at control, however, the other flinched as if struck.

"Is this an infection?" Amric asked. "Am I sick, or mad?"

The other looked at him with a pained expression, and shook its head. Amric chuckled at the folly of his own question. How could he trust the word of what might be a figment of his own imagination to determine if he was mad nor not?

"How long have you been... with me? Since Stronghold, and the exposure to the Essence Fount?"

A slow shake of the head.

"Longer?"

A barely perceptible nod. Amric frowned as he walked.

"Why do you not speak?" he said. "It was you calling to me when I lost consciousness in the grip of the Nar'ath queen, was it not? Urging me to release you, to fight together?"

The other nodded.

"Then why do you not speak now?"

His double gave a helpless shrug. Amric stopped and turned toward it, brow furrowing in confusion. The other immediately shrank before his intent gaze. Even as the warrior stared, the figure's outline shimmered and grew indistinct, beginning to fade from view.

"Wait!" Amric cried, reaching toward it. The form blurred, darting away from his outstretched hand like a windblown curl of dark smoke. Amric gritted his teeth and pulled up short, fighting his desire to give chase. He drew a deep breath and closed his eyes.

"Please wait," he said in as gentle a tone as he could manage. "I just need to understand."

He waited there for long seconds, breathing slowly. He struggled to keep his mind clear of the anger and loathing that threatened to seep in again at the thought of another creature inhabiting his body like some incorporeal parasite. In desperation he drew upon his warrior's training, seeking the calm in which he wrapped himself at the center of battle. Very gradually it came to him through his own layers of resistance, and he sank into that void, shedding hesitation and fear, stripping away denial and prejudice. He needed the truth if he was to survive, in this as much as in the chaos of battle, and he would cut away what obscured it until truth was all that remained.

This strange entity had been with him for some time now, of that much he was certain. Certainly since the cataclysmic events at Stronghold, when proximity to the Essence Fount had affected him so. And he could not deny that some unknown force had acted through him to collapse the massive chamber at the core of that fortress when all had seemed lost. That same power had kept Valkarr from the very edge of death long enough for him to be saved. It had been all too easy for him to attribute the episode to the Essence Fount, since it was a huge, powerful manifestation of purest magic and utterly beyond his ken. Grelthus and Bellimar had both insisted that the Fount was not a live thing capable of intelligent action, however. It was a rupture in a ley line—a veritable river of magical energy—and no more sentient than an erupting volcano.

He had ignored all they said and refrained from further examination of the alternatives, because he had feared the conclusions to which they led. It might have been the Essence Fount, or merely coming to a land where all magic was rising to run rampant, that awakened this entity within him, but for some reason he believed its response that it had been with him since before that time.

A lifetime's aversion to magic rose like bile in his throat, threatening to dislodge him from the center of the void. He was a warrior, raised among the Sil'ath. Magic was a perverse thing, an addiction for less disciplined races. An image appeared in his mind of Valkarr, his closest friend since childhood, with reptilian features twisted in shock and revulsion. Then came more flashing images: Innikar, Sariel, Prakseth—but no, Prakseth was dead. Amric shook himself, and sought the calm within once more.

It was not that simple. Whatever lurked inside him might be killing him or driving him slowly mad, it was true. But it had also saved Valkarr in Stronghold, had in fact saved all their lives. And while the strange dizzy spells had occurred at inopportune times, during periods of high stress and in the face of deadly threats, it seemed as if the other had been offering help each time.

Release me, it had told him. From what? To fight together, it had suggested. But how? By taking over his body? He felt another chill. Would this creature then assume control, never to relinquish it? Would Amric then become the entity within, little more than a persistent shade lurking at the back of its consciousness?

He shook his head. The thoughts sent fear lancing through him, but they did not match what he had seen and felt. The other had not wrested control from him in Stronghold, when he had been injured and at his most vulnerable. Instead, it had joined with him somehow, brought him unimaginable power at his time of need, and bolstered him to achieve the impossible. Afterward, it had retreated into seeming nonexistence again, fleeing before his scrutiny as it had done every time since, and as it had done here. These were not the actions of some unseen tyrant or assassin, awaiting only opportunity to strike him down. And the haunting, wounded look in its—in *his*—eyes had been disturbingly genuine.

The familiar presence gathered at his side. Even with his eyes closed, Amric could feel a tentative hand reaching for his shoulder, and an overpowering sense of worry washed over him. He opened his eyes to regard the other, once more his mirror image, and the hand froze in mid-reach.

"The dream, with the hidden cottage in the forest," Amric mused. "That was *your* dream, not mine."

The other hesitated, and then nodded.

"You fear me, fear my discovery of you," he continued, fumbling for comprehension. "I can *feel* it in you, just as you react to my own state of mind. You have been remaining ever close, but evading my direct attention, terrified that I will find you and strike you down somehow, just as in the dream."

The other drew back, almost cringing.

"That is why you come to me only in moments of distraction or weakness," Amric said, eyes narrowing. "Only then are you bold enough to act. You seek to protect me, and yet you have this terrible fear of my wrath."

His own grey eyes stared back at him, wide with apprehension. Amric burst out laughing, and the other started and blinked at the sudden sound.

"I still do not know what you are, my mysterious friend," he said with a shake of his head. "But I can see that you are as scared of me as I am of whatever it is you represent."

The other flashed a hesitant smile at him, but remained at arm's length.

A harsh sound echoed faintly in the distance, shrill and grating. It was an alien shriek filled with rage and pain, and sudden memories of the waking world flooded back to Amric. The hive, his friends, the Nar'ath queen and her minions, the arrow fired by Thalya and the concussive explosion that had resulted; how could he have forgotten? His life and the lives of his friends hung in the balance as he wandered this surreal landscape.

"If I can hear that monster out there, at least I know I am still alive," he said grimly. "I need to wake. I need to go back and fight. Now."

His dark leather and oiled chain armor appeared, sheathing him in its fierce embrace. His fingers curled around battle-worn hilts, and the steel of his blades gleamed before him. The creeping white mists of the dream began to curl about him. The other drew away from him and vanished like smoke scattered before the wind, though whether it fled his weapons or his sharpening focus, he was not sure.

The mists swirled in a tightening funnel around him, faster and faster, bearing flickering images. Amric caught glimpses of the dark interior of the hive, illuminated by the pulsing green glow of the pools. He saw the huge and menacing figure of the Nar'ath queen, thrashing about while her skulking minions milled about with confused and uncertain movements. He saw the hunched figures of his friends isolated amid a storm of sand. And there were other images as well, hallucinations that made no sense to him: the forest, the hidden cottage, an intangible presence hovering fretfully within the cottage above a sleeping child. The door to the cottage cracked open to reveal a blinding sliver of sunlight…

Amric shook his head, and the chaotic images receded. These were not his visions alone, he knew, but also the memories of the other tangled with his own. He clenched at the recognition, wanting to push it all away from him, to be alone once more in his own mind. But the thought continued to nag at him: whether or not he was at risk of losing himself, if this elusive entity could help him save his friends, would he not do it? The situation was dire, if indeed it was still possible to win out. He had already admitted the possibility of the worst that could happen to him, and yet he knew that he would give his own life in an instant if it meant saving the others.

Why, then, not his sanity as well?

He smiled grimly. There would be time enough to seek a cure, if he survived.

"I am going out there to slay that monstrosity, if it can be done," he called into the air. "You offered to fight together, before. Will you do so now?"

There was no response to his query aside from the echoes of the Nar'ath queen's fury, which were growing louder by the moment. The mists curled tighter around him like a cocoon.

"Will you come if I call upon you?" Amric shouted.

He looked around for the shadowy figure, but saw no sign of it. He closed his eyes, seeking the insubstantial presence that he knew was nearby, and yet he could not find it. There was nothing. The harder he looked for it, the less certain he was that he had ever felt it, that the whole experience had ever been anything more than a muddled, lingering dream. Perhaps he really was going mad after all.

He tightened his grips on the swords and braced himself, looking upward into the narrowing funnel of mist above him. The shrieks of the Nar'ath queen hammered at him in waves now. The soft caress of the mists felt more and more like the howling bite of a sandstorm. He closed his eyes, pushing back doubt and fatigue, seeking the center of the void he would need to survive in the maelstrom awaiting him in the waking world above.

He exhaled slowly.

"Are you with me?" he whispered.

Yes, I am with you.

Rough hands shook him.

The ingrained instincts of the warrior took over, and he lashed out before he was fully aware, before his eyes even opened. A grip of iron caught his forearm in motion and clamped there, holding him firm. Amric's eyes flared wide to find Valkarr crouched over him. He could read the relief in his friend's tight expression even through the swirling, wind-borne sand. Behind Valkarr stood the hazy figures of Sariel and Innikar, peering down at Amric.

A broad grin creased Valkarr's scaly face. "If you are done resting, warmaster, your warriors are quite ready to leave this place."

Amric lurched up to a sitting position, and helping hands boosted him to his feet. His head spun and his body ached in more places than he could count, but he managed to stand on his own. His face and hands stung as if burnt, and there was a stabbing pain in his left side when he took too deep a breath.

To his surprise, he found his swords back in his hands, just as in the strange dream. He frowned. His weapons had been lost in the sandstorm as he fought the Nar'ath queen, tumbling from his numb fingers and scattered in different directions. How, then, had they found their way back to him while he was unconscious? The waking world was not like the dream landscape, where he had summoned his belongings with desire alone. Had his friends found them on the chamber floor and pressed them into his unresponsive hands as he was lying there? Whatever the cause, he was grateful for their return.

A sharp tremor shook the ground, accompanied by an ear-splitting peal of agonized fury. The center of the chamber was enveloped in a great cyclone of sand, and from it came waves rippling along the ground like low-hanging smoke. It seemed the Nar'ath queen was injured and angry, and had once more cloaked herself with her eerie control over the wasteland. As Amric studied the tempest, wondering if they could find their way through it to strike at the monster, another tremor ripped through the hive and almost threw him from his feet. There was a sound like the breaking of dry branches, and a network of cracks spidered through one side of the dome overhead. A piece of sandstone the size of a horse cart fell away from the high wall and shattered into a thousand shards of rock upon the ground. Several more followed, and the cracks in the dome began to spread and widen.

"The hive is collapsing," Sariel shouted. "We need to leave now!"

Amric threw another glance toward the dark, raging heart of the storm, and then nodded. "Let her pull the place down on her own head," he said. "We will wait for her above, if she emerges."

They ran for the nearest of the winding stairways. At the foot of the stairs, Amric paused and spun about.

"Bellimar!" he said. "Did you find him as well?"

Valkarr shook his head, his expression grim. "We found no sign of him, but it is hard to locate anything out there. We were very fortunate to find you, once the queen raised the sandstorm again."

Sariel grabbed at Amric's arm, pulling him toward the stairs. "There is no time to look again," she hissed. "We can only hope that he found his way out on his own."

Amric hesitated, lifting his gaze to the shaking dome above, then gave a reluctant nod and turned back to the stairs. The old man had shown himself to be canny and tough; hopefully that would be enough to see him free of this place of death and destruction.

The warriors sheathed their blades and raced up the curving stairway. The ground fell away below, and they were soon above the roiling clouds of dust and sand, but their ascent proved no less harrowing than the battle below had been. The whole place trembled and heaved, threatening to throw them from the narrow stairs with every step. Twice the steps began to crumble away beneath their heels, and only quick leaps and the clasping hands of their comrades allowed them all to continue climbing toward the night sky.

They were partway up when a fluttering shadow shot free of the maelstrom below and rose through the air in an impossible leap. It clamped to the wall below the stairs ahead of them, clinging like some ragged spider. After a moment's pause, the figure began to move, scampering up the sheer stone wall. Amric reached over one shoulder for the hilt of a sword as he neared the thing, but then he froze as he recognized the pale, slender hand that reached over the edge of the stairway.

"Bellimar!" he cried.

The old man pulled himself onto the stairs with a grunt, and then rose shakily to his feet. His clothing was torn and he bore countless gashes and scrapes, though his wounds were all puckered and bloodless. He swayed for a moment, clutching his side, and then gave the warriors a rueful look.

"Remind me never to do that again," he muttered. "I suppose I should be grateful that I am already dead."

Below, the angry cries of the Nar'ath queen rose to a crescendo. The swirling sands drew together across the hive and toward the core of the storm, leaving the chamber floor bare as they receded like a sudden tide. It all hung there for a moment, dense and dark, and then exploded outward with a sound like a thunderclap. The concussive force pressed them all to the wall of the hive for a moment as the sands bit at their exposed flesh. Then it subsided, and the sand sheeted down the outer wall. The chamber was clear to view once more, as was the Nar'ath queen.

She stood hunched in the center of the hive, seething with rage. She was surrounded by a dozen of her heavyset black minions, which milled about her in fretful uncertainty. The queen's face was a charred ruin, and her heavy outer jaws hung twisted and useless from the lower part of her elongated skull. From the midst of that blackened visage, however, her green eyes burned with brilliant and unremitting malevolence. Those glowing slits raked over the room, searching for her prey. Her head lifted toward the tiny figures high above her, and her eyes narrowed. With a harsh, gurgling hiss, she burst into motion, surging for the foot of the stairway. The hive, which had become still momentarily, began to shake again with renewed vigor.

Amric's brow furrowed. The stairs were narrow and unstable; there was no way they would support her bulk. He was about to say as much aloud when the Nar'ath queen reached the wall, and the words died in his throat. The stone wall warped at her approach, twitching and rippling like the hide of a beast. The ground lifted before her, and the stairs near the bottom melted and flowed slowly together to form the beginnings of a ramp. Amric felt a chill. The monster was reforming the place to meet her will, and it would not be long until she was able to pursue them out of the hive.

Amric glanced down. The stone beneath him had begun to shift, as when a strong ocean current pulled the sand out from beneath one's feet. The edges of the steps were becoming less definite, rounding and disintegrating before his eyes. He shared a quick glance with the others.

"Run!" he barked. "Now!"

They raced up the stairway as it eroded and crumbled, by turns running and scrambling on all fours. When at last they reached the lip of the dome's opening, Amric could not recall a time when he had been more grateful to stand beneath the open sky. A roar of frustration followed them as the Nar'ath queen continued her climb. Thalya, Syth and Halthak were waiting for them with the frightened horses.

"Where are the captives?" Amric asked.

"Marching back toward that outcropping of rock we camped on last night," Thalya responded. "They are weak, and the desert may be no friendly place, but the men seemed to find it preferable to remaining near the hive."

Amric nodded. "Nice shot, by the way. You have my thanks."

"You are welcome," she said. "And you owe me for that arrow."

But she flashed a smirk as she said it, and he grinned back. Then her gaze strayed to Bellimar, taking in his bedraggled state, and her smile faded. Bellimar met her emerald eyes with an unblinking, unreadable expression. Amric tensed. The huntress had expended two of her powerful ensorcelled arrows, but she had a third remaining. It might look to her as if Bellimar was evincing a moment of vulnerability worth exploiting, but Amric had seen the vampire's unnatural speed and strength firsthand below. In addition, the Nar'ath queen would reach the top of the dome in short order, and the battle would be resumed. They might need every weapon in their arsenal to stop her, if it was even possible to do so. A confrontation between the two of them here and now would prove disastrous for them all.

Before he could step between them, however, Thalya took a deliberate look up and down Bellimar, her cold expression promising a future reckoning, and then she turned her back on the old man. She stepped into the saddle of her black mare.

Amric let out a slow breath and swung atop his bay gelding. Sariel vaulted up to sit behind him. The others mounted their own horses, with Valkarr and Innikar riding together again, and the group began to pick their way around and down the dome as rapidly as its steep slope allowed. The horses seemed to be having an easier time on the descent than they had when climbing the structure, and Amric realized that the slope was less severe. The hive was slowly sinking, settling as it shook, almost deflating. The riders picked up speed, coaxing the horses to a sliding trot over the crumbling surface.

With a shriek like tearing metal, the Nar'ath queen burst from the hive. Her baleful gaze fell upon the riders, and long black claws tore into the stone as she surged forward after them.

"I hope you have a plan to stop that thing, swordsman," Syth called as he cast worried looks over his shoulder. "That arrow only seems to have made it mad."

Amric turned in the saddle to find Valkarr.

"We cannot face her directly again," the Sil'ath said. "Our blades were little more than annoyances to her. We need to wear her down."

"Agreed," Amric replied. "Ride on to the ground and lure her away from the hive. I think she draws power from this location, somehow. Spread out so that she can only chase one at a time, while the others dart in and out quickly. She's too big for a single killing stroke. Try to bleed her with smaller wounds instead. Weaken her slowly, and then finish her."

Valkarr's eyes narrowed, but he nodded in response as he rode. Behind him, Innikar gave Amric a questioning look.

"You talk as if you will not be there," Sariel hissed into his ear, giving voice to their puzzlement.

"I am hoping it will not come to that," Amric said with a tight smile. "But those are my orders—my suggestions—in case this does not work." He handed her the reins.

"In case what does not—" she began.

Amric whipped a leg over the saddle and dropped from the horse.

Sariel shifted forward into the saddle and pulled back on the reins, slowing the big bay, but Amric waved them all on.

"Go!" he shouted. "I think I know how to stop her, but follow Valkarr's lead if I am wrong."

The riders exchanged glances, hesitating precious seconds more before spurring their horses onward down the outer surface of the hive. Syth lingered last, clearly torn as mad admiration shone in his eyes. Finally, he threw a long look toward the retreating form of Thalya on her mare, and he turned his horse after the others. Amric smiled; he wondered if Thalya knew.

"You are going to need a bigger weapon!" Syth called back as he rode away, and then Amric was alone.

I know, Amric thought. I am hoping I have brought one.

He turned to face the charging Nar'ath queen.

The riders had made good time, aided in large part by the gradual sinking of the dome. Amric now stood significantly closer to the wasteland below than to the top of the hive. The queen had gained ground on them, certainly, but her own mass and the decaying surface was hampering her progress. The fringe of small appendages skirting her huge form dug into the stone beneath her, keeping her from sliding out of control. She released and grabbed anew in a rippling, insect-like crawl. It brought her toward Amric at an alarming pace, but he was grateful to find it was nowhere near the blinding speed she had exhibited below.

He would need the time, if this was even going to work. If he was not insane after all.

Amric reached inside, searching for the presence he knew was there.

I need you now, he thought. You wanted to fight together. This is our chance.

For long, sickening seconds there was nothing. Amric watched the Nar'ath queen, radiating power and rage, clawing her way toward him. Then the familiar presence filled his mind, drowning his senses. Feelings of fear and urgency hammered at him, wrapping his own emotions and amplifying them until he was all but crushed beneath their weight. He staggered and almost went to one knee as a wave of dizziness struck him.

No! he commanded, gritting his teeth. If we fight for control, we will both die. This time we work together.

The pressure receded and the presence became hesitant, confused. It seemed to Amric like a wild animal, uncertain whether to attack or flee. He needed it to do neither of those, and instead accept a third alternative. His alternative.

I have done my best to deny your existence, he thought. Well, no longer.

The hive shook beneath his feet, and the Nar'ath queen came on.

You have hidden from me within my own mind, and sought to overwhelm me by acting on my behalf, he continued fiercely. No longer.

The Nar'ath queen drew near, glaring her hatred from a ruined face. She crouched low with her torso, squatting with forelimbs outstretched like a massive spider, while the serpentine rear part of her form gathered and tensed for the final pounce.

This time we work together, Amric repeated, lifting his arms.

Power roared within him, filling him like an ocean of white fire.

The Nar'ath queen's glowing green eyes widened in sudden fear and outrage. "Adept!" she screamed. "Deceiver!"

With thunderous force that shook the dome anew, she catapulted into the air toward him. Amric raised his hands, palms outward, and made a sharp pushing motion. The monstrosity struck an invisible force in midair and careened backward to slam into the stone. Fine cracks snaked in every direction from the point of impact. She twisted back into an upright position in an instant, but he was not done. Operating on pure instinct—his or the other's, he was not certain which—he reached out with hands flared open to send tendrils of power threading through the disintegrating stone of the hive. The dome began to rumble even more violently than before. The Nar'ath queen scrabbled with her talons over the bucking surface, seeking enough purchase for another charge.

"We will destroy your kind, Adept!" she spat. "My minions will—"

"Let us see if you can command your minions from hell, fiend!" Amric snarled back.

He clenched both hands into fists. A deafening roar shook the hive, and the top half of the massive dome fell away before him in an avalanche of stone. The Nar'ath queen vanished from sight, clawing and shrieking, sucked into a growing vortex of rock and sand. The hive continued to fracture and tumble in after her, and her screeching was lost in the thunder.

A meandering crack split the stone at Amric's feet. The vast hole that had been the top of the hive was growing rapidly; the ragged edge crumbled toward him like a voracious, widening maw that meant to consume him as well.

Amric turned and ran.

His body was bruised and battered, his every nerve tingling, and it felt as if he had been somehow singed from the inside. He pushed it all from his mind as best he could. Right now, to run was to live, and the fates be damned but he was going to *run*. He ran down the slope at a reckless pace, hurdling cracks as they yawned before him and skirting the sinkholes that opened like sores in the earth. The surface of the dome was decaying, softening from stone to sand, and seemed to catch at his boots as he pounded over it. His footing was far too treacherous to risk a look back, but his fevered imagination put the collapsing edge at his very heels.

He hurled himself past the last bit, leaping through the air to strike the sand of the wasteland. He rolled several times and came to his knees, gasping for breath. He was just in time to see the last remnants of the hive vanish beneath a crashing wave of sand, sending a plume of dust high into the night sky. Where the imposing structure had been, there was nothing left but a broad, shallow crater in the desert.

Amric sagged back on his haunches, shuddering with reaction. The strange presence flitted and circled within him, almost giddy, while he only felt a chilling numbness inside. He turned his hands over, staring down at them as if they were not his own. Wisps of smoke rose in slow curls from his fingers.

The whicker of horses caused him to lift his head. The others drew rein a short distance away, their eyes wide as they stared at him. Valkarr rode at the head of the group. Amric searched his friend's expression, seeking any clue as to what he was feeling at the moment: revulsion, fear, anything. But the Sil'ath's face was frozen in shock, and revealed nothing.

Bellimar urged his horse forward, edging past Valkarr's blue dun. Incredulity and triumph warred within his ancient eyes.

"Swordsman," he whispered. "Your aura—"

"I know," Amric mumbled, looking back at his hands. "I know."

In truth, he could feel the power still radiating from him like the heat from a bonfire. He closed his eyes, trying to shut it all out. He had asked for this, had invited it to emerge, had all but demanded that it fully join

348 | MICHAEL J. ARNQUIST

with him. But it was too much, too fast, and it felt like it was consuming him from the inside. The strange presence within him faltered, sensing his rejection. Its elation faded, eclipsed by rising puzzlement and concern.

Amric heard several of the riders slide from their mounts, heard the thumps as their boots hit the ground. Tentative steps approached him where he knelt. He felt them gathering around him, but no one touched him, and nothing else broke the silence except his ragged breathing.

Nothing, that is, until a sharp crackling began in the night air.

Amric's head snapped up. He felt a jarring sense of panic come from the other within him, and that brimming presence fled, winking out of existence so quickly that Amric was left reeling at its sudden absence. He expected to feel an abiding sense of relief to be free of it, and instead he felt only... empty.

A fiery rift appeared in the air above the crest of a nearby dune. It split wide like an opening wound, and through it stepped a man in black robes. The rent closed behind him with a sizzling hiss. The stranger was tall, with a dark beard, and he held himself like a man prepared for war. His gaze swung toward them, and a humorless smile spread across the hard edges of his features. Amric could feel the man's power even over the distance, blazing like a beacon in the night. Somehow he knew, without the slightest hint of doubt, what type of creature they were now looking upon.

This, then, was a true Adept.

This was the creature that struck fear in the black heart of the Nar'ath queen, the monstrosity that had nearly killed them all.

And it might well be his own kind.

CHAPTER 23

Borric skimmed at the surface of consciousness from the underside. To his fevered imagination, it seemed he was being carried in the belly of some great shuddering beast as it raced over hill and valley, and he wanted to scream out in defiance at his fate. For brief moments he would propel himself upward to crest that surface and steal breath from the waking world. Each time he was rewarded by the cool night breeze whispering across his face and the barest glimpses of tall, rustling grasses waving at him as he passed over them. Then jaws of darkness would close over him once again, and he was back in the belly of the beast.

Borric crashed to the ground, and white-hot pain lanced through his broken arm. An involuntary cry escaped through his clenched teeth as he was expelled into full consciousness at last, and he writhed onto his back to remove the weight from his crushed limb. He began to push himself upright with his uninjured arm when he looked up and his surroundings swam into focus. He froze in place.

He had no idea how long he had been unconscious since the frenzied battle in the streets of Keldrin's Landing, but the night was still deep and absolute and untouched by any interference from the dawn. He was lying atop a low hillock in the rolling grasslands, far from the city now. An insistent moon soaked the thick clouds above from behind with a soft, silvery glow, and if not for that muted light he would have been hard pressed to see even a hand's breadth before him.

As it was, however, he had no trouble at all discerning the black creature looming above him.

Borric's breath lodged in his throat as he braced for an attack, but the fiend stood motionless, nearly astride him, silhouetted against that argent sky. A long strip of its ragged, cloth-like wrappings trailed across his leg, and he had to fight the overwhelming urge to fling the loathsome object away from him. He realized the monster was not even looking in his direction. Instead, it faced to the south and was poised as if listening intently to some distant sound. He cast a surreptitious glance about, seeking the means to strike a blow while his captor was distracted, but his own weapons were gone and he could not see so much as a rock nearby in the darkness.

When the creature moved, Borric started so hard that he nearly left the ground. It took a dragging step forward, its vacant ebon face still raised to the south. A chorus of dry rustling sounds on all sides brought Borric's head whipping around, and the captain of the city guard realized with a sinking feeling that hundreds of the creatures were all around him. They were all standing taut, seemingly uncertain, just as the one above him. Scattered moans and sobs revealed that other captives had been dropped to the earth as well.

The creatures all surged forward in unison, a sudden black wave that went from standstill to sprint in the blink of an eye. Borric's erstwhile captor vanished from sight, swallowed by the tall grasses. The grizzled soldier had but a moment's flicker of relief before the muffled thunder of hundreds of black feet brought him around. A steady stream of the creatures rushed by him on either side, heedless of his presence, and he twisted and dodged as best he could from his position on the ground to avoid their passage. One struck him a glancing blow as it rushed by him; it was not an attack but rather an incidental collision, but it was enough to spin him halfway around and send him sprawling. His shoulder throbbed like it had been struck with an iron bar as he rose with caution from the dirt, but the creature ran on without sparing a backward glance. Sharp cries from all around told him that others were not so fortunate in avoiding the stampede.

It seemed an endless number of the foul creatures had flowed around him when finally it ended, and the last of the attackers passed into the night. Borric rose to unsteady feet and looked around. More dim figures were rising from the grasses, and he saw a number of people pulling others to their feet or supporting them to stand.

Borric blew out a breath. He did not know why the creatures had so suddenly abandoned their prey, and for the moment he did not much care. He and the others had been granted a welcome reprieve, and he would make the most of it. He only hoped that the fiends would not return just as suddenly. Even if they did not, the open night held many other dangers for a straggling group of unarmed refugees. It would be a long and harrowing trek back to the city.

The townsfolk were already drawing together into small groups. He started walking toward the nearest. He held himself straight-backed and did his best not to hobble; his men and the citizens of Keldrin's Landing would need him to be strong. He raised a shout for members of the city guard, and several voices responded at once. He allowed himself a grim nod of satisfaction, and then he began the process of organizing the survivors, calling out directions in a clear, commanding voice.

Amric rose to his feet, never taking his eyes from the man in black robes.

The newcomer raised one hand over his head to point skyward, and a brilliant, fist-sized globe sprang into existence high overhead, bathing the entire area in cold, blue light. The man surveyed them all for a long moment as they squinted against the sudden illumination. Then his face darkened in apparent anger, and he started forward, striding down the dune and toward them. He walked with a measured pace, his taut posture an incongruous mix of arrogance and prowling caution.

"I am Xenoth, Adept of the Third Circle," he announced. "I am the Hand of the High Council of Aetheria in this matter."

Amric frowned. He glanced at Bellimar and raised an eyebrow, but the old man gave an almost imperceptible shake of his head. It seemed the string of names and titles meant nothing to him either.

The man drew to a halt twenty yards from them. The Sil'ath warriors moved away from Amric in wary crouches, spreading out to form a semicircle around the stranger, but he appeared not to notice. Instead, his deepset eyes shifted in all directions beneath a dark brow as he seemed to be searching for some unseen threat.

"Which matter?" Amric asked, and the man's hawk eyes turned to him.

"I seek the rogue Adept," Xenoth said. "Where is he?"

"I am not certain of whom you speak. Perhaps if you could describe this—"

"Do not toy with me, boy," the man snapped. "I felt the power that was employed right here, moments ago. Not even you simpletons could fail to notice a display of that magnitude. Where is he hiding?"

Xenoth's tilted his head to one side, regarding Amric with narrowed eyes. "Yes," he murmured. "I think you know something." The man's arms hung at his sides, and his long fingers twitched. "Time to share what you know, boy."

Amric tensed, measuring the distance between them. His palms itched for his swords, but he wondered what good they would be against the likes of a true Adept. In his mind's eye, he saw again the Nar'ath hive swallowed by the ravenous ground, so much like the thunderous collapse of Stronghold's core; could he even close with Xenoth before the man brought such terrible power to bear against him and his friends? He hesitated. Perhaps he should be considering another defense entirely. But as he searched within for the mysterious, lingering presence, he found nothing.

"Forgive the lad," Bellimar interjected, stepping smoothly in front of Amric. "He thinks with his sword arm, more often than not."

"And what have we here?" Xenoth mused. A humorless smile twisted his sharp, angular face, and he raised one hand in a beckoning gesture. Bellimar stiffened with a grunt as he was lifted from the ground by some unseen force. Amric started forward, one hand reaching over his shoulder, but Bellimar stopped him with a warning look. The warrior let his hand fall, and he watched in helpless frustration as the vampire's rigid form, suspended several feet in the air, drifted over to the black-robed Adept.

Xenoth clasped his hands behind his back and tilted his bearded chin upward as Bellimar floated to a halt before him.

"Fascinating," he murmured. Then, louder, he said, "Do you know what I see before me, vampire?"

"I can only guess," Bellimar said through clenched teeth.

Xenoth chuckled. "I see a corrupted being, caught on the knife's edge between life and death, held there by a powerful enchantment. This is marvelous work, intricate and thorough. This could only have been accomplished by Adepts. Do you recall when this was done to you?"

"As if it was yesterday," Bellimar hissed.

Xenoth met his eyes and gave a slow, grave nod, as if processing some sobering bit of information he found there. "Yes, indeed," he said. "It is no secret that my kind have visited this world over the millennia, when the occasion warranted. You must have drawn considerable interest from my ancestors for them to devote such special attention to you."

"Your kind forced this torment upon me," Bellimar snarled. "If not for their interference many centuries ago in the affairs of this world—in *my* affairs—I would have cast all the lands beneath my shadow."

"Ah, that would be it, then," Xenoth said with a dismissive wave of his hand. "They were merely protecting their investment."

Bellimar hesitated, taken aback. "Protecting...? What investment?"

"The spread of Unlife, if left unchecked, can eventually taint the core energy of a world, like a parasite in the water supply," Xenoth replied. "This world had to be allowed to ripen unhindered."

Amric went cold at the man's words in a way that had nothing to do with the cooling night breeze. Allow this world to ripen? For what purpose? He could not see Bellimar's expression, since the old man was still hovering and facing away from him, but the Adept was studying that expression with piercing intensity.

"Does it soothe your anger to know that there was little nobility in what they did?" Xenoth asked. "No, I thought not."

"What they *did* was leave me in torment for more centuries than I can now recall," Bellimar spat in a venomous tone, "cut off from my powers and afflicted with a hunger that I could no longer satisfy. They layered crushing guilt and conscience upon my existing curse, and amplified my suffering a hundredfold in so doing." His voice faltered and dropped to a near whisper. "And I cannot say any of it was undeserved, given my crimes."

Xenoth's laugh was a harsh, pitiless thing. "Wretched, foolish creature," he chided. "You continue to delude yourself, even after all this time. Do you not see? The Adepts dampened your connection to all magic, that much is true, and somehow they managed to do it without ending your existence. A fine, delicate touch, that. However, while you could no longer tap your sorcerous powers, such as they were, your vampiric affliction was also suppressed. But that is all. Any quaint sense of morality that emerged at that point, any penance that you believed you had to pay, was your own."

Amric saw Bellimar stiffen at the man's words.

"I see you do not fully believe me," Xenoth said with a chuckle. "Consider another point, then. The enchantment imposed upon you should have lasted a century or so at most, and yet you say it has lasted many. Why do you think that is, vampire?"

The Adept let the words hang there for a long moment, remorseless and still as a coiled serpent, even as Bellimar hung in the air before him.

"You know as well as I, vampire. Your own will, your own tenuous access to Essence, is sustaining this *curse*—as you call it—now."

Bellimar gasped and hung his head, shaking it in silent denial, but Xenoth pressed on. "Can you not appreciate the irony? Some part of you is convinced that you deserve this suffering, and so you maintain it all this time, with increasing effort on your part, without even being consciously aware of how you are sabotaging yourself."

The old man raised his head and stared, mute and helpless, at his captor.

"There is no need for your continued suffering, however," Xenoth continued. "The enchantment is ages old and decaying now, even with your bolstering. No doubt you can feel its hold upon you slipping more and more as the years pass. I cannot say for certain how much longer it will last. I can free you, here and now. The scant time remaining to this world is insufficient for you to do any material damage. How would you like to be free?"

Bellimar's head twisted to the side, and his stricken eyes found first Amric, and then Thalya. His gaze caught on the huntress and remained there.

"What say you, vampire?" Xenoth said softly. "The Adepts did this to you, long ago. Surely there is no guilt in letting an Adept free you now. Tell me what I wish to know, and you can be unfettered once more. You can rule the twilight days of this world. Tell me where the fugitive Adept is hiding."

Thalya stood rigid, staring back at the man—the monster—that she held responsible for the death of her father, and for the destruction of her entire life. She appeared to be waiting for him to utter the words that would deliver final condemnation in her eyes.

"What say you, vampire?" Xenoth repeated. The words, so like the ones Bellimar had demanded of Amric back in the inn at Keldrin's Landing when they had first met, struck at Amric's core. He opened his mouth to say something, anything, to distract the Adept and draw his attention away from the old man, but the words lodged in his throat and his limbs seemed frozen, unresponsive.

Syth took a sliding step forward, his fists clenched at his sides. The strange winds emanating from his person swept the sands back from him in a spiraling halo. "Leave him alone," he grated.

Xenoth turned toward him, blinking as if had entirely overlooked the thief's presence. He flicked one hand and Bellimar was cast away in an arc. The old man landed in a catlike crouch on the barren ground and stayed low with his grey robes pooled about him. His features were a frozen mask as he stared at the Adept. Xenoth held up one hand and curled it into a loose fist, and Syth's fluttering cloak suddenly pressed tight to his rigid body as his feet left the ground. As Syth floated toward Xenoth, wide-eyed and struggling against his invisible bonds, the latter looked him up and down with a critical eye.

"Unstable," he remarked with a note of disapproval in his voice. "The halves of your nature are in constant conflict, much like your vampire friend there. It is a wonder you survive at all, but you are calmed at the moment. Is this some subtle working of the rogue Adept, perhaps?"

Xenoth looked to the others, and Syth flinched when his dark gaze fell upon Thalya.

"Ah, I see," the Adept murmured with a cold, knowing smile as his eyes lingered over the huntress. "Something much simpler, in fact." He gestured toward the black, jointed gauntlets that Syth was wearing. "Does she know the price you pay in wearing those dreadful devices? Do you even know, yourself?"

The muscles in Syth's jaw clenched as he glared defiance down at the black-robed man. Xenoth gave an unfriendly chuckle. "No matter," he said. "You know the information I truly seek, and I now know what you truly value. Do I need to be so crass as to state the obvious?"

Thalya gave a startled yelp as her arms were pinned to her sides. She was pulled taut to her full height until the toes of her leather boots just grazed the surface of the sand beneath her. Syth gave an incoherent growl of rage and threw himself against the unseen force binding his limbs. He twisted and thrashed, but to no avail.

With an effort of will, Amric wrenched free of his paralysis and burst into motion at last. He stepped forward, reaching for his swords, and the other Sil'ath warriors started toward Xenoth in the same instant. The black-robed man barely spared them a glance, making an impatient gesture with one hand in their direction. The ground rose before the charging warriors in a thick crescent and smashed into them, hurling them all backward and crashing over them like a wave.

The last sounds Amric heard before weight and darkness closed over him were the frightened screams of the horses as they thundered away, deeper into the wasteland. A detached part of his mind was relieved that the beasts had not been caught in the wave, even though rounding them back up for the trip home would be no easy task. That was a matter for another time, however. At the moment, he was tired and battered, and needed just a few moments of rest before...

He cleared away such drifting thoughts with an abrupt shudder, and quelled a moment of panic as he realized just how close he had come to losing consciousness there, buried in an earthen tomb. He forced himself into motion, clawing in the direction he had last seen the night sky, squeezing his eyes and mouth shut to deny the seeping sand that strove to invade. He had not had time to fill his lungs before being buried, and his chest burned with need. His outstretched hands broke the surface first, followed by his head, and he sucked in a sweet breath. The Sil'ath were emerging on either side as well, gasping and shaken.

Xenoth was still focused on Syth and paid them no more heed than so many insects, swatted away and then forgotten. A throaty bellow from Halthak, however, brought him around with one dark eyebrow raised. The Half-Ork ran forward with his gnarled staff held across his chest, as if he meant to push Xenoth back from the others through sheer force. The Adept's hard features twisted into a sardonic smile.

"Another scrub talent," he sneered. "More than a spark, but highly limited in utility. This pitiful world certainly does suffer its share of mongrels."

He flicked a finger at Halthak, and a sharp snapping report wrenched a scream from the healer even as it spun him from his feet. "Let that occupy you for a time," Xenoth said, as Halthak collapsed in a heap upon the sand. "And be grateful for my mercy. With your particular talents, I could make your end far longer and more arduous than you could ever imagine."

Amric pulled himself from the sand and stood just as Xenoth was returning his attention to the struggling form of Syth.

"Xenoth!" he shouted. Inwardly, he was grateful that his voice rang out clear and strong, not at all like the croak he had suspected might emerge. "Let them go. I am the one you are after."

The Adept spun toward him. He wore an irritated, disbelieving scowl, but then his eyes narrowed in sudden suspicion.

"Could it be?" he mused. "Yes, it just might, at that. I should have spotted you at once, even in that barbarous garb. Your aura is not just weak like these other brutes, but non-existent. You are too perfectly concealed, and that should have alerted me from the start. The right age, yes, and you even look a bit like…. Come here, boy!"

Xenoth thrust one hand toward him in a lunging strike, and a vice-like pressure closed around Amric with crushing, irresistible power. A pulsing arc of force sent the others, including the floating figure of Syth, flying away from the Adept to tumble like so many dry leaves across the ground.

Amric glared at the black-robed man as he glided toward him. Xenoth peered back, his heavy brow furrowed in concentration. The warrior tried to shift and flex, seeking some room to move within his invisible bonds, but there was none to be had; he might as well have been encased in cold, unforgiving stone. His swords, an inviting weight at his back, might as well have been back in Keldrin's Landing for all the chance he had to reach them now.

As he drew closer, Amric studied his assailant. The cold light from the globe overhead cast a portion of the man's countenance into craggy shadow, and further deepened the hard planes of his face. Amric was surprised to note the creases of age and weariness woven into those bluff features, and the streaks of iron grey that shot through his dark beard. The man's eyes, however, remained intense and pitiless; his was the hooded stare of a practiced hunter studying his quarry without a trace of emotion. Almost no trace, Amric corrected himself. There was a smoldering anger to the man, a bitter tightness to his features that he kept behind an outward mask. And, as he stared at Amric, a slight widening of his eyes that betrayed something akin to genuine surprise as well.

"Remarkable," Xenoth breathed. "Truly remarkable."

Amric eyed him. "What is remarkable?" he demanded, but the man continued as if he had not heard the question.

"The trail you left behind shows you are quite strong, if clumsy, and yet had I not looked more closely...." Xenoth trailed off, pursing his lips. Then he shook his head. "Even now I cannot be certain. I could just kill you. Perhaps I should. Perhaps this is some elaborate trick." He stared at Amric with distrust and hate in his eyes, but then his brow clouded and his gaze wavered. "No, I have to be certain. There can be no mistakes, this time."

His frown of concentration deepened, and Amric felt a strange probing at the edge of his senses, as of a low sound just beyond his range of hearing that tickled at his inner ear, or a feathery touch hovering just above his skin.

"Remarkable," Xenoth muttered again. "Very few full Adepts can conceal themselves so well. Did you truly learn this on your own, without tutelage?"

Amric remained silent, glaring at his captor. He still lacked the context to form a meaningful reply anyway, and if the man interpreted his reticence as indication of the presence of some powerful teacher or ally, then so much the better. Perhaps it would cause him to proceed with greater caution. The probing grew stronger, more invasive. It blossomed into hot, needle-sharp talons that plucked and pried at his psyche. Amric gritted his teeth, fighting the urge to flinch with each sharp new twinge. He could endure this violation, for he had endured greater pain. After all, it was all in his mind; it was not as if this attack would inflict any lasting damage, like a physical weapon—would it?

An eternity later, Xenoth rocked back on his heels and blew out a frustrated breath. The stabbing pains ceased, and Amric sagged against his unseen bonds. He hoped that the man did not notice the prolonged shudder that ran through his rigid frame.

"However you learned this trick," said the black-robed Adept, "and whether you managed it yourself or it was laid upon you by another, it is magnificently done. I cannot pierce it." The troubled lines on the man's face hardened once more into a venomous resolve. "Fortunately, there are other methods available to gather the proof I require."

There was a grey blur of motion at the edge of Amric's vision, and Xenoth spun in that direction, raising a clenched fist before him. Bellimar's hurtling form halted in mid-air, hands extended like claws, teeth bared in an enraged, frozen grimace. The vampire's fangs, so carefully concealed all the time by restrained expressions and half smiles, were bared beneath narrowed eyes that glowed like red embers. Bellimar hung suspended in the air, straining in helpless fury toward the Adept. Xenoth, for his part, stroked his dark beard as he studied the vampire with cold, deliberate amusement.

"That is the second time you have intervened on the boy's behalf, creature," he said. "Shall we see if he feels the same concern for you?"

Xenoth brought his hands forward and together, as if plunging them into Bellimar's midsection, though several yards still separated them. The old man convulsed, his eyes flaring wide in sudden shock. Then the Adept whipped his arms apart in a sudden ripping motion. A rush of energy washed over Amric like a warm wall of mist and was gone, dissipating into the air. Bellimar bent like a drawn bow, arching backward with his head thrown back as every muscle in his body went taut. The scream came an instant later, an inhuman shriek of agony.

"Stop," Amric grated. "Stop whatever it is you are doing to him."

Xenoth threw a glance at him, and his mouth quirked up in an icy smile. "Ah, boy, do not be a fool. This was the easy part. I have only just begun this one's torment."

Bellimar's scream continued. It went on and on, rising into the night air to hang there unending, as if refusing to be bound by the need to draw breath. Amric added his own voice, shouting forth incoherent rage as he strained against his invisible prison.

"Perhaps I am not casting my net wide enough, however," Xenoth said, his words vibrating with power as they cut through the din somehow without him raising his voice. "If this one's plight does not move you, then we will try another."

He turned toward Halthak, who had regained his feet on a leg that looked to be fully repaired. The Adept made a sharp gesture, palm up as if scooping something from the ground, and angry blue fire erupted from the wasteland beneath Halthak's feet and crawled up his limbs. The Half-Ork uttered a cry of pain and dismay, and he staggered back, slapping at the flames. The blue fire spread hungrily to his hands and arms, writhing along his limbs like a live thing. In its wake, the healer's skin blackened and cracked. Halthak stumbled to his knees, a look of concentration freezing his coarse features into a rictus of pain. The flesh began to heal beneath the licking blue flames. Halthak scooped sand onto his limbs, seeking to smother the spreading fire, but when the sand fell away the fire still remained, slithering over his figure to blacken new flesh. Halthak groaned and squeezed his eyes shut, and the skin knit shut and healed once more. The fire, however, was an implacable foe, and continued to crawl over him.

Amric roared his fury, throwing himself into his efforts until his vision swam and darkened at the edges from the exertion. Something cracked in the back of his mind.

Get out here, he panted at the presence hiding within him. *He is killing them! Get out here and join me, or we all die, here and now!* The only reply was a mindless, gibbering terror, distant and muted.

"Or perhaps another," Xenoth continued in a hard tone. He flung out one hand and great gout of brilliant white fire erupted from it. The fiery display was blinding, and for a brief moment it lit up the wasteland around them in stark relief. Amric, squinting against the sudden illumination, was able to catch a glimpse of the sprinting form of Innikar, rushing forward with blades upraised, before the fire engulfed him in mid-stride. The Sil'ath warrior did not even utter a cry, so quick was his demise. The white fire flared once, dazzling and fierce. When it faded, Innikar was simply gone. His abandoned blades glowed and hissed in the sand, no more than warped pieces of metal, and the remains of the warrior's armor were a blackened and shriveled mass.

Amric's throat cracked and closed on a scream he had not even realized was his own. He saw Sariel and Valkarr approaching from opposite sides, their mouths open in horror. Xenoth turned toward Sariel. Without hesitation, she hurled one of her swords to spin in a glittering arc toward the black-robed Adept. The spinning weapon struck some invisible barrier in mid-air and ricocheted to the side, but Xenoth flinched away from it with a grunt nonetheless, and it saved her life. She had thrown herself to the side as soon as the sword left her hand, and another long breath of white flame seared through the space she had occupied a moment before.

Halthak uttered frantic cries of pain as the blue flames writhed all over him. Bellimar was still suspended in the air, bucking and convulsing, his scream becoming hoarse as it echoed on and on. Sariel rolled on the ground and came up in a dead sprint, running parallel to Xenoth. Valkarr did the same from the other side. The Adept tracked their movements with calculating eyes.

Something broke in Amric's mind. The barrier that had cracked moments before shattered into razor shards, which then shattered into so much dust. He could not say for certain whether he drew forth the other within him and shook from it the blind, unreasoning fear that held it paralyzed, or whether it rose to meet him, buoyed by a rising explosion of power and vengeful fury. There was a jarring collision that shook him to the core as they joined, exquisite pain and pleasure interwoven in an instant, and the other suddenly filled his awareness. Before, when they had interacted, it had felt like two wary combatants circling one another, seeking some way to occupy the same space without breaking some fragile truce. There had been an impression of passing control from one to the other, a grudging relinquishing of self.

This time was nothing like before.

An alarmed part of Amric quailed at the sensation, at the *permanence* he felt in the action of merging; there would be no return to normality this time. That part of him felt dismay for what he had just sacrificed and loathing for the thing he had just become. In the end, however, that disapproving part of him was like a scholar clearing his throat at the center of a battlefield between colliding armies—just a small noise lost amid a maelstrom.

Power continued to surge and gather within him, building into a white-hot core that permeated his being until his very flesh tingled and he thought he might be incinerated if he drew upon more. Amric flexed outward with the power in a jerking shrug, and the bonds that held him ruptured, cast aside like so many brittle sticks. He staggered as his boots hit the ground. Then he and the other within him turned their attention together to their foe.

Xenoth stiffened, some arcane instinct warning him of the forces gathering at his back. He spun away from hunting the Sil'ath warriors, his eyes widening.

Amric hit him with everything he had.

He lunged forward with both hands extended, and from them leapt forth a torrent of white flame that filled the night, hammering into Xenoth. The black-robed Adept cursed and crossed his arms before him, lowering his head and bracing against the surge. Sand went up in great, spiraling plumes as the man was driven sliding backward a dozen yards across the ground.

The tenacious blue flame coursing over Halthak's body dwindled and died, and the healer sagged to all fours. Bellimar's scream came to an abrupt end as whatever force was holding him suspended in the air released him at last. He crashed to the ground in a heap. Valkarr and Sariel each slowed to a halt, staring in disbelief at the display of power going on between them. Valkarr's dark eyes threw back a reflection of dazzling white light as his gaze darted between his childhood friend and the river of eldritch flame emanating from him.

Amric clenched his jaw and continued to pour energy out into the night, sending it washing over the black-robed Adept. Where it was coming from, he neither knew nor cared; he would burn Xenoth to a cinder, just as that monster had done to Innikar and tried to do to the others.

A deep fatigue, starting at the roots of his senses, began to steal over him. He shook it off and continued, but his outthrust hands began a traitorous trembling. Perspiration beaded his forehead and ran into his eyes, and he blinked it clear with a growl. With a sinking sensation, he realized that the flames were not as bright, not as voluminous, as they had been moments before. His mind grew clouded, and a strange wordless clamoring intruded, trailed by a dull comprehension; it was the other within him, pulsating with panicked warnings.

The jet of flame sputtered and died, and Amric fell panting to his knees, more exhausted than he could recall having been in his entire life. He raised his head with a monumental effort to regard the damage he had done.

A smoking crater gaped before him, twenty feet across and three times that or more in length. The near end was a scorched ramp downward into a blackened pit, starting narrow and broadening to its full width at the bottom. The far end was scalloped deeply and polished to a dark, glass-like finish. The edge of the crater glowed like an ember thread, fading as it cooled in the night air.

At the center of the basin stood the black-robed Adept, unharmed.

Xenoth's arms were still crossed before him, and he let them fall to his sides. His teeth gleamed in the soft, silvery light of the globe hanging high overhead. It was the grin of a peerless predator on familiar ground.

"You have ample power, boy, I will grant you that," Xenoth said, speaking slowly as if savoring every word. "But you lack the training to use it, and you exhaust yourself with such ineffective, unfocused displays. You very nearly killed yourself there and saved me the trouble."

He began a purposeful march up the scorched ramp.

"Now let me show you how it is done."

The Adept's hands began to glow.

CHAPTER 24

The black-robed Adept spread his hands out before him without breaking stride, and Amric found himself fighting for his life.

The attack came from every direction at once, bewildering, dazzling, faster than thought. Streaks of light leapt from Xenoth's splayed fingers and arced through the sky. They fell toward Amric like sparkling gossamer threads, graceful in their descent, and yet some nagging instinct warned him that their touch would mean his death. He tried to rise from his knees, but the ground buckled and shifted beneath him like a live thing, throwing him off balance. His attacker made a curt back-handed motion, as if casting something away, and a crackling ball of energy the size of a fist came hurtling at him. He hurled himself to the side, rolling from its path and trying to keep a wary eye upon the falling threads. Rather than continuing past, however, the orb swerved to follow him in a sudden burst of speed.

Amric's hand darted over his shoulder for one of the swords in a reflexive but futile gesture, but the fiery missile was too close. He threw up his hands, as if mere flesh could somehow ward off the thing's destructive power, and he braced for the impact. To his surprise, the crackling ball struck some unseen barrier mere inches from his hands. The blow sent a shudder of force through him, but the ball deflected aside. His relief was short-lived, however; the orb looped through the air in an unsteady arc and came at him again, picking up speed.

His mind raced, trying to discern how he had defended himself from the attack, but his thoughts were interrupted as something struck him from behind. His back tingled and went numb, and he stumbled forward from the blow. The treacherous ground rippled and rose to catch at his foot, and he was sent sprawling. A flare of instinct warned him of the next attack, and he spun onto his back, thrusting out a forearm to block it. One of the deadly threads landed inches above his arm and pooled there upon an invisible surface. Several more followed, hissing as they struck. They began to spread, seeking the edges of the shield above him.

Amric gasped for breath, his mind muddled with fatigue. The other within him was a constant, frantic presence now, yammering in fear.

If you can do better, he thought in weary frustration, feel free to step in at any point.

A rumbling blow shook the shield around him, and then another, and then another. Three of the blazing orbs wobbled away from him, dim for a moment and then brightening once more. They were expending their energy against his invisible shield, he realized. Their energy for his; small wonder that he felt more tired by the moment, then. How had Xenoth held up so well beneath Amric's onslaught of magic, then? The Adept had emerged from the attack, uninjured and infuriatingly unperturbed.

Xenoth's laughter floated to him.

"You cannot keep this up for long, boy," the man called to him. "You are untrained, weary, slow to react." As if to punctuate his point, another thunderous blow shook Amric's shield and the cold, tingling sensation seeped through his right side. The glowing threads continued to fall above him, spreading and probing for weakness.

Xenoth chuckled. "You see, boy, fighting with magic is like using any other weapon. It requires skill and strategy as well as strength. It requires discipline, and a lifetime of practice. To conquer your foes, you cannot simply hoist the largest sword you find and swing it as hard as you can. Victory goes not to he who roars the loudest."

The orbs blurred toward Amric, and three more crashing strikes buffeted him. His forearms, still raised above him, were quivering and numb. His breath burned in his throat and whistled between his clenched teeth. The presence within had subsided to feverish, insistent murmurings. Through a mental fog, Amric realized there was coherence to what it was saying. It was articulating a desperate plan.

"To be certain, there is a time and place to hold nothing back," Xenoth continued. By the direction of his voice, the man was moving around Amric in a slow circle. "However, in this case it is hardly required, since you are a minor threat at best."

Amric ground his teeth at the naked derision in the Adept's voice. He knew that Xenoth was trying to taunt him, but it galled him that the man was right. Would Xenoth leave once he had slain Amric? Or would the black-hearted bastard feel compelled to finish Amric's friends as well?

The presence was still adamant within the warrior's head. I do not like our odds, Amric thought back in grim response, but neither do I have a better plan. Everything in one strike, then. Be ready.

Three more hammering strikes rang against his invisible shield, and the glowing spheres drifted away in unsteady orbits. Amric closed his eyes, sucked in a breath, and burst into motion.

Guided by the mysterious presence within, he *pushed* outward with explosive force, casting away the clinging energy of the threads. He surged to his feet, cursing both the lethargy of his movements and the way the world tilted and swayed around him. He found the dark figure of Xenoth no more than a handful of paces away, and he gathered his will for a single surprise strike that would encompass the entirety of the strength remaining to him.

The chilling smile upon the Adept's hard, angular features was the first true indication that the plan had already failed. Amric strained, drawing upon the power of Essence that surrounded him, the lifeblood of this world, and it responded to his call. Unlike the raging torrent of before, however, it gathered in sluggish, grudging response, as if sharing his weariness. Not enough, he realized, and not fast enough by half.

There was a flash of movement from the black-robed Adept that failed to fully register upon Amric's dulled senses, and the impact followed an instant later. A sheet of blinding light filled the warrior's vision, and he was hurled backward. It felt as if a massive, armored war horse had hammered into him at a full charge. He flew through the air and slammed into the ground, sliding to a stop on his back.

He could not recall any sound accompanying the explosion, but his ears rang now with the echoes of a deafening roar and there was a warm trickle at each ear that could only have been blood. The world wavered and fractured above him and darkness leaked through the cracks, but he struggled to hold the fragments together as he clung to consciousness.

An infinite instant later, the tall figure of Xenoth loomed over him. His voice was alternately an intimate whisper and a distant shout.

"What is this, then? Still alive, boy? Your instinctive defenses are impressive indeed. Perhaps there is something to be said after all for not holding back—"

The other within Amric struck out like a coiled serpent, sending a lance of white fire at Xenoth from the warrior's trembling hand. With a startled curse, the Adept slapped it aside and leapt back. It was the last feeble strike of the exhausted entity, however, and the incorporeal presence withdrew to swirl protectively around Amric's mind.

"A wilding!" Xenoth exclaimed, his tone heavy with both wonder and revulsion. "You are a *wilding!*"

Wilding? Should that mean something to him? Amric tried to focus upon the word, upon his foe, upon anything at all, but it kept slipping through his grasp like quicksilver. There was a trio of staccato reports nearby, somewhere past the periphery of his vision. Xenoth flinched and turned away, raising his hands. A searing flash of light came from that direction, followed by a brief but intense wash of heat.

"Interrupt me again with such pathetic attacks, woman," Xenoth snarled, "and I will come find you out there in the darkness. Your life hangs upon my whim, and your end will not be pleasant if you try my patience further."

The man loomed over Amric once more, cold triumph illuminating his harsh features. He shook his head and looked over Amric with narrowed eyes, as if facing a particularly colorful and venomous creature, and yet unable to resist the temptation of further study.

"A wilding," he breathed. "I have never been so close to one."

A searing jolt ran through Amric's frame, and he stiffened in pain. The other within him lashed out again, weaker yet, and Xenoth laughed. An invisible weight settled upon him, pressing him to the earth.

"Fascinating," Xenoth crowed. "This must be how you managed to evade my search all those years ago. Could it be? Could your wilding magic have shielded you somehow on sheer instinct, even at that age? Such power and subtlety from an infant, an ignorant creature—it strains belief! And yet, with your parents slain, there was no one else on this primitive world that could have concealed you from me."

Parents? Amric's head spun as he tried to orient on the Adept's words. He recalled nothing of his parents or his time before he lived among the Sil'ath. Years later, when he had been old enough to frame the proper questions, his adopted family had responded in the laconic manner for which the Sil'ath were known: he had been found, alone and helpless, and they had chosen to take him in. This terrible man was the first he had encountered who knew anything of Amric's origins. This man had known his parents, and he knew as well what fate had befallen them. The warrior pressed his lips together, forming them around the first of many questions, but only a low groan emerged.

Above him, Xenoth's face had grown pensive, and his gaze drifted in pursuit of some distant memory. "This also explains your parents' sudden defiance of the Council and their persistent interest in this remote world. It must be why they fled here in the end. They were trying to hide *you*."

Xenoth rocked back on his heels, stroking his short-cropped beard in thought.

"The question at hand, then, is what to do with you," he mused. "Wildings are executed at birth by edict of law, and yet the opportunity to study one who has managed to survive to adulthood could have considerable value to an interested few. You are sentenced to die twice over, however, as both an affront against nature and as the offspring of traitors. I am forced to anticipate the Council's wishes on the matter, in the face of this unexpected development. Would they wish the long-delayed sentence carried out immediately, or would they wish you brought back as a unique specimen?"

He leaned down toward Amric and spoke in a lower, conspiratorial tone. "It seems you compel some measure of loyalty among these lesser creatures with which you surround yourself. Even now they approach again, skulking about in the darkness like rats circling a lion with all the ferocity they can manage." The Adept chuckled, a harsh sound devoid of warmth, but his dark eyes glittered with satisfaction. "Fear not, boy, I have a surprise in store for them. I only hope that I am not forced to slay them all, one by one, before it is ready."

Amric went cold inside, and in his mind's eye he bore witness once more to hungry flames devouring the lean figure of his friend, Innikar. Xenoth was correct; his companions stood little chance against this powerful monster. Amric tried to lift his head in a dizzying effort, tried to force a shout of warning from his throat, tried to tell them all to stay back, but the result was scarcely more than a bestial growl even to his own ears. He made another attempt, twisting his head to either side and giving it a frantic and vehement shake of negation. He almost lost consciousness; only by laying his head back against the ground again and pulling in deep breaths did he manage to stave off its departure. He had seen no motion in the darkness beyond the silvery pool of light from the globe overhead, but he had to hope that the others had seen him and recognized the warning.

"No, I cannot bring you back alive," Xenoth said at last. There was a forced conviction to his tone that punctuated whatever internal conflict had been playing out in his head. "Your existence would become known to the public eventually, and the Council can ill afford a rekindling of past insurrections." The Adept leaned closer still to him, and the hesitation in his voice vanished, burned away in a forge of bitter anger. "I have to admit some personal preference in the matter, wilding. Ever since that day, all those years ago, when I returned from this world empty-handed and unable to prove your death, I have suffered in the Council's esteem. You have cost me much, boy. I am an instrument of the Council above all, and though I took no pleasure in the execution of your parents, you can rest assured that I will take great pleasure in yours."

Amric panted and glared up at the man. His head whirled as much from trying to piece together the information he was hearing as from any physical ailment. His foe was close enough to strike, if only he could move. If his limbs would obey him, they would know in the blink of an eye if an Adept could survive the loss of his head, or if he would perish like any other man. The invisible weight pinning him to the ground was unrelenting, however, and so Amric could only grind his teeth in helpless frustration as Xenoth stepped away from him, and the opportunity was lost.

"Time to die, wilding."

The Adept's clenched fists began to glow once more.

Thalya raised her head and risked peering over the low ridge that sheltered her from the Adept's sight. At her side, Syth did the same.

"His hands are glowing again," Syth reported in a tight voice.

"I can see that," the huntress said.

Syth leapt to his feet, his jointed gauntlets flaring open with a metallic rasping sound. "We have to do something! He will finish Amric for certain this time."

"I *am* doing something," she snapped.

She rose, placing a foot upon the ridge, and lifted her bow. Her hand snaked over one shoulder and found an arrow in the quiver slung across her back. From the instant her fingertips brushed its fletching, she knew it for the last of her enchanted black arrows. It was the one she sought, and yet she hesitated. One left. It had taken everything she and her father had scraped and saved, over all those years of meager, nomadic living, to have those three arrows crafted. She had used the first of the three to slay that Nar'ath drone back on the night they had captured her. She had expended the second earlier this very evening, to free Amric from the clutches of the Nar'ath queen. There was but one remaining. It was her final chance to fulfill the mission that had consumed her life. It was her only hope of vindicating her father's obsession and ridding the world of Bellimar the Unholy at last.

How could she bring herself to waste it on any other purpose?

And yet, when she looked upon the black-robed man standing over Amric, her conviction faltered. She recalled her father's tales of the ancient Vampire King, a slavering monstrosity whose malevolence and hunger knew no bounds, who raised legions of the walking dead—and worse—to grind humanity under his remorseless heel. The stories were scavenged from dim and dusty histories, it was true, and yet her father had spoken with such fervor that it was easy to think perhaps he had been there to witness it all firsthand. This man, this Adept, certainly did not compare to the horrid visions her father had conjured for her, at least in appearance.

But then, neither did the silver-haired old man she had finally found at the end of her long hunt. There was a darkness lurking beneath his stately exterior, of that she was certain; she had expected as much, though she had not thought to find it so well concealed. Her father had warned her of his superhuman strength and speed as well, but she had not expected to see it exhibited only to save, rather than harm. Above all, she had not expected to see a gentle, abiding sadness in him, and a kindness in his sparkling eyes that unearthed memories from her childhood. It was perhaps the most insidious thing about him that she could no longer look upon him without seeing the grandfatherly man who would always pause with a warm smile for her as a little girl, and who would trail a finger down her cheek and gently tweak her chin before returning to study with her father. She fought a sudden urge to raise her hand to her cheek now, as she had then.

No, Bellimar had not proven to be the monster she expected. Not yet.

She had seen the incredible power wielded by the Adept, however. She had watched in horror as he incinerated the Sil'ath warrior, Innikar, in mid-stride. She had hidden in the darkness, seething with helpless anger, as this monster in the guise of a man tortured her companions with savage amusement. The contempt in which he held their lives was almost palpable, and he spoke of the destruction of their world as if it was a foregone conclusion. If there was any truth to his words, then this creature was every bit as much a threat to her world as was the demon of her father's darkest fears.

And Amric was going to die if she took no action. It was clear that the swordsman was possessed of his own mysteries, but he was courageous, honorable and compassionate, and she refused to withhold the shot that might save his life.

The black arrow seemed to leap forth into her hand, humming with power and intent. In one smooth motion, she nocked it and drew the bowstring until her hand touched her cheek. She sighted in on her target. Xenoth was focused upon the supine figure of Amric before him, and brilliant white fire flared and curled about the black-robed Adept's hands, spread at his sides. It was a long shot in poor light, but she could not get much closer without sharing Innikar's fate. And even if she could, there was no more time for subterfuge.

Her lips pressed together in a grim line. The man had somehow sensed her attack before and managed to deflect her normal arrows. Stopping this missile would be another matter. It had not killed the enormous Nar'ath queen, but it had incapacitated her for a time and made an utter ruin of her face.

Let us see, then, what it does to a man who appears quite mortal, Thalya thought to herself.

Syth waited beside her, tense and expectant. The ceaseless winds around him whipped at his clothes, almost lifting him from his feet in his eagerness to charge forward. Xenoth raised his fiery hands, advancing a step as he did so. The wicked, glinting tip of the arrow shifted a hair to follow. Thalya let out a slow breath, and her fingers tensed for the release.

A rumbling roar shook the ground. Thalya swayed, thrown off balance, and lowered her bow to avoid loosing a wild shot into the night. Her target staggered as well and cast about wildly for the source of this new disturbance.

The sand over the collapsed Nar'ath hive erupted less than thirty yards from Xenoth and Amric, and a billowing cloud climbed into the sable sky. With a shriek like metal tearing, the Nar'ath queen burst forth. Her claws left long furrows as she dragged her massive form free of its earthen prison. She was ragged and torn, and viscous green ichor seeped from her many wounds. Several of her appendages hung broken and useless, but she dropped into a menacing crouch on the remaining limbs. Her serpentine coils gathered behind her. The queen bared her fangs in a slavering hiss, and her gaze raked over the supine form of Amric to fix upon Xenoth.

"Another Adept!" she shouted. "So it was no idle threat after all." The huntress raised her bow and then hesitated. Which to target? And what good would it do to slay one when the other would then be their undoing? She muttered an oath and dropped down behind the low ridge again. Syth knelt beside her.

"What do we do now?" he breathed, his eyes scanning the scene beyond like a caged animal.

"We wait," she whispered back, "and hope for the right opening."

"What trick is this, wilding?" she heard Xenoth demand. "What manner of creature is this?"

"You are looking upon the fall of your kind, Adept," the queen snarled in response. "We are the Nar'ath. We are your doom made flesh."

Xenoth snorted. "From the look of things, you are only a pace or two from your own doom. If you truly know my *kind*, creature, you should know as well how easily I can send you the remaining distance. Begone, then! Enjoy what time remains to you and to this pitiful world."

"Indeed, we know your kind, Adept," the queen answered with a low, sibilant laugh. "You gave birth to us, all those centuries ago, and then tried to end us, but you failed. We have been preparing to face you again, ever since, on more even footing this time. We are nearly ready now, and it is not *this* world that interests us."

"Do not trouble me with your riddles, creature," Xenoth snapped. "Speak your meaning before I destroy you where you stand."

The Nar'ath queen gave another ugly chuckle. "You will not find me such easy prey, Adept. Even now, my minions return at speed to defend or avenge me. They will wash over you like a tide. You cannot hope to slay them all."

"I have no need to slay them all," Xenoth said. "My business here will be concluded long before your forces arrive." His voice rang with confidence, but Thalya noted that he threw a glance to either side, probing the darkness of the wastes.

"And then you think to return home, to your world, through the Essence Gate nestled amid the ancient ruins of Queln?" The Nar'ath queen's harsh voice almost purred with satisfaction.

There was a long pause as the black-robed Adept stood, still and silent, regarding the monster swaying in a spider's crouch before him. "You cannot use the Essence Gate," he said at last.

The queen's laugh was booming, triumphant. "I see that the colossal arrogance of the Adepts has not diminished in all this time!" She leaned forward, and her voice dropped to an almost intimate whisper that somehow still carried to Thalya's ears. "We have already used the Gate, sweet enemy mine, and countless times at that."

"Impossible. You are lying."

"I would not hesitate to harm you with lies," the Nar'ath queen sneered, "but when the truth will suffice, it is a much sharper weapon. Years ago the Essence Gate began to draw, ever so slightly, upon the energies of this world. My sisters and I were feeding upon the ley lines to restore our strength and to increase our numbers. We were proceeding with utmost caution, remaining well out of sight. The Gate drew tremendous power to it, swelling the lines as it drained the land. It was nothing at all for us to trace the flow of power to its origin in Queln, where so many of the lines meet in a great nexus. We could feel the power flowing through the Gate, and we were quick to divine its purpose. We moved but a few token forces through at first, testing our ability to use the passage. We grew bolder when we saw how poorly the Gates were protected on your side. Now many of my sisters have already passed through with their armies into your world, and our forces build on both sides."

Xenoth did not reply, and the queen laughed in disdain. "What power you have bestowed upon us, all unknowing! You tapped into the arteries of this world, unable to rein in your appetite, and were unaware of the parasite you fed as you did so. The Nar'ath have grown stronger in recent years than in all the centuries that came before. Your greed and conceit have at last paved the way for your downfall, and for our ascension."

Xenoth growled something in reply which Thalya was unable to discern, but the Nar'ath queen rumbled another laugh that grew hard and brittle at the end. "Do you take me for a fool?" she demanded. "You cannot change what will be. Your world is lost, and it gives me pleasure to have you die not in ignorance, but in despair!"

On the last word, her voice rose to a terrible shriek, and she sprang at the Adept. The black-robed figure threw his arms wide, and fire lanced from his fingers to slam into the charging queen. She crashed to the ground with a bellow, but pushed herself upright in an instant, cackling and fixing her emerald glare upon Xenoth. Tendrils of smoke rose where the fire had scorched her flesh. She hurtled forward, impossibly quick for a creature of such mass, and fire streaked out again to lash at her in response. This time she hunched forward, shielding her head with claw and limb, and drew most of the fire upon her heavy shoulders. Some of it struck home, but most glanced away from her plated armor.

The Nar'ath queen peered between her crossed limbs with a devil's grin, eyes narrowed to slits. "Oh yes, Adept," she hissed. "We have built up some resistance to your arsenal since last we met."

She lunged toward him. Xenoth stabbed his hands toward the sky, and a thick wall reared from the wasteland ground before him. With a thunderous crash the Nar'ath queen hammered through it. She lashed out with a long, many-jointed limb at Xenoth. He crossed his arm in a warding gesture, and though her claws rebounded from the empty air before him, the Adept was sent flying through the night in a flutter of black robes. With a hiss of pleasure, the queen slithered after him.

"Come on!" Syth exclaimed, bounding to his feet.

Thalya tore her gaze from where the Nar'ath queen was leaving the pool of light, and blinked up at him. "Where?"

"To the swordsman! He is no longer bound. This is our chance to be away from here while those monsters tear each other apart."

The huntress snapped her gaze back to Amric, abandoned for the moment on the sands. It seemed true; the warrior was no longer pinned flat on his back, but rather had risen to one elbow and was holding his head with his other hand. Thalya sprang to her feet and followed Syth, who was already sprinting across the sands.

As she ran, the titanic struggle between the Nar'ath and the Adept continued. The concussive force of a distant explosion nearly lifted Thalya from her feet, and the Nar'ath queen slammed to the ground partially in the light. She rose and twisted toward her foe, lurching into sinuous motion once more. Green fire sprang into sight across her armored carapace, spreading with voracious speed. The queen shrieked her rage but otherwise paid it no heed, and the unnatural fire dwindled and died away as she slithered back into the darkness beyond. Arcing threads of light illuminated her silhouette, raining down upon her like a volley of flaming arrows, and she swatted at them as she bore down upon her prey.

Thalya shuddered and ran on.

Syth, moving swift as the wind that was a part of his nature, reached Amric first. The Sil'ath warriors, Valkarr and Sariel, seemed to appear from nowhere and were at his side moments later. The three of them had the swordsman on his feet by the time Thalya reached them all. Amric swayed in their grip, but his voice was level and steady when he spoke.

"You have to find Halthak and be away from here," he said. "The Adept means to kill you all by some scheme he has devised."

Valkarr and Sariel exchanged a glance, and both opened their mouths to reply, but whatever they were to say was lost beneath a sudden, keening scream by the Nar'ath queen. Sand sprayed over them in a rolling cloud as her massive form was driven back into the light. Fire streaked from the darkness and tore at her flesh, and she twisted from side to side in a futile effort to avoid each new strike. The Adept appeared, following her and pressing the attack. Even as the fire continued to flay at her in relentless strokes, the ground about her rippled and hardened into great thorns of stone that speared into her serpentine body and held her fast. The queen roared in fury and tried to wrench loose for another charge, but a towering spike shot upward to pierce her midsection, transfixing her. She quivered with the blow and slumped forward onto the spike. Only then did the rain of fire cease. The Nar'ath queen drew short, ragged breaths and lifted her fearsome head to glare hatred at her foe.

Xenoth stalked further into the silvery light, dirtied and disheveled and panting with exertion. Perspiration ran across the hard planes of his face, drawing veins of flesh in the dust there. "Now you die, fiend," he said in a low growl.

"You call us monsters, Adept, and yet it is not we who have destroyed worlds to sate our appetites." She tilted her head toward him in a hideous grin as dark green ichor seeped between her fanged teeth. "At least, not yet." The Nar'ath queen convulsed with harsh, gurgling laughter.

Xenoth's jaw clenched and he shot both hands skyward. Another huge pair of spikes erupted from the ground and met at the queen's chest, and the laughter came to an abrupt end. The giant form sagged and went still. The Adept eyed the motionless creature for a long moment before turning toward them. Thalya felt a chill play along her spine at the murderous rage writ plain upon the man's features. Xenoth stabbed a finger at Amric.

"You, wilding, are coming back to Aetheria with me. The Council needs to hear of this new threat, and I will bring them all that you know on the matter."

"That," Amric replied, "will be a disappointment to all involved."

Xenoth's eyes narrowed. "Nevertheless, before you die, you will do this service for the world that birthed you. Come here, boy!"

He made a sharp beckoning gesture, and Amric stiffened. Torn from the grasp of his comrades, he hurtled through the air to hover before the Adept. Steel rang as the two Sil'ath warriors drew their swords and started forward, and Syth crouched and clenched his gauntleted fists, preparing to launch himself as well. Thalya raised her bow, reaching over one shoulder for her quiver.

"No, wait!" Amric shouted, halting them in their tracks. Thalya's hand froze with her fingers brushing the fletching of an arrow. "He will burn you to cinders, as he did Innikar!"

"Listen to the boy," Xenoth warned. He made a gesture, and a brilliant seam of light parted in the air behind him. The huntress caught a glimpse through the aperture of another sliver of night, elsewhere—of murky grey mists curling about tumbled masses of bleached stone. "There is no need for me to slay you all. Not when someone else is so eager to do so."

Something about the Adept's dark chuckle made the hair at the nape of her neck stand on end; it was a sound laden with both malice and conviction. Then another sound caught her attention, a dry rustling at the edge of the darkness. She turned her head toward it, and her flesh turned to ice.

Something blacker than the night was pooling there, and shadows rippled from it in waves that lapped hungrily at the meager light. A figure rose at the deepest heart of the shadow, powerful and timeless, and twin pinpoints of scarlet swung toward them. A wave of cold washed over her as that unblinking gaze settled upon her, pushing at her like a physical thing, peeling away her defenses and leaving her trembling like a child. Then it slid across her and was on to the others. The huntress heard their startled gasps and knew they felt it as well, but she could not turn away from the thing in the shadows. She realized her hand, still hovering at her quiver, was shaking so much that the arrow she touched was rattling among its fellows.

The dark figure rose in a slow, silken movement, and the caressing darkness flowed to it and enfolded it like a mantle. The mantle of the Vampire King, the Lord of the Night.

Bellimar the Black had returned.

CHAPTER 25

Thalya stared, unable to move, the very breath frozen in her throat.

"What have you done?" she heard Amric demand.

Xenoth turned his head a fraction but did not take his eyes from the dark figure at the center of the gathering shadows. "I promised a surprise for these lesser creatures, wilding. Look on a moment, before you and I depart, and witness what I have prepared for your companions."

Bellimar—or rather, the monstrosity that now stood in his place—shifted his gaze over to the Adept. Bloodless lips parted in a smile too broad by far to be human, revealing long, curving fangs beneath. "And where will you flee, Adept?" he whispered. Thalya flinched as the velvet words, vibrating with insidious power, caressed at her ears.

Xenoth lifted his chin. "I flee from nothing and no one."

Bellimar made a deep inhaling sound, and the silvery light from the globe above dimmed for a moment as tendrils of shadow slithered across the sands. Xenoth flicked a glance at the tiny ball of light, and then back to the vampire. "And yet you are fearful, Adept," Bellimar pressed. "I can taste your fear, and it is a heady thing to one so long denied his appetites."

"I do not fear you, fiend," Xenoth sneered. "My concern is for Aetheria alone. The Nar'ath filth must not be allowed to cross over into my world."

"By the queen's own words, many already have. You are too late."

"Then I will prevent any more from crossing over."

"And how will you accomplish this, Adept?" Bellimar asked in a chiding tone. "The magic you expended on the wilding and the Nar'ath queen has left you more drained than you wish to show. You are weary, and you have faced but one of the Nar'ath."

"I have no need to defeat them all myself, fool. When I bring word of this threat to the Council, they will authorize me to activate the Gate, and this wretched world will be drained of its Essence. The Nar'ath will perish along with everything else. We can then hunt at our leisure whatever smattering of those creatures already made it through."

Thalya felt a new chill at the Adept's words. This, then, was the destruction of their world he had been referencing in that cold, vindictive manner. Worse, it appeared that the night's events had only served to accelerate the dire fate of her world. Her gaze darted between Bellimar and the Adept. They were intent upon each other, while she and the others were all but forgotten for the moment. Her fingers closed upon the shaft of the arrow and began to remove it from the quiver in a very slow, deliberate draw.

"Come, wilding, it is time for us to go," Xenoth said. He half-turned toward the glowing rift in the air and made a peremptory gesture that brought the suspended form of Amric drifting after him.

Bellimar moved. So sudden and silent was the motion that the huntress blinked in momentary disorientation as her eyes struggled to follow it. She was struck by a memory from her childhood, one of many occasions when her youthful exuberance had shrugged free of the limits imposed by her father's cautionary words. Playing in the forbidden territory of his study, she had knocked over a large inkwell on his desk, and watched in dawning horror as the jet-black ink raced in spreading rivulets over the papers scattered across its oaken surface. Bellimar's movement was like that, quick and liquid. One moment that heart of darkness was seething at the edge of the light twenty yards away, and then it simply *flowed* a dozen yards closer in the span of a breath. His eyes never left the black-robed Adept, and his fangs were still bared in a terrible grin.

Xenoth spun around with a snarl. "Do not think to pit yourself against me, vampire! I freed you from your binding so that you might enjoy a brief return to your former glory, but do not forget your place."

Bellimar drew back into the roiling mass of shadow until only his eyes were visible as scarlet pinpoints burning with feverish intensity. "Fear not, Adept, I will never forget what your forebears did to me. Still, they demonstrated might on a scale to dwarf your own. Perhaps the Nar'ath queen was correct, and the Adepts have grown weak and complacent over the centuries. Perhaps you are indeed but echoes of your former glory. Perhaps the time of the Adepts is nearly past."

Xenoth's expression darkened further yet. "You wish to test my strength and judge for yourself?"

A low, silken chuckle rumbled out of the darkness. "Are those the ancient ruins of Queln I see behind you?"

"Where I travel next is of no import to you," Xenoth snapped in response.

"Ah, but there, I am afraid, we must disagree." The core of shadow seemed to fold in upon itself and vanish, drawing the tendrils of darkness along with it. Thalya froze, glancing around, and Xenoth stiffened as well. Bellimar reappeared in a black cloud, this time on the other side of the ring of light, closer still to the Adept and this time nearly between him and the huntress.

"You see," he continued as if uninterrupted, "you have given much back to me, much that I thought never to experience again. Now you speak of depriving me of it all once more, and this time forever. I am not certain I can abide it."

"It is not your choice to make, creature," Xenoth stated in a flat tone. "You cannot affect what will come, and if you cross me now I will burn you to ash. Embrace the gift I have given you, and the time remaining to you. I have even gone so far as to provide the means to slake your thirst." With a sweeping gesture and a sardonic smile, the man indicated Thalya, Syth and the Sil'ath warriors. One of the Sil'ath hissed in anger, and Syth uttered a quiet oath under his breath.

Bellimar glanced at them all over one shoulder. Thalya felt the weight of his burning gaze press upon her, saw him take in her upraised arm and the black arrow in her hand. They locked eyes for a split second, and her stomach plummeted as the corner of his mouth quirked upward in a knowing smirk. Then, with a deliberate gliding motion, he crossed between the huntress and the Adept, turning his back fully to her.

"Yes," he murmured to Xenoth. "So you have."

Thalya's mouth fell open. He was all but inviting her to strike at his exposed back! Was it a trick? Bellimar was within the argent ring of light, but the shadows moved with him like a shroud, and the light itself seemed to recoil from his presence like waves from a darkened shore. Still, she could discern the outline of his figure with enough clarity to place the shaft between his shoulder blades. Was he taunting her to take the shot, intending to foil it with inhuman speed as he had before? Perhaps he was confident that the missile would not prove powerful enough to do him lasting harm, now that he had been transformed. That seemed foolish, however; the other two arrows had slain one of the Nar'ath soldiers and gravely wounded the massive queen, and all this despite the queen's boastful words to Xenoth of her kind's resistance to magical assaults. Why, then? Was Bellimar truly courting his own destruction?

"Come, wilding," Xenoth said. "It is time we left your friend to his appetites."

The man backed toward the rift, which had begun to shimmer and pulse at the edges. Was it her imagination, or was it slightly smaller and less bright than when it had first appeared? Amric grunted as he began to float after the Adept once more, and then his motion faltered and stopped.

"No," he said through clenched teeth.

Xenoth looked up at him, raising one dark eyebrow. "Impossible," he breathed.

"I am *not* going with you." Amric's voice was low and growling with strain.

The Adept's short beard bristled as he thrust out his chin, and his eyes narrowed in concentration. Amric quivered, still hanging in the air, but did not move any closer. The heels of his boots settled a few inches closer to the ground. This time the grunt of effort belonged to Xenoth, and Amric's slow descent was halted. Thalya felt the hairs on her arms and the nape of her neck rise as the air began to hum and crackle with energy.

"Impossible," Xenoth repeated.

"I would surrender myself to prevent further death, but you mean to see my friends slain and my world destroyed regardless of my fate." The warrior bared his teeth in a snarl. "Not while I draw breath, Adept."

"That is easily remedied, boy," Xenoth snapped, his features twisted with fury. "You may have caught your breath now, but I can convince the Council without the evidence you bring. Die, wilding!" On the last words, his voice rose to a frenzied shout. His arms flung outward, sending his black robes billowing, and his hands clenched, claw-like, around sudden writhing flame.

And then, it seemed to Thalya, everything happened at once.

Syth left her side in a rush of wind, charging toward the Adept. Valkarr and Sariel surged forward at the same instant with a throaty battle roar, silver light glinting from their blades. As quick as they all were, however, quicker still was Bellimar the Black. He launched at Xenoth like an ebon spear, silent and lethal in flight. The Adept fell back a step with a startled curse, twisting about to face these new threats. Fire leapt from his hands to lance at Bellimar, but the vampire flowed to one side in his swirling cloak of shadow, evading the strike. More fire followed, streaking after him in the night, and he faded back from it in sinuous, graceful motions, like thick black smoke cast before a storm wind.

A sharp gesture from the Adept sent a scything blast of air into the charging warriors, tearing them from their feet. Thalya staggered at the concussive force, though she was a good distance behind them by then. As she regained her balance, she felt a familiar tugging sensation through her arm and shoulder. She realized she had nocked the black arrow to her bow and drawn it back until the ridge of her hand brushed her cheek. She followed the shifting figure of Bellimar through his darting movements. The old man—the black fiend, she corrected herself—eluded streak after streak of fire, but each killing strike drew closer to him than the last.

Amric dropped to the ground and fell to all fours. Whether Xenoth's concentration had lapsed or the warrior had somehow broken the bonds on his own, she could not say. His chest heaved with exertion as he pushed himself to one knee and began to rise, but the power cascaded from him in shimmering waves. With an incoherent cry of rage, Xenoth wheeled to face him.

For one fraction of a second, time stood still for the huntress. Every detail of the frenzied scene yielded itself to her with startling clarity. Syth and Valkarr struggled to their feet, dazed. Sariel was a crumpled, unmoving form upon the sallow ground beyond them. Bellimar, target of a lifetime of vengeance, crouched like a dark bird of prey with the talons of one pallid hand sunk into the sand before him. He looked at her, framed for that one perfect moment by the wickedly curved blades of the arrowhead. He flashed a smile, and the corner of one eye crinkled in a fleeting wink. And then, as before, he turned away in a deliberate motion and left himself defenseless to her.

The ensorcelled arrow strained at the bow, humming with eagerness. The missile had grown warm to the touch, and then hot, as if losing patience at her hesitation. It bathed her cheek with heat and threatened to sear the tips of her fingers. The last of the three, the last with a chance to fulfill its destiny, it had been meant for this moment since its creation. It sang at that moment with a singular joy of purpose.

And what of her, then? She had been waiting for this moment even longer, no less crafted and sharpened and aimed than the arrow itself. Why had she not already taken the shot? Why did her heart not thrill to the same sense of fulfillment, of fate? Why did her fingers refuse, even now, to release the black arrow to its deadly flight?

Xenoth lifted hands that blazed with fire. Amric was still rising unsteadily to his feet, and some detached part of her mind noted that the swordsman would not be in time to ward off the coming attack. Bellimar knelt with his back to her, motionless, waiting.

Thalya released her breath as she released the arrow, just as she had been trained to do. It struck her as peculiar that it came out almost like a sigh of relief, like a parting kiss to speed the weapon on its way. The string thrummed and the arrow leapt from her bow. That elusive sense of fulfillment flooded her at last as she watched it go with a grim smile. *Fly true*, she thought fiercely after it.

Xenoth saw it coming at the last instant. He froze, and his features twisted from murderous intent to an almost comical surprise. He threw his hands up in a warding gesture, and the missile struck an unseen barrier less than an arm's length from his face. There was an ear-shattering detonation, and green fire coruscated over an invisible dome-like shape before the man. Xenoth staggered back with a cry and dropped to one knee. A wave of hot air washed over Thalya and brought a biting cloud of dust and sand with it. She raised an arm to shield her eyes, and when she lowered it again, Xenoth was staring at her, shaking with incredulous rage.

"You *dare?*" he thundered. "You insolent—"

Amric attacked in a roar of flame. He stood, braced forward, arms extended and palms outward as if he meant to push Xenoth away through sheer force of will.

And push him he did.

Brilliant white light erupted from Amric's hands and fountained into a column of energy as thick as a man. It was bright as the sun, but more narrowly focused than the uncontrolled torrent he had called forth before. Xenoth managed to lower his head and cross his arms against it, but the strike slammed into his defenses, lifted him from his feet and threw him backward. The Adept flew through the glowing rift he had opened and disappeared into the mists beyond in a flutter of black robes. The fissure wavered at his passing, and then its fiery edges contracted and came together like a great winking eye. The seam flared once in the night air, then faded and was gone.

Xenoth blinked, and dragged in a shuddering breath. A steady ringing sound droned in his ears, and he felt strangely weightless. Pale mists curled about him in a cool embrace, but he caught glimpses of the night sky through that shroud, and it seemed to him that the world was tilted the wrong way. For that matter, the damp, lanky grasses intertwined with his beard and tickling his nose and lips seemed out of place as well.

A soft rustling sound approached. Large, almond-shaped amber eyes regarded him behind a thin veil of mist, and he blinked back at them, uncomprehending. A scratching noise came to him, claw upon stone, and an eager mewling escaped the creature. It was answered from a smattering of other directions, all drawing nearer.

It was those sounds that jarred the Adept from his stupor. They carried notes of need, of intent, of hunger. The danger of his situation crashed in on him.

Xenoth lurched upward to a sitting position with a thin shout, sweeping an arm around in an arc to wave them back. The nearest creature shrank away from him, its rabid eyes narrowed, and it turned as if to leave. The Adept pushed to his feet and staggered for a moment, shaking his head to clear it. The creature gave a rumbling hiss of unmistakable pleasure at this show of weakness and took another slow step toward him. Xenoth felt a momentary stab of fear that gave way to burgeoning rage.

"Back, you carrion-feeders!" he shouted, whirling his hands in a wide circle that sent lashes of fire into the mists. The lurking shapes scattered, keening in fear and frustration. They melted back into the murk, and then Xenoth was alone.

He slapped at his robes with more vigor than necessary to dust them off. He could not decide if he was more furious at the defiance of lesser creatures such as the wilding and his companions, or at his own foolishness for being caught by surprise like that. In the end, he concluded he had fury enough for both at the moment. The boy had made a quick recovery, and had shown surprising strength and focus in that last attack. Xenoth knew little of wildings; perhaps that wild, instinctual nature to their magic enabled them to adapt with unnatural swiftness. Doubtless it was merely one of many reasons the Council had eradicated them with systematic precision, throughout the years. And where had the woman procured a nasty little surprise like that arrow, anyway? This primitive world was proving to be full of unpleasant surprises.

He clenched his fists and spent a long moment contemplating the idea of ripping open another Way to go finish off the wilding. No, he decided at last with a sigh. As much as it would bring him pleasure, it was a poor plan. Opening a Way to unfamiliar territory was a taxing endeavor, and he had already done it twice this night in rapid succession. Another trip to and from the wastes to capture the wilding, after all that he had spent that night, would leave his strength ebbing to a dangerous level.

Xenoth frowned. It galled him to admit it, but that damnable vampire had been correct: he was weary. Subduing the wilding had been no real challenge. The boy was strong and unpredictable, but he lacked any semblance of craft that would make him a true threat. The Nar'ath monstrosity, however, had been another matter. The fiend had hardly been slowed by attacks that should have torn it asunder, and Xenoth had been forced to put more and more energy behind each strike to affect it at all. In the end he had resorted to indirect means, pouring energy into the creature's surroundings to batter at it, to weaken it, and to slip past its armor at last. He considered its intimations that its kind had built up some resistance to magic over time in preparation for facing the Adepts, and he shuddered to think of untold numbers of the monsters already lurking within his world.

He knew what must be done. He knew as well that it might well mean his life to do it.

When the flare of magical activity here—power that could only have been an Adept—had drawn the attention of the Council, it had confirmed his greatest shame at the same time it offered his chance at redemption. Find and eliminate the boy, an enemy of the Council by extension, as he had failed to do all those years ago. It was made quite clear that Xenoth's life was forfeit if he returned empty-handed again.

That, however, was exactly what he had to do.

A new, higher priority had surfaced, and it could not wait upon his original mission. He had to close the doorway used by the Nar'ath to enter Aetheria and warn the Council of the hidden threat already harbored there. Would his masters understand the choice he faced? Would they show lenience for the decision he was about to make?

Xenoth took a deep breath and turned to look upon the Gate. It towered above the fog, a massive arch of stone that stood silent and majestic atop its marble platform. A faint nimbus of light surrounded it and imbued the crawling mists in all directions with an eldritch glow. The weathered sigils carved into its surface, each as tall as a man, pulsed in a slow rhythm as if the ancient construct was drawing breath. Within the arch, a shimmering surface stretched and rippled like dark waters kissed by moonlight. Even standing hundreds of yards from it, Xenoth could feel the power of the Essence Gate pulling at him. The power to give or take on a cataclysmic level. The power to share or to destroy. The power to unmake.

The black-robed Adept let his eyes travel over the Gate, following the curve of the great arch and lingering upon each luminous glyph. He knew in principle how to proceed, though he had never thought to perform the actions himself. What he was contemplating carried its own penalty of death or imprisonment. The Essence Gates transmitted the lifeblood of Aetheria; the Council did not tolerate tampering with their operation except under its own express orders. And yet, it had to be done. It was the only way to be certain, the only way to protect Aetheria.

With that much decided, he had one more choice left to make: close the door entirely, or throw it wide open? The door was open a crack at the moment, figuratively speaking; Aetheria was sipping at this world's essence through the Gate. He could disable the Gate, which would simultaneously sever the flow of magic through it as well as prevent its use as a transportation portal between the two worlds. Aetheria required the sustenance it received from its feeder worlds, however, and the Council would not be pleased to lose one that was drawing at this level.

If the door could not be closed, then, that left only the other option: he could open the door wide by fully activating the Gate. This world would be drained of its magic in rapid, catastrophic fashion, and all life here would perish. Rather than a reduction of its intake, Aetheria would receive a veritable flood of new energy to meet its needs for a time. The Nar'ath scourge waiting to cross over would be dead, and the troublesome wilding as well. A hard smile spread across Xenoth's features. It was a way to protect Aetheria and fulfill his mission at the same time. In any event, the Gate's current activity level was an indication that this world was scheduled for harvest soon. He would merely be accelerating the schedule somewhat. He could only hope the Council would see it that way as well.

The Essence Gate seemed to beckon to him from its platform. The device was an ancient and formidable magic, but it would take some time to reach full operation. It would take longer still for it to drain the essence from this world. The sooner he started, the sooner Aetheria would be safe.

Xenoth squared his shoulders and strode into the mist.

"Did you kill him?"

Amric tore his gaze from where the glowing rift in the air had vanished, and shifted it over to the huntress. The wilding magic was flitting about inside him in a state of wordless elation, and the sensation, akin to a persistent buzzing in his ears, was very distracting. "What did you say?"

"Did you kill him?" she repeated. "The Adept, with that last attack of yours."

Something inside the warrior flinched at the wary mask she wore as she regarded him. He shook his head. "No, I do not think so," he said. "It was a weak strike, but it caught him off-balance and gave him a good push while his attention was elsewhere." He gave her a steady look. "You have my gratitude for your intervention, Thalya. I owe you my life."

Her cheeks colored and she lifted her chin in a clipped nod.

"Foolish girl," hissed a voice that brought them both sharply around. Bellimar had withdrawn to the light's edge, and was once again wreathed in deepest shadow. His eyes burned blood-red from the darkness. "You had your opening, girl. You should have taken the shot. I may not have the strength to offer you another."

Thalya's features hardened. "I made the choice to save Amric's life over ending yours, Bellimar," she snarled. "I hope I chose the greater monster for that last arrow. Do not prove me wrong!"

The huntress spun on her heel and stalked away, muttering about the need to find Halthak so they could depart this place. Syth was weaving a drunken path toward them, and she brushed past him without a word. He craned his neck to watch her stomp into the darkness.

"What is she so angry about?" he demanded in a too-loud voice, knuckling his ear and shaking his head to clear it.

"She questions herself over the shot not taken," Bellimar responded. Then he gave a dry, sibilant chuckle. "And she wishes for one more such arrow."

Syth eyed the old man, exchanged a meaningful glance with Amric, and then turned to follow Thalya. "I will help her look for the healer," he called over his shoulder. "He cannot have been thrown far."

Amric faced the vampire, and they regarded each other without speaking. At last, Bellimar broke the silence with a whisper. "You already know what must be done, swordsman. Freed of the binding that suppressed my demonic nature, I will once again be more monster than man, soon enough. You will be forced to end me, if you can, or I will slay you all."

The warrior shivered at the quiet conviction behind the old man's words. He opened his mouth to speak, but Bellimar was already shaking his head. "There is no salvation for me this time, Amric. Last time, it took a group of Adepts, each far more powerful than the one we just fought, to change my very nature in this way. Even if the Adepts of today are still capable of such acts, we simply do not have the time before I once again become a scourge of death upon this world—starting with all of you."

"How long can you hold out?"

"Not long, I am afraid. My hunger has been long denied, but its victory is now inevitable. My control erodes with each passing moment, and I find it harder and harder to remember why I should fight against it."

Amric folded his arms across his chest, fixing storm-grey eyes upon Bellimar. When he spoke, his voice was level and edged with the steel of command. "You staved it off for centuries, holding together a failing enchantment through sheer force of will. You have risked yourself for all of us more than once. Even Thalya, looking upon you just now, found something worth saving." The pinpoints of scarlet blinked and shifted in the direction the huntress had gone, before settling back upon the warrior.

"We must tend to our fallen," Amric continued. "We must be gone from here before either the Adept or the Nar'ath minions return. We can regroup with the survivors from the hive at the crag where we camped last night, and make our plan there. Xenoth must be stopped. I need you to hold out that long."

Bellimar snorted. "You cannot stop him. You were fortunate to survive this encounter."

"Still, I mean to try, and I will need your counsel if I am to stand any chance at all."

There was a pause, and then Bellimar whispered, "And what then, swordsman?"

"There has to be a way," Amric said quietly.

The vampire gave a slow shake of his head. "You ask the impossible, many times over."

"Still," the warrior repeated, "I mean to try."

Bellimar drew back into the shadows until even the crimson glimmer of his eyes all but disappeared.

"I need you to hold out that long, Bellimar. What say you?" Amric's mouth quirked upward at the corner as he echoed the old man's own words from when they met in the inn at Keldrin's Landing, what seemed an eternity ago.

"I will strive to do as you ask," Bellimar replied at last. "But when the time comes, promise me you will act without hesitation. Promise you will do what must be done, if you can."

Amric inclined his head in a grave nod. "I will."

He turned his attention to helping with the fallen. Valkarr had already assisted Sariel to her feet, and though she was groggy from the concussive blast that had knocked her unconscious, she bore no serious injuries. The two of them greeted him as he approached. On the surface they sounded no different than the friends he had known since childhood, but there was an unfamiliar hint of reserve to the bearing of each that sent slivers of ice deep into his chest.

A brief search for the horses proved fruitless. The animals had either fled too far to hear their calls, or had fallen prey to the denizens of the wastes. Syth and Thalya had better luck locating Halthak, at least. The healer had been hurled away in the chaos and partially buried under a mound of sand. He staggered back with the support of the others, and his own bruises and abrasions were scarcely healed before he began fretting over everyone else.

The remains of Innikar were so blackened and distorted as to be un-recognizable, little more than warped blades and bits of metal in a pile of ash and cinder. The swords were in no condition to return to his family back home, so they buried them with him, there in the wasteland. It was a futile gesture, given the ephemeral landscape of rolling sands all about them, but one they performed by unspoken agreement. They had no suita-ble means by which to carry the remains anywhere else, and Sil'ath tradi-tion held that their heroes should lie where they fell in battle, so that they could continue the fight from the spirit world. Amric pictured the irre-pressible Innikar shrugging off an inconvenience like death as if it were some ill-fitting cloak, drawing his swords once more with the joy of battle alight upon his lean features. He smiled to himself. The Sil'ath were ever a stubborn, pragmatic people, and their beliefs were a firm reflection of that. The smile faded. The Sil'ath. *His* people.

The strange, silvery orb Xenoth had left hanging above them had be-gun to wane by the time they gathered to leave. Its light was but a glim-mer when they crested the first rise. It was gone by the next.

They trekked through darkness that was hemmed in below by the pale sands of the wastes, and above by the thick blanket of clouds laying siege to the moon. Bellimar kept his distance from the party as they marched. Amric forbade him from ranging too far ahead for fear that encountering the weakened captives from the hive while alone would prove too great a temptation. Even so, the vampire vanished for uncomfortable stretches of time before reappearing in some new and startling direction. Several times it seemed a great winged shape, blacker than the night, passed over them in a wake of bitter cold. More than once, the wilding presence within Am-ric roared to the surface in response to something out there that he could not see. Each time it would gibber and bristle at the unseen threat, mak-ing his entire body tingle with tension, and then it would slowly subside.

More than once, he caught Bellimar's penetrating red eyes, out in the darkness, following their progress with an inhuman hunger.

In the earlier ride from the crown of rock to the hive, they had taken a circuitous route to conceal their approach from the Nar'ath exodus. As they trudged the reverse route, they made no such effort. As a result, the return trip took almost the same time, despite being on foot. When the rocky crag finally reared up before them, stark against the subdued luminance of the clouded sky, Bellimar was already crouched at its base.

"I cannot go up there," he called as they approached. "Blood has been spilled."

Amric pulled up short, facing him. The hair rose at the back of his neck as he caught the rough, throaty character to the old man's voice. "What have you done, Bellimar?" he demanded.

Bellimar laughed, and there was little humanity in the cold sound. His chin was tucked low, and beneath eyes that blazed with hunger was a mouthful of fangs gaping wide enough to engulf a man's head. "I? I have done nothing, warrior." He spat the last with a note of contempt, eyes narrowing to slits. "You can be assured that if I had done it, I would not have wasted their precious fluids like that. It is cooling, spent, the life in it already departed. Useless to me. It fans my hunger, but it is the blood of the living that truly calls to me like a siren's song."

The black mass roiled and seethed and seemed to lean toward him by some small degree. Amric tensed. His wilding magic screamed a warning, but it was unnecessary; he recognized a predator about to rush when he saw it. With an effort, he kept his hands from twitching toward his swords.

"Is this to be it, then?" he asked in a low voice. "Is Bellimar the man lost entirely?"

Bellimar froze, then the glowing eyes dimmed a bit and he pulled back into his mantle of shadow. "Not yet, warrior," he said, and some of the guttural growl was gone. "Not yet, but all too soon."

Valkarr drew abreast of Amric, with gleaming steel bared in both fists. He did not remove his gaze from Bellimar as he spoke to Amric, "Perhaps the men fought amongst themselves."

"Or were set upon by some other horror out here," Halthak put in, glancing about.

"Perhaps," Amric agreed. "I see only the tracks of the men at the base of the path, over our own and those of the horses. Whatever violence occurred up there, they either brought it with them, or it found another way up."

"Or it leaves no tracks," Thalya offered, casting a pointed look at Bellimar.

"Whatever the case, it is time we found out," Amric said.

Bellimar retreated into the darkness and agreed to remain below until called. Amric went first, swords drawn. He felt the weight of the vampire's gaze pressing at his back until the curve of the path took him out of sight. He reached the peak and stepped into the broad crown of rock, dropping into a low crouch. Valkarr and Sariel joined him an instant later.

All was quiet. Too quiet, he decided. The pool of water was undisturbed, an unbroken mirror nestled at one end. The thin copse of trees stood untouched by any breeze, and six of the seven men were sheltered there in various states of repose. Two sat with their backs to the boles of trees, heads bowed, and the other four were lying on their sides with their heads resting on their arms. Of the seventh, there was no sign. Amric studied the scene for a long moment. They were too still. No rustle of breath, no twitch to discourage a persistent insect, no slight stirring to find a more comfortable position on the ground. Not a single chest rose and fell to indicate life. These men were all dead.

Amric signaled to the others and started forward. Valkarr followed on his heels. Sariel dove into the underbrush and Thalya leapt up to the lip of rock and began to walk the perimeter in a half-crouch with bow drawn. Halthak put his back to the rock, clutching his staff before him, and Syth remained there with him, his jointed metal gauntlets curled into fists as he swept his gaze over the area.

The two warriors crept near the motionless bodies of the men. Valkarr stretched out one arm, and with the flat of his blade, lifted the bearded chin of one of the men sitting upright against a tree. Half-lidded eyes stared forward, unseeing, and blood seeped from a slit throat.

"No talon did this," Valkarr commented in a whisper in the Sil'ath language. "Only a keen steel edge cuts so clean."

Amric nodded, glancing around. Each of the other men bore similar marks, a single stab to the heart or a single slice to the jugular, and each was sitting or lying in a congealing pool of blood. "Efficient," he remarked in the same tongue. "Each death by a single stroke, no bruising or defensive wounds. Even their expressions are serene. There is no indication these men had any time to fight back."

Valkarr peered at the slack features of one of the men, then turned to study another. "Do these men look familiar to you?"

"Morland's men," Amric said with a frown. "I thought I recognized them earlier tonight in the hive, from our visit to that bastard's estate. They are—or were—members of his personal guard."

"Something is not right," Valkarr said, lifting his head to scan around. "Where is the seventh? Could one man have done all this? A trained assassin, perhaps, who took them all in their sleep?"

Amric shook his head; he had no answer. An uneasy sensation was crawling between his shoulder blades. His friend was correct, something was not right here. He had the persistent feeling that they were being watched. The wilding magic stirred within him.

Thalya gave a low whistle, and the warriors rose to their feet. The huntress was standing at the far edge of the crag, across the shallow pool from them. She motioned downward. "I found the last one," she called. "He is draped over the rock here. I think he is dead."

She began to kneel, and sudden instinct screamed a warning to Amric. He shouted, "Thalya, no!"

The attacks were swift as lightning, their timing without flaw. Amric had taken half a step when a cloud of smoke erupted behind him. A slight gust of warmth caressed at his skin, and a sulfurous smell burned at his nostrils. Steel sang in the crisp night air, and Amric twisted with the reflexive speed only a Sil'ath warrior could manage. A talon of fire raked along his ribs, parting the links of his mail shirt like so much paper. Amric caught a fleeting glimpse of pale skin, an unruly white shock of hair, and delicate features twisted in a primal mixture of murder and ecstasy. He continued his spin, lashing out with his sword, and Valkarr stepped into a lunge of his own from a few paces away. There was a soft thump in the air as the assassin vanished in another swirl of smoke, and the warriors' blades crossed in the space he had been.

Thalya started to straighten at Amric's shout and then went rigid, her back arching as she was lifted to her toes. Blood burst from her chest, and she looked down, eyes wide with disbelief. A thorn of steel sprouted there, glistening red. The blade was withdrawn with a jerk, eliciting a strangled gasp from her, and she collapsed to the rock. The second Elvar assassin stood behind her amid a veil of smoke. He watched her fall, a feral grin alight on his narrow face.

"Brother, I am most displeased," he purred. "Its vulgar bellow spoiled my clean kill."

His twin appeared next to him in a dark cloud. He cocked his head at the crumpled form of Thalya. "No matter, brother. It is a long way back to the city. We can claim them all one by one, at our leisure." He raised his voice, calling to Amric. "Our lord Morland sends his regards. He wishes it to know that it dies tonight by his decree. By now the city has fallen, but it must understand that our lord is most thorough and cannot permit word of his arrangement with the Nar'ath to spread."

"Our lord is wise," the other agreed. "Witness his justified caution in that it has not only survived the Nar'ath, but sought to steal away his gift to them."

"Morland, that snake!" Amric snarled. "So he is the traitor the Nar'ath queen mentioned. He betrayed the city and his own men, his own kind, to those monsters!"

Just then, a strangled sound resolved into an incoherent scream of loss and rage. Syth rushed toward the assassins with a wild-eyed look of madness, and the violent winds whirling around him flattened the foliage and propelled him along in great bounds.

"Syth, wait!" Amric cried, starting forward. "We must attack together, or they will kill us all, one at a time!"

Syth gave no indication he had heard the warrior. He leapt to the ridge of rock and raced along it at a breakneck pace, heedless of any danger to himself. The Elvaren roared with laughter, their faces alight with their own madness.

"Come ahead to your death, fool," one said, beckoning with a long, slender blade. "Now or later, it is all the same. You cannot hide from us, for we will be waiting in the next shadow you fail to check. We are creatures of the night—"

A wave of blackness rose over the edge. It flowed like ink over the rock and sent sinuous tendrils into the basin. The night air thickened with sudden, biting cold. A figure coalesced there, spreading a cloak of writhing shadows. Its eyes burned scarlet and fierce, furious and vengeful. Every living creature present knew it at once on some instinctual level; this was death incarnate, merciless and ravenous beyond measure. The Lord of the Night turned the full weight of his gaze upon the assassins, and the rumbling hiss that issued forth bore not the slightest trace of humanity.

The Elvaren gaped, their eyes bulging, and they both vanished in a flash of smoke.

Syth rushed to Thalya's side and cradled her in his arms. Halthak splashed through the shallows of the small pool at a run, and threw his staff aside as he reached her. The Sil'ath warriors arrived an instant later, watching every direction for the return of the assassins.

"She lives," Halthak moaned as he placed his hands on her. "But there is so much damage, and she is so weak...." He squeezed his eyes shut, concentrating, and Amric's senses tingled as the healer's magic came into play. Syth cast frantic looks from Thalya to Halthak. Her breathing was quick and shallow, coming in tiny, bubbling gasps. The flow of blood from her chest slowed as the healer worked, but did not stop, and the wound shrank somewhat but remained open.

The warrior ground his teeth in helpless fury. On sudden impulse, he closed his eyes and focused on sending energy to the healer, offering it gently for his own use. The wilding magic flared in response, and he heard Halthak gasp. The hum of the healing magic against Amric's senses intensified.

A minute went by, then two. At long last the Half-Ork sagged back with a groan, and Amric's eyes snapped open. When Halthak looked up, his expression was tormented.

"No," Syth whispered.

"I am so sorry," Halthak said. "The strike was true, she is too far gone. There is not enough of her own spark left in her to fan back into a flame. I can die with her, but I cannot save her. I have given her a few more moments, but it is all I can do."

Syth swallowed and nodded, and Halthak fell back against the rock, putting his head in his hands. Valkarr and Sariel each gripped him on the shoulders, their faces stony as they stared down at the huntress.

Syth continued to hold her, rocking slowly in place. Thalya drew in a ragged breath, and her eyes fluttered open. They glistened like emeralds as she looked up at him. "Syth," she breathed.

He opened his mouth to reply, but his voice cracked and the words were lost. Thalya gave a wan smile.

"I wish we had more time, love," she murmured. "I wish we had met sooner. Much... could have been different."

"I would change nothing, but for the end," Syth replied.

She smiled again, this time wider. Blood seeped between her teeth. "You see? You are better with people than you are aware, Syth."

He made a choking sound and nodded.

"I need to speak with Bellimar now, love. Something... left unfinished."

Bellimar, cloaked in shadow a short distance away, lifted his head at the words. Syth threw a scathing look at the vampire, but Thalya whispered something to him, and he gave a reluctant nod. He kissed her forehead and stepped back. Bellimar hesitated, looking at the others, and then glided forward. As he did so, the darkness writhing about him seemed to retract, to diminish somewhat, and the slender figure that knelt at her side could almost be mistaken for the silver-haired old man he had been. The bones in his face jutted a bit too sharply, however, and the fever-bright flames of hunger in his eyes were unmistakable. There was a tremble to his movements as he took her hand, and Amric could see that he was at the frayed edge of his control as he leaned down close to her.

Her drooping eyelids flared open at his touch, and her green eyes sought his face. They stared at each other in silence, and then her blood-flecked lips moved. "Do not prove me wrong, Bellimar."

A few droplets of blood sprayed to his cheek at her words, and Bellimar flinched as if burned. The huntress held his gaze for a moment longer, and then her labored breath left her in a long sigh. Her hand went limp in his grasp, and she was gone. Syth uttered a moan of anguish, but Bellimar remained poised over her, motionless, his eyes searching her still features. He extended his other hand and closed her staring eyes. He started to withdraw his hand, hesitated, and then drew one slender finger along her cheek and gently tweaked her chin.

"Release her, monster," Syth grated, his voice quavering. "I will not have her defiled by your foul touch. She would never consent to become a black fiend like you."

Bellimar did not glance at him, but he laid her hand upon the stone and stood back. Shadow gathered to him once more like ebon sands flowing into an abyss. "Calm yourself, thief," he said. "Even if I wished it, she is beyond my influence now."

Syth growled something at him and knelt again by Thalya's side.

"Wilding."

Amric turned at the single word, spoken with iron determination. He faced the old man, who had fixed upon him with an unwavering gaze.

"Come," Bellimar said. "We have much to do, you and I, and precious little time left to do it."

"What is your plan?" the warrior asked.

"To do the impossible." Bellimar's eyes were like windows into a blazing forge as he shifted them to the fallen huntress. "And to fulfill her last request."

CHAPTER 26

"Are you out of your mind?" Syth demanded.

Amric did not reply. He wanted to smile at the irony of the man's words, but he thought it would merely agitate him further, so he refrained. He sat cross-legged on the ground, hands resting upon his knees. The dawn was still hours away, but the gibbous moon found its way at last through the thinning cloud cover to spill light down upon them. It gave the wasteland a bleak, otherworldly cast, and left Amric feeling like a wayward ghost intruding upon a world in which he was no longer welcome.

Caught between worlds, he mused, as ever.

Valkarr and Sariel stood at Amric's shoulders, flanking him. They appeared relaxed, but he knew better. There was a tension to their stances that was only obvious to one who knew them well. Taut as bowstrings, he thought with a sad smile as he thought of Thalya. So many lost already. Of the warriors he and Valkarr had set out to find, only Sariel now remained. And countless more would perish if this did not work. Some distance behind him, the grating sound of rock against rock informed him that Halthak was still fretting at the crude cairn they had built, as far to one end of the crag as had been possible. It had taken precious time to dig even a shallow grave for the bodies and cover them with rocks, and to rake sand over the spilt blood as well, but it had seemed a judicious precaution.

Amric's jaw clenched. He was about to put his life and his sanity in the hands of a creature consumed with demonic hunger. The less temptation at hand, the better.

Directly opposite him, perched upon the outermost rim of rock, was Bellimar. Whether he sat as Amric did, or crouched like some great black bird of prey, the swordsman could not say. A pallid face, a leering nightmare apparition, hovered amid the enveloping shadows at a height that could have been either. Red eyes remained fixed upon the warrior in an expectant stare.

Syth stepped in front of Amric, breaking his line of sight. The troubled winds swirling around the man sent cool night air washing over him. "This is a *terrible* plan," Syth insisted.

"And yet, we have no other," Amric returned quietly.

"You cannot let that—that *thing* into your head," Syth spluttered, gesticulating at Bellimar.

Amric sighed. "You know the situation as well as I, Syth," he said. "Xenoth means to activate this Gate device and destroy our world. It would take us several days to ride there, even if we manage to recover the horses. On foot, it would take us much longer, and we would be without the provisions we lost in the packs that left with the horses. The land between here and there is crawling with Nar'ath and worse, and we have seen almost no water or game. We could detour to Keldrin's Landing for mounts and provisions, but the city may be overrun. If the Nar'ath queen words were true, we would be marching right into the bulk of her returning forces as well." He lifted his eyes to the other's face. "When we rode to Stronghold, the forest became more and more dangerous the further in we went. According to Bellimar, the ruins of Queln are deeper yet into that forest. And if we survive the journey, we would likely be too late to stop Xenoth."

Amric watched objection and doubt war in the man's expression. "Do not misunderstand me, Syth," he said. "I would be walking even now, if there was no other alternative. But Bellimar says he has another way, and I have to try."

"By laying yourself open to him?" Syth asked in disbelief. "Are you mad? Do you even believe he can make you a match for the Adept?"

"I never made that claim," Bellimar interrupted, his voice a raw, guttural growl. "I mastered sorcery over years—nay, centuries—of study and use. No, I can only implant a minute portion of my knowledge in the time we have, and even at the height of my powers I could not have faced the likes of Xenoth directly. I can give you the means to seek out the Adept, and perhaps the basic tools to live a few seconds longer than you otherwise would. The rest will be up to you." He grinned. "You have a penchant for the unpredictable, swordsman, and for surviving against all odds. You will need it."

"And what of you, Bellimar?" Amric asked. "Will you not fight with us at Queln?"

Bellimar shook his head, the death's-head grin fading. "Regrettably, I cannot. I can no longer endure the direct touch of sunlight, as my protection from its effects was removed with the last vestiges of my curse. Dawn is mere hours away now, and we will consume most of that time in your preparation. I would be of no use to you, there."

Amric's eyes narrowed. "Then where will you go?"

"There is something more I must do, before I become lost entirely," Bellimar said.

Amric regarded him in steady silence for a long moment. "I cannot let you become a plague on this world again, Bellimar. I will not stop one monster only to free another."

The red eyes brightened, blazing with defiance, and the shadows gathered and rose to spread over them all like huge black wings. Valkarr and Sariel dropped into crouches, swords flashing free, but Amric did not move. Bellimar shuddered, faltered, and then sank back, his eyes dimming to their low, feral glow once more. "It will not come to that, warrior," he said in a strained whisper. "You have my promise."

Syth stared at Bellimar, and then rounded again on Amric. "Look at him! See the monster he has become, the fiend of legend once more. If you let him in, how do you know that he will not strike at you while you are vulnerable? What assurance do you have that he will ever relinquish your mind once he is in there?"

"Only my word," Bellimar hissed. "And the fading strength of my will. We should be about this, before I lose even that. Look to the east. Our time draws short."

Amric followed his gaze. The clouds extended in a ceiling high above, churning like a storm-tossed sea. In the wasteland, the cover had thinned, and fitful gaps had appeared, permitting the light of the moon and scattered fragments of star-flecked night to show through. Far to the east, however, the clouds were knitting together, growing dense and dark. An ember glow flickered there among them, and Amric might have thought it the first touch of dawn if it were not still some hours too early. As he watched, he felt a curious tugging sensation, akin to the inexorable pull of the earth below him, but pulling at something *within* him toward that distant site. The wilding magic stirred, uneasy.

"Yes, you can feel it," Bellimar murmured. "What has been a slow, steady stream is becoming a torrent. The magic of the land is being drawn to Queln, even stronger than before. It seems Xenoth has made good on his threat to activate the Essence Gate. We have very little time now. It may already be too late."

Amric swung back to face him. "We had best get to it, then."

Valkarr looked down at Amric, his lean, reptilian features pinched with concern. "You mean to go through with this, then?"

Amric's jaw tightened as he nodded. Syth threw up his hands with a snort of disgust and stalked away.

"Very good, swordsman," Bellimar said. "Let us begin."

The vampire fixed upon him with a rabid gaze, and Amric met it, unflinching. Glowing red eyes narrowed to pinpoints, burning with new intensity, and then began a slow widening, like a rising pool of flame. The warrior felt himself drawn into their depths. Every instinct flared at him to break the contact, but he fought the impulse and forced himself to remain steady. Bellimar's voice rolled out of the shadows, and the raw edge to it was gone. Instead it was rich and deep, smooth and purposeful.

"We will enter a trance state together, you and I. When you are ready, I will enter your consciousness. You must lower your defenses and allow me in. I must go deep enough to implant knowledge where you will retain it, at least long enough to serve you in your battle against the Adept."

There was a soothing, hypnotic quality to the man's voice, something lacing his speech that numbed the senses and made Amric's eyelids grow heavy. It stole over him so quickly that he had to shake himself to alertness in order to focus upon what the other was saying. The wilding magic stirred within him, uneasy.

"With most anyone else, I could just force my way in," Bellimar continued. His words fell in a steady, rhythmic cadence. "But you, my friend, represent a unique challenge. In any event, there can be damage incurred in such a boorish, aggressive approach. No, our situation demands an expert touch, and fortunately for us both, I can provide one."

Amric drifted, sinking into the molten pools that were the old man's eyes. There was a note of anticipation, of hunger in the vampire's tone that triggered a small warning at the back of his mind, but it was a distant annoyance and easily ignored.

"You must realize that there is no small risk to me in this venture," Bellimar murmured as his mesmerizing voice dropped ever lower. "While you know the necessity of this, your wilding magic may not react well to the perceived intrusion. If it acts on its own to strike out at me while we share your mind, the consequences could be disastrous for us both."

Amric swayed where he sat, his eyes half-lidded.

"Are you ready, swordsman?"

He mumbled something that might have been an affirmative, and there was a hiss of muted triumph in response.

Bellimar entered his mind like a knife.

The pain was sharp and sudden, a sliver of ice stabbing into his skull. Amric jerked upright, and a bestial growl escaped through his clenched teeth. An unfamiliar presence writhed in his mind, something dark, cold and unclean. Foul tendrils snaked through his consciousness, lodging there with thousands of tiny hooks like a creeping vine laden with thorns. Anger rose within him, primal and powerful, burning away rational thought. His wilding magic roared its outrage. As if from a great distance, he heard the exclamations of those around him, and the keening edge of bared steel.

"Warrior!" hissed Bellimar's voice, and this time it came from within his own head. "Amric! Remember our purpose here! I cannot afford to be gentle in the time we have, not against a mind as strong as yours. Even though you try to leave yourself open to me, it is like trying to worm my way in through a crack in a fortress wall. Call them off, or all is lost!"

Amric hesitated, the pyre of gathered power burning in his chest. He grunted something unintelligible, but the sounds around him stopped. He tried again. "Wait," he gritted. His voice sounded harsh and alien in his own ears. "Do not interfere."

"Good," Bellimar assured him. "Now bring your magic under control. I do not like how it is eyeing me."

Amric took a deep breath, and his throat felt dry and raw. He sent a pulse of reassurance to the bristling wilding, and calmed it over long seconds of effort. It faded back, grudging and tense, still vigilant. Amric had a moment to catch his breath, and then the cold presence of Bellimar flowed the rest of the way into his mind, eliciting another gasp of shock and filling his head until he thought it would burst. More dark coils slithered forth, and lancing pain followed each as it dug in. Amric clenched his jaw and waited.

The agony subsided, replaced by a numbing sensation that flooded his limbs. He tried to curl his hands into fists, and nothing happened. He realized with a flicker of panic that he was no longer in command of his own body.

"Now then," Bellimar said with a chilling note of satisfaction. "Shall we finally get some much-needed answers?"

"W-what?" Amric demanded. His thoughts were scattered, sluggish, but he forced the fragments together.

The other's dark presence swirled about. "Mystery is your constant companion, warrior. I believe the answer to one of those mysteries, at least, is buried deep within your own mind, in your earliest memories. I intend to find that answer."

"Is this a betrayal, Bellimar?" Amric made no attempt to keep the threat from his tone.

Bellimar snorted. "Hardly. Now that I am established, I do not know that you could unseat me, but even so, I have no interest in a contest of wills with you."

"Then what is the meaning of this change of plans? I thought we had no time to spare."

"We do not," the vampire confirmed. "But time runs at a different pace in here, in your mind, than it does out there. And I suspect the information to be gained will prove crucial to your survival in the days to come. I think we have to take the risk."

Amric hesitated. A sting of anticipation mingled with icy dread coursed through him. "And what if I do not want to know?"

There was a pause, and then Bellimar said, "You may have suppressed an inner magic for the better part of your life, Amric, but I do not think you are capable of turning away from the truth, once you know of it. Even a painful truth."

Amric grimaced. It was true. He had spent his life in open honesty with all he encountered, and most importantly, always with himself. Or so he had thought. Still, he had never been one to back down from what had to be done, no matter the personal cost. Could he do any less now?

"How do we proceed?" he whispered.

Bellimar made a pleased sound that contained notes of eagerness and what might have been admiration. "As I mentioned, I will not have the luxury of being gentle."

The hooks constricted, and the pain began again.

Captain Borric stormed through the courtyard in the shadow of the city's massive southern gate. The wounded continued to straggle in, and his soldiers directed those with the most grievous injuries to a hastily constructed triage station where a handful of weary physicians had been pressed into service. Borric paused at the station and surveyed their work for a moment in silence.

One of the physicians, a slender fellow with a tapered beard, approached to check on the crude sling supporting the captain's broken arm, but Borric shook the man off with a dismissive growl. The grizzled soldier turned away and surveyed the courtyard.

His soldiers moved among huddled masses of the townsfolk, providing a show of strength and comfort to which they could cling. Very few of the citizens had dispersed deeper into Keldrin's Landing yet. Instead, they sat in a stony silence punctuated by occasional moans and muffled weeping, as they waited for Borric's men to finish scouting ahead to confirm that the black fiends were indeed gone. Most were careful to keep their eyes on each other or on the soldiers, and avoided looking at the bodies of the dead, carelessly strewn about the courtyard like leaves scattered before a storm wind.

Borric, however, forced his gaze to linger upon each and every one. Their deaths were on his hands, and he could do no less.

A shout interrupted his grim reverie. One of his men burst into view from an eastern side street, pounding along the cobbled stone of the courtyard toward him.

"What news, Gilsen?" Borric called.

"Captain!" the man gasped as he drew near. "More trouble from the east!"

The townsfolk nearest them gasped, and a low murmur built in the courtyard as word spread like fire through dry grass. Borric kept his eyes on the man, letting none of the dread he felt show in his expression. "What sort of trouble?" he asked in a crisp tone.

"Sir, I climbed to the wall-walk and saw it myself," Gilsen said, still panting.

"Saw what, soldier?"

The man drew a deep, steadying breath. "There is a strange light in the sky, far to the east, like a huge fire in the forest, but hanging high above it instead—"

"Gilsen," the captain interrupted gently. "We have a ravaged city full of dead and wounded, and our gates lie open to the next attack. Of what import is a distant light in the sky to us, at this moment?"

"Sir, that is not the whole of it," Gilsen insisted, his eyes wide. "Between that strange fire in the sky and the light of the moon, one can see a fair distance over the countryside right now, despite the dark hour."

Borric's breath caught in his throat. "And?" he managed.

"The land to the east is crawling with all manner of twisted creatures. They are coming from everywhere, like before, like the night of the attack on the city gate!"

The captain's spine turned to ice. He swept his gaze around the court-yard, at the weak and the wounded. *Not now*, he thought, *not now*. A bone-deep stab of pain coursed through his useless arm. "How many?" he asked, keeping his voice low.

The man did not appear to hear him. His words continued to tumble out, one atop the other. "Maybe they are all stirred up by this fire in the forest, the way they are gathering, so many more than before—"

"Gilsen!" the captain barked, bringing the man up short. "How many?"

Gilsen looked at him with a haunted expression. "Sir, if I had to guess—all of them. Many times more than before, too many to count, and they are coming fast."

Captain Borric closed his eyes. He had read the knowledge in the young man's face. Gilsen expected to die. The soldier felt—*knew*, with a certainty—that he was describing his own imminent death. The city was not defensible. The southern gate had been breached this night and dam-aged beyond their ability to repair in time. The eastern gate had been re-stored since the first assault, days ago, but it had only just withstood then against a smaller force than what Gilsen described was coming now. The mighty perimeter wall of the city, their beachhead against this savage and untamed land, was broken. The wild, it seemed, had decided to strike back at the hubris of civilization.

He was in charge of the city's defense, and yet he knew he could not stave off its destruction this night.

But he might be able to save the lives of its people.

"Sound the alarm, Gilsen," he said. "City wide, and be quick about it."

"Sir?"

"We will take everyone we can find to the docks, commandeer every available ship, and abandon the city. We cannot stop them from taking Keldrin's Landing, but if we make haste, we do not have to be here when it happens."

"But Captain," Gilsen objected, "there are not enough passenger ships for everyone. Most of the ships at the docks are cargo vessels, loaded with trade goods."

"Dump it all over the side," Borric said. "Keep only the foodstuffs. And we will need to take what provisions we can as we flee the city, as well."

Gilsen gaped at him. "The lords and merchants will not like that, sir."

The captain gave him a cold smile. "Then I welcome them to take up the issue with the city's new residents. I, for one, will thank the fates if we survive long enough to lament any lost profits."

Gilsen squared his shoulders and clapped fist to chest in a salute. His eyes crinkled at the corners, but no other sign betrayed the grin he was stifling. Borric returned the salute, and then pointed back in the direction from which the man had come.

"Carry my orders to the others," he said. "Have the men sound the alarms. We need to get these people moving if we hope to see the dawn. Now, soldier!"

Amric rose through layers of darkness, cut by the unforgiving shards of memory. The fragmented images assailed him, whirling and spinning, disjoint and out of order.

Scaly Sil'ath features looking down upon him, regarding him with an eye that is skeptical but not unkind.

Fierce, flickering swordplay with his childhood fellows; a cry of triumphant pleasure as he presses the attack, ever faster.

Watching, troubled for reasons he cannot name, as five of his finest warriors—Innikar, Sariel, Prakseth, Varek and Garlien—depart to investigate the source of the disturbances coming from the mysterious north. The last time he would see some of them alive.

The images spun again.

Climbing a sheer face of rock, racing Valkarr to its peak.

The heads of human men and women swiveling to follow him as he strides through the streets of Lyden as a tall stripling. Pink, soft and civilized, they are; baffled and suspicious as they gaze upon him.

Gliding through the underbrush, long-spear in hand, moving like the wind itself as he and his fellow warriors stalk the ravening pack of greels that had been attacking homesteads on the outskirts of Lyden.

The images spun.

Three score swords raised to the sky by strong Sil'ath arms, hailing Amric as the tribe's new warmaster. The throaty roar of the tribe as he lifts his own sword in response. No other upturned face glowing with as much pride as that of the previous warmaster, save perhaps that of his son and Amric's closest friend, Valkarr.

Clasping forearms with his sword-brother, Valkarr, sworn in blood.

The images spun.

The thunderous clash of battle against an armored host, a remorseless foe of the Sil'ath. The terrifying and graceful dance of the battlefield. Outnumbered but victorious; the first of many such victories.

The images spun.

A cottage in the deep woods of strange and alien design. The door opening to spill sunlight inward. A shadow cast across the threshold.

The images spun and blurred and came to a jarring halt. The chilling presence of Bellimar seeped around him once more.

"I think I lost consciousness for a time," Amric gasped, still reeling.

"Indeed, you did," Bellimar said. "Not for long, but much has been accomplished in that time. And I believe I have found what we seek."

The scene swam into focus. Or, rather, it tried to. He was looking upon the interior of the strange cottage, but his field of view shifted and flickered back and forth between two vantage points. The effect was dizzying, disorienting. There was an infant boy child in an ornate basinet; his was one of the perspectives. The other was an invisible presence circling in fretful motions above the child.

He was seeing the same scene from two different perspectives at once, he realized: that of the child—himself, as an infant—and that of his wilding magic. He concentrated, trying to sort out the juxtaposition of the images.

The child was very young, and was thin and weak from hunger and dehydration. As a result of one or both factors, there was a foggy quality to the child's vantage. He leaned in listless repose against one wall of the basinet and his face was blotched red from earlier tears, but he was calm and clear-eyed now. Crying had done no good; help was not coming to his call. He was too young to take further action toward self-preservation on his own. Without help, the child was doomed.

The memory of the wilding magic was much stronger. There was a simple, childish quality to its thoughts as well, and its frantic concern grew to a fever pitch as the child grew weaker and weaker. It had broken the spell that bound them both in extended slumber, but it knew not what action to take from there. Some primal instinct nagged at it in persistent warning. Something was wrong, and danger was coming.

The magic reached out, questing beyond the bounds of the cottage, looking for aid of any kind. Life teemed in the surrounding forest, but it offered no succor. There was a myriad of tiny creatures, from insects to rodents, too primitive to be of help. It found a large life force, a sleek predator, but touching its mind revealed only boundless hunger and a resulting singularity of purpose, and the wilding shied away from it.

The wilding swirled in frustration and kept searching. Then it found them, a handful of minds moving through the nearby forest with resolve. They were hard and complex, but their camaraderie toward each other was palpable. The wilding rushed to contact them, but it found no kindred magic to answer back. Instead, they felt something of its clumsy attempt at contact, and the reaction was immediate and violent, a surge of rejection, superstition and prejudice. The wilding recoiled, frustrated at the failure. It withdrew until they were calm once more, and then tried again.

Slower this time, softer, the gentlest of touches. It focused upon the leader alone, soothing the rough edges of that creature's distrust and fanning its curiosity. It led them to the cottage by small degrees, nudging dozens of minor impulse decisions in favor of a path that led there. It was slow, frustrating work, and the wilding magic fluttered in panic at every minute setback. At last, however, the group drew within sight of the cottage. The wilding reached deeper into its flagging strength, and, with a surge of effort, parted the veil of magic that concealed the structure from without. The group gasped in surprise, brandishing weapons and hesitating at this sudden wonder. The wilding froze. It was exhausted and spending all its remaining energy on suspending the veil. There was little it could do at that point but wait and hope.

The leader studied the cottage for a long moment, and then prowled in a slow semi-circle around it before advancing to the door. Inside, in the basinet, the boy child looked up as the door eased open to spill sunlight and a long shadow inward. A tall, powerfully built figure approached and loomed over him. The child gazed up into a strong, reptilian face, and the Sil'ath warrior looked down upon him with a dispassionate eye.

They stared at each other in silence for several seconds, and then the warrior turned to leave. The wilding magic pulsed once in a panic.

Amric, watching, held his breath. To an outside observer, the actions of the Sil'ath warrior would seem callous, but he knew better. The reclusive Sil'ath were assiduous in their efforts to avoid interfering in the affairs of the other races, and it would take much to cause one to cross that line.

But then the warrior paused, looking back with an unreadable expression. He took in the gaunt condition of the child, and the level, steady stare of his grey eyes. The Sil'ath grunted, and there was a note of admiration to the sound.

"You do not cry or show fear, little one," he said. His words were in the Sil'ath tongue, and though the infant Amric could not then understand, the incorporeal Amric watching the scene did. "Do you have a warrior's spirit?"

Perhaps in response to the gentle tone, the child reached a hand toward the warrior with tiny pink fingers outspread. The warrior's answering grin was fierce.

"You want to live?" he said. "You shall have your chance."

Scaly, muscular arms lifted the boy from the basinet. With a final glance around the place, Verenkar, Valkarr's father, turned and left, holding the child against his broad chest.

The wilding magic flared with joy and relief. In its elation, it again brushed against the entrenched disdain for magic in the minds of the Sil'ath warriors. Acting on primal instinct, it quickly retreated back into the recesses of the child's mind. There it curled in upon itself, shifting and tightening like the intricate coils of a complex knot being drawn through one another. Smaller and smaller it became, folding inward, and the child's radiant aura shrank with it. Finally it dwindled to a pinpoint, inverted itself in a spasm of effort, and vanished.

The Sil'ath hunting party moved through the undergrowth, swift and sure. From the crook of one iron arm, the child Amric glanced back to where the cottage had been, and saw only the thick green shroud of the forest once more.

The scene dissolved and Amric drifted, stunned.

"It saved my life," he said in disbelief. "Not just recently, at Stronghold and the Nar'ath hive, but from the very beginning."

"That appears to be true," Bellimar agreed. "I regret that the memories go no further back, but between this one and Xenoth's statements, I think we can now piece together your origins."

"Xenoth slew my parents, and meant to slay me, back then," Amric said, his thoughts racing. "My... magic lured the Sil'ath to me, and then hid itself so thoroughly that no one—not even I—knew of its presence. And since the Sil'ath took me in, Xenoth never found me."

"And where does that chain of thought lead you?" Bellimar pressed.

"Xenoth mentioned my parents' defiance of his Council. They fled to this world, for some reason."

Bellimar waited and said nothing.

"My parents are from this other world, this Aetheria," Amric said at last. "And so am I."

"All of which implies that you, Amric, are an Adept as well."

He started to deny it, but his vehemence flared and then died. He thought of the power that had coursed through him at Stronghold when their lives hung in the balance, and how he had sought it out and called it forth at the hive. He had access to powers he had never known, that much was certain. He could no longer pretend to blame it on phenomena like the Essence Fount. But was he an Adept? He was *not* like that monster, Xenoth, killing indiscriminately and reveling in the use of power. And the Adept had called him a *wilding*, had used the appellation with scorn and repugnance. Surely that meant that they were nothing alike. If his magic was emerging again after lying dormant so long, however, could it be that he would become a creature every bit as loathsome as an Adept? Could a wilding be even worse?

He had been raised by the Sil'ath to abhor the use of magic, and now there was no question that he was infused with it. It was a part of his nature, hidden all these years, concealed among the very people who would never tolerate its presence. He was everything that the people who had saved his life and given him a home both feared and detested. Had Verenkar known back then, he would have left the child to die alone. Had Valkarr known, he would not have sworn brotherhood. The Sil'ath had been manipulated into accepting him. How many other ways had they been affected over the years, without their knowledge?

The wilding magic within Amric stirred and shrank back from the pain and confusion that coursed through him. He sighed and sent a wave of warmth and reassurance at it. *This is no fault of yours,* he thought. *You acted to preserve us both.*

Sharing his thoughts, Bellimar spoke. "You may be a unique form of Adept," he said, "but you come from a world of Adepts and you wield great power. Whatever a wilding may be, you are also one of them."

Amric heard the bitter emphasis on the last word. One of *them;* he was a descendant of the beings that had stripped Bellimar of his power, so long ago, and left him in a cursed half-existence. Not for the first time, it occurred to Amric just how vulnerable he was to the vampire at the moment. Before Amric could object, however, Bellimar continued.

"Fear not, swordsman. I spent countless years nursing my hatred for what the Adepts did to me, but no longer. Whatever Xenoth might have claimed, the Adepts of that time bore little resemblance to the mean-spirited creature we faced tonight. Just as *you* bear little resemblance to him. This tells me that, even if today's lords of Aetheria have fallen to the depths of corruption, it need not be so. No, the Adepts struck down a monster, and I will not become that again."

Amric was silent for a moment, contemplating the quiet certitude in the old man's words. "How will you prevent it?" he finally asked.

"I know of only one way," Bellimar responded. "There is something else I must do first, however."

Amric caught a glimpse into the other's thoughts, and he understood at last.

It dawned upon him as well that the drifting sensation had direction and inexorable purpose, that as they conversed, they had been floating up-ward. It was like rising to life-giving air from the depths of the sea, and when he broke the surface, he sagged back into his body in the waking world. He heard sharp inhalations and sudden movement on either side of him. The vast funnels of flame that were Bellimar's red eyes withdrew from around him and then shrank back to hooded, blazing pits within folds of shadow.

"It is done," Bellimar announced.

Amric gave him a sharp look. "What of the training you were to pro-vide?"

"Done," the old man answered with a twist of a smile. "Putting any false modesty aside, I am a master at this, and I accomplished much while you were unconscious. I was able to implant the knowledge to open a Way, as Xenoth did, but to Queln. It is always easier if you have been there be-fore, and I experienced Queln long ago, before its majesty had faded so. You now have something of my memories of the place." His smile broad-ened into a vicious grin. "And I did my best to plant a nasty surprise or two for you to offer Xenoth, when you face him. Please send my regards."

Amric's eyes narrowed as he regarded Bellimar. He was unnerved at the prospect of the vampire enjoying free reign in his psyche while he was defenseless, but there was little help for it now. Somewhat skeptical, he reached for the expertise to open a Way, focusing on his desire to reach the Adept, and to his surprise it came to him readily. It was as if it had always been there, a task that was now every bit as familiar as drawing his sword or riding a horse. His wilding magic roused and flared with eagerness at the prospect of calling up the power necessary for the act, but Amric shuddered at the violation. What else had Bellimar hidden within his mind?

Bellimar stared back with that infuriating grin, as if daring him to ask the question aloud. Amric ground his teeth, but held his tongue. He had agreed to the process, after all, in a desperate grab at salvation for his people and his world. He had known the risks.

Instead he said, "I thank you for your efforts, Bellimar. May they prove sufficient, for all our sakes."

Bellimar responded with a solemn nod. "We must part ways now. The dawn is coming, and I have far to travel before I lose the cover of night."

Amric pushed to his feet, and in the simple act he uncovered yet another revelation: his weariness was gone. The battles with the Nar'ath queen and Xenoth had left him exhausted in mind and body, but he felt as if he was somehow waking from a full night's rest. He was not fully recovered, but he felt fit enough for the coming conflict. His brows knitted in puzzlement. It made no sense; his time locked in the trance had not been long enough to account for the change, and in any event, it had not felt in the least way restful. Then he glared at Bellimar with sudden suspicion.

"You shared more than knowledge," he accused. "You gave me some portion of your vitality as well."

"I can assure you that it came without price or taint," Bellimar said. His grin broadened even further, and closer inspection revealed what the shadows had concealed until then. The vampire was even more wasted and gaunt than before. His eyes burned from sunken black pits, and his narrow face was so hollow-cheeked as to appear skeletal. When he smiled, the white skin tightened like parchment over a bleached skull.

"That is strength you can ill afford to discard," Amric said with a frown. "It will make your curse all the more difficult to bear."

"Indeed it does. Another reason I must be away from here."

The vampire's voice quavered slightly as he spoke, and the hunger rolled from him in palpable waves. They faced each other for a moment, and then Amric said, "So be it. Fare you well, Bellimar."

"Fare you well, Amric."

"What madness is this?" Syth cried, sweeping in from the direction of the cairn. "Should we not try to stop him? Thalya wanted him—"

"Dead or redeemed," Bellimar interrupted with quiet conviction. "And though she could not know it, she may well have achieved both, in the end. Do not worry, Syth, the night is not over yet."

The dark figure turned to depart, then hesitated, and swung back.

"She would want you to remember, Syth, that love is a gift, and its magic is in the giving and receiving rather than the having. What you were given can never be taken at the hand of another."

"What do you know of love, fiend?" Syth snapped. "Are honeyed words supposed to soothe my pain?"

"No," Bellimar responded with a sad smile. "But there will come a time when the truth behind them will restore a measure of your inner strength. Grieve until then, my young friend. No one can take that from you, either."

Before the other could form a retort, Bellimar whirled away and flowed over the rocky edge in a cascade of midnight, vanishing from sight. Moments later, a shadow rose against the light of the moon and spread great black wings to wing its way rapidly north. Amric watched until it dwindled to a speck and was lost against the dark leaden grey of the night sky. Then he turned to Valkarr. His friend reached out and clasped his shoulder, but hesitated at the look on his face. One scaly brow ridge rose in question.

"There is something you need to know," Amric said, and his tongue felt thick in his mouth. "About me. It may affect your decision to join me in what comes next."

Valkarr snorted. "I think not."

"Hear it first."

The Sil'ath warrior folded muscular arms across his broad chest. "Are you going to tell me that you do not wish me at your side in this battle?"

Amric swallowed. "No, of course not. Never that."

"Then it can wait until afterward," Valkarr stated. "We all know what is at stake, and we stand ready, sword-brother. Lead the way."

Sariel stepped to his side in silent accord. She lifted her chin and met his gaze with a fierce glint sparkling in her eye. Halthak drew up behind them, and though his knuckles were white as he gripped his gnarled staff, he stood unbowed and his features were set into hard, resolute lines.

Syth cast a final, lingering look at the solitary mound of rock. His hair and clothing fluttered and waved toward it, as if the ever-present breeze surrounding him meant to pull him back in that direction. When he turned back to the others, his expression was stone. "Let us finish this," he said.

Amric drew a deep breath and concentrated, calling forth knowledge that was not his. He drew upon power that was, and it filled him in a ready, burning flood. In his mind, he held an image of the ancient ruins of Queln, and it was a composite of Bellimar's borrowed memories and the remote scene he had glimpsed earlier behind the black-robed Adept. He focused his will on a point in the air before him, there atop the crown of rock, and he made a cutting motion with one hand. A tall seam of light appeared, and with another gesture it split open. Amric felt a tearing sensation, as if he was parting heavy cloth with his bare hands, and the effort drained at his energy, but the Way opened before him like a thick set of curtains spreading to reveal an open doorway behind.

Beyond the fiery edges of the aperture, he could see Queln.

Mist curled everywhere amid great tumbled ruins, flowing over, between and through. A roaring sound came to him, vast and unfathomable like the thunder of the ocean, and light of every hue danced within the mists. The air crackled with power, raising the hair on his arms and the nape of his neck as stood there. His wilding magic prowled and snarled with impatience in the recesses of his mind.

Amric did not look around at the others, but he could feel their stares heavy upon him. He reached over his shoulders and drew forth both swords. Power suffused him, continuing to build, and at his touch mystical flame sprang across the blades. The others flinched, and he clenched his jaw as he watched the heatless flame writhe along the naked steel.

Some knowledge, once gained, could never be forgotten. Some actions, once taken, could never be undone. That it was necessary did little to lessen the pain.

He plunged forward and through the portal.

CHAPTER 27

Amric stepped through the portal and onto a forest-backed hill that over-looked a scene out of madness. Black clouds gathered overhead in dense folds, colliding and joining together to form a titanic spiral that spanned the sky and turned with a slow, ponderous grace. A mountainous funnel began at the center of that great wheel and reached for the earth below. Lightning clawed at the clouds and wound its way down the dark vortex, and all of it was permeated by a sullen, volcanic red glow.

On the ground, the mist stirred and flowed in response, though whether it fled the storm or rushed to meet it, Amric could not tell. It moved in a way that seemed at once both erratic and yet somehow pur-poseful, stalking and then swift, like the prowling of some starving beast. The shattered ruins of Queln, the skeletal remains of a civilization long forgotten, pushed their way through the vapors. Whatever forces had torn the ancient city apart had done so with vehemence; some of the towering structures had been worn and humbled at the merciless hand of time, but many appeared to have been blasted apart, leaving naught to mark their passing but jagged boulders of marble strewn about.

Dark and twisted shapes moved through the ruins, skulking behind the veil of mist. They shambled in fitful bursts, emitting occasional shrieks and keening cries. Those inhuman calls were laced with pain, fury and madness, and they were answered by more inhuman throats in the surrounding forest.

The air itself trembled with a continuous roar of magic, and Amric's knees buckled as everything hit him at once. A sense of desperation and agony threatened to engulf him, as if the land itself recognized its immi-nent demise and was laboring for each remaining breath.

The others stepped up beside Amric. He straightened, ignoring their sharp looks of concern. He released the Way he was holding open, allow-ing it to seal with a hiss, and a mental weight lifted from him.

The initial assault against his perceptions had been overwhelming, but he steeled himself against it. With the sensory onslaught came a rush of vitality, filling him until his breath caught and his nerves burned. Magic flooded this place, just as it had in the core of Stronghold near the Essence Fount. Where that phenomenon had been ruptured and raw, however, the flow of energy here was controlled, directed, bound. Amric concentrated and found he could sense the invisible currents converging from every direction. They ran like vast rivers through the ground beneath his feet and the sky above, rushing all around and past him.

They ran directly to the Essence Gate.

He knew it the instant he saw it. A massive arch of stone, it sat atop a high platform directly beneath the tip of the dark vortex. Broad, weather-worn steps climbed out of the mist to reach it. The Gate was wrought with sigils that burned with hellish light, and its interior churned and shone in a dazzling sea of fire. It could have been the ravenous maw of the gods, vengeful and all-consuming, and all of the magical energies were drawn to and into that luminous arch.

Amric's fists clenched upon the hilts of his swords until his hands shook. That thing was feeding upon their world, holding it helpless as it killed, visiting untold suffering upon the land and its creatures. It was time to end this.

"Well," Syth remarked, "I guess we know where we need to go." He cast a dubious eye at the intervening ground between them and the platform, where misshapen figures skulked in the mists. "How do we plan to not die until we get there?"

Amric frowned in thought. He had planned to keep Xenoth occupied while the others destroyed the Essence Gate, but even at this distance he could see the massive scale of it. Their weapons would have little effect on the huge ring of stone. But perhaps there would be some other means of disabling it until the tools required to destroy it could be brought to bear. He turned to the others, driving the point of one flaming sword into the ground to free one of his hands.

"We will go in this way," he said, indicating their path. "We stay together at first. I will do what I can to shield us from the Adept's initial attacks, and I will draw his fire from there. Once Xenoth is focused upon me, slip away into the ruins. Stay in pairs, stay out of sight, and watch each other's backs. Valkarr and Sariel, circle around and look for an opening to strike at Xenoth, or at least distract him enough to give me an opening. Syth and Halthak, make for that raised platform and find a way to disable the Gate."

Amric received a chorus of grim nods in response. He faced Valkarr. "Maintain cover until you can strike with certainty. Remember Innikar, my friend. Xenoth does not give second chances."

"Would you like to show me which end of the sword to hold as well?" Valkarr inquired with a fierce grin, though his eyes were hard and sober as they clasped forearms. "For those who have fallen," he said in the Sil'ath tongue, his tone solemn.

"For those who remain," Amric answered in the same language, completing an old Sil'ath exchange for luck in battle. He clasped forearms with each of the others as well, meeting their eyes, hoping that his gratitude and his pride in their courage was easily read there. He retrieved his sword from where it stood jutting from the ground, and they strode together down the hill and into the swirling fog.

They moved in loose formation with Amric on point, gliding through a ghostly landscape of mist and stone. Crags of shattered marble loomed over them, and piercing cries echoed all around, but nothing approached. The few creatures they passed near enough to see were too consumed with their own torment to pay any mind to the group's passage; they snarled and shrieked and clawed at themselves, and it was a simple matter to skirt wide around them in the murk.

Amric raised frequent glances toward the Gate as they moved. He did not do so in order to maintain their heading—far from it, in fact. The construct was a persistent, thundering presence tugging at his senses, and he could have walked a direct path to it with his eyes closed. He kept a wary eye out for the Adept, to be sure, but it was more than that as well. Each time he looked upon the terrible majesty of the Essence Gate, it seemed he could see more of the forces at play around it. At first he saw faint currents curling toward and into it that he took for the capricious movements of the mists. They continued to sharpen with study, however, until they became phantasmal patterns of flowing light.

A hushed query revealed that none of the others could see the patterns, though asking the question earned him cool, appraising looks in return. He found himself mesmerized by the streams of light, and the more he concentrated, the more of them he could see. It was like another view onto reality, hidden behind—or woven into—the primary façade, as if he had somehow opened a second pair of eyes capable of seeing past the surface. Something clicked in his mind, and he realized he was looking upon the movement of primal energies, the raw forces of life and magic, flowing from every direction as they were drawn to and consumed by the Gate.

Whether it was instinct or another gift of Bellimar's knowledge, he did not know, but it felt oddly natural to look upon the world this way.

He should have felt a twinge of his old revulsion, he knew, to see the pervasive threads of magic. They were everywhere, tangled and intricate, unavoidable. They connected every living thing in a latticework of energy, from the smallest spark of life in a fluttering insect or a coarse blade of grass to the more pronounced auras of his companions. He had once thought to hide from magic, to spurn its touch in all capacities by strict choice, or to tolerate only brief exposure when required. He could see now how absurd those intentions had been. Magic was everywhere, surrounding them, inside them, inherent, inextricable. Bellimar had tried to tell him so when they first met, though he had not been ready to hear it. That force could be used for great destruction and evil, as he had seen, but at the same time it was the essence of life at its purest. Looking upon its beauty and complexity with newfound sight, it was hard to see it as anything other than a gift. He could scarcely bear to look away from it, even for a moment.

And so it was that he had an instant of warning when the first attack came.

Tendrils of power came snaking through the mist toward them. Silent and invisible, they did not register to his mundane sight, but to his magical sight they stood out in stark relief and writhed with violent purpose. They darted toward him, grasping, and he struck out with both swords on pure reflex. The naked steel blazed and parted the tendrils of light as it would flesh, and Amric felt a surge of savage joy. He ducked under a sweeping hook and slashed through the coil behind it, and the last of them blackened and faded.

He glanced back to find the others in wary crouches, looking around with expressions of bewilderment. They could not see such concealed attacks, and so it would be on his shoulders to protect them.

Mocking laughter drifted to them. "Crude, but effective," Xenoth called. "You are full of surprises, wilding."

The white mist billowed and swirled, ebbing back from either side of their path like waves pulling at the shore. A huge tunnel opened in the fog, giving them a clear line of sight all the way to the foot of the stairs which led to the raised platform upon which the Gate rested. Only one thing obstructed their path, a lone figure in black robes with arms spread to part the gathering mists.

"There is no need for this, Adept," Amric shouted. "No need for further destruction and death. You have no place in this world, and we want no part of yours. Shut down the Gate and leave here forever."

"You are wrong on all counts, boy," Xenoth sneered in response. "You may want nothing of my world, but it is still the world that birthed you. For it to live on, it requires all that this one has to give. As for my *place*, as you put it—" Flame erupted from his hands and curled up his arms. "My place is wherever I choose to set foot."

Xenoth threw his hands forward and sent gouts of fire hurtling toward Amric.

Borric paced the docks, and with each heavy stride he lowered a booted heel with a sharp report. He bellowed orders to his tired men as he moved, punctuating his imperatives with the occasional cuff or shove to spur greater haste. Hard at work alongside the city guard were a number of men from the private forces of the lords and merchants. Some had seen the necessity of his plan, and had contributed their manpower toward the salvation of all.

He scowled out at the mouth of the harbor, where flecks of lantern light bobbed with the waves, marking the staggered departure of over a dozen ships. Others had looked only to their own needs.

He raked his gaze over the throngs of people crowding the docks and trailing away into the city. More arrived every moment, laden with their belongings. Borric shook his head. Piles of such possessions were mounting near the docks, where the people were forced to discard them before boarding the ships. Only food, people, and the clothes on their backs would be permitted; there was no room for anything else. Even so, the entire operation was moving far too slow for his tastes. At any moment, he expected to see a swarm of fang and claw overtake the back ranks of the crowd, and the screams to begin. Borric swallowed, blinking rapidly to clear the sudden, vivid vision.

A shout rang out nearby, and Borric flinched, half-turning toward the sound. It was just the captain of the cargo ship, however, declaring it full. Borric looked it over and then nodded to the men on the docks. With efficient motions, they cast the lines free and sent the ship lumbering into the bay.

Borric counted the remaining ships for the hundredth time that night, weighing them against the straggling multitudes of people. He pursed his lips. He was no seaman, but by his rough estimations it would be a close thing indeed. Even purged of their trade goods as well as anything else that could be sacrificed for space or weight, many of the vessels were already riding quite low in the water, overburdened with human cargo.

And the stream of people continued, disgorged from the city at a maddening pace.

Borric turned on his heel and thundered down the docks, raising his voice to a bellow again.

Amric ducked behind a crumbled wall as a spray of rock showered down around him. He leaned against the cool, pitted stone, panting for breath. Xenoth's scornful laughter followed him.

"Your friends have deserted you, wilding. What did you expect of such insects?"

Amric remained silent. The Adept's initial assault had buffeted him like a thunderstorm, but he had held his ground long enough to cover the retreat of his companions. That short, furious exchange had almost been his undoing, however. Xenoth attacked and changed tactics with such speed that one strike had barely registered before the next was worming past his defenses from another direction. Only a combination of his instinctual wilding magic and the knowledge from Bellimar had kept those killing forces at bay for the seconds he needed to escape.

He looked down. One of his swords still burned bright with flame. The other had become a blackened, useless twist of metal, destroyed in deflecting some strange volley of sticky, clinging fire the Adept had thrown at him. He cast it aside.

"Come now, boy!" Xenoth shouted, a note of impatience souring his tone. "We have already proven that you are no match for me. Let us dispense with the games and finish this. You may have lived like a beast, but you can still die like a man."

Amric ground his teeth. It was evident that he could not fight a defensive battle here. The Adept was a master at this form of combat, while he was only beginning to understand the fundamentals involved. Well, if the game could not be won, it was time to change the rules.

He drew in power, took a deep breath, and lunged out from behind the wall. The Adept was stalking toward him, and his hard features lit with triumph. Amric thrust out his free hand, fingers splayed, and focused his will. Ribbons of light writhed toward the man, and his foe's expression turned to one of concentration as he warded off the attack with rapid motions.

"Now where did you learn that, boy?" Xenoth demanded, his brow furrowing. "I do not—"

And Amric hit him with the other attack. With the frontal assault to keep the Adept busy, he had sent a hammer-blow of energy to the side, around and through the ruins, looping back to approach from an unexpected direction. It struck Xenoth with a detonation of such force that Amric felt it like a blow to his chest, and it threw the black-robed man sideways. Xenoth lurched to his feet, livid with fury. He had opened his mouth to voice some new threat when Amric pulled a thick marble column down onto him.

It fell with a resounding crash, and a cloud of dust rose to mingle with the mist as tons of cold rock settled to the turf. The warrior watched, holding his breath. Had he managed to catch the Adept by surprise?

Sudden instinct flared in warning, and he dove to the side. A lance of flame sizzled through the space he had been only moments before, coming from behind just as his own attack had done. With an ear-splitting report, the center of the column exploded, sending jagged shards of marble the size of a man hurtling outward. Xenoth rose from the wreckage with teeth bared in rage and murder in his eyes. He took a step toward Amric, then staggered to the side and put his hand to the rock for support.

Good, Amric thought with grim satisfaction. The man was not invincible after all.

The moment of weakness was fleeting, however. Xenoth straightened and glared his hatred. "For that, boy, I will make your death a slow and painful one."

The man spread his arms like black wings, his hands formed into claws. In an instant, Amric was fighting for his life. The attacks came from every direction, everything from towering walls of force to needle-sharp talons of fire. They rained down upon him, circled him, drove at him from all sides. They slammed at him, staggered him, bloodied him. He slapped some away with warding gestures, writhed between darts of death with cat-like grace, and sent his sword whistling through ribbons of fire to send them crumbling into ash. His blade, wreathed in flame, wove a glittering net around him, and his movements became a blur. He gave himself over to pure instinct, lost himself in the dance of battle, and gave his wilding magic free reign. The presence within answered his call, roaring to the surface with primal fury, and the two became one as never before. Amric lashed out with both steel and magic, faster than the eye could follow, in total unison of body and mind.

The moment seemed at once endless, poised forever on the edge of a razor, and yet over all too soon. The attacks ceased, and Amric spun to one knee at the center of a blackened crater. He held his sword held back and swept outward, and each breath seared in his chest.

Xenoth stood frozen, his eyes wide. He raised his hands again and hesitated for only the briefest instant, but it was enough. Amric burst into motion, darting from view and disappearing into the ruins. He staggered and clutched his side as he ran through the mists, but he wore a grim smile. They had each drawn blood in this first clash, and he was still standing. Moreover, he had seen something new and unexpected in the Adept's expression, there in those closing seconds.

He had seen fear.

The men on the docks paused in their work, craning their necks back toward the city. Borric looked at the upturned faces. Their eyes were wide with apprehension, and shadows played across their smudged features, snared between the cold light of the moon and the warm light of the flickering torches. The captain turned to look as well.

He let out a slow breath. There was nothing to see yet. The city streets ramped down to the docks in a series of wide switchbacks and stairways carved into the slope, and the buildings and boulevards all stood dark and empty. The steady stream of humanity had slowed to a trickle and then stopped altogether, but many still stood flocked together on the quays, seeking places on the remaining ships. As Borric watched, a ripple of motion passed through the throng of people as the citizens of Keldrin's Landing turned to gaze back into the city's heart as well.

The eastern gate could not be seen from the docks, but all could hear the approach of the swarm. A low, unearthly sound had been building as a background hum for long minutes, and it was rising to a fever pitch. It reached a crescendo, and the crowd held its collective breath.

Something slammed into the distant gate with thunderous force, and the sound rang out in the night like hammer upon anvil. Metal screamed and wood split with a cracking report, and it seemed to Borric that the very ground beneath his feet trembled from the blow. The sound of the advancing swarm of creatures, muted before by the mighty city wall, was freed. The shrieking roar of countless bestial voices, raised together in mindless fury, echoed over the city.

Borric's blood ran cold at the sound. There was nothing of nature or reason in that sound, nothing even of predators hunting for survival. Rather, it was a chorus of torment and madness, of pain and blind, lashing rage. The primitive part of his mind that screamed for self-preservation wanted only to find a deep, dark hole and hide in it until death had passed him by, but he shook himself with an effort. He looked around and found the people rooted in place, frozen with terror.

He climbed onto a nearby crate, drew a breath, and boomed a wordless shout as loud as he could manage over the crowd. The men and women blinked, startled from their stupor, and turned to him with blank stares.

"Faster now, people!" he bellowed. "Make your choice between the belly of a boat and the bellies of those fiends up there. One or the other will have you by the morning light!"

The crowd surged forward, pressing onto the docks.

He shouted, "Keep it orderly and help your fellows, or you will be swimming instead!"

Borric jumped down from the crate and pushed one of his men into motion, then stooped to help a citizen who had stumbled back to her feet. He strode down the docks, shouting orders and casting frequent looks up at the darkened city looming above.

Amric peered through a crack in the stone, watching the tall figure of the Adept move through the ruins with a wary stride. Without warning, Xenoth whirled and sent fire lancing into the mist. The warrior's heart skipped a beat, fearing one of the Sil'ath had been found. After a moment, however, the Adept turned back with an angry oath, and Amric let out a breath of relief.

Xenoth stalked back and forth, scanning the ruins for his prey, but he did not roam far from the stairway leading to the Gate. Amric cursed. He had allowed the man to catch fleeting glimpses of his movements between piles of rubble, and though he had drawn occasional fire, the Adept had refused to be lured away from the platform. He had to find some way to divert Xenoth's attention to such an extent that Syth and Halthak could slip behind him and up to the Gate. This was proving difficult enough, but it was only the first step. Assuming those two could find a way to shut down the Gate, the Adept would doubtless react by slaying them both and reactivating the device. Fundamental to the success of the plan was preventing Xenoth from taking such action, and Amric had to find the way.

He raised his voice and shouted, "This is madness, Adept. What gives you the right to end an entire world?" He then spun and glided away, staying low and out of sight.

Xenoth cocked his head, orienting upon the sound, and turned his steps in that direction. His hands twitched and clenched at his sides. "You know why it must be now, wilding," he shouted. "The Nar'ath threat must be contained. They cannot be permitted to gain a foothold in Aetheria." He tilted his head, listening. "But that only made the matter more urgent. This pitiful world has been scheduled for destruction for some time now, and therein, I think, lies your true question."

Xenoth neared the tumble of rock and raised his hands in anticipation, but spun around in shock when Amric's voice came from a different direction. "And your answer, fiend?"

The Adept gave a cold smile and a rueful shake of his head, and altered course. "Are you a fiend when you hunt game, boy?" he called out. "Are you a monster when you draw nourishment from the flesh of a lesser creature?"

"It is not the same," Amric snarled in response. "You are planning the death of an entire *world*. Countless lives snuffed out."

"So that countless others may live," Xenoth insisted, his eyes narrowed as he searched the mist-shrouded darkness. "Aetheria is home to the greatest civilization in all the stars, and the wonders it has achieved throughout the millennia do not come without cost. Our world alone cannot support our needs. Sacrifices must be made. This world is not the first to give its life to the greater good, nor will it be the last."

Amric knelt in a tall patch of damp grass, peering around a fallen column. There, near the foot of the stairs leading to the Gate, a flicker of movement. A pair of dark figures crept toward the foot of the stairs, hiding in the mantle of shadow in the lee of the platform.

"The greater good?" Amric demanded, putting all the scorn that he could muster in his tone. "All your achievements are steeped in the blood of innocents. No amount of noble intent can justify such a price!"

Xenoth barked a laugh. "Your perspective is skewed, boy. Doubtless the game you slew for sustenance would put a higher price on its own life as well, if it could."

"It is not the same," Amric repeated, flushed with anger. "A hunter takes what he needs so that he and his family can survive, but he takes one of many, and the herd replenishes. You speak of taking in order to achieve greater wonders, and of leaving behind a world barren of all life. There is no comparison."

"Perhaps not," the Adept growled, sliding around the end of the column to face Amric. "Then again, to us, perhaps your world is just one of the herd to be culled for our use."

He lunged forward with a triumphant shout, and fire roared toward Amric. The warrior, awaiting his appearance, rolled to one side and sent a lance of light at the other in return. The blow shattered on a glittering shield raised at the last instant by Xenoth, and Amric sprinted further into the ruins. Xenoth spat an oath and started to follow, then caught himself and glanced back at the platform. Syth and Halthak were scrambling up the steps, twin shadows against the pale marble.

With a scream of outrage, Xenoth ran for the platform, unleashing strike after strike as he went. Lashes of fire tore great gouges out of the stone, and Syth and Halthak darted back and forth upon the stairs in a frantic effort to avoid them. A blazing whip sheared through a section of the stairway beneath Syth, and it began to fall away. He sprang from the falling segment in a prodigious leap, and sudden wind caught him at the apex, propelling him toward the stairs. Before he could land, however, a snaking blow hammered into him and sent him spinning over the side, into the darkness.

Amric reappeared in a mad sprint. He had doubled back when he realized that the lure had failed, and he struck out with a sledge of force that threw Xenoth from his feet. The black-robed Adept rolled into a crouch, facing the warrior with a snarl. He swept out with an arm, and a huge boulder ripped free of the turf and catapulted toward Amric. The latter dove to one side, raising a hasty shield to deflect the giant missile, but it collided with such force that he was sent flying back and to the side. He slammed into a marble boulder, and his world exploded in pain and flashes of light as he fought to retain consciousness.

Valkarr and Sariel appeared as if from nowhere, twin specters darting at the Adept from either side with flashing steel. Rather than try to stop them individually, however, Xenoth brought both fists together and slammed them to the ground, sending a circular wave rushing outward that threw them back into the mist. The Adept stood and extended one hand toward Halthak, still clambering up the stairs. The step beneath the Half-Ork's foot exploded in a spray of rock and he fell, tumbling end over end on the punishing stone until he came to a crashing halt at the bottom.

Halthak spat out blood and pushed to all fours as Xenoth strode toward him. The cuts and bruises on his craggy face faded and vanished, and his breathing grew steadier.

"Ah yes," the Adept sneered. "One of the insects. The scrub talent, the lay healer. I warned you once not to cross me, that I would make your end far more agonizing than you could imagine. Insect, you will find now that I am a man of my word."

Xenoth put his hands together before him, and his brow furrowed in concentration. A ball of sickly green and black energy gathered there. It blazed and grew like a tiny sun of malevolent purpose. Xenoth growled with the effort, and his hands began to shake.

Amric rose to his feet, his legs wobbling beneath him. He found his sword a dozen feet away, its flame extinguished. He blinked, trying to clear his vision, as his wilding magic railed within him.

Halthak bared his tusks in defiance, and gathered to spring at the Adept. Xenoth lashed out, and the sphere of dark energy struck the healer full in the chest. Halthak was blown back onto the stairs with crushing impact. He slumped there for a moment, dazed, limbs splayed out on the marble steps. Then he lifted his head to stare at his torso in shock. The robes covering his midsection had been blasted away to form a gaping hole, and the edges of the cloth were blackened and smoking. Underneath, a circle of the same foul green and black energy was boiling and churning as it gnawed away at the Half-Ork's torso. It grew, widening and deepening, chewing an ever larger hole in his bare, grey flesh. Halthak slid to his knees at the base of the steps and screamed, a wrenching sound of exquisite suffering, and his head fell forward in concentration. The growth of the cavity slowed, and it began to shrink as the flesh knitted around it. The green blazed even brighter in response, however, and the energies within swirled faster. The void began to expand again, more swiftly than before.

Xenoth gave a harsh, pitiless laugh. "It feeds on magic. The more you draw upon, the more you pour into healing yourself, the faster it will grow and consume you. And the more pain you will feel. A fitting punishment, I think, for a meddling insect like yourself."

Halthak screamed again and fell to his side in the grass, curling around his injury. The Adept stepped back with a cold smile.

"I warned you fools," he said. "I deal out retribution and death at the behest of the Council. It is all I do, and there is nothing on this pathetic world that can stop me."

"Xenoth!" The shout brought the Adept around in a swirl of black robes. Amric stalked toward him, down the center of the tunnel carved from the mist. There was a slight limp to his gait, but his stride was purposeful. His sword jutted from one fist, and his storm-grey eyes were hard as steel. His gaze flicked to the struggling form of Halthak for an instant, and then returned to fix upon his foe. White flame, bright as the sun, burst out around the blade and kindled within his eyes.

"Bold words," he growled. "Come prove them."

Morland stood alone at a towering window in the great hall of his mansion, his hands clasped behind his back. His dark eyes were unfocused and saw nothing of the majestic scene wrought in colored glass before him, or the lush, exotic gardens beyond.

Distant, muffled shouts and a soft thump against the great double doors at the end of the hall broke into his reverie, and he turned toward that end of the room with an expectant scowl. The doors remained closed, however, and the sounds were not repeated. He muttered an oath under his breath and turned back to the window.

What was taking those incompetent fools so long, anyway? He had been very clear about the need for haste, but such reinforcement of the obvious should not have been necessary, in any event. His watchmen had brought back word that the townsfolk had returned, having somehow eluded the grasp of the Nar'ath, and that the city was being overrun by some new, overwhelming force. That news had spread like wildfire through his men, and there had been no hesitation to comply when he ordered them to prepare for flight.

The escape plan was simple, and one he had prepared well in advance in case this tumultuous night came to the worst. His stewards and private guards were to collect the most necessary of his belongings, and then escort him to the docks. There, he would signal in the clipper that was anchored out in the bay, a very swift personal vessel that would carry him away from this wretched place. It was time to pursue his fortune elsewhere.

The clipper was large, but it would not carry all those still in his employ. No matter. Many swords would need to remain on the docks anyway to keep the rabble from viewing his ship as their own salvation. He permitted himself a small, cold smile. He would simply tell those left behind that they would be well compensated for their bravery, and that he would send in the next ship once his was safely away. They were coarse men with credulous minds, after all.

Morland flinched as one of the torches sputtered and died in its sconce at the far end of the room. That corner of the hall fell into deeper shadow, and Morland stared for a long moment. Nothing moved there, and the tension eased from him. A sudden shiver caught him by surprise. When had it become cold in the room? He eyed the cavernous hearth, devoid of its usual fire at the moment, and then shrugged it off. He would be leaving soon; there was no time to bother with such worries.

He forced his attention to other matters, and wondered if Nyar and Nylien had completed their mission. It was a pity they had not returned yet. He had become somewhat accustomed to the twin Alfen assassins lurking about, and they had a way of turning up at just the right time, but it seemed unlikely this time. They were utterly mad, the both of them, but they had proven to be very useful tools, peerless at dispensing death at his command. They would be difficult to replace.

The merchant crossed the room, his silk slippers whispering on the vast, intricately woven rug. He stood before a window opposite the first, one that looked out onto a portion of his estate grounds rather than onto his gardens. He squinted into the darkness, and then sighed. He found himself wishing he had been less efficient about disposing of the farseer once the Nar'ath had retreated. The young fool's talents would have proven useful in monitoring the progress of the creatures now invading the city, and in choosing his escape route. But alas, the lad had known or guessed too much regarding Morland's arrangement with the Nar'ath, and he could not risk such rumors following him to more civilized regions. Plan for every eventuality, leave nothing to chance.

Another torch died with a hissing pop, and Morland whirled about. Three more followed in rapid succession, and he took an involuntary step back. The far end of the room descended into darkness so absolute that he could no longer discern the gleaming brass that bound the doors.

"Is someone there?" he asked.

Laughter, soft and rich, drifted out of the darkness. Morland jumped at the sound and then remembered himself. He was the lord of this manor, and there would be hell to pay if one of his men was interrupting him with anything other than news of readiness for their departure. He drew up to his full height with fists clenched and demanded, "Who is there?"

The blackness drew together like an eddying pool and formed into the shape of a man. With one long step, the man broke into the light, but wisps of shadow seemed to cling to him still, as if the darkness was reluctant to be left behind. He was a tall man, sharp-featured and broad of shoulder. He was clad in dark greyish robes, with hair as black as polished jet. He regarded the merchant with a faint smile upon his lips.

Morland opened his mouth, hesitated, shut it again. The stranger radiated cool assurance, and there was an august quality to his bearing that left the merchant with an involuntary desire to bend his knee before him. This was a man in the prime of his power, accustomed to rule. And, Morland thought with a frown, he looked somehow familiar.

The stranger began a slow stroll around the enormous room, considering the lavish furnishings in silence. He paused before a huge tapestry that brushed the floor at his feet and soared to the ceiling high above. He looked it up and down, tilting his head to one side, and then resumed walking. Morland took a few shuffling steps, studying the man's profile.

Morland's eyes narrowed. "I know you," he said.

The stranger gave a soft laugh that sent a chill crawling along the merchant's spine. "You may remember me. You may recall meeting me in this very room, mere days ago." The force of the man's gaze turned upon him, pinning him in place for an instant, and then slid away once more. "But you do not know me, merchant."

"You bear a strong resemblance to that Bellimar fellow, who came here with the swordsman," Morland said. "Are you some relation of his?"

"I am that man," the other responded. "I am Bellimar."

"Impossible," Morland said with a derisive snort. "That one was bent with age, with hair of silver. You are decades younger."

"Only in appearance," the stranger said. He smiled, and there was nothing of warmth in the expression. "I have fed very well, this night."

The merchant blinked and shook his head. "Believe what you will, I have no time for such games. The city has fallen, and any who wish to live must flee Keldrin's Landing immediately."

"I know," said the man who called himself Bellimar. He began to walk again.

Morland's brow furrowed as he watched the stranger's gliding, unhurried progress around the room. His tone hardened as he stated, "My personal guard will be coming through those doors at any moment to escort me to safety."

"No," Bellimar said. "I am afraid they will not."

"And why not?" the merchant demanded.

The other chuckled. "Someone gave them the notion that you would be remaining here, instead. That you were, in fact, already dead."

Morland's breath caught in his throat. "My men would never believe such a ludicrous falsehood."

"I prefer to call it more of a temporal inaccuracy," Bellimar said with a dismissive shrug. "Regardless, some elected to leave, while others chose instead to remain and voice their skepticism." He turned to the merchant with a smile, and the torchlight danced in his eyes, causing them to give off an eerie, lambent glow. "As I mentioned, I fed well tonight."

"What do you want here?" Morland demanded, suppressing a shudder.

"I came to fulfill a promise, Morland. I came for you."

It took a few tries before the merchant could make any sound pass his lips. "I do not understand," he finally managed.

"Someone I cared deeply about perished by your hand tonight, merchant," Bellimar said, and his tone had become as cold and hard as ice. "Which reminds me, I found some instruments you appear to have lost."

The man's dark robes fluttered and a pair of heavy, oblong objects tumbled across the ornate rug toward Morland. They took irregular bounces, and one veered to the side in a semi-circular path, rocking to a halt. The other rolled to a stop against his slippered foot, facing upward. Glassy eyes stared up at him, unseeing, and the mouths gaped in frozen, unending screams. The severed heads ended at the neck in ragged flesh, torn from their bodies by main force. The skin was sunken and bloodless, but there was no mistaking the slanted features or the white shocks of hair that had belonged to the Elvaren assassins, Nyar and Nylien. Morland stared in horror.

"They fancied themselves creatures of the night," Bellimar mused with a dark chuckle. "*My* night. Imagine their surprise to encounter the Lord of the Night himself." He tilted his head, studying the grisly objects. "Actually, you do not have to imagine. You can still see that surprise in their expressions."

Morland wrenched his gaze away from the horrific sight at his feet and found something even worse awaiting him. Bellimar had not moved, but the shadows gathered to him in crawling, serpentine movements. The light in the great hall dimmed to a ruddy twilight as the remaining torches burned low, coughing and sputtering and fighting for life. The stranger's smile widened to reveal rows of long, gleaming fangs. His eyes burned scarlet and feral.

An inhuman voice hissed from that roiling mass of shadow. "We will not be disturbed, merchant. There is enough time left to us to ensure that you feel a measure of the suffering you have caused. And I will make certain that you cause no more."

Morland's mouth worked in terror, but only a strangled gasp emerged. His breath frosted in a wisp before him.

"Come now, Morland," Bellimar said, his words raw and guttural and pulsating with hunger. "You are a man of business. You of all people should know that, sooner or later, one's debts must always be paid."

The shadows rolled forward at a slow, inexorable pace, closing around him.

Morland found his voice at last, but there was no one in the mansion to hear the screams.

The ruins of Queln blazed with light and thunder as Amric and Xenoth fought. There was no longer any semblance of guile or strategy to their actions, and no more words were exchanged. None were necessary. Each man stood his ground, hurling his rage and determination at the other in the form of primal energies, seeking to hammer his foe into oblivion. The Essence Gate towered above them on its high platform of stone, a continual, roaring presence that made the very air shimmer with the power being drawn into it. It looked down upon the battle below with an uncaring eye.

Amric gave himself over to the fury of battle, fighting on purest instinct, and his wilding magic was a fierce ally in tune with every fiber of his being. He became a melding of man and beast, of steel and magic, and he could not have begun to say where one left off and the other began. His sword flickered, slicing and deflecting too fast for the eye to follow, and he sent attack after attack lancing toward his foe.

He drove forward.

Without even knowing how he did it, he drew upon the rising tide of magic within him and all around him. He pulled it from the air that crackled and sang at the point of overload, and he reached deep into the ground beneath his feet to tap into the immense ley lines coursing there. He drew it in until his body burned and he thought he must surely burst into flame, and then he reached for still more.

Amric pressed the attack, strike and counterstrike at lightning speed. Xenoth's eyes grew wide. Perspiration ran freely down the hard lines of his face, and his dark hair hung damp and lank across his brow. Step by grudging step, the black-robed Adept was forced to give ground. Amric bared his teeth in a wordless snarl and pressed harder.

He took another arduous step forward, and Xenoth took another back. He pummeled at Xenoth's defenses in wave after wave. He felt the other's shield crack before his onslaught and uttered a growl of triumph. Another slow step, like walking against a hurricane wind, and his foe's heels were against the marble steps that led up to the Gate. Xenoth felt behind himself for the first step, and then the second. He stumbled and fell back against the cold marble, his motions frantic. Amric put another foot forward, pressing the advantage.

His legs wobbled beneath him.

The world tilted and dimmed for a sickening instant, and Amric shook himself with a curse. Not now. Not when victory was so close. He had been pushing too hard, running up against the mortal limits of endurance and punishment all night. Now it seemed that even Bellimar's gift of borrowed vitality was waning at last. Even the darting presence of the wilding magic within him had grown sluggish and confused. His eyes fell on the crumpled form of Halthak, lying too still in the tangled grass at the base of the stairway by the Adept, and his jaw clenched. He thought of all that had been sacrificed for this moment. He would not succumb now.

He brought the world back into focus with an effort, but the damage had been done. Xenoth was on his feet once again, and there was an exultant glint in his dark eyes. Both men sent blazes of light lashing at each other, and for long seconds they traded frenzied blows, neither giving ground. Then Amric's defenses faltered, his exhausted reaction too slow by a bare instant, and a coil of energy snaked through, rocking him back on his heels. The next blows fell less than a heartbeat later, before he could recover his balance, and they slammed him to the ground with crushing force. His sword slid away into the grass, its flame extinguished.

Abrupt silence fell over the ruins, except for the background hum of the forces being drawn to the gate and the labored breathing of the two combatants. Amric rolled to his side, dizzy and disoriented, his unfocused eyes rolling about in an attempt to determine from which direction the attack would come.

"You are even stronger than I thought, wilding," Xenoth panted after a moment, bracing his hands upon his knees as he gasped for breath. "You would be fearsome indeed, if you had even a modicum of skill. But I warned you before about overextending yourself. This battle ends now." The man straightened with obvious effort and started toward Amric.

"Damn right it does," growled a voice from the ground.

A gnarled hand of pebbled grey flesh lashed out from the grasses at Xenoth's feet and wrapped around his ankle.

"What the—" The Adept staggered, caught by surprise, and almost fell. He spun to find the fallen figure of Halthak looking up at him. The Half-Ork's talons tightened, digging deep into the man's flesh. Xenoth cried out in pain as his leg buckled beneath him.

"Fear not, Adept," Halthak said, baring crooked teeth in a broad, grim smile. "Nothing down here but us insects."

With a clap of impact, the healer released his magic into the Adept.

It was just as he had done to the mad Wyrgen Grelthus in Stronghold, reversing the normal flow of his healing magic and sending his own injuries slamming into the other. By that point, the boiling mass of greenish energy had spread to cover Halthak's entire torso. Sickly black tendrils wound into his extremities, climbing his neck to his jawline and threading along the flesh of his forearms that showed past the sleeves of his robes. All of this withdrew as if time itself had reversed to undo the damage. The corruption retreated from his limbs and crawled across his chest, contracting to a burning hole of seething energy that dwindled and vanished. Halthak let out a gasp of relief even as Xenoth cried out in new agony. The Half-Ork released his grip on the man's leg and scrambled back from him.

The Adept stumbled a few steps and stood with legs braced wide apart, swaying in place. A ravenous green glow lit his tunic from beneath, and blight crept up over his throat, darkening the skin there. His eyes bulged with disbelief as he clawed at his chest. His uncomprehending stare leapt from himself to the healer and back.

"It feeds on magic, I believe you said." Amric dragged himself to his feet, leveling an iron gaze at the Adept. "The more you pour into it, the faster it grows and consumes you."

Xenoth whirled to face him, fear flooding his features.

"Earlier this night," Amric continued in a pitiless tone, "you also told me that there is a time and place to hold nothing back." He gave the Adept a wintry smile. "I could not agree more."

The warrior stepped forward in a lunge and thrust out both hands. He called up every last ounce of power he could muster and hurled it all at Xenoth. Light and flame roared at the Adept, hammering into him, driving him back against the marble stairs. The black-robed man howled and thrashed beneath the torrent, trying to deflect it or wriggle free, but it seized him and pinned him in place. Rather than incinerate him, however, the flood of energy was drawn into him, feeding the sinister affliction that consumed him. The blight spread at a fiery pace, green and black strands writhing across his limbs, gnawing and tightening with predatory swiftness. Xenoth's cries rose to an inhuman shriek and then cut off abruptly. His tall form collapsed in on itself, then withered and burned. In mere moments it became unrecognizable as anything that had ever been human.

When only black ash remained, scorched across the pale marble of the stairway, only then did Amric allow the torrent to cease. He fell forward to all fours, the breath searing in his chest. His wilding magic swirled and darted in weary jubilation, and he allowed himself a small smile in response. *Well done, my friend,* he thought. *Surviving to this point was all part of my plan, but I did not much care for our chances.*

The magic pulsed back at him with a sensation very much like humor, and Amric blinked at the sly intelligence he sensed. It seemed there was more to this mysterious presence than he had realized.

Such matters would have to wait, however. Their work was not yet done.

He tried to stand, failed, tried again. Strong but gentle hands clutched at his arms and helped him on his third attempt. Faces swam before him: Halthak, his coarse features pinched with concern; Syth, bruised and battered but alive; Valkarr and Sariel, the visages of home. He mumbled something about the Gate and made for the platform.

Amric remembered little of their ascension to the Essence Gate. At the time, it seemed an eternity of climbing and stumbling, of lifting hands and distant, encouraging voices. The sounds rose in volume, became sharper, resolved into a single insistent voice, repeating his name over and over.

"No time," he insisted, his words slurred. "Have to reach the Gate."

"We are here, sword-brother," Valkarr responded in the patient tone of repetition. "And we have found no way to shut it down."

The statement caused a chill within him and Amric sobered, felt the fog lift in grudging stages. He blinked and looked around. His friend's statements were true. He sat on the raised platform, and the others were gathered around him.

The Essence Gate loomed over him, and he was awestruck by its ancient majesty. The massive arch of stone towered sixty feet or more into the air, and each of the worn sigils carved into its broad surface was the height of a tall man as well. An aura of brilliant light surrounded the device, radiating from it in measured pulses as if the device drew long, ponderous breaths. The sigils pulsed with an orange-red glow to the same slow beat. Within the arch stretched a shining surface, almost too bright to look upon. Amric's second sight showed rivers of energy running into that rippling aperture, flowing into as to a giant drain, never to return.

"We have found no controls, on or around it," Valkarr said, his jaw muscles tightening as he regarded the mammoth device. "It continues to empty our world of life."

"We thought you might be able to..." Sariel trailed off, ending with a vague gesture.

Use magic, Amric thought with a bitter grimace. Of course.

He studied the Gate, observing the movement of energies around it. His wilding magic stirred and quivered, though whether with trepidation or eagerness, he was not certain. Not knowing how to proceed, he reached out with his senses, seeking to touch it and better understand it.

To his surprise, something touched back.

An expansive presence followed that initial contact, flooding him with its awareness, and an eager murmuring pattered against his mind. Amric's mouth fell open in shock. It was an ancient thing, timeless and patient. It was vast and powerful, but oddly compliant—and it was very much alive. It whispered to him, eager to yield its secrets, and there was a soft susurration at the back of his mind as it conversed with his wilding magic as well.

Hardly daring to hope, he inquired after the information he sought, and the Gate responded to that encouragement with a surging desire to please. A score of voices babbled at him in cheerful cacophony, and he struggled to single out one at a time to follow. In moments he understood how to return the mighty Gate to a state of quiescence, and he knew how to travel through it to Aetheria, the master world on the other side. He also knew, beyond a shadow of uncertainty, that there was no way to destroy or permanently disable the Gate from this side. A cold pit opened in his stomach.

The roar of the Essence Gate lessened, and its radiant corona diminished to a faint, clinging nimbus of light. The surface within the arch darkened until it no longer blazed like the sun, and instead resembled the moon-kissed ripple of the sea at night. The sigils dimmed until they burned low, like dying embers.

Amric let out a slow breath and exchanged a weary glance with his companions.

The Gate was dormant once more. Their world was safe, for the moment.

CHAPTER 28

The *Silverwing* carved through the waves. It was a squat and ungainly ship, wallowing in each trough and showing little of the grace its name implied as it carried its burden of refugees out into the Vellayen Sea. All the same, Borric decided as he stood on the aft deck and watched the docks of Keldrin's Landing grow smaller in the distance, right at this moment the sturdy vessel was a thing of beauty to him.

The *Silverwing* was the last ship to slip away from the land, and thus it had an unobstructed view of the trap that had closed its jaws just behind them all.

In the half-light of the yielding night, the city teemed with motion. Dark, twisted shapes slithered through the streets and crawled over the buildings. Some moved together in seething masses, like great swarms of angry insects. Others, larger and heavier, stalked amid their smaller brethren, brushing them aside as they moved. Still others appeared as glimmers of cold light, wraiths that flickered here and there like whispered tales. The creatures tore at the structures and raised their voices in furious shrieks that carried across the water to those on the boat.

Borric watched, mesmerized. His broken arm hung in its sling, seeming to throb in time with the rolling motions of the ship, and he gave a shudder that owed nothing to the salty breeze. The escape had been a close thing indeed. It would be quite some time before he closed his eyes without seeing the burning hatred in their bestial stares or hearing the rasp of their talons on the docks as the sailors threw the last of the ropes that bound the ship to shore. He hoped that no one had been foolish enough to remain behind, hoping to weather the invasion. If so, there was nothing to be done for them now. He forced his mind to other matters.

What had happened to drive the magical creatures of the area, normally so reclusive, to such lengths of madness? It was a question that had been asked often over these many months since the troubles began, but he found himself no closer now to an answer.

The worst of it had always emanated from the east, somewhere in or beyond that vast, terrible forest. The ominous storm brewing over it was only the latest evil to gather there. Borric glanced in that direction, squinting into the distance, and blinked in surprise. The sullen, reddish glow on the horizon had diminished, and the black mantle across the sky had broken into fragments. Even as he watched, the storm clouds clotted together in lesser groups and continued their grudging dispersal.

The captain of the *Silverwing* stepped up beside Borric. The grizzled old sailor had a lean, pitted face that resembled a barnacle with a greying beard. One knobby hand extended to caress the ship's rail in a familiar, unconscious gesture filled with pride. In all the chaos, Borric had not even caught the captain's name, despite working shoulder to shoulder with the man for long, frantic minutes during their escape; somehow it seemed absurd to ask after it now.

"Did well for a one-armed man," the captain said in a rasping tone. "Pulled your load. You'd make a fair sailor, if you've a mind for it."

Borric chuckled. "Let us just say that I did not lack for motivation, especially there at the end."

The captain gave a dry chuckle. He jerked his chin toward the retreating city. "They are calming, now."

It was true. The frenzy of activity at the city was slowing. The creatures were no longer incensed and destructive, but rather were milling about. They appeared more restless and confused than angry.

"What do you make of it?" the captain asked.

Borric shrugged one shoulder and shook his head. "Perhaps they only wanted to see us gone," he said. "Perhaps we were never meant to be there in the first place."

The captain gave a noncommittal grunt. They watched for a time in companionable silence as each plunge and rise of the *Silverwing* carried them further and further away. The heavens brightened steadily with the coming dawn, and at last the creatures, no more than tiny motes in the distance by then, melted away into the ravaged structures of the city to take cover from the day.

"I am told that you are in command here," the sea captain said. There was a question behind the words.

Borric, erstwhile captain of the city guard for Keldrin's Landing, rumbled a laugh that began in his belly. "No sir," he said with a broad grin. "As of this very moment, I am just another soldier seeking safe return to my family and my home, having been away from them much too long. I am at your service for the duration of the journey, Captain."

The old sailor lifted his bearded chin in a nod, and ran another possessive stroke along the rail. Then he gave the weathered wood a pat and turned away, barking orders to his crew.

Borric remained on the aft deck for quite some time. He stood there, unmoving, until the city was no more than a hint of shadow against the sweeping majesty of the coastline. He stood there until the ghostly fingers of dawn spread across the sky, and the new day began at last in a crown of gold on the eastern horizon.

Only then did he turn away as well.

Bellimar sat cross-legged on the huge expanse of ornate rug in the great hall of Morland's estate. To his left, a pool of crimson seeped into the lavish material, casting a spreading shadow across the rich colors of its pattern. He did not spare it a glance. That work was done, and nothing remained there to hold his interest. To his right, a long, golden sliver of light stretched across the rug where the morning sun knifed its way between the heavy drapes that otherwise masked the towering window. His eyes traveled along that fiery line to where it passed within a hand's breadth of him. His skin tingled and crawled beneath his robes, as if his very flesh sought greater distance from the killing light.

It was strange to fear the sun's light again. He recalled when, all those centuries ago, he had forsaken such mundane pleasures as admiring the splendor of a sunrise in favor of a darker path, the path to power. After the Adepts struck him down and twisted his nature with their magic, he had been able to bear its touch once more; there had been some pain, certainly, but no lasting damage. He had been far too consumed with regaining his power and solving the mystery of what they had done to him, however, to waste time on such trivial victories. He found it ironic that now, with the restraints imposed so long ago lifting at last and his power rapidly returning, he craved most what was forever lost to him.

His hunger surged within, perhaps in response to his yearnings, and it railed against his inaction. It spoke to him, not with words but with inviting sensations. It was low and fierce and insistent, calling for him to follow the deaths he had dealt tonight with thousands more, and then a thousand times more after that. He was ancient and powerful, and only the blood of the masses could slake a thirst as mighty as his. He was fearsome and indomitable, and he would grind the trembling thrones of the world once more beneath his dark, remorseless heel.

It stirred ecstasy and need within him, and he was swayed. It burned through him like liquid fire, fuel for his ascension, and he exulted in the rapture of it. He closed his eyes, nostrils flaring, a cruel smile twisting his handsome features.

But he did not move.

With a twinge of regret, he pushed it all away, pushed it to the back of his mind and locked it behind a barrier of iron will. His hunger shrieked and clawed and hissed in impotent fury. *Why fight the inevitable?* it demanded, and it was no small part of him that roused in response to the thought. The barrier cracked, but held.

Soon it would be over. No need to fight it much longer.

He summoned images to his mind's eye. Amric, dauntless and driven, radiating a compassion and resolve that lent strength to those around him. Halthak, whose innocence and heart somehow withstood all manner of darkness around him. Syth, lost and mourning, drawing time and time again upon a well of courage and empathy he did his best to conceal. Thalya, as a wide-eyed child and later as the woman who was in some ways still a child, driving her conviction deep into him until it struck home and could not be dislodged. Her father, Drothis, a kind man driven out of fear and duty to actions that did not suit him. There had been others over his many lifetimes, but these were enough. They had changed him somehow, here at the last, and he built his fortitude upon his memories of them.

He would not become the monster that they feared, that he himself feared. He was strong enough to do what was required. All things must one day end to allow for new beginnings, he reminded himself. Sometimes it was necessary to have faith that a carefully planted seed would someday bear fruit.

Bellimar opened his eyes. He stretched his hands out before him, and there was only a faint tremble before they grew still. His hunger clamored at him, alarmed, but it was a distant, muted thing, of no particular import to him now. An abiding sense of serenity stole over him, and he smiled.

It was time to see the sunrise one last time.

He threw his arms wide in a sweeping gesture. Across the room, the heavy drapes flew open in response, flooding the great hall with the brilliance of the morn. Golden light washed over Bellimar where he sat, and he gazed in wonder upon the beauty that shone down upon him. The demonic part of him went berserk, howling in panic. Every instinct screamed for self-preservation, to writhe away from the killing light while there was still time. He convulsed in involuntary response to that most primal of directives, but he refused to succumb. He gritted his teeth and held himself rigid, motionless.

The light of the sun assailed him like a living thing, determined to seize him in its vicious grip and exact revenge for his centuries of defiance. It flayed at his flesh with relentless strokes. His pale skin cracked, blackened and burned, and still he did not avert his gaze. His shining black hair withered and fell from his head. Searing flame blossomed in his chest. His flesh began to fall away in flakes of black ash, and his robes sank inward as his tall form became wasted and skeletal.

There was less pain than he had expected, he noted with detached interest; a small mercy, that. Falling ash obscured his vision for a moment, and he waited patiently for it to clear. His sight continued to darken, however, and the golden light contracted as if the sun drew back from him. No matter.

Rest well, Thalya, thought Bellimar. Your mission is complete at last.

Then awareness faded, and the cavernous hall stood empty but for drifting black ash and the fading resonance of death.

Amric lay stretched out on the cool marble of the platform, gazing upward at the calming sky. He knew he had been dozing by the fitful, uneven leaps of the sun as it climbed to its mid-morning height.

The immense shadow of the Essence Gate fell across him. He did not glance at it. He did not need to. The Gate had not ceased its low murmurings to him since those first moments of contact, and he did not need to look upon it to sense its steady, quiescent thrumming. It was a marked transformation from the raging nexus of power it had been, but still it radiated deep, eternal patience that bespoke a readiness—an expectation—to awaken once more when called upon. Amric's jaw clenched at the thought.

A less distinct change, but no less real, was evident all around the Gate. The storm had vanished; the clouds above continued to thin, and they had lost much of their sullen glower. The white mist, insolent in the face of the rising sun, still clung to the ruins of Queln below, but the eerie cries of its tortured inhabitants had subsided. An idle breeze wound its way through the forest that encircled the ruins, like a rustling sigh of relief.

It had been only a few short hours since the Essence Gate had been shut down, but the land was already breathing easier. Perhaps it marked the beginning of recovery. Even the pulsing rivers of energy far beneath him had begun to ebb somewhat. Several major ley lines converged here, and so Queln would always be a place of power, but it was no longer the crashing maelstrom of before.

Amric sighed. He was stalling.

He rolled to his feet and stood. The others were resting a short distance away on the platform, farther from the Gate. Valkarr and Sariel were on their feet an instant after him, their expressions expectant. Halthak lifted his head and blinked large, owlish eyes. Syth was sprawled out with his head on one folded arm, and his chest rose and fell to a light snoring sound. Amric smiled as he looked upon each of them, but he sobered as he met Valkarr's gaze.

"We should have that conversation now, my friends," Amric said.

Valkarr started on a good-natured retort. Then he paused, studying his friend's expression, and merely nodded instead. Amric joined them, and they sat in a circle at the platform's edge. The warrior considered his words for a long moment, and then began speaking in a soft tone.

"When Bellimar was... inside my head, he unearthed memories of mine, truths that I either never really knew, or somehow managed to bury and forget. My earliest memories, of where I came from and how I came to be among the Sil'ath."

Amric took a breath, frowning. The others watched him, saying nothing.

"What Xenoth said was true," he said. "I was not born on this world. I was left alone as an infant, presumably when my parents were slain as Xenoth claimed, and I would have died as well if my wilding magic had not acted of its own will to save me." He held Valkarr's gaze. "It saved me by reaching out and touching the minds of the Sil'ath hunters it found nearby."

Valkarr's brow ridge rose slightly, but otherwise he betrayed no emotion whatsoever.

Amric continued, "In particular, the magic concentrated its efforts on the leader of the hunting party. It soothed his distrust of other races, and it pulled at him to investigate the concealed dwelling that held me. Once it had persuaded the Sil'ath leader to take me from there, it buried itself so deeply within my mind that even I was unaware of its presence thereafter. I think it somehow sensed the dislike of magic felt by the Sil'ath as well as the danger of something else pursuing it and meaning us harm, so it hid from both. As you already know, Valkarr, that Sil'ath warrior was your father."

He paused, waiting for a reaction. Valkarr regarded him steadily, without expression, and then asked, "And what have you concluded from these revealed truths?"

Amric swallowed and shook his head. "It was all based on a lie," he whispered. "Your family took me in because my magic compelled them to do so. The Sil'ath abhor the use of magic, and I hid that very thing in your midst. I have magic—I *am* magic—and I understand now that I can no more separate that part of me than I can put aside my own mind." Amric's voice grew hard, bitter. "Would your father have saved the life of some human infant if he had known what he was bringing into the fold? Would you all have accepted me as one of your own, as a Sil'ath warrior? Would you have made me your warmaster, and followed me into battle?"

His wilding magic stirred within, uneasy in the face of his cold anger, but he ignored it.

"No," Valkarr admitted. "None of these things would have come to pass, had your true nature been known then."

"Exactly, and that is why—"

"And that is why I am glad we did not know," Valkarr interrupted.

Amric's words tumbled to a halt. "What?"

Valkarr grinned. "I agree with you that we would have made different choices, had we known. However, in this case, we are better for the choices we *did* make, not knowing."

"You cannot mean that," Amric protested. "Think about the evidence, looking back on it now. You had a human warmaster, and closer ties with the people of Lyden than any other Sil'ath tribe permitted with outside races. You know that caused the other tribes to question your father's judgment on more than a few occasions."

"Indeed it did," Valkarr responded with a grave nod. "And yet we prospered when other tribes did not. We had the trust and aid of our human neighbors, enjoyed active trade between our peoples, and we stood together when the troubles began from the north. Moreover, our success in battle was unmatched, even among much larger tribes. I maintain that we are better for the strengths you forged among us, and I remain proud to have called you both warmaster and friend."

Amric stared at him. "How can I claim credit for anything I achieved, when it may have simply been the result of my magic influencing others on my behalf?"

"You, who worked hardest among us?" Sariel interjected with a silvery laugh. "Besides, you said yourself that your magic was hidden away all these years. Do you think it could have acted without you sensing it? Think on the effect it has had upon you since we came to this region."

"And if it did," Valkarr put in quietly, "what of it? As you said, it is a part of you. If your magic had a subtle hand in things now and again, it is not so different from Prakseth making use of his own great strength, or Varek relying upon his keen eye as a marksman."

They fell silent for a long moment at the mention of their fallen comrades.

"I appreciate your words, my friends," Amric said at last. "You cannot know how much they lift my heart. But we all know things cannot be as they once were. I can no longer be warmaster for our people."

"That is..." Valkarr began, hesitating and then lowering his gaze, "probably for the best."

Amric leaned forward and spoke with quiet vehemence. "You must be warmaster, Valkarr."

The other's eyes snapped up to find his. "Me?"

"My friend, there is no one better suited for the role. No one better able to guide our people through whatever dark days may come before the threat of the Nar'ath on this world is ended. The Nar'ath forces will not grow so swiftly, I think, without the activity caused by the Gate to feed upon. You must warn the Sil'ath and spread word of this lurking menace to the other races as well, before the Nar'ath find another source of power and become too strong to face."

Valkarr's eyes narrowed. "And you? Where will you be?"

Amric took a deep breath. "I must travel through the portal, to the home of the Adepts, and put an end to the threat of the Essence Gates."

A stunned silence greeted his statement.

Syth sat up, rubbing his eyes and squinting into the sunlight. "Are you mad?" he demanded.

"I managed to shut the Gate down, for now," Amric said, "but I see no way to disable or destroy it from this side. We are at the mercy of the Adepts as long as those devices can be used to leech the life from worlds such as ours. The Adepts, the Gates, the Nar'ath, they all owe their origins to Aetheria in some way. Aetheria holds the key to our survival. It must be done, and there is no one else."

"You will need swords you can trust to guard your back," Valkarr insisted, folding his arms across his chest. At his side, Sariel gave a fierce nod of agreement.

"And no one could ask for better than the two of you," Amric said with a sad smile. "But you are needed to lead our people, and a world steeped in magic is no place for Sil'ath warriors. You saw what just one Adept was able to do. I need to lose myself among them and seek out their secrets, not put them to the sword."

Valkarr set his jaw and regarded Amric with a deepening scowl. Amric's steel-grey eyes did not waver. There was both warmth and regret in his tone when he said, "If I must, I will make it my final command as your warmaster."

"And as the new warmaster, I will promptly disregard the order," Valkarr growled.

Amric shook his head. "Your head and your heart are giving you different advice, my friend. A leader must listen to both, and yet hold duty above all."

They stared at each other, unmoving. A minute slid by, followed by another. At last, Valkarr blew out a long breath and said, "As you wish." He jabbed a finger at his friend. "But this is not farewell, merely farewell for now."

They stood and clasped forearms, and then Valkarr drew him into a very human embrace. Sariel did the same by turn, her dark eyes shining.

"There is one more thing I can do for you," Amric said. "If you will permit it."

He stepped back and faced away from them on the platform, focusing his will. It was more difficult than before; the borrowed knowledge was elusive for a moment, and he grasped at it like a fading memory. With a sharp gesture and a grunt of effort, he opened a Way in the air before him. An ache rose in his chest as he looked through the glowing aperture and beheld the sun-dappled woods of home. The plain, stalwart spires of Lyden were white in the distance, and the tall grass rippled in a breeze that carried familiar, comforting scents through the portal. His gaze lingered on the well-worn path that led, in no more than half a mile, to the simple dwellings of his Sil'ath tribe.

He wrenched his gaze away. The Sil'ath warriors were staring as well, transfixed.

"Unless, of course, you would rather trek through this forest and the wasteland beyond without supplies or mounts," Amric said with the corner of his mouth quirking upward.

"I do not trust magic," Valkarr said with a chuckle. "But I trust you. And I have had my fill of the creatures in this forest for a time."

Sariel stepped through the Way, and Valkarr moved to follow. At the last moment, he hesitated and turned aside to Amric once more. "Return safely," he said softly. "We will be waiting."

"I will, if it be within my power," Amric responded. "And perhaps I will have discovered something of myself, on the other side."

Valkarr let out a roar of laughter. "I have known you all my life, my friend, my brother. Wherever you go, you bring change and draw others together. Your heart and your spirit, however, do not change. I think it is this Aetheria that will do the discovering."

His friend clapped his shoulder and then passed through the opening. The Sil'ath warriors broke into a loping, mile-eating run on the path, never looking back, and were soon lost to sight. Amric closed the Way and stood in silence.

Halthak drew his attention with a gentle clearing of the throat. "He was right, you know."

"How do you mean?" Amric asked with a slight frown.

"You brought us together," the healer responded. "Each of us a half-breed in our own way, caught between worlds just as you are, at home in none. Some of us cannot hide our heritage, like me and Syth. Some carry deeper secrets, like Bellimar. Like you. And then there was Thalya, never truly allowed her own existence. You drew the best from each of us, gave us purpose."

Amric laughed and shook his head. "You do me far too much credit, Halthak. You make it sound as if I had some grand plan all along, when you know I did not."

Halthak rolled his shoulders in a shrug. "You drew together those you needed at the time you needed them most," he said with a crooked smile. "Call it magic or fate, instinct or leadership, it was somehow enough."

Amric shook his head, but did not pursue the matter further. "And what of you two?" he asked. "Where can I send you before I go?"

Syth leapt to his feet, anger twisting his features. "I wish to pay Morland a visit," he snarled. "That putrid piece of filth will answer for what he has done, for what he did to my Thalya."

"He already has," Amric answered gently. "I read Bellimar's intent, when he shared my mind. That was the reason for his haste in departing. It was the last task he had set for himself."

Syth froze, searching Amric's expression. His fury guttered and died as comprehension stole over his drawn features, and his eyes became once more windows onto his grief. "Oh," he muttered, sagging back. "I see. I am going to miss that old man."

"And I as well, Syth," Amric replied in a voice that was almost a whisper. "I as well."

Syth lifted his chin, some of the fire returning, and said, "Then I am going with you. There is nothing left for me here, and I would leave this world behind to tread upon another."

Amric started to object, but Halthak cut in with soft, adamant words. "I am going with you as well."

The warrior looked from one to the other. He knew he could bring them through the portal with him, if he chose. The Gate itself had been eager to share such secrets with him. He had no idea what to expect on the other side, however, except that it would be dangerous beyond measure. It was an unknown world of high magic, peopled by powerful, ruthless beings. Xenoth had made it clear that wildings were not suffered to live in Aetheria, and he did not yet know if he could conceal his nature there. Even if he could, someone had ordered his parents slain long ago, and him as well, in a standing order that had lasted to this day. There was no guarantee that he would be able to blend in, and even less assurance that these two could. They would all be intruders in a strange land.

Furthermore, if neither his wilding nature nor an old vendetta against his family was enough to get them all killed, there was the matter of their mission; they would be there with the express purpose of disabling the ancient artifacts upon which that world depended. Artifacts they would fight to preserve. Artifacts he had no idea how to destroy.

And, lest he forget, there would be the growing scourge of the Nar'ath there, planning the destruction of all.

As comforting as it would be to have friends on the other side, he might well be leading them directly into death's gaping maw. The wry thought arose, unbidden: *And how would that differ from everywhere else you have led them?* Next time, however, would he be able to lead them back out again?

He sighed, closing his eyes. He kept coming back to Halthak's words, just moments ago. *Caught between worlds just as you are, at home in none.*

He opened his eyes, and looked upon his companions again. They stared back with quiet resolve. He could see that they knew as well as he did what they all faced, and that they recognized the consequences failure would bring. They did not have a lifetime of battle experience or a new-found wild magic to rely upon, and still they were determined to accompany him.

Amric turned to face the Essence Gate. Syth and Halthak stepped up to either side of him. They gazed up at the solemn majesty of the ancient device, and its rhythmic pulsing seemed to quicken almost imperceptibly in anticipation. The wind whispered through the forest once more, though whether it spoke encouragement or warning, he could not say. Amric began walking toward the Gate, and the two men matched his pace. He gathered his will as he went, extending it to include the others. The portal shimmered and beckoned before them.

Endings and new beginnings, he thought to himself as they passed beneath the shadow of the great stone arch. Farewell, and hello again.

He strode forward and into its embrace.

THE END

ABOUT THE AUTHOR

Michael J. Arnquist works as a software engineer, mostly because he heard the phrase 'starving artist' a few too many times while growing up. His true loves, vocationally speaking at least, have always been fiction writing, cartooning and illustration.

Michael lives in the Pacific Northwest with his lovely wife, two beautiful daughters, and entirely too many dogs and cats for any one household.

Made in the USA
San Bernardino, CA
27 January 2013